"I've come to expect wonderful books from ... historical romance, *Words Spoken True*, doesn't disappoint. In this novel, Ms. Gabhart gives readers a peek into the lives of two news reporters—one a man and one a woman—both intent upon creating the best newspaper in Louisville, Kentucky. Amid unsolved murders, riots, and adversity, the ability to trust each other and trust God is put to the test. Ms. Gabhart weaves a story that is a page turner from beginning to end. This is one you'll highly recommend to friends."

—**Judith Miller**, author, Daughters of Amana series

Praise for *Angel Sister*:

"What a jewel of a story. Reminded me of *To Kill a Mockingbird*. Like a Kentucky summer, *Angel Sister* starts slow and easy but by the end, roars along, leaving the reader breathless and wanting more. "

—**Lauraine Snelling**, author, Red River series,
Daughters of Blessing, and *One Perfect Day*

"This book will leave you changed as it uncovers family secrets and draws you into the days following the first World War and the Great Depression. It will astound you how the characters persevere while making difficult decisions amidst heartache, and their determination to make it through the toughest of hard times."

—*RT Book Reviews*

"An amazing reminder of how we lean on our own strength and understanding—and then are surprised at our inability to overcome obstacles."

—*CBA Retailers + Resources*

"Angel Sister paints an inspirational portrait of forgiveness and grace in the midst of trial and hardship. . . . It reveals how forgiveness brings freedom, not so much for the one forgiven as for the one doing the forgiving. Two major strengths to Ann Gabhart's writing include her deeply textured characters and rich atmosphere. She moves the plot forward by weaving the past with the present. . . . There are many levels to this deftly written novel."

—*Crosswalk.com*

"Gabhart is one of the best Christian-oriented historical fiction authors writing today. Her characters have depth, her plots are complex, and there are no easy answers. Praying does not always work, at least not in obvious ways, and her characters struggle with their faith the way any sane person would when confronted with war, alcoholism, abuse, and abandonment. *Angel Sister* is the beautiful, sometimes difficult, story of a family using love, faith, and forgiveness to hold itself together."

—*Historical Novel Review*

Books by Ann H. Gabhart

The Blessed

Angel Sister

The Outsider

The Believer

The Seeker

The Scent of Lilacs

Orchard of Hope

Summer of Joy

WORDS SPOKEN TRUE

A NOVEL

ANN H. GABHART

R
Revell

a division of Baker Publishing Group
Grand Rapids, Michigan

Published by Revell
a division of Baker Publishing Group
P.O. Box 6287, Grand Rapids, MI 49516-6287
www.revellbooks.com

Printed in the United States of America

Library of Congress Cataloging-in-Publication Data
Gabhart, Ann H., 1947–
    Words spoken true : a novel / Ann H. Gabhart.
      p. cm.
    ISBN 978-0-8007-2045-2 (pbk.)
    1. Kentucky—History—1792–1865—Fiction. 2. Louisville (Ky.)—History—Fiction. I. Title.
PS3607.A23W67 2012
813'.6—dc23   2011041472

Scripture quotations are from the King James Version of the Bible.

Published in association with the Books & Such Literary Agency, 52 Mission Circle, Suite 122, PMB 170, Santa Rosa, CA 95409-7953.

12   13   14   15   16   17   18   7 6 5 4 3 2 1

To my readers who have followed my story trail
from Hollyhill
to Harmony Hill
to Rosey Corner
and now . . . Louisville

Historical Note from the Author

*I*n 1850, Louisville, Kentucky, was the tenth largest city in the United States. Its population had been swelled by immigrants from Germany and Ireland after the failed German revolution and the Irish potato famine. Many of these immigrants were of the Catholic faith, and the predominantly Protestant white population in Louisville began to fear their influence in the political arena. The decline of the Whig Party allowed a new power, the American Party, to enter the national political arena in 1854. The American Party was commonly known as the "Know Nothing" party because its secretive members often answered questions with "I know nothing." By 1855, the Know Nothings could count fifty thousand voters in Kentucky. The party supported limiting immigration, allowing only native-born Americans to be elected to political office, and strictly curbing the alleged influence of the Roman Catholic Church.

Prior to the invention of radio and television, newspapers were how people kept up with what was happening in their cities and country. Newspapers grew by leaps and bounds in the 1800s. In 1855, Louisville had at least four daily papers and several weekly papers as well. Many of the editors of these papers had agendas. They picked sides on the hot issues of the day and churned out papers full of stories and fiery opinion pieces to support their positions. Editors with disparate viewpoints dueled in words and on occasion with pistols. Editorials were often written with the intent to inflame the populace and goad the people into action. After the election riots of 1855, many placed some of the blame for the civil disorder at the door of newspapers. At least twenty-two people were killed in these riots in Louisville on August 6, 1855, a day that came to be known as Bloody Monday.

While the actions of my characters are completely fictional, the political unrest of the day and the riot scene I dropped them into was entirely too true. We can't hide from history— what happened, happened—but we can hope examining our past will make us wiser as we face our future.

1

*A*driane Darcy's heart pounded as the darkness settled down around her like a heavy blanket. Her eyes were open. Open as wide as she could stretch them, but she could see nothing. The dark was claiming her. She wanted to fight it, but what good would it do? The dark always won. Better to sit quiet as a mouse and accept her punishment. That's what her stepmother told her when she pushed her inside the closet under the stairs and slammed shut the door.

Forcing her hand up through the thick black air, Adriane dreaded the feel of the rough inside corners of the closet door. She tried not to make any noise, but something rattled the door. She jerked her arm back and was suddenly fully awake.

It was only a dream. Adriane kicked free of the bedcovers and sat up to fumble for a candle. She needed light.

She gripped the waxy candle but stayed her other hand before she could feel for one of the newfangled matchsticks. She thought of the welcome flare of light the match would bring, but she tightened her jaw and turned loose of the candle. She was no longer a cowering child trapped in dark fear, waiting for the moment light would spill into the closet when her father came to rescue her. She needed no rescue now.

She pulled in a deep breath and blew it out slowly. Familiar shapes began to emerge from the night shadows—the chest with the blue pitcher and basin on top, her small writing desk piled with books and papers, and her wardrobe with the door a bit ajar.

The panic of the dream receded, and she was settling back on her pillow when something clattered against her window. That was the sound in her dream.

Adriane popped up in bed again and stared at the window. For one crazy moment she thought it might be Stanley Jimson come to propose to her in some foolishly romantic way. He certainly needed to do something to make amends to her after totally deserting her at last night's social, not to mention asking her father for her hand in marriage without one word to her first.

Not that she wanted to marry Stanley Jimson. She certainly did not. She had yet to meet the man she wished to marry, or more troublesome—her father was wont to say—the man who wished to marry her. Now it appeared there was such a man. Her father had scarcely been able to contain his joy and relief while telling Adriane about her marriage-to-be the night before as if she had no choice in the matter. As if she'd be as happy about it as he so obviously was. After all, Stanley was from one of the most prominent families in Louisville. It was rumored Stan's father, Coleman Jimson, planned to run for state senator in the August election, and money was certainly not an issue.

"What more could any girl want?" Adriane's father asked her.

"A proposal might be nice," Adriane shot back.

Now Adriane grabbed her wrapper and smoothed her dark hair back into some reasonable order before she pushed up the second-story window and peered down at the street.

All thoughts of Stanley Jimson vanished from her mind when she saw Duff Egan getting ready to pitch another pebble toward her window.

The young Irish boy stopped his windup and called softly, "Miss Adriane, they found another body. You told me to be letting you know soon's I heard."

"The river slasher?" Adriane kept her voice low, not much more than a whisper.

"The same."

"Wait there. I'll be right down."

Adriane eased the window closed to keep from waking her father. He'd never allow her out on the streets this time of night for any reason, much less to go to a murder scene. It would be shockingly improper.

In fact her father had denounced the very stories about the murdered Irish girls as somewhat scandalous and not something a respectable newspaper should print. Of course, he did print the stories. A lot of readers liked scandalous, as the *Herald* and its new editor, Blake Garrett, had proven well enough over the last several months. The *Herald*'s headline scoops on the murders were pushing up its circulation numbers until it was actually beginning to rival the *Tribune*'s numbers. Her father's paper, their paper, had been the leading newspaper in Louisville for over a decade. She planned to keep it that way in spite of the winds of change sweeping through the city.

While her father kept battling against the *Herald* in his editorials, Adriane thought the real war would be won or lost in the headlines. So she'd had Duff on the lookout ever since the last girl was murdered down in Shippingport.

Adriane yanked on a pair of her father's old trousers and a shirt she had stashed in the bottom of her wardrobe for just this purpose. With a few deft twists, she pinned her thick dark hair flat against her head.

The clock struck two as she slipped out of her room and

made her way down the stairs, doing her best to avoid the squeaky boards. Halfway down she caught the acrid smell of ink from the freshly printed editions of the *Tribune* stacked in the pressroom waiting for morning delivery. Soon people all over Louisville would be opening up the *Tribune* to find out the news for March 22, 1855.

Adriane could almost hear the rustling papers and see the expressions on the faces of the people reading her and her father's words. The familiar thrill Beck said all good newspapermen felt when they put a new issue on the streets pushed through her.

At the thought of Beck, Adriane held her breath and stepped even more gingerly on the stairs. Beck, her father's right-hand pressman since before Adriane could remember, slept in a small room just off the pressroom. He would tie her to a chair before he'd let her out of the building to chase after a story about a murdered Irish girl. Dear Beck. Like a favored, fond uncle, he'd probably sent up a thousand prayers while he worried over her and did his best to protect her. Mostly from herself.

In the front hallway, she grabbed a hat and jacket off the rack and slipped silently out the front door.

"Miss Adriane, is that you?" Duff appeared out of the shadows beside the front stoop, the whites of his eyes shining as he took in her getup.

"None other," Adriane said. "I'm ready to go."

"Could be you shouldn't ought to be going down to the river with me. It won't be no place for a lady." Even in the dim light she could see his troubled frown.

"You're right, Duff, but I won't be a lady. I'll be just one of the fellows."

"Folks ain't always that easy to fool." Duff gave her a hard look. "You may have on breeches, but you have some to learn about how a feller walks."

"Then give me a lesson."

"You have to be throwing your legs out free and easy without worrying about no ruffled petticoats and such." He walked away from her with a swagger.

Adriane stifled a laugh as she followed after him, copying his stride.

"Not bad," Duff said. "But ye'd best keep to the shadows and let me do any talking that needs to be done. There be some things loose clothes can't hide."

"Right," Adriane agreed as the boy turned to lead the way down the street.

Ever since Duff had shown up on the *Tribune*'s doorstep begging a job several months ago, he'd been more like a little brother to her than a regular hand. It had taken some doing for Adriane to convince her father to take the boy on since Duff was only twelve and, even worse, one of the Irish immigrants her father railed against in his editorials. Her father worried the rapid increase in the city's immigrant population was going to bring them all to ruin. He believed some privileges, such as running for elected office, should be reserved for men born in America. Immigrants excluded.

Adriane didn't always agree with her father's politics, but nobody cared what she, a woman, thought. Women were excluded right along with the immigrant population. Women weren't even supposed to bother their heads over such issues. Too much thinking on serious matters was reputed to be injurious to the female brain. Nor were women supposed to go chasing after stories on the wrong side of town in the middle of the night. Her father would be furious if he found out. She took another look back at the building that housed the *Tribune* offices and their home. No signs of anybody stirring.

With a breath of relief, she hurried after Duff toward the riverfront. Beyond the pools of light from the gas streetlamps, the black night lurked and put out fingers of darkness to claim her. Her heart pounded up in her throat, but she told herself it was only the dream remnants bothering her.

She hadn't had one of those nightmares for years. Her stepmother, Henrietta, was long dead, and no one locked Adriane in dark places anymore. Nothing in the night was threatening her. She was only chasing after a story. That by itself was enough to make her heart beat faster. With excitement. Not fear.

In front of her, Duff slowed and edged closer to the buildings. He grabbed her arm to pull her back beside him before he pointed ahead to where men were milling about in the street.

"Don't be getting too close to any of the watch," he warned her in a whisper. "They favor booting you toward home if they get half a chance."

Adriane moved when Duff moved, melted into the shadows when he stopped as they crept closer to the scene. The quarter moon slipped out from behind the clouds to reflect a bit of light off the river beyond them and give the night an eerie gray look in spite of the streetlamps. It was far too easy to imagine the poor murdered girl's ghost in the misty shadows.

A shiver walked through Adriane as her eyes fastened on a grimy blanket covering what had to be the body. All at once, it wasn't just a story for the *Tribune* she was trying to beat the *Herald* to, but a real girl who wouldn't awaken when the sun came up to go about her life as she should.

"Did you know her?" Adriane whispered in Duff's ear.

"No, but one of me sisters did. Kathleen O'Dell's her name. She worked down at the Lucky Leaf. The story I heard said she left early last night, but didn't give no reason why. Nobody saw her after that."

"Nobody but the murderer." Adriane's eyes were fixed on the body. At the sound of footsteps on the walkway, Duff jerked her back into a dark doorway as a man in a rumpled suit hurried past them.

The man spoke to a few of the policemen before he slowly approached the body. He stared down at the covered shape as though gathering his nerve before he knelt down to lift an edge of the blanket. After a long moment, he very carefully let the cover drop back down over the body.

Without proper thought, Adriane stepped out of the doorway to get a better look at the man's face. He might be the girl's father or perhaps a brother. As if the man felt her eyes on him, he stood up and looked directly toward her. The terrible anger on his face made Adriane catch her breath.

Duff grabbed her arm again and pointed in the other direction toward one of the watch. "It looks like Officer Jefferson has spotted us, Miss Adriane." His whisper in her ear was urgent. "We'd best make a run for it. Now."

A large man in uniform was heading their way, swinging his truncheon menacingly as he yelled, "Hey, you two, get on out of here. This ain't no entertainment feature."

Duff tugged on her arm, but Adriane hesitated. She hadn't seen enough yet. That hesitation cost her. The man who'd been looking at the body covered the space between them faster than Adriane thought possible. She gasped as he grabbed her other arm and yanked her out into the light. Duff pulled her back toward the shadows.

Adriane tried to jerk free of the man's hold. When he held on grimly, she kicked his shins. He paid the blows no mind as he tightened his grip on her arm. "You know something, don't you?"

His words so surprised her she ceased struggling and looked directly into his dark, intense eyes.

Adriane was about to say something when Duff saved her from her own foolishness by shoving between them to ram his shoulder into the man's middle.

"Run!" he yelled.

When the man staggered back, Adriane was finally able to jerk free. With a worried glance over her shoulder at Duff, she took off up the street, but she had no need to be anxious about the boy. He slipped away from the man's hands as easily as an eel escaping a net. In a matter of seconds, he caught up with her.

"Stick close, Miss Adriane," he said as he passed her.

Adriane didn't need to be told. She stayed right on Duff's heels. It wouldn't do for her to be discovered down here.

Behind them, the man shouted, "Wait! We won't hurt you."

They kept running as Duff led her around and between buildings. Once they ran right through the middle of a warehouse, crawling in a window on one side and running out an open door on the other. After that, they didn't really have to worry about anybody catching them, but Duff didn't slow down until they reached the street leading up to the *Tribune* offices.

"Too close," Duff gasped as he leaned up against Harrod's Dry Goods Store to catch his breath.

Adriane held her side and pulled in deep breaths. She hadn't run like that since she was a child playing tag with the neighbor kids, but now every nerve in her body was screamingly awake until she was aware of the slightest noises, the depth of the shadows around the *Tribune* offices across from them, and the very air against her skin.

When she caught her breath, she said, "But we made it."

"Only because nobody but fat old Officer Jefferson chased us, and he can't run more than five minutes without taking the wheezes." The boy looked at her, and even in the shadows she could see his concern. "I shouldn't of ought to have taken you down there. If Mr. Darcy finds out, he'll fire me for sure."

"Don't worry. I won't let Father fire you, Duff." Adriane touched the boy's shoulder. Behind them, the sky was already beginning to lighten, so she went on. "Come on in and nap in the pressroom till time to take out the papers."

"Can't," Duff said. "I got to be going home to check on me sisters and me mother." He turned to go but then looked back, a smile stealing across his face again. "It was some chase for sure, wasn't it, Miss Adriane?"

"That it was." Adriane laughed and gave the boy a little shove down the street. "Now go on with you. I don't want to have to explain to Beck why you're late to get your papers."

The minute he took off in an easy jog, Adriane remembered she hadn't asked him if he knew the name of the man who'd grabbed her, but she didn't call him back. Instead, after noting how the eastern sky was turning a pale pink, she took off her shoes and slipped through the front door. Without a sound, she crept past the pressroom, but she didn't make it. Beck grabbed her by the collar.

"Hold it, you scalawag," he growled. When he spun Adriane around to face him, her hat fell off. He blinked his eyes a couple of times and leaned down closer to her face as if he couldn't believe what he was seeing in the dim morning light. "Addie?"

"Shh, Beck. Don't wake Father." She looked from Beck to the stairs and then back at Beck.

The old man took in her trousers and tried to look cross, though one corner of his mouth twitched up. "I reckon as how that wouldn't be a good idea right now." Beck shook his head with a heavy sigh. "I'd ask you what you've been up to, but I ain't all that sure I want to know."

"I was just trying to beat Garrett to a headline for once."

"And what headline you been out chasing?"

"They found another Irish girl stabbed to death down on the riverfront." Adriane turned her eyes from Beck to the pile of papers just inside the pressroom that were nothing but old news now.

All signs of a smile vanished from Beck's face. "Addie, tell me you didn't go down to the riverfront."

"Oh, don't look so shocked." Adriane touched the old man's wrinkled cheek. "Nobody knew it was me."

"What were you thinking, Addie?" Beck frowned at her.

"That maybe we could beat Garrett to that headline."

"All the headlines in the world ain't worth you taking that

kind of risk. You'd best be sending up a thankful prayer that your guardian angel was watching over you."

"I know, Beck. I will and you'll be sending them up with me, won't you?" She gave him her best smile. She knew Beck couldn't stay upset at her.

"It's a fact you need praying over." He shook his head again as his frown faded. "I don't reckon it's any use fussing at you. You're too hardheaded by far to listen to nothing nobody says anyhows."

"I've always listened to you, Beck."

"Then listen to this." He gave her shoulder a firm shake. "You'd best get on some decent ladies' clothes before the boss catches you in this getup."

Adriane looked down at the trousers damp from the river mist. She sighed. "You're right as always. Father would tell me I'm ruining my chances for a decent match and here when someone has at last asked to marry me."

"What's this about marrying?"

"You haven't heard?" Adriane kept her voice light. "Stanley Jimson asked Father for my hand in marriage last evening. Father's ecstatic."

"You don't say. Well then." Beck wouldn't quite meet her eyes as he went on. "It's said the Jimsons are one of the finest families in Louisville."

"Richest anyhow," Adriane said.

"Money comes in right handy at times."

"So I've heard." Adriane looked at Beck and stopped pretending. If there was one person she could be honest with, it was Beck. "You don't like Stan, do you?"

Beck finally looked back up at her. The wrinkles around his eyes tightened some as he reached out and laid his hand on her cheek. "It don't make no matterance who it is I like, Addie. What you got to worry about is who it is you can take a liking to."

2

*B*eck's words echoed in Adriane's head as she exchanged her trousers for petticoats and skirts.
Would she be able to do what he said? Take a liking to Stan
Jimson. At least the proper kind of liking. She and Stan had
been keeping company for months. As she'd told her father
the evening before, Stan made a very convenient escort to
the social functions where she gathered little tidbits on the
social scene to print in the *Tribune*.

The ladies of the town so enjoyed seeing their names in
print, properly surrounded by flattering adjectives, that several months ago Adriane had begun writing a "Sally Sees All"
column devoted entirely to who wore what accompanied by
whom to which social.

Often as not, Adriane had to hide her yawns behind her
fan as she feigned interest in the chatter of the ladies at the
gatherings, but the increase in the *Tribune*'s readership numbers more than made up for a few hours of boredom.

Adriane jerked the pins out of her hair and let the dark
strands fall down around her shoulders. As she began brushing out the tangles, she met her eyes in the mirror. She dropped
her hands to her side and stared at herself. Would everyone expect her to become one of those ladies worried about nothing

more than the latest bit of gossip or what she'd stitch on her next sampler?

Adriane almost smiled. Gossip she could handle, but she couldn't sew. She'd never learned even the most basic stitches. The only thing she was good at was helping put out the *Tribune*, and she wasn't ready to give that up. She had to keep being part of the push to get the news in front of the populace. It was what she lived for.

The tangles in her hair forgotten, Adriane went to stand in front of her small desk where her journal lay open. She stared at the words on the page as if she hadn't written them there herself the night before. *I am to marry Stanley Jimson.*

She wanted to turn the page to a blank sheet where she could write of her morning's adventure with Duff. Then she was ashamed for thinking of it as a lark. The poor girl under that grimy cover would have no opportunities to seize happiness in the days ahead. Those days, her very life, had been taken violently from her. Here Adriane was being offered every chance—money, position, love. Why did she keep feeling as if someone was trying to shove her into a dark closet the way Henrietta used to do when she was a child?

What other choice did Adriane have except marriage? She was twenty-two, several years past the prime marrying age. As her father said, she was surely fortunate to be getting an offer at all, especially since he'd not been able to put aside any kind of dowry for her. There was always a new and better press to buy, such as the one he'd been talking about lately that could print twelve sheets at once.

And every woman wanted to be married, didn't she? It was the natural state of life for men and women to marry. Didn't God tell Adam and Eve to go forth and be fruitful? Fruitful and marriage went together. Her father himself planned to marry the lovely Lucilla Elmore in the fall when her self-prescribed two-year mourning period for the late Mr. Elmore was properly observed.

Lucilla had positively beamed at Adriane the night before when her father announced the news of Stan's impending proposal, and deep inside Adriane, the first fluttering of something very near panic had awakened.

She could perhaps have convinced her father she had no desire to marry, that he needed her to help him with the *Tribune*. Hadn't he always told her she was worth two hired hands? But Lucilla would have stronger powers of persuasion. While it was rumored the late Mr. Elmore had not left Lucilla as much of his estate as she had expected when she married the man twice her age seven years earlier, he had left her with a comfortable income.

With that money practically in reach, Adriane's father had already been in touch with some of the manufacturers in the East. A press that could print twelve sheets at a time would be better than two hired hands.

So if Lucilla had decided Adriane must marry, there would be no way she could fight it. She would have to marry Stanley Jimson. She made herself read the words on the page of her journal aloud. "I am to marry Stanley Jimson."

At the sound of his name in her ears, she had the odd feeling a box was closing around her. She pushed the feeling aside. She was no longer a child to be terrified by imagined monsters in the dark.

She would face what had to be done. If she had to marry, then so be it. And why not marry Stanley Jimson? Now, when she thought about it, she realized he'd been trying to ask her to marry him for weeks, perhaps months. She had simply put him off. It surprised her that he had gone to her father. She smiled a little. Perhaps it would be good to marry a man with a few surprises.

It could even be that if she had to marry, and it appeared she did, then Stan might turn out to be the ideal man. She could surely persuade him she would never be happy unless she could keep writing and in some way helping with the paper.

He would want her to be happy. Wasn't that what he was always telling her? That he had an undying affection for her and that her happiness was of the utmost importance to him.

Adriane picked up her pen, dipped the nib in the ink, and wrote "Mrs. Stanley Jimson" on the page of her journal. She so disliked the way the words looked she almost marked them out, but she stayed her hand. Instead she stared at the name and remembered all the times she'd heard people say what a lovely couple she and Stan made. She could not agree.

They were opposites in all ways. Stan was so blond and fair that she feared when she was in his company her own dark hair and rosy complexion caused him to look even more pale and delicate than he might have if he were keeping company with someone whose coloring more nearly matched his own. Even his eyes were pale, a kind of shadowy gray. Somewhat like the misty fog rising off the river that morning, Adriane thought suddenly. Her own eyes were as blue as a deep summer sky.

While she never thought much about it, she knew it was true when people told her she was pretty. Those few who remembered her mother said she was the exact image of her. When she asked her father once if this was true, he had studied her for a long moment before he answered. "I suppose it is true that you look like Katherine on the outside, but you are like me on the inside."

Those had been his exact words. She'd written them down in her journal, but she didn't need to turn back the pages to remember them. She knew what was important to her father and what was important to her. It was not what was on the outside.

Which had attracted Stan? She had little doubt of the answer to that question. He claimed to be quite entranced by her looks. Young men were always ready to flock around her at any event, but she'd had few serious suitors. Her beauty was not enough to make up for her lack of money and, even worse, her outspoken and determined character. The only one to persevere was Stanley Jimson.

Why? That was the question Adriane really needed to answer. It wasn't as if Stan didn't have plenty of other choices. That was assured by his family's money in spite of the way the girls sometimes giggled and mocked Stan behind his back. The poor man did often appear to be weak beside his father who practically radiated power. Not only that, but his own mother had a way of making him seem fawning by demanding Stan attend to her slightest whim whenever they were out in public together.

The thought of the old dragon brought a tight smile to Adriane's face. Meta Jimson hated Adriane and had devised numerous ploys to protect her precious son from such an unsuitable match. Adriane stared down at the name she'd written in her journal and tried not to wish the woman had succeeded.

She slammed the book shut, shoved it into its place on the shelf. Then without looking back in the mirror, she pulled the brush through her hair a few more times before tying it back carelessly.

She didn't have time to worry about any of this now. The newsboys would be coming for their papers and she wanted to write down what she'd seen in those predawn hours on the riverfront before she lost the intensity of the images. For a minute she remembered how the eyes of the man who had grabbed her burned into hers, and in spite of herself she couldn't keep from comparing them to Stan's eyes. Feeling had almost exploded from that man's eyes. She'd never seen anything exploding from Stan's eyes.

Stan was always so perfectly in control, his emotions contained as neatly as his cravat was tied. In contrast, at times Adriane felt as if her own emotions were loose cannons apt to shoot off in who knew which direction. Hadn't Stan just chided her last week for heatedly responding to Mrs. Hafley when the silly woman had made a totally inane remark about Adriane's friend Grace Compton? Just because Mrs. Hafley was living in the lap of luxury didn't mean all women were. And it was for all women that Grace was in the East making a valiant effort to promote a woman's right to vote.

Adriane sighed as she headed down to the pressroom. She would have to remember better control of her tongue this afternoon when they attended Mrs. Wigginham's benefit. It would not do to have Mrs. Wigginham angry with her or more importantly the *Tribune*.

With automatic movements, Adriane stirred up the cookstove fire, made coffee, and fried bacon and eggs. In the pressroom she could hear Beck straightening the trays of type before the new day's rush began. Adriane slipped out the back door and whistled softly. An ugly spotted mongrel crept out of the shadows to take yesterday's stale bread from her. When she patted his head, his crooked tail moved back and forth in a ludicrous sort of wag that never failed to make Adriane smile. Then with the bread in his mouth, the old dog melted back into the shadows.

Adriane watched him go and wondered what stories the old dog might be able to tell. For a minute, she considered writing something for the paper from the dog's viewpoint. She smiled a little at the thought of her father agreeing to publish such foolishness in the *Tribune*. That would never happen.

Back in the kitchen, she put her father's breakfast in the warming oven and carried Beck's to him in the pressroom, along with the pot of coffee. Adriane was at her desk struggling to come up with the right words for what she'd seen that morning when the newsboys showed up for their papers.

The minute Beck opened the door, Duff slipped inside in front of the other boys to help hand out the bundles. Before he took out his own bundle, he came over to Adriane and pulled a newspaper out from under his coat.

"You seen the *Herald*?" the boy asked as he spread the paper out on Adriane's desk.

The sight of the *Herald*'s masthead brought the usual flush of anger. Adriane's eyes fell to the three-inch headline. *RIVER SLASHER STRIKES AGAIN.* Underneath in smaller headline type was *THIRD GIRL'S BODY FOUND.*

"How does he do it?" Adriane said more to herself than to Duff as she quickly scanned the account.

"It's a puzzler, but I'm figuring he must have had his men holding the presses for the story when we were down there," Duff said.

"But how does he find out everything so soon?" Adriane said.

"It's said he walks the streets all over town talking to folks about what might be happening or going to happen." Duff poked the headline with his finger. "I'm told he pays good money for all kinds of leads even if he don't never make a story out of it, as long as them doing the telling promise not to let none of the other papers in on it. People who know I'm working for the *Tribune* won't hardly give me the time of day no more. They're scared somebody from the *Herald* will see them talking to me and Garrett will stop paying them for their stories." Duff looked up at Adriane with a frown wrinkling his small, round face. "Looks like we wasted our time this morning."

"No, we'll have a story to run tomorrow." Adriane looked down at the *Herald*'s headlines with a sigh. "Even though by tomorrow it'll be old news. But keep your ears open, Duff. You might hear something new we can use."

"I'll be listening for sure, Miss Adriane, but Garrett will be bound to hear it first. He always does." Duff shrugged his shoulders a little.

"You said one of your sisters knew her."

"Aye."

"Was this poor girl Irish same as the other two?" Adriane touched the girl's name on the page.

"Aye. Some are saying that's why nobody's in much of a dither about it all."

"That's not true," Adriane said, even though she knew it was. Before Blake Garrett had come to town and begun printing the most sensational stories he could dig up, this girl's murder probably wouldn't have even made it into the papers, much less been a headline story. After all, not only was she an Irish immigrant, she worked in a tavern.

"Maybe not, but if you ask me, the watch ain't got a clue as to who's doing it all and ain't looking too hard to find out." Anger tightened Duff's young face. "I talked to a sister of the first girl what was killed a couple months back, and she says they've yet to see the first policeman around their way. She was scared. Me own sisters are scared."

"Who can blame them?" Adriane quickly skimmed the article about the murder. The girl had been stabbed the same as the others. Adriane's eyes settled on a quote from the girl's brother, saying how his sister had never hurt anyone and had always done whatever she could to help her family out. Adriane felt tears prickling her eyes. Garrett knew how to pull at the heartstrings of his readers.

Duff pointed toward the paper. "You want to keep it? He has a piece inside about how there be no guarantees the slasher's next victim might not be some lady who lives out on Walnut or Broadway instead of just a poor girl down on the riverfront."

"Really? That should cause some discussions in the parlor rooms today." Adriane peered down at the paper and then began quickly folding it up. "But you'd better get this out of here before Mr. Darcy sees it."

"Before Mr. Darcy sees what?" Adriane's father spoke up behind them.

Adriane spun around keeping the paper behind her. "Oh, Father, I didn't hear you come downstairs."

"So I gather." He peered at her over the top of his spectacles. "What is it you're hiding behind your skirts?"

"Nothing important. Just a copy of the *Herald* Duff happened across on the way over this morning." Adriane brought the paper out from behind her back reluctantly.

Her father's face turned grimmer at the sight of it. "And what does our Mr. Garrett think the news is this morning?"

"Another girl got killed last night, Mr. Darcy," Duff said.

"Let me see." Her father held out his hand.

Adriane handed the paper to her father and tried to think of a way to avert the storm that was sure to come. She pointed Duff toward his pile of papers. "You'd better get the news out on the street, Duff."

Duff took one look at Wade Darcy's face, grabbed his papers, and disappeared out the door.

Wade stared after him a moment. "I don't know why I ever let you talk me into giving that Irish pup a job. If the party men find out, I'm apt as not to lose half my readers."

"He's a hard worker," Adriane said.

"And a wizard with this newfangled equipment," Beck put in as he came over to join them.

"He's a boy. Still wet behind the ears," Wade said.

"But a wizard nonetheless," Beck insisted. "I ain't never figured out all these new contraptions, but he can stand and watch one run a few minutes and figure out which screw or whatever needs tightening."

"I know. We need him. If only he didn't look so Irish." Wade blew out his breath and shook his head before he dropped his eyes back to the paper he was holding.

"You say Chesnut's man has done beat us to the headlines again," Beck said.

"He'll sell his papers today," Wade said without looking up. "People nowadays don't want to read the real news. They want to be shocked and scandalized."

Beck peeked over at the *Herald*'s headlines. "I reckon as how that should do it then. You got to admit it's more of a grabber than the mayor's order to keep hogs off the streets."

"What do you know about what's news?" Wade glared at Beck.

"Not a thing, boss. Not a thing." Beck didn't seem a bit put off by Wade's bad humor. "I just set whatever you or Addie here tells me to. And there'll be plenty of people out there that will want to know what you've got to say about the elections coming up. Your editorials could sell a paper even if nothing else happened anywhere in the world."

"Maybe so, Beck. Maybe so, but something's always happening. We just need to start finding out what before the *Herald* does."

"We will, boss."

"That's right, Father," Adriane put in. "You're always on top of whatever's happening in the political arena."

"That's true." Wade Darcy's frown eased back. "And that's the real news. Did we get anything in from Colonel Storey for tomorrow's issue?"

Adriane turned back to her desk and picked up a letter. "As a matter of fact, we did. As usual, he doesn't completely agree with your views."

"That's fine. A little controversy is good for circulation." He folded the *Herald* and smacked it in his palm.

"You want me to get rid of that?" Adriane asked.

"No. I want to read over Garrett's editorials. It's always best to keep abreast of what the enemy is up to."

"Have you met him, Father?" Adriane couldn't help but be curious about this man who was making such an impact on the town's newspaper business even though he'd only arrived in Louisville a few months ago. It was common knowledge he'd worked for a big daily up in New York City. Another reason for Adriane's curiosity. Why would he leave a New York paper for one here in Louisville? So far she hadn't heard the first bit of reliable information about that.

"Of course I've met him. If he wasn't such a young pup,

I'd call him out." Her father twisted the paper as though he might rip it in two.

"Father!" Adriane's eyes popped open wide. "We've been campaigning for an end to duels."

"Don't look so shocked, Adriane." Her father waved the rumpled paper at her. "I didn't mean it. The only way I'll shoot him is if he shoots at me first on the street."

"Oh, Father, go write your editorial. Just gun him down with words."

"You want to save some space for the murder in tomorrow's paper?" Beck asked before her father moved away toward his office.

He hesitated as though wanting to say no, but there was only one answer. "I suppose we'll have to," he said with a sigh. "Garrett's headlines will convince even our readers that it's news. I'll get a report from Chief Trabue before we go to press."

"I don't think the police are doing much about any of it," Adriane said.

"I wouldn't wonder, the kind of girls they were. Decent young ladies shouldn't even be reading about such things." A new frown furrowed her father's brow. "Young ladies like you."

Adriane quickly changed the subject. "We could try to find out if any of the steamboats are trying to make a record run to New Orleans and back. I hear Captain Overstreet on *The Belle of Paradise* has been tying down his valves."

Her father's eyes narrowed on her. "Where did you hear that?"

"I don't know. Around," she said vaguely.

Her father's frown lines deepened as he said, "You hear entirely too much for a lady, Adriane. You must be more circumspect about appearances now that you're to marry Stanley."

"I don't care about appearances, Father," Adriane said.

"Of course you do, dear. All young ladies care about appearances." Her father's frown was replaced by an indulgent smile. "By the way, Lucilla is sending her dressmaker over with a special gown for you to wear tonight. She had her woman make it as a surprise for just such an occasion."

"I have dresses."

"Not proper ones, according to Lucilla, and I'm sure Lucilla knows best about such things."

"Yes, Father." Adriane had little choice but to give in gracefully.

So when Lucilla's dressmaker, Nora, showed up with the boxed dress, Adriane left the pressroom, scrubbed the ink off her hands, and submitted to the fitting. As Nora fussed over her, admiring her hair and her figure, and praising Mrs. Elmore's fashion sense that had made her pick the perfect deep blue for the dress, Adriane wished she could be the boy Beck had sent down to the docks to check out the steamboats.

She remembered the exhilarating freedom she'd felt that morning in those borrowed trousers as she'd followed Duff through the streets to the river. In contrast, she felt a helpless captive swathed in the beautiful silky dress she was to wear to the party that night to announce her engagement to Stanley Jimson.

3

After Nora made all her measurements and tucks and settled down in the tiny sitting room to, as the seamstress said around the pins in her mouth, "make the dress even more perfect," Adriane checked the time.

Stan would be arriving any moment to pick her up for Mrs. Wigginham's Library Aide Society meeting. Adriane toyed with the idea of going back downstairs to help Beck. When Stan showed up, she could always claim she'd forgotten about the meeting.

Adriane sighed. Stan might believe her. Her father would not. Besides, she'd promised Mrs. Wigginham she'd come, and Mrs. Wigginham was not a person who forgave broken promises. She liked seeing her name in the paper associated with whatever noble cause she was supporting at the time.

Opening the door of her wardrobe, Adriane studied the dresses hanging there. She smiled a bit as she selected a deep cranberry dress with only a touch of cream lace at the high neck for ornamentation. She might have to go, but she didn't have to look pretty.

After she slipped the dress on and shook the skirt down over her petticoats, she stood in front of the small square mirror on her wall and carelessly caught her hair back with a matching cranberry ribbon. Stan would want a wife who was a decoration on his arm. So perhaps her very plainness today would discourage him from speaking or at least make him hesitate for a few weeks. A few weeks, even a few days might give Adriane time to get used to the idea instead of feeling as if she were being swept toward the altar in a flood of other people's wishes.

It wasn't that Adriane had never thought of love and marriage. When she was younger, she had pored over the love stories serialized in the popular magazines that told of ladies captivated by handsome men who loved them devotedly.

Adriane stared at her reflection. Perhaps Stan did love her devotedly. The problem was with her. She supposed she was fond of Stan, but she couldn't see herself ever being captivated by him. She'd never even allowed him the favor of a kiss. She felt no desire to do so now.

Adriane ran her fingers through her dark hair to tousle it just a bit more and glanced down at the plain lines of the dress with satisfaction. But when she passed through the sitting room on the way to the stairs, Nora looked up at her and exclaimed, "Ma chère, what a perfect color for you. I will inform Mademoiselle Elmore that we must have a length of that very color in a shining satin for an evening gown. We'll cut it low." Nora motioned with her needle. "With your dark hair and lovely neck, you will be the most beautiful belle in all of Louisville."

"This is the plainest dress I have," Adriane protested.

Nora looked at her knowingly. "With one as beautiful as you, the plainer the dress the better. It is only the simply pretty ones who need ruffles. You, ma chère, should always be different."

That was easy enough, Adriane thought as she hurried down the steps. At least it always had been before. Now it appeared she was going to be forced to conform to society's norms.

Stan was waiting in the small entrance hallway at the bottom of the stairs. One look at his broad smile, and she knew a plain dress and a careless hairdo would not be enough to slow the force of the flood carrying her toward the altar.

"My dearest Adriane, you look charming as always." He lifted her hand to his lips, but kept his eyes on her face.

After a moment, she attempted to gently pull her hand away, but he held it more tightly.

"We'll be late," she said.

"No one will notice." He surrendered her hand at last but continued to almost devour her with his eyes.

Adriane had to fight the urge to shrink away from him as she noted the uncommon color in his cheeks and the almost feverish look in his eyes. "Are you feeling well, Stanley?" she asked. "You look flushed."

He put a hand to his cheek and laughed. "With excitement, my dearest. It is a wonderful day for the two of us. Perhaps we could skip this tiresome tea and spend the time getting better acquainted."

He reached out to capture her hand again, but she pretended not to notice as she picked up her wrap. "I'm sure that would be delightful, but I did promise Mrs. Wigginham the *Tribune* would carry some mention of her event, so I do need to at least make an appearance."

"Of course." Stan gave in as he held her cloak for her. "We can talk on the way. We have much to discuss, you and I." His hand lingered on her shoulder for an instant before he opened the door and allowed her to precede him out into the street.

An early morning shower had left puddles in the street, but now the sun was shining. Adriane raised her face to the sky a moment to gather in the sun's warmth before she allowed Stan to hand her up into the carriage.

Adriane didn't enjoy riding in closed carriages at any time, but today she felt as if all the air was being shut outside when Stan climbed up beside her and the driver fastened the door.

She could feel Stan's eyes on her as the carriage began to roll. With her brightest smile, she began to chatter about how the spring flowers would soon be blooming, as though nothing at all was unusual or different about the day.

After a moment Stan broke in on her words. "Your father did speak with you last night, did he not?"

"I generally speak with my father every day." Adriane had no intention of making it easy for Stan.

"Of course," Stan said. "I spoke with him myself yesterday about a matter of some importance."

She dropped her eyes to her gloved hands clenched in her lap and reminded herself that the man beside her was only Stanley Jimson. Without looking over at him, she pictured him there beside her. Sitting straight, holding his hat on his lap. Perfectly dressed with blond hair carefully slicked back. His gold watch chain would be hanging just so across his vest. He adjusted it constantly to be sure it stayed in correct alignment. His buttons would be gleaming. She frowned a bit and wondered if he still had his small, neat moustache, but she didn't peek at him to see for sure.

Stanley Jimson was not a man she needed to fear. She rather doubted anyone would look on the man with fear of any sort. In fact he was so slender and pale, that at times he seemed to almost fade into the background at the socials so that she had difficulty finding him when she wished to leave. It could be she had often failed to take him seriously enough, but she needed to do so now. Not because she feared him, but because she feared the sort of wife he might expect her to be.

She kept her eyes on her hands folded in her lap as she picked her words very carefully. "So my father said. Do you not think it would have been more appropriate to speak to me first?"

Stan laughed. "I wanted it to be a glorious surprise."

She raised her head and met his eyes directly for the first time since she'd come down the stairs and noted the difference in him. She had thought he would be the same Stan as

34

always, quietly willing to go along with whatever she said, but there was a new confidence in the way he held his mouth. It was not altogether unattractive, simply unfortunate at this moment in time when Adriane needed to be sure that their union, if it were to take place, must be formed in accordance with her desires and wishes.

"I'm not at all sure I'm ready for marriage." She kept her eyes steadily on his face as she noted he did indeed still have his moustache.

Again there was the smile and that new look in his eyes that was making Adriane uneasy. "Your father appears to believe you are."

"Yes, but in this matter, it is surely more important what I appear to believe." Her look did not waver as she refused to think about the scarcity of air to breathe inside the carriage.

The flush of victory drained from his cheeks, and when he spoke again, it was with his normal timidity. "You're not refusing my offer of marriage, are you, Adriane?"

In spite of the fact it was what she wanted, Adriane couldn't help but be a bit disappointed at how easily she had been able to deflate Stan's confidence.

"No, of course not," she said quickly. "Although it might have been nice if you could have made the offer to me face-to-face."

"You know I adore you, Adriane, and I've tried to ask you to marry me dozens of times, but you would never allow me to say the words." A familiar whine worked its way into Stan's voice.

"I am certainly ready to listen now."

"But my dearest Adriane, I can hardly make a proper proposal in a moving carriage, especially with the way Jack seems to be finding every bump and rut in the road."

"Very well." Adriane turned her eyes back to her gloved hands in her lap. "Perhaps on another occasion when the surroundings are more ideal."

"My father is announcing the engagement tonight." The whine in Stan's voice carried an edge of panic now.

"What engagement?" Adriane asked sweetly.

Adriane could feel Stan's eyes on her, but she refused to look up at him. After a long moment, Stan rapped on the front of the carriage and shouted at Jack to pull to the side of the street. When the driver jumped down to open the door for them, Stan informed him shortly that they merely needed a rest from the bumps of the road and when they were ready to proceed on to their destination, he would signal him.

With a puzzled expression, the man closed the door, and the carriage tilted a bit as he climbed back up on the driver's seat. All the noises of the street faded away as inside the carriage the silence grew and became almost overwhelming.

Just when Adriane thought Stan was going to simply rap on the carriage front and have his driver continue on to the benefit, he spread his handkerchief on the floor of the carriage, slipped off the seat onto one knee, and took Adriane's hand. "My dearest Adriane, will you do me the honor of agreeing to be my wife?"

Adriane looked at him and laughed. She couldn't help herself as she pulled him back up on the seat. "Oh, Stanley, I am sorry. I don't know what sort of madness came over me, making you do such a thing. Can you forgive me?"

Stan did not smile. "I am waiting for my answer."

Adriane's own smile disappeared. "And I will give you an answer if we can come to an agreement on certain matters pertaining to the event."

"This is not a business deal, Adriane."

"Of course not." Adriane allowed the first hint of a blush to come into her cheeks. Now that she had things under control, she could afford to show a bit of weakness. "It's just that I would not want to marry until September. The summer is so hot for weddings, don't you think? And I would need time for proper planning and to have my dresses made. You do understand, don't you, Stan?"

"September seems a good month. I think my mother will approve."

Adriane turned her eyes back down to her hands to hide the smile wanting to play around her mouth at the thought of Meta Jimson approving of anything to do with this whole affair as long as Adriane was the bride. Adriane swallowed her smile and quickly struck her second and even more important bargain. "Also, I must be able to continue writing."

"Really, Adriane, I don't—"

Adriane interrupted him before he could word a refusal. "I know you will be able to provide wonderfully for us, Stanley." She peeked up at him from under her long dark lashes. She knew how to use her charms if necessary. "But I do so enjoy my writing. Perhaps I could continue my Sally Sees All column for the paper or find some other creative outlet."

"I suppose a bit of poetry writing would not be improper. At least until the babies begin arriving." He took her hand again and put it to his lips. That unsettling look was back in his eyes.

The panic fluttered inside her. She couldn't think about babies yet or how they came to be. She would have to get used to the idea of marriage to Stan first. "There may not be babies right away."

His eyes slid away from her face down to her bosom encased in the plain dress. "There are always babies," he said softly. "You'll enjoy that."

She knew he was not meaning the babies, and though her cheeks flamed, she managed to keep her voice calm and level. "Stanley Jimson, I'm surprised at you."

"People often are, my dearest Adriane," he said with a laugh that wasn't altogether pleasant.

Adriane was relieved when he gave the signal for the carriage to begin moving again. He began talking about the party in their honor that night, and she managed to smile and nod at the appropriate moments. He took her hand in his, and Adriane could think of no good reason to pull it away.

As they proceeded on toward Mrs. Wigginham's house, the air in the carriage seemed to be running out, and Adriane began to feel faint. She kept watching Stan as his words bounced off her ears and wondering how in the world she would be able to live the rest of her life with him. The rest of her life.

Perhaps she would be glad for the babies to come and bring her the chance of escape through death. Henrietta had once told her that Adriane's own mother had embraced death the night Adriane was born. That she had wanted to die because she knew Wade Darcy deeply regretted the day he had married her. It was a lie. Not that her mother had died giving her birth, but that her father had regretted their love. By this time Henrietta's every thought had been darkened by the bitterness of grief. She had lost three babies, and Wade no longer went to her bed. Adriane had only been ten, but she had known. As Henrietta sometimes told her before shoving her in the dark closet under the stairs, Adriane always knew too much.

But now Adriane did not know enough. What did she really know about this man sitting beside her? What did she know of marriage? Worst of all, she knew no other choice. For a few seconds she couldn't breathe. As she fought to keep from gasping for breath, she fingered the carriage door handle and considered throwing it open. She needed more air.

She forced herself to breathe in and out slowly. It would not do to fall apart in front of Stan. With effort, she pushed the fluttering panic back into a dark corner in her mind and took control of her emotions. She might be swept away in a flood toward the altar, but she could at least try to swim a little to see if she might make headway against the force of the current.

First she would talk to her father that afternoon before any official announcements were made. Maybe there remained a chance she wouldn't have to be swept away to the altar at all. Her father had always been one to see reason. Adriane would just have to come up with some very good reasons not to marry Stanley Jimson, or at least not marry him so soon.

Adriane made herself smile over at Stan and really listen to what he was saying about the house his father was planning to build for them. When he paused to take a breath, she said, "But doesn't it take a long time to build a house? Perhaps September will be too soon for the wedding. We could wait until next spring."

"Don't bother your pretty little head over such things, Adriane. We are to live with Mother and Father until the house is finished."

"They have agreed to that?" Adriane wasn't able to keep a hint of disbelief from her voice.

"Of course. Father is very pleased with the whole arrangement. He likes you very much." Again Stan looked at her in a way that made Adriane want to shrink away from him before he went on. "He was the one who suggested perhaps it would be best if I consulted your father first."

Adriane frowned a bit. "Your father scarcely knows me."

"But he thinks you are lovely. As you are, my dearest." Stan caressed her hand with his thumb. "He and your father have become very close as they've worked together building up the American Party here in Louisville."

"Father has been attending a lot of their meetings, but he doesn't say or even write much about what goes on there."

"Of course not. The party leaders feel it is better if we form our policies in secret."

"But why?" Adriane asked.

The American Party had been gaining strength in Louisville, and her father was sure their candidates would sweep the city elections next month. The party, dubbed the Know Nothings by a New York editor because of the way members

39

claimed to "know nothing" when asked about the party's aims, did have a few stated objectives. The members took an oath to vote for no candidate who was not a native-born American and they favored a twenty-one-year wait for immigrants to become citizens.

Coleman Jimson, who hoped to be the Know Nothing candidate for state senator in the August elections, had been courting the *Tribune*'s support for months. So now Adriane waited for Stan's answer with considerable interest and hoped he wouldn't simply laugh at her question about politics as he sometimes did.

For the moment, he seemed to forget she was a woman who could not possibly understand nor be interested in anything political as he explained. "No battle was ever won by the general riding over to the opposing general and spreading out his battle plan in front of him. And this is a battle. Those of us who are true, native Americans have to fight against the influence of the immigrants who haven't had time to learn the ways of our great country. We have to make sure the country is preserved for those who founded it, for those who have fought in her wars."

His words echoed a bit in her mind as she remembered one of her father's recent editorials stating almost the exact same sentiments. It bothered her that she didn't know who was parroting whom.

She said, "The Irish and Germans just want a place to live and work."

"But at what cost to the true American? We cannot allow the city to be controlled by men who would answer to their pope before they would answer to their president." He glared over at her, the flush back in his cheeks.

"Do you think the pope tells them how to vote?" Adriane asked.

Instead of answering her question, he laughed as he said, "You do have a way of turning a conversation, Adriane, my sweet. A moment ago you have me down on my knees in a carriage, of all places, proposing, and the next you're plying me with questions on political matters you can't possibly understand. Sometimes I think you only do these things to tease me."

Adriane bit back the other questions she had. She wanted to know more, but she had to be circumspect in gathering political information to use in her Colonel Storey letters. No one knew she was Colonel Storey. Certainly not Stan or her father. Sometimes she thought Beck suspected, but he'd never said anything. A woman wasn't supposed to bother her pretty head in regard to anything political. Not only was it unseemly, it was rumored that the strain of thinking on such matters caused madness in females.

At least Colonel Storey could survive her marriage to Stan. She could still send his letters to the *Tribune*, and there would no doubt be more gatherings, more chances to overhear bits and pieces she could form into letters from the opinionated colonel.

She managed to smile over at Stan, but her smile faded when he began to look her over as if she were a new pacer he hoped to acquire for his carriage. "You look lovely as always, my sweet, but I do hope you will get some new gowns with a few ruffles and of a more comely color, say a soft pink or yellow. And perhaps you should keep your gloves on today."

Adriane held her tongue with effort as her determination to talk to her father before the evening grew stronger. Perhaps there was yet a way out of this dilemma. But as Stan kept talking, her heart grew heavy, and she felt the floodwaters sweeping her off her feet again.

4

*B*lake Garrett hurried along the street, trying to avoid anyone's eye who might want to talk. He was usually more than willing to stop and pass the time of day with people on the streets since it was one of the best ways he'd found to gather information, especially from those who disagreed with the editorials and stories in the *Herald*. That is, as long as they weren't waving a gun or knife about.

Blake tried to avoid those kinds of encounters and hadn't done too badly since coming to Louisville six months ago. In fact there had been so few run-ins with angry readers that Chesnut told him he must not be getting enough fire in his editorials.

But today he kept his eyes on the street in front of him. He was already late for Mrs. Wigginham's Library Aide Society meeting. When he'd first promised Mrs. Wigginham the *Herald*'s support of her worthy cause, he'd thought she would be satisfied to send him a letter telling of the proceedings, which he could then publish in a prominent place in the next issue of the *Herald*. But no, she'd insisted he must personally attend the meeting if he wanted to remain in her good graces.

Dear Mrs. Wigginham. She might smile and bat her eyes as if she were still a young belle of eighteen instead of well into her sixties, but Blake recognized power when he saw it, whether it was in the social arena or the political one. Someone not in Mrs. Wigginham's good graces would not find himself invited to important social gatherings. Someone not in her good graces wouldn't have much chance of becoming a respected editor in the town. So Blake was rushing along to her house even though he'd much rather be digging for news out on the streets.

Of course the old lady was also an indefatigable matchmaker. She'd no doubt have some friend's sweet-mannered daughter lined up to make cow eyes at him today. Blake sighed at the thought. When he'd tried to tell Mrs. Wigginham as diplomatically as possible that he was much too busy with the *Herald* right now to give the proper attention to the fairer sex, she had delicately touched her lace handkerchief to her lips to hide a smile while claiming that men always gave their attention to the ladies. It was their nature. She was simply trying to help him meet and attend to the proper young ladies.

When Blake edged past a pile of crates in front of Simpson's Candle Works, water splattered down on his head from the eaves still dripping from an early morning shower. He ran his hands through his black hair to shake out the dampness. He'd left his hat somewhere again. Probably in one of the taverns down in Shippingport, but there was no time to go back for it now. He had to make his appearance at the meeting not only to appease Mrs. Wigginham but also because he was sure Wade Darcy of the *Tribune* would be there. The Library Aide Society might not be sensational news, but it was becoming a matter of honor to Blake that Wade Darcy not beat him to any story.

Blake smiled a little to himself. Darcy would have seen a copy of the *Herald* by now and would know Blake had scooped another headline story. Blake had picked up a copy of the *Tribune* down in Shippingport that morning. There was no mention of the murders in it at all. Instead its columns had been filled with political news, readable and important enough, but not the kind of thing a man had to read first thing in the morning even if it made him late to work.

Wade Darcy had had things his way for a long time in Louisville. Too long. The *Tribune* still had the highest circulation of the dailies in the city, but it wouldn't be long before the *Herald* caught up. Blake was beginning to think he might pass the *Tribune* in another month, at least three months ahead of the schedule he'd originally set for himself when John Chesnut, the owner of the *Herald*, had hired him on as editor. Chesnut rubbed his hands together with glee and laughed out loud every time Blake reported the rising sales numbers to him.

Chesnut, an editor of the old school, didn't always agree with what Blake printed, but he gave him a free hand.

"As long as you keep nipping at Wade Darcy's heels, you can print stories of frog fights, for all I care," he'd told Blake even while shaking his head at the first murder story. "But son, are you sure folks are going to want to read this? I mean, it's not as if the poor girl was exactly a lady, and she was Irish besides. You know how most of the folks in this town feel about the immigrants."

"They'll want to read it," Blake had assured the old man.

And they had. While plenty of people thought the stories more than a little scandalous, they read them. There were those who accused Blake of reporting the details of the murders for the sole purpose of increasing the *Herald*'s circulation, a position Wade Darcy was glad to expound on. Just a couple months back the man had written an editorial attacking Blake for his "insensitivity and impropriety."

Worse, Darcy had hammered home to his readers the fact that Blake was a Northerner. Not something that would endear Blake to many of Louisville's finest citizens who liked to think of themselves as Southerners. Blake blew out his breath and recalled Darcy's words.

While New York City might have no standards of decency ruling its editors, Mr. Garrett might do well to remember that he presently abides in the South where gentility and consideration of our fair ladies' high sensibilities are much more to be considered than how many newspapers this type of sensationalism might sell.

Blake had always been able to remember most anything he read word for word. A blessing for a newspaperman, his father used to say. Or a curse when a man wanted to forget. Not that Darcy's words bothered Blake all that much. Readers would be disappointed if the editors didn't sling a little mud at one another in their editorials.

Plus it was hard to be convinced of Darcy's sincerity when a rehash of that first murder story in the *Herald* had been on the *Tribune*'s front page in the very same issue as the editorial.

Blake frowned now, thinking about that first murder. At the time, he'd thought it was a freak happening. The girl had been pretty and young, and though no one would come out and say it in so many words, she'd probably been making money the only way she could to help her family eat. Nobody had been too worried about it. A girl like that had to expect a bad end, and certainly nobody had thought it would happen again.

But it had. Twice now, with the poor woman found last night. Even the police were beginning to pay some attention to the murders. That morning, he'd stumbled across Sergeant Wentworth actually asking questions down in the latest victim's neighborhood. Blake thought with satisfaction that at least part of this newfound interest in keeping the law even in the Irish communities was due to his reporting of the crimes.

Blake didn't care what people thought. He hadn't written the stories only for the shock of the headlines. A woman getting murdered, whether she was considered a lady or not, was something that should concern the authorities, and three women murdered should be enough to set the whole town on its ear.

He had known this last woman. Kathleen O'Dell worked at the Lucky Leaf Tavern where Blake often stopped for a meal when he was down along the riverfront nosing about for stories. While the poor girl hadn't exactly been a beauty, she'd been pleasant enough and always quick with a wink and a laugh in an attempt to stir Blake's interest.

"Aye, twill be the lucky girl that ever catches your eye, Blake Garrett," she said the last time he'd seen her. "Or perhaps it is you already have a proper miss somewhere a-waiting for you. But there's plenty who need a girl not quite so proper as well." She raised her dark eyebrows and brushed her body close to him in invitation. "I could show you a good time."

"Just bring me my meal, Kathleen. Just the food," he told her with a laugh. "You know a newspaperman doesn't have any money left for fun after he has to pay for leads to his stories."

Little did he think that two days later he would be paying for news of her death. The ragged Irish boy had come banging on the door to his offices after midnight the night before. They'd already run the first issues, but when Blake heard what the boy had to say, he'd shouted to Joe to stop the press. They'd pulled half the front page out of the galley, and Joe had waited while Blake set the new type, composing the story on the spot.

Then, to be sure the story was genuine, Blake had gone down to the riverfront where he'd made himself look at what was left of Kathleen O'Dell. As he'd stared at her mutilated face, a cold resolve hardened inside him to do everything in his power to bring the woman's murderer to justice.

Kathleen and the other two murdered girls might not have been ladies, but they didn't deserve to die like this. He'd use the *Herald* to push that at the mayor and the chief of police in every way possible until there were some results. And in the

---

meantime, he'd search for his own clues. People sometimes told a newspaperman things they'd never tell anyone else if that man asked the right questions.

That morning, he'd hunted up all his regular contacts to get some leads on what those right questions might be, but even the people who usually made up some kind of tale rather than have nothing to say seemed to be at a loss when it came to the murders. It was becoming too apparent that no one had the first idea as to who the murderer was except the poor girls who could not tell and the murderer himself, who wasn't likely to admit to the heinous crimes.

So there was no one to accuse or even suspect. Worst of all, the killings seemed to be on some sort of schedule, about a month apart. Blake was determined to at least bring enough attention to the murders to make the monster, whoever he was, hesitate to strike again. Blake already had the death of one young woman on his conscience. He didn't relish having another.

Blake frowned as the noise of the street faded away. He didn't like to think about Eloise Vandemere. Pretty, silly Eloise. Blake might even have been foolish enough to marry her if her father hadn't deemed him such an unsuitable suitor.

Her death shared no similarities to the deaths of these poor Irish girls. Eloise had been a lady. That fact more than any other had been the reason Blake had no way to see that those who caused her death were brought to justice. He couldn't even be sure he shouldn't share in the blame.

Blake pushed thoughts of Eloise away. He could do nothing for her now. He'd had his chance before her death and failed her. He had to live with that and someday meet his Maker with that dark spot on his soul, but dwelling on it wouldn't bring Eloise back to life. He had moved on. Left New York behind and begun over.

Louisville was a new town, with new people and new problems. And he was a new person, nothing like the young pup who had imagined himself in love with Eloise. He'd landed on his feet with John Chesnut and his *Herald*. Some might call it luck. Pure, blind luck that had Blake knocking on Chesnut's door the very day the doctor had warned the old man to quit chasing the headlines if he wanted to keep breathing.

That was all right with Blake. If he could draw only one card as a newspaperman, then luck might be the best card to draw. It had served him well that day. Made Chesnut give him a second look. Ended up with him being an editor, the one who could decide what would be printed and what would not. A level of newspapering it might have taken him years to rise to in New York.

At last he saw Mrs. Wigginham's stately brick house down the street. Carriages surrounded it, but a quick check of his watch told him he wasn't overly late. He shoved the watch back in his pocket and straightened his lapels before he ran his fingers through his dark hair again. His last-second grooming did little good as his hair fell back into the same lines with a few curls lapping down on his forehead. He brushed at a bit of dirt on his trousers, checked his shoes for mud or worse, and bounded up the steps where a black servant opened the heavy wooden door before he had a chance to lift the brass knocker.

Mrs. Wigginham's large double parlor was full of ladies in frothy yellow, pink, and blue dresses with here and there the dark suit of a gentleman among them.

Mrs. Wigginham advanced on him the moment he stepped through the door. "Ah, Mr. Garrett, I'm so pleased you managed to work my little benefit into your busy schedule."

"Never too busy for you, madam," he said as took the old lady's hands. When she held up her cheek for Blake's kiss, he caught a whiff of perfume that reminded him of roses beginning to wilt.

With the obligatory kiss out of the way, she stood back and looked at him knowingly. "But you bring the odor of the riverfront with you."

Blake looked down at his clothes in embarrassment. "I do apologize if I'm offensive."

"No, my dear boy. You could never be that. I rather like the breath of fresh air you bring into my parlor, and I must confess that I guessed about the riverfront. I read of the latest tragedy in your newspaper this morning." She took his arm and led him across the long parlor. "Come, sit with me and tell me all about it."

He followed her meekly enough, glancing around a bit warily to see which young lady was bearing down on them.

Mrs. Wigginham noticed him surveying the room and laughed softly as she perched on one of the settees and patted the spot beside her. "Do sit with me a moment." Once he was seated, she went on, an amused smile lingering in her eyes. "I regret you'll have to pick your own young lady today. I did plan for sweet Mary Sutcliffe to entertain you with her charms, but alas, her mother sent word Mary was not quite herself this afternoon."

"That is regretful." Blake remembered sweet Mary Sutcliffe from other occasions and felt no regret at all. She was a vapid little girl of a woman with a nervous giggle and a clinging hand he was never able to escape once she'd placed it on his arm.

"Perhaps you could call and leave your card so she will know you missed her."

"Perhaps," Blake said with a noncommittal smile. "But now you have my undivided attention, so please tell me about this latest cause of yours."

"Oh my dear boy, please. You make me sound like one of those Northern reformers who take up their causes." She held up her hands as though to ward off his words before picking up her folded fan to tap a slim volume of poetry on the table beside them. "I'm only attempting to interest the local citizenry in expanding the library's book collection."

"Of course. A very worthy endeavor and one that seems

to have considerable support, especially among the ladies."
Blake glanced out at the people around them and then back
at the woman beside him.

"I've found our local ladies sincerely eager to help broaden
the interests of the community in proper ways. I do hope your
newspaper will see fit to join in support."

"You need not worry on that account, Mrs. Wigginham.
The *Herald* stands ready to support any worthwhile community activity."

"I never doubted that." Mrs. Wigginham smiled and laid
her hand on his arm. "Now don't think you have to dance
attendance on me. You can go capture one of the young
beauties."

"I fear none of them are as entertaining as you, dear lady."

"You have a silver tongue, Mr. Garrett, and you should be
ashamed, using it on an old lady like me." She laughed with
pleasure. "But please don't stop."

Blake managed to hold his smile in place. Underneath all
those layers of social fluff was a shrewd old lady who knew
more about the people of Louisville than anyone else was ever
likely to know, and most of the time he enjoyed talking to her.
But there were times when he wearied of the social games.

A stir at the door caught his attention. An odd hush fell
over the double parlors for just a second as a new couple
entered before a buzz of whispers circled the room.

"Our couple of note today," Mrs. Wigginham said. "It's
supposed to be a secret, but everyone here has already heard
they plan to announce their engagement this evening. They
do make a lovely pair, don't you think?"

Blake didn't answer. His eyes were still on the girl in her
rather plain reddish dress. There was something different
about her as she surveyed the room quickly, her eyes resting
for a moment on Mrs. Wigginham but passing almost without
notice across him. When she turned to allow her escort to help
her off with her cloak, her dark hair spilled carelessly down

her back as if she hadn't had time to properly arrange it. The man spoke into her ear, and the girl pulled up a smile that looked somewhat forced as they turned to face the people.

"She's beautiful," Blake said.

He didn't realize he'd spoken aloud until Mrs. Wigginham looked at him with raised eyebrows. "So she is. But I fear young Stanley Jimson has gotten rather more than he bargained for when he bargained for our dear Adriane's hand in marriage. And his mother has quite taken to her bed." Mrs. Wigginham's smile became a chuckle. "The whole situation is just too delightful."

"Stanley Jimson?" Blake watched the man tucking the girl's hand under his arm. He'd met Stanley, a pale shadow of his father, Coleman Jimson, who was being advanced as the Know Nothing candidate for state senate. Coleman Jimson had come to the *Herald* early on courting Blake's support. Blake hadn't trusted the man then and nothing he'd seen or heard since had caused him to change his mind. But he was treading softly. Coleman Jimson was a powerful man with an army of friends, and Blake wanted to have his facts rock solid before he took him on in the paper. He had time. The election for state senator was not until August.

"You surely know Stanley." Mrs. Wigginham was taking obvious delight in sharing every detail with Blake. "He's at all the socials, quite the life of the party if the ladies can talk him into playing the piano for them."

"I've met him, but not the young lady with him."

"You're impressed." Mrs. Wigginham's smile lit up her eyes as she touched her lips with her handkerchief. "The first woman in Louisville to impress you turns out to be none other than Adriane Darcy. This is getting more delightful by the moment."

"Darcy?"

"Oh yes, my dear boy. Wade Darcy's beautiful, opinionated daughter. The volumes I could tell you about that girl and the unorthodox way Wade has raised her. They say she's been setting type since she was ten, and was never properly educated. I doubt she even knows how to do needlework or play the piano."

"I suppose young Stanley can do that. Play the piano, I mean."

"Now, Mr. Garrett, don't be naughty." Mrs. Wigginham reached over to give his arm a little shake as though to upbraid him before she went on, her eyes dancing with amusement. "Stanley is a very sweet young man. Always gallant, especially to his mother."

"Who is not so happy over the upcoming union, you say."

"I surely didn't say that. You must have misunderstood, my dear boy," Mrs. Wigginham said with another pleased laugh. Her hand tightened on his arm. "Oh look, they're coming over to speak to me. I'll be able to introduce you properly."

The little woman's eyes were sparkling and color bloomed in her cheeks. Blake thought she looked ten years younger than she had when he came in. "You planned this whole thing, didn't you?"

"Why, I'm sure I don't know what you could mean, Mr. Garrett, but of course I wanted Adriane to come. She writes such wonderful notices of my little benefits. You should really read them to get some pointers."

"That sounds like excellent advice," Blake said as he started to stand up. "And now if you'll excuse me, I'll get us something to drink."

"I'm not the least bit thirsty, Mr. Garrett, and I would think you'd enjoy meeting the competition." Mrs. Wigginham kept a firm hand on his arm to keep him from making his escape. "It is whispered that our sweet Adriane writes half of what appears in the *Tribune*. While that is shocking to be sure, it also makes her rather interesting, don't you think?" Mrs. Wigginham leveled her eyes on him as she went on without waiting for an answer. "Now do be a good boy and allow an old lady her fun."

5

*A*driane could hardly believe her eyes when she looked across Mrs. Wigginham's parlor and saw the man who had grabbed her down at the riverfront that morning. It couldn't be, but there he was. Staring directly at her. Her heart began pounding madly as she fought the urge to flee back out the front door before the man could recognize her.

She might have lost the battle and run like Cinderella at the stroke of midnight if she hadn't caught a glimpse of herself in one of Mrs. Wigginham's many mirrors. Her breathing slowed as her panic receded. In spite of his sharp eyes, the man would hardly make the connection between the ragged Irish boy he'd grabbed in the dim light of the streetlamps and the picture of a lady she presented now. And what did it matter if he did? No one would believe him even if he were ungentlemanly enough to speak of it.

She lifted her head a bit defiantly, but did not look in the man's direction in spite of the way she could practically feel his eyes burning into her. Perhaps it had nothing to do with her early morning visit to the murder scene but was simply because she looked so out of place in her dark cranberry dress among all the pastel skirts of the other young ladies. He looked as out of place himself in the same rumpled suit he'd had on that morning, but it wasn't just his unpressed coat. It was more that he seemed too large for the room, as though he'd had to corral his energy in order to play attendance on Mrs. Wigginham.

Adriane had the crazy desire to raise her eyes and meet the man's brazen stare directly to challenge his memory. Saner thoughts ruled. She kept a polite smile firmly on her lips and pretended not to notice him at all while Stan helped her off with her cloak.

Yesterday she might have whispered to Stan to ask who the man might be, but today everything was changed. Stan was no longer simply a convenient escort but the man she was to marry. As Stan handed Adriane's cloak to the servant, whispers frantically circled the room. Adriane kept her smile firmly fixed on her face even as her heart sank. It was more than obvious that their pending engagement was far from a secret.

Her head high, Adriane pretended not to notice the curious stares as she crossed the long parlor to greet Mrs. Wigginham. Stan kept Adriane's hand tucked tightly under his arm as though he feared she might try to escape him.

Oddly enough, Mrs. Wigginham seemed to be holding on to the man by her side as if fearing the same thing about him. In fact, the man did appear anxious to escape as he began to rise from his seat beside the old lady. All around the room, Adriane noticed young ladies poised, ready to rush the man whenever Mrs. Wigginham removed her hand from his arm.

If she did. Adriane looked directly at Mrs. Wigginham. A happy flush of red spread across her cheekbones and her eyes sparkled as though she'd just discovered a potion to recapture her youth.

There was no denying the man was handsome, Adriane thought, as she slid her eyes quickly past him again. Black hair curling across his forehead. Eyes almost as dark. Skin that showed he was outside in the weather a lot. A dark moustache that surprisingly sprouted a few red hairs. A mouth that seemed to want to curl into a smile but did not. Broad shoulders stretching the material of that wrinkled coat. He was not the typical guest at one of Mrs. Wigginham's afternoon functions.

Yet everyone else in the room, including Stan, seemed to know him. In fact, Stan muttered under his breath as they crossed the room, "What is he doing here?"

She might have asked Stan for information then, but she felt the eyes of the assemblage too strongly on her. An odd feeling of charged expectation seemed to be radiating in the air. At first Adriane had thought it was the knowledge that her engagement was supposed to be a secret until the announcement that night, but the closer they got to the man and Mrs. Wigginham, the surer she became that the tension had something to do with him. It was almost as if everyone in the room knew of their moonlight encounter and was practically holding their breath, waiting to see what might happen next.

Adriane decided she would not give them the pleasure of seeing her show any kind of shock or surprise, no matter what this man said or did. Already his manner was quite brazen as his eyes continued to bore into her. For the briefest second she allowed herself to look directly at him. A spark seemed to sear the air between them, almost as if they shared some kind of familiar bond. But that was foolish. Adriane quickly averted her eyes. She had no idea who he was, and their encounter that morning hardly made any sort of bond between them. Even if he did recognize her.

"Mrs. Wigginham." Adriane ignored the man who had risen to his feet as she leaned down to speak to the old lady. "It is so good of you to open your house for such a worthy cause. I'm sure all the patrons of the library will greatly benefit from the added volumes that will be donated as a result of your efforts."

"How kind of you to say so, Adriane. And so good of both you and Stanley to come to my little gathering when I know you must have many plans to make." Mrs. Wigginham smiled over at Stan before returning her eyes to Adriane.

Adriane kept her smile firmly in place even though her heart sank a bit at the woman's words. "Plans? I'm sure I don't know what you mean, Mrs. Wigginham."

"Now, Adriane, you needn't pretend with me. We all know your delightful little 'secret.'" Mrs. Wigginham looked at Stan again. "I have to admit I was beginning to wonder if you were going to be able to capture her, Stanley."

"I never had any doubts." Stan sounded smug as he glanced at Adriane before looking back to Mrs. Wigginham to trot out his best manners. "And it's always a supreme delight to come to one of your events, my dear lady. My mother asked me to extend her regrets on not being able to attend today. As you say, there is much to plan."

"Of course," Mrs. Wigginham agreed easily. "I'm sure it will be the event of the year."

Adriane listened to them, her smile firmly fixed on her face. It was growing more and more difficult to believe she could somehow change her father's mind about this marriage being necessary. Especially with the whole town practically already invited to attend the ceremony before she was even consulted. A fluttery finger of panic tried to edge back out in her mind, but she shoved it away from her thoughts.

She could hardly give in to panic right now, not with Mrs. Wigginham watching her so closely. And it wasn't only Mrs. Wigginham's eyes on her. The man beside the woman continued to stare at Adriane without the first hint of politeness. She glanced over at him coldly, her smile gone for the moment as Adriane decided to take matters into her own hands. If the man recognized her, so be it.

"I beg your pardon, sir. I fear we have not been properly introduced."

"No, indeed, we have not," the man said with the beginnings of a smile that showed he knew much more about Adriane than she knew about him. "But we mustn't cheat dear Mrs. Wigginham out of the pleasure."

Mrs. Wigginham laughed delightedly. "Oh, do forgive me, Adriane. It appears I have been lax with the social niceties, but I assumed the two of you were already acquainted."

Adriane tore her eyes away from the man to look at Mrs. Wigginham. Could the man have already revealed their meeting that morning? No, she thought not, for Mrs. Wigginham didn't look shocked, only amused.

Mrs. Wigginham rose from the velvet settee to touch Adriane's arm as she made the introductions. "Dear Adriane, this is Blake Garrett. Mr. Garrett, Adriane Darcy. Mr. Garrett is the new editor of the *Herald*, as I'm sure you're aware, Adriane."

Red spread across Adriane's high cheekbones as her eyes flashed back to the man beside Mrs. Wigginham. No wonder the old lady was having so much fun. Adriane glanced over at Stan. He could have warned her. A whisper as they were crossing the floor wouldn't have been too much to ask.

With effort, Adriane managed a polite smile. "How nice to meet you at last, Mr. Garrett. I have to admit I was beginning to wonder if I had a smudge on my cheek, the way you were staring at me. It's a relief to know it's only because I am from the enemy camp."

"Dear Adriane, you do say the most wicked things." Mrs. Wigginham's smile lit up her whole face.

Adriane hadn't seen the old lady this animated since the rumor had gone around town that the mayor's wife was leaving him. And it seemed she was not through with her fun for the day. She took Stan's arm and leaned heavily on it. "My dear boy, would you mind helping an old lady over to the table? I do need to be sure the refreshments are holding out."

When Stan looked from Adriane to Blake, Mrs. Wigginham

quickly said, "Don't worry about the two of them. They no doubt would enjoy a few minutes to get acquainted, and I think we can trust them not to duel in my parlor." She began moving off with Stan in tow. "Now do tell me all about what sort of event your mother is planning for this evening. Perhaps there would be some way I could help. If not tonight, then with some other event. A tea in Adriane's honor might be appropriate, don't you agree?"

Stan, used to doing his mother's bidding without complaint, let Mrs. Wigginham lead him away with no further resistance. Mrs. Wigginham was the one who looked back at Adriane, a mischievous glint in her eyes.

"You have to admire a hostess who enjoys her parties," Blake Garrett said.

"Mrs. Wigginham is a dear." Adriane had a polite smile firmly in place again as she looked up at him. She had wanted to meet Blake Garrett for weeks, and now she'd had two encounters with him in one day. "It's so nice to finally meet you, Mr. Garrett. I've heard so much about you."

"I daresay some of it should not be repeated." A smile broke over his face and practically exploded from his eyes, which were much bluer than she had at first thought.

Adriane's knees went a little weak just from the power of it, but she pulled herself together. It had been a busy morning, and she had forgotten to take time to eat. That surely had more to do with her weak knees than Blake Garrett's smile.

Even so, there was no denying he was handsome. And not at all what she had expected. He looked more like one of the daring riverboat captains rather than an editor. But then most of the editors she knew were her father's age or older.

Acutely conscious of the scrutiny of those around them, Adriane laughed lightly before she said, "You're staring again. I'm still not sure there's no smudge on my face. It wouldn't be the first time, I regret to say."

"Nor the first time some man stared at you because you're beautiful."

"Not usually so boldly," Adriane said.

"I must apologize, Miss Darcy. I admit I'm often too bold for proper manners, but I find it can be an advantage in the newspaper profession, don't you agree?"

"I'm sure my father would." Adriane kept her voice light. "I am more of the opinion that boldness is important in any profession a gentleman might choose."

"And how about for the ladies?"

"I rather fear that boldness for the ladies is limited to a daring neckline or a hint of paint on one's cheeks." Adriane carefully lowered her eyes and pretended a blush. She knew she should hate this man. Loyalty to her father demanded that much. But everything about him intrigued her. Surely she could hate him more effectively once she knew him better, and as Mrs. Wigginham said, they could hardly duel in her parlor.

"In the North, a few of the ladies are becoming much bolder than that. A few are even speaking out for women's rights." His voice seemed to be trying to challenge her.

"Yes, I've seen the articles in the papers. We rarely reprint them because Father is of the opinion that our city is not yet ready for such radical thinking."

"And what is your opinion, Miss Darcy?" He sounded sincerely interested.

She searched for a safe answer, one that would be honest yet not shock anyone who might be eavesdropping on their conversation. It would not be a good day to start a controversy in regard to the rights of women. Today it seemed the only right she had was the right to be glad a socially proper young man desired to marry her.

She quickly scooted her thoughts away from Stan and smiled at Blake as if they were discussing nothing more important than which spring flower should be her favorite. "I believe a young woman should have the same opportunity to be educated as a young man."

He peered down at her as though her answer surprised him. "Correct me if I am wrong, but aren't there a dozen young ladies' academies in this city alone?"

"So there are. As a matter of fact, I attended one once for several months. Most of them are very good at teaching a young lady to be charming."

"A most necessary skill," Blake said.

She knew he was baiting her, but she played along anyway. He would not get the better of her with words. "Without a doubt, sir. Perhaps even essential to a woman in these days."

"And if you were, God forbid, not of the fairer sex, but one of the gentlemen with a choice of professions, which profession would you choose? To edit a paper as your father does?"

"That might be an interesting possibility, but I do believe, since we are merely dreaming, that first I'll spend a few years as a riverboat captain. Perhaps I could make a record-breaking run to New Orleans."

He laughed. "I'm afraid, my dear Miss Darcy, that not all riverboat captains are gentlemen."

She smiled slightly and looked straight into his dark blue eyes. "Neither are all editors."

The laughter was suddenly gone, but in its place was a considering look as Adriane knew he was seeing beyond her pretty face now. It was not a bad look, and she didn't shy away from it but met it fully in spite of the fact she still feared he might recognize her as the Irish boy he'd grabbed that morning. It was a look she'd never seen in Stan's eyes or one she was ever likely to see. Again the panic reared inside her, and she looked away from Blake Garrett for fear his quick eyes would catch some glimpse of her worry.

"Your father has taught you well, Miss Darcy," Blake said at last.

"Not all would agree with that assessment. Sometimes not

even my father." Adriane wished the words back at once, but words spoken could not be edited and changed. So instead she hurried on. "Now if you'll excuse me, I do believe Stan needs my help with Mrs. Wigginham."

"I'm sure he does. I wouldn't be surprised to discover young Stanley needs someone's help with everything," Blake said. "You have my sympathy."

"I beg your pardon," Adriane said coldly.

He did not take back his words. "You heard what I said."

"Stanley is a wonderful young man from a very influential family." Adriane was careful to sound as if she meant each word and then wished she hadn't bothered to defend Stanley. What difference did it make what this man, Blake Garrett, thought?

"With a great deal of money, I hear. Congratulations, Miss Darcy. Your future should be quite comfortably secure." His dark blue eyes burned into hers.

Adriane knew she should look away, but she couldn't. She did manage to keep smiling even as the word "secure" echoed emptily in her mind. She felt anything but secure as the flood pushed against her, threatening to rip her away from all she'd ever held dear.

"So it seems," she murmured. *Dear Father in heaven,* she thought, *how will I survive this?* No answer came to her silent prayer as the man's eyes kept probing her as though he could see beyond her words.

"Yes." His smile disappeared as he pushed his next words at her. "Just think of it. In forty years you may very well be the next Mrs. Wigginham, playing your parlor games with the people who come to pay you homage for being so rich. What causes do you think you might espouse, Miss Darcy?" He raised his eyebrows at her.

His words and look infuriated her, but she refused to give him the pleasure of seeing he'd been successful at upsetting her. Instead she smiled coolly up at him. "It's been an interesting experience meeting you, Mr. Garrett. I'm sure our paths will cross again in the months to come."

"I certainly hope so." His smile returned, wide and unforced. "I enjoy a good duel of words whether I win or lose."

Adriane laughed sweetly. "Why, Mr. Garrett, I have no idea what you could mean. If there is any dueling of words, I'm sure I must leave that up to you and my father." Quickly before he had a chance to respond in any way, she turned away from him and began making her way across the room to Mrs. Wigginham and Stan.

Because she didn't want to seem to be fleeing the man, she stopped to chat with this or that group of ladies. She asked several of them about the efforts to acquire more books for the library, and they all answered with care just in case their words should appear in the *Tribune*.

No one mentioned her engagement to Stanley Jimson. After all, that was supposed to be a secret until evening. But the old women beamed at her as if she'd succeeded, at last, in doing something right, and the younger ones hid their giggles behind their fans while their eyes darted from Adriane to Stan and back.

By the time she joined Stan and Mrs. Wigginham, Adriane's face hurt from so much smiling, but she dared not stop. Mrs. Wigginham sent Stan after some fresh tea and waited until he was out of earshot before she said, "I trust you found Mr. Garrett amusing." She was regarding Adriane closely.

"Yes, indeed. I've looked forward to meeting him." She didn't let her smile waver as she looked at the woman. "How kind of you to arrange an introduction."

"I fear I may have delayed my kindness too long," Mrs. Wigginham said.

"Delayed too long in what way, madam?" Adriane asked, totally puzzled by the old lady's remark.

Mrs. Wigginham didn't seem to hear Adriane's question as she stared across the room toward Blake Garrett. He was surrounded now by young ladies who were perhaps hoping one of his flashing smiles might be directed their way. After a moment, Mrs. Wigginham said, "He is a charming man, don't you agree? My young friends practically faint from pleasure if I pair him with them at my parties. If I were only thirty years younger myself."

"I fear he didn't pull out too many of his charms for me." Adriane looked back at Blake Garrett for the first time since she'd left his side. He seemed to sense instantly when she looked his way, and their eyes met. Again there was that strange flash of feeling between them even though Adriane immediately turned her own eyes back to Mrs. Wigginham. Mrs. Wigginham's delighted smile had faded. In fact she looked a little sad.

"Is something wrong, Mrs. Wigginham? Perhaps I should help you to a chair."

"No, no, my dear. I was just regretting my lost youth. I do hope you won't regret yours."

"I don't know what you mean," Adriane said.

"I think you do, child." Mrs. Wigginham's eyes bored into her. "You must know how very fond I am of you. For a truth, you remind me a great deal of myself when I was younger. Things have not changed so much, you know."

Suddenly Mrs. Wigginham tiptoed up to touch Adriane's cheek with her dry lips. "Do try to be happy, dear Adriane."

Stan returned with their tea in time to hear the old lady's last words. "You need not worry about that, Mrs. Wigginham," he said. "I plan to devote my life to making Adriane extremely happy."

"I'm sure you will, Stanley." Mrs. Wigginham's polite smile looked a bit strained when she turned to take her tea from Stanley. Without the first sip, she set the cup down on a table beside them. Her smile vanished as she put her hand on Adriane's arm and gave it a slight shake as though to make sure Adriane listened to her next words. "But never forget. True happiness must come from within. It is the one gift only we can give ourselves."

6

When Stan walked Adriane to her door after the Library Aide Society meeting, he told her how much he looked forward to the evening's events and how he knew she would look her most beautiful. She hadn't mentioned anything about Lucilla having a dress prepared for her, but he already knew.

She wanted to ask him once again to delay the announcement, but she did not allow the words to pass her lips. She'd already made her request in the carriage on the way home from Mrs. Wigginham's.

With her nicest smile pasted on her face, she'd allowed him to hold her hand as she explained in her sweetest voice, "It's just that I feel we both need time to get used to the idea, Stan."

"I've been used to the idea for months," he said.

"But I have not. I've hardly considered marriage at all."

"I find that hard to believe, my dearest Adriane. Young ladies rarely ever consider anything else." He laughed before he lifted her hand up to touch his lips to her fingers.

Adriane resisted the urge to jerk her hand free as she searched for the right words to make her point. "I fear you will find I am not your typical young lady."

"No, you certainly are not. I think even Blake Garrett agreed with that."

"What do you mean?" Adriane asked carefully. She didn't really want to talk about Blake Garrett.

"I saw the way he looked at you. It was not a bit proper, and I can't imagine what Mrs. Wigginham was thinking when she insisted on dragging me away to leave you alone with him." Stan's smile disappeared as his eyes narrowed and he tightened his hold on her hand. "I shall have to insist that you not speak with him again."

His demanding tone irritated her, but she bit back an angry reply. She needed to carefully pick her fights today. So instead of telling him she'd talk with whomever she pleased, she said, "You need not worry about that. I doubt Mr. Garrett and I will have many opportunities to speak with one another since he and Father are practically sworn enemies. Besides, I found the man rude and insensitive."

"He's that all right." Stan frowned slightly. "The man has no regard for the sensibilities of his readers, else he wouldn't print those shocking murder stories in his paper as if those poor unfortunate girls were ladies."

"Ladies or not, their deaths are distressing, and the police should do all they can to catch the murderer." At last Adriane managed to ease her hand away from Stan's. She felt quite confined enough simply being in the carriage with him without having to submit to him holding on to her.

"Of course," Stan agreed easily as he sat back in the seat and eyed her. "But even if the villain's not caught, I doubt the fair young ladies of our town have any reason to worry in regard to their own safety. Garrett is merely trying to stir up fear among the population in an unseemly attempt to sell his newspapers."

"But there's no way for anyone to know that for sure, is there?" She frowned a little. "I mean, about whether there will be another victim and who that might be."

"I suppose you're right. Who could know that except the one responsible for the dreadful crimes?"

The scene she'd seen that morning flashed through Adriane's mind, and she couldn't keep from shuddering.

Stan scooted closer to her and slipped his arm around her shoulders. "My dear Adriane, you have nothing at all to be concerned about except looking beautiful for the announcement tonight. From now on, I will always be close by to protect you."

Adriane had barely stopped another shudder from shaking through her, and she had been completely unable to keep the panic from slipping back out into the open and flapping its wings of worry until it filled her mind.

Ten minutes after Stan left her at the door, Adriane had on her old work dress and was downstairs in the shop proofing the galleys. The story of the latest murder was a calm repeat of the facts in the *Herald* with a quote from the mayor that everything possible was being done to track down the killer. The chief of police promised security would be stepped up all over the city and assured the good people of the community that they were safe.

Her father's editorial made no mention of the murders. Instead he expounded on the qualifications any voter needed in order to make an intelligent choice in an election. Colonel Storey's letter attacked the Know Nothing party for its secretive ways and asked what possible reason a political party could have for keeping its aims and purposes unknown to the general public. The letter carried just the slightest hint that something illicit might be going on.

Her father had fired off a response to her Colonel Storey letter, claiming it to be a sacred right of Americans to assemble as they pleased and to promote the good of the country in whatever manner the assemblage deemed best. She read his words with a slight smile.

This editor has attended some of the "secret" meetings our dear Colonel Storey refers to, and I can attest to my readers that the members of the Know Nothings, more correctly called the American Party, are simply working to preserve the special God-given freedoms to which all true Americans are entitled. Note that this editor speaks of true Americans. That means those men who were born here on our sacred soil and have fought and bled for the freedoms we hold so dear. I have to wonder how the good Colonel came by his military title. From his words it doesn't seem as though he knows the value of serving his country.

Her father had responded to her Colonel Storey letter just as she'd expected. In fact she could probably have written the words for him. Sometimes she did. She knew how he would think. She knew how her imaginary Colonel Storey would think. What she sometimes didn't know was how she herself thought.

The words in front of her eyes faded away as she remembered again the party that night. She couldn't allow this to go any further. With a deep breath for courage, she stood up to go face her father. She could not marry Stanley Jimson. At least not so soon. Perhaps she might be able to learn to care for Stanley in a way that might lead to marriage, but she needed time to develop such feelings. Surely her father would understand.

Her father was holed up in his small office off the pressroom with the door closed. That meant he was working on a story, but Adriane knocked anyway.

"Come back in half an hour," her father shouted.

Risking his anger, Adriane cracked open the door and said, "I need to talk to you now, Father."

His voice changed, lightened. "Adriane, of course. Come in."

She pushed the door the rest of the way open and carefully sidestepped the stacks of old papers, books, and flyers to stand in the narrow bit of free space in front of her father's desk. Makeshift shelves full of more books and papers lined the wall behind his desk. Boxes of old type and who knew what else gathered dust behind the door. There was one ladder-back chair intended for visitors, but it too was piled high with papers. Her father had tossed the rumpled copy of the *Herald* on top of the pile, and just seeing it sent a strange little jolt through Adriane.

She couldn't think about Blake Garrett. Not now. She needed to come up with the right arguments to convince her father she wasn't ready for marriage. To Stanley Jimson or anyone. She stared at her father as she tried to organize her thoughts.

Wade Darcy's desk was an island of neatness in the midst of all the other confusion of paper in his office. The last week's issues of the *Tribune* were stacked neatly on the right-hand corner of his desk as always. Blank paper waited on the left corner. His pens and ink were laid out and ready in front of him just above the dark green blotter. A couple of New York papers, some telegraph messages, and a few letters lay within easy reach as he worked on a story.

Even the page full of handwritten words in front of him was neat with few scratch outs. Adriane had always been awed by how her father was able to get his stories and editorials the way he wanted them the first time, while she had to rework anything she wrote at least twice before she could bear to think of seeing it in print. He told her he'd learned to write it right the first time through practice and because of deadlines, and that someday, with practice and dedication, she might have the same control over her own written words.

Adriane had been writing long enough to doubt that, but she did need to be sure she got these words she was about to speak right the first time. As she looked at her father, smiling up at her from behind his desk, she wished she'd taken time to practice what she needed to say. For a minute she considered racing upstairs to her room to argue her case in front of her mirror or perhaps even try the words out in her journal before she spoke them aloud to her father. She sent up a quick prayer that the words she needed would find their way to her tongue.

"Forgive me for interrupting you, Father," Adriane started.

"That's no problem. This story is practically writing it-self." Her father waved at the paper in front of him and then smiled at her. "Have you come to talk about the party tonight? Lucilla's woman, Nora, showed me your dress. It's very elegant. You'll have to be sure to thank Lucilla properly."

"Of course."

"Oh yes, and I was supposed to tell you that Lucilla will send one of her maids over to help with your hair. I am to send one of the hands to fetch her."

"That's hardly necessary. I'm quite capable of fixing my own hair." Adriane had a sinking feeling in her stomach. The conversation was not starting out well.

"If you prefer, but you do want to look your best." He pulled his watch out of his vest pocket and checked the time. "So you may need to be getting ready soon."

"That's what I want to talk to you about, Father."

"Don't worry if you didn't get something done. Beck can handle whatever it is."

"I know he can," Adriane agreed. "And everything's run-ning on schedule in any case. The quotes you got from the mayor and chief of police were just what the murder story needed and should reassure the townspeople." Adriane's eyes strayed to the *Herald*. She thought about telling her father about meeting Blake Garrett, but bit back the words. She had to concentrate on getting a reprieve from this sentence of marriage.

"That was my aim," her father said. "The *Tribune* doesn't print stories just for the sensational value but for the good of our readers. The citizens of our town need to be assured that the authorities have things under control."

"Do they?" Adriane couldn't keep from asking.

"You aren't concerned, are you, Adriane? I mean for your

own safety." Her father took off his reading spectacles and peered up at her face. "Chief Trabue tells me the murders are localized in the immigrant areas of the town and that none of our ladies have any reason to doubt their safety. Besides, you shouldn't be worrying about anything but your own happiness today. I assume Stanley did speak with you."

"He spoke with me. It appears someone else has already spoken to the rest of the town. Everybody at Mrs. Wigginham's gathering was whispering about us."

"Such good news is hard to keep secret." A smile spread across her father's face again.

In the face of his obvious happiness over the whole affair, Adriane hesitated. She had no desire to disappoint him. Ever since she could remember, she'd always tried to please her father whenever she could. After all, he was the one who had rescued her from the dark closets and Henrietta. He was the one who had taught her history and encouraged her reading. He was the one whose love she'd never had to doubt.

And yet there had always been a kind of reserve between them. She couldn't remember him ever swinging her up in the air when she was a little girl. He never complimented any of her stories in the *Tribune*. Indeed he hardly seemed aware of the work she did on the paper or to keep the household running smoothly. Until Lucilla had come along and perhaps pointed out the value of having an attractive daughter to make a proper marriage, Adriane doubted her father had given the first thought to her appearance.

Now as he sat waiting for her to speak, he fingered his spectacles and let his eyes stray back to the page in front of him. She knew she'd best hurry out her arguments before she lost his attention altogether. "Father, I wonder if it might not be possible to wait awhile on the announcement."

He looked puzzled, unsure of her meaning at first. "Which announcement is that? No candidates have officially filed for office yet, have they?"

"No, Father. I mean the announcement of Stan's and my engagement." The smile fled his face, and Adriane rushed on before he could speak. "I need time to get used to the idea."

"What is there to get used to, Adriane? You've been seeing Stanley for months. He's a good man from a fine upstanding family, and he'll be able to provide well for you. Your future will be secure."

Again the word "secure" echoed hollowly inside her head. Her heart was beating too fast and her hands felt clammy, but she made herself put forth her best argument against the union. "I don't love Stan, Father."

Her father frowned and with his hands on the blotter pushed himself up to a standing position. He leaned across the desk to stare straight at her. "Love? What romantic nonsense is this?"

Her heart began pounding even harder, but Adriane stood her ground. "Marriage should be a union of love."

"You'll learn to love Stanley," her father said.

"I'm not sure that I can, Father."

He pushed away from his desk and tried to pace back and forth, but there wasn't room between the shelves of books and stacks of papers. So instead he stood still a moment and stared at the wall.

Adriane had seen him do the same thing a thousand times when he was searching for the right way to word his arguments in an important editorial. When at last he began speaking again, it was slowly and with great care, as though she might not be capable of understanding. Adriane had heard him speak to opposing editors in the very same tone, and her heart sank. He was going to refuse to understand.

"My dear, I think you have some misconceptions about the union of marriage. You mustn't believe what you read in those ladies' magazines or the silly novels some women are writing these days. Love is not the most important factor in a marriage. Far from it, in fact."

Adriane started to say something, but her father cut her off. "You can't argue with me on this, Adriane. I have more experience than you. I've been married twice."

"I know," Adriane said quietly. "I lived through one of those marriages. I saw how it destroyed Henrietta."

They had not spoken of Henrietta since her funeral over ten years ago, and now her father's eyes burned into Adriane even as he answered in his calmest voice. "It was not the lack of love that destroyed poor Henrietta but the lack of babies. And there was nothing I could do about that. The fault was with her."

Adriane wanted to ask what it was that had destroyed her own mother, but she dared not voice the question, even though Henrietta's words that her mother had wanted to die echoed in her head. Instead Adriane said, "And do you love Lucilla?"

Her father met her look directly. "I am very fond of Lucilla. She's a lovely woman, but love is not the most important consideration in our decision to marry."

"What is, Father?"

"Comfort. Security. Lucilla has both to offer me. Stanley Jimson has both to offer you."

"I'm happy with my life the way it is."

At last his eyes softened on her. "But you can't stay my child all your life, Adriane. Lucilla says it's not proper to have you working so much on the paper and neglecting the more important things a young lady your age should be doing. She says it's time you married."

"And what do you say, Father?"

"Lucilla is a woman. She knows more about these sorts of things than I."

"I am a woman too."

Her father came around the desk to take her hands. "You are. A very beautiful woman, but Lucilla tells me I have neglected your proper upbringing. That you know more about being a man than you do a woman and that you are very fortunate to have someone like Stanley Jimson who adores you as you are."

"I'm not at all sure that is true."

"But it is. He thinks you're the most wonderful girl he's ever known." Her father was smiling again now. "Remember, he talked to me yesterday."

"He doesn't know the real Adriane Darcy."

Her father squeezed her hands a bit and laughed gently at her. "There is only one Adriane Darcy, my dear. And since he's been keeping company with you for a good while, I'm certainly sure he's aware of the type of person you are. He respects and admires your talents and individuality."

"His mother has taken to her bed." Adriane wasn't sure why she brought up Meta Jimson except that she was running out of other arguments.

"Meta has always been too possessive when it comes to Stanley. She would be upset no matter whom he had chosen to marry, but given time, she will learn to love you."

"It appears we all have a lot of learning to do." Adriane squared her shoulders as she looked directly into her father's eyes. "I'm not sure I can go through with it, Father. Not unless I have time to adjust to the idea."

"The marriage won't have to be right away. You'll have plenty of time to appreciate all the advantages of marriage to Stanley Jimson, and by the day of the happy event, you'll be eager to join with him in holy matrimony."

Adriane pulled her hands away from her father's touch. She studied his face a moment longer before she said, "What if I refuse? What if I say I cannot marry Stan?"

"Cannot?"

"All right." She lifted her chin defiantly. "Will not."

He looked at her sadly for a moment. "You're twenty-two, Adriane. There are decisions that I suppose I cannot make for you anymore. This may very well be one of them, but you know how I feel. I want you to marry Stanley. I think he will make you happy, and I know it would make Lucilla and me very happy to see you in such a good situation before we marry ourselves. I don't think you should make any kind of foolish decisions just because of a silly, romantic notion about love."

"And what happens if I do make the 'foolish' decision not to marry Stan?"

Her father's sadness now was mixed with a bit of anxious concern as he began to realize how serious Adriane was. "I really don't know. I suppose I might be able to help you obtain a position as a teacher in one of the female academies in the North, although that wouldn't be what I would wish for you, my dear." Again he frowned. "And the Jimsons will naturally be upset. Coleman Jimson might withdraw his support from the *Tribune*, perhaps even insist on replacing me as editor."

"How could he do that? The *Tribune* is your paper."

Her father went back to stand behind his desk. He stared down at the papers there for a moment before he answered. "A little over a year ago we were short of cash and Coleman loaned me some money. I haven't been able to repay him as yet." He looked up at Adriane. "I will, of course, but he has been very considerate and has allowed me to take my time gathering the necessary funds. You understand, don't you, Adriane?"

And at last she did. The words came hard, but she said them. "Yes, Father. And perhaps you're right. Perhaps I am being too romantic."

"You are fond of Stanley, aren't you, Adriane?" Frown lines wrinkled his face as he peered across the desk at her.

"Of course. We've been friends for a long time."

So much relief washed over her father's face that Adriane feared he hadn't told her everything, but she didn't ask any more questions. She simply listened as he said, "I feel very sure Stanley will make you very happy, Adriane. I wouldn't have agreed to any of this, no matter what, in any other case."

"I know, Father." Adriane forced a smile. "Now, if you'll excuse me, I'd best begin dressing for the party tonight."

Again he came around the desk, this time to lay his hand on her cheek. It was the most affectionate gesture they ever exchanged, and Adriane wished for one crazy moment that he would hug her. "You will look beautiful in your new dress," he said.

Adriane turned away from him and fled the office before he could see the tears in her eyes.

Upstairs in her room, the beautiful blue dress spread across her bed mocked her. Adriane blinked away her tears and ran her fingers across the sleek fabric. She had to wear the dress. She understood that now. Slowly her hand moved up to touch one of the small bows decorating the neckline. Adriane had wanted Nora to take the bows off, but the dressmaker had assured her they were the latest rage on all the most fashionable dresses.

Adriane brushed away the last trace of tears and found her small sewing scissors on top of her bureau. With great care she snipped the threads holding the bows and pulled them off the dress. She might have to wear the dress. She did not have to wear the bows.

7

*B*lake Garrett sat at his desk and stared at the blank paper in front of him. He should have had the piece about Mrs. Wigginham's little benefit written an hour ago. All he had to do was wax eloquent about Mrs. Wigginham's noble desire to expand the holdings of the library and the fine support the ladies of the community were giving her efforts. He ought to be able to write the piece in his sleep, but thoughts of Adriane Darcy kept pushing everything else out of his mind.

He'd stayed at Mrs. Wigginham's far longer than the half hour he had planned, talking to a dozen pretty young things who tried to enlighten him on the meaning of the flowers a gentleman might send a lady. Silly little Cordie Fricklan had even found a copy of a book detailing this gentle art of expression in Mrs. Wigginham's parlor to show Blake. He feigned interest, all the while secretly watching Adriane Darcy.

He kept thinking he must have seen her somewhere before. Something about her was so familiar, especially those wonderful eyes, but he would remember if he had. No man was likely to forget meeting such a beautiful woman. While his eyes were pulled to her like iron filings to a magnet, she ignored him completely as she worked her way through the guests with young Jimson dancing attendance on her.

Every time Jimson caught Blake's eyes on Adriane, he glared across the room at Blake. Blake merely smiled back, half taunting the man. Stanley Jimson was a milksop, a mama's boy. The talk around town was that even his father had little use for him in spite of the fact Stanley was his only son.

Blake stared across his desk at the posters and news articles tacked to the wall in front of him without seeing any of the words. Behind him Joe was shouting at one of the hands, but Blake was only vaguely aware of the noise.

He shouldn't have told Adriane she had his sympathy. Still, he wasn't sorry he'd said what he had. A woman like Adriane Darcy should not even consider marrying a man like Jimson. Blake wondered what would have happened that afternoon if he had charged across Mrs. Wigginham's parlor to forcibly remove Adriane from the man's clutches and help her make her escape.

He smiled a little at the foolish thought. She, no doubt, had no desire to be rescued, since women generally set great store on marrying well. If he'd learned nothing else from his tragic affair with Eloise, he learned that.

He'd had nothing to offer Eloise but the infatuation of a foolish young man with dreams of someday running his own newspaper. Her father wasted little time pointing out to his daughter that dreams could not supply fancy dresses and servants, much less a house in the better parts of town where society ladies would stop in to leave their cards.

Any hint of a smile vanished from Blake's face as he rubbed his forehead. He didn't often think of Eloise, but here she had come back to haunt him twice in one day. It was the murders that brought her to mind, he supposed, but it did little good to think of her now. She was beyond his help, and perhaps had been ever since she'd made her choice.

"You do understand, don't you, Blake?" she'd told him

that day almost five years ago as tears wet her pale cheeks. "It's not that I don't love you. I do. Desperately. But I must do as Father says."

While Blake hadn't understood at the time, he accepted her choice and, surprisingly, had not mourned that choice very much. Instead he embraced his newfound freedom and decided love was a distraction he could do without until after he managed to achieve his goal of having his own paper.

It remained a distraction he could do without. He picked up his pen and wrote a couple of sentences on the paper in front of him as he tried to shove thoughts of Adriane Darcy out of his head.

So what if she intrigued him? Lots of things intrigued him. Such as who the river slasher was. Such as whether or not the Irish boy he'd grabbed that morning knew anything about the murders. Such as deciding which political candidates the *Herald* should support in the spring elections. Such as making sure he beat Wade Darcy to every important headline and making the *Herald* the most widely read paper in Louisville.

"Hey, boss." Joe came over to his desk. "Ain't you got that piece ready to go yet? You said it wouldn't take you five minutes."

"It's ready." Blake scribbled down one last line, then glanced quickly back over the paragraph he'd written and hoped it would please the old lady. It mentioned her name three times and the good cause twice. Still, it was short and not very flowery. Adriane Darcy's story would be better.

He handed the page to Joe who was watching him with a worried look on his face. "You ain't sick, are you, boss?"

"I'm fine, Joe." He smiled at the short, wiry man.

When Joe came around begging a job shortly after Blake took over the *Herald*, Blake had been ready to send him on his way, but Joe started talking before Blake could say the words.

"I need the work, Mr. Garrett, and I'm good at it. Just give me a couple of weeks to prove it to you." Keeping his eyes on the ground, the man had twisted the rim of his hat as he went on. "I guess maybe you might've heard I once upon a time had a problem with the drink, but I'm married now and she's got two little ones by her late husband—God rest his soul—and we need what money I can make for food, not the drink."

Blake hesitated. "What experience do you have?"

"I reckon at one time or another I've worked for nearly every paper in town," Joe said.

"The *Tribune*?"

"Some years back. But Mr. Darcy or his man Beck don't put up with much in the print shop. So I didn't last long." Joe's eyes darted up to Blake's face and quickly away. "You understand that was before I give up the drink."

"I understand," Blake said thoughtfully. "Well, Joe, it just so happens that some of the hands walked out when they heard Mr. Chesnut had hired some fellow down from New York City."

"I heard some talk on it. That's why I come over." Joe raised his head and looked directly at Blake for the first time since he'd come to the door.

Blake studied him intently. "I plan to make the *Herald* the biggest paper in this city, and in order to do that I need the right kind of men to back me up here in the shop."

"I know just about everything there is to know about printing a paper, boss. You learn a lot moving around the way I have."

Blake reached behind him and took an apron off the rack. "All right. You've got the job. We've been late with the last two issues. I don't want to be late again."

"Won't be no late issues while I'm here, Mr. Garrett. You can count on that."

Joe had been true to his word, staying sober and becoming as loyal to Blake and the *Herald* as a stray dog who'd finally found a home. Before a month was gone, he was practically running the shop. He knew all kinds of tricks to make the printing go faster and had a way of keeping the other hands on task. Best of all, he knew most of the other papers in the city inside and out, and he was just as anxious to see the *Herald* pass them by as Blake was.

Now Blake looked at Joe and said, "I met Wade Darcy's daughter this afternoon."

"Adriane?" Joe's face softened a little. "She's something, ain't she, boss?"

"What do you know about her, Joe? I mean, did you meet her back when you worked for the *Tribune*?"

"Meet her?" Joe's voice went up a level as if Blake's question surprised him. "The girl was always in the shop helping do this or that. Beck used to say he had her setting type before she was ten. I reckon when I was there she might have been about thirteen. Pretty as a picture even back then. Not that she did much girlie stuff. She was already living and breathing the news. It was right unnatural when you thought about it." Joe frowned a little.

"Unnatural? How do you mean?" Blake watched Joe intently as the man twisted his mouth to the side and thought about his answer.

"I don't know," he said after a moment. "I guess that a little girl like she was then could know what folks would want to read in the paper and what they wouldn't. She had a feel for it, right enough. There's plenty of ink in her blood, and that's a fact."

"Didn't she go to school?" Joe's answers were making Blake even more curious.

"Oh, I suppose she might have. I don't rightly remember. I do remember Beck used to worry about her some, especially when he heard people talking about her."

"What kind of talk?" Blake thought about pulling out his pencil and scribbling down a few notes the way he did when he was working on a story to make sure he kept his facts straight. But this wasn't for a story, and it was unlikely he'd forget a word of anything he heard about Adriane Darcy.

"You know how folks are. And I don't suppose it was exactly proper a little girl like that spending so much time working with us fellows. 'Course at that time there wasn't nobody but me and old Beck, and I reckon we'd a both died on the spot before we'd have let any harm come to little Addie." Joe smiled a little. "That was Beck's pet name for her."

"What do you think about her now?"

"I ain't seen her for a long spell, but they say she grew up real pretty. 'Course I still hear talk about her."

"What kind of talk?"

"Same old stuff." Joe waved his hand in dismissal. "How this or that ain't proper. How she'll never find no decent gent to marry her because of the way she don't mind telling a body what she thinks without worrying about who she's talking to."

"I guess they were wrong about that." Blake pushed back his chair and stood up from his desk. "There's a big party tonight announcing her engagement to Stanley Jimson."

"Is that a fact? Stanley Jimson." Joe looked thoughtful. "Who'd a thought it? But maybe she got tired of setting type."

"I wouldn't bet on that." Blake watched Joe's face as he went on. "You sound like you were really fond of her."

Joe looked down at the floor, then back at Blake. "Now, boss, I know how you feel about the *Tribune,* but I ain't gonna say nothing bad about the girl cause there ain't nothing bad to say. I don't care if she is Wade Darcy's daughter."

"Ease down, Joe." Blake smiled and held his hand palm out toward Joe. "I was just curious about her. Besides, I don't think you need to worry too much about defending her. She's capable of that all on her own."

"Sounds like the two of you might have had a little run-in. I wouldn't want to make no wagers on which of you bested the other." Joe grinned.

Blake laughed a little. "If we'd had pistols, we'd both be bleeding. That's for sure."

"And you say she's planning to tie the knot with Stanley Jimson." Joe's smile disappeared. "I'll bet poor old Beck is grieving some over that."

"Why do you say that?" Blake's eyes sharpened on Joe.

"Well, you know Stanley Jimson, boss. And old Beck fairly doted on the girl. He'd want better than that pantywaist for her. For a fact, I'd wish better than that for her my own self."

"And who would you match her up with, Joe, if you were playing matchmaker?"

"Oh, I don't know." A wicked little glint lit up the man's eyes as he stared at Blake. "You maybe, boss. The two of you together might start a newspaper dynasty. Why, you'd have your kids setting type before they could walk."

Blake threw his head back and laughed. "Wade Darcy would shoot me first."

"Now that could be a fact. And I reckon he's happy as a pig in mud with the whole setup. With Jimson behind the *Tribune*, he won't have to worry much about the *Herald* overtaking him."

"And with the *Tribune* behind Coleman Jimson, Jimson may think his way's clear to the state senate house." Blake's face tightened at the thought. He wasn't going to let that happen without a fight.

"You saying he has another think coming, boss?" Joe raised his eyebrows.

"Could be."

Joe suddenly looked worried. "Things could get ugly if you take on Jimson and the Know Nothings. They've pretty well got the town wrapped up right now. Most of the old Whigs is going their way, and the Democrats ain't got nothing to stop them."

"Don't worry, Joe. I'm going to step easy till I know exactly which way I want to go with the *Herald*. But once I've got my facts gathered, I'll slam them so hard and fast they won't know what hit them."

Joe shook his head. "It may be you not knowing what's hit you. I've heard talk, and some of them Know Nothing fellows is ready to do whatever it takes to make sure their candidates come out on top. You know yourself there's done been some riots in other cities. It could happen here."

"Then we'd better make sure we're on the right side."

"The right side or the one that sells the most papers?" Joe peered at him across the desk.

"We have to hope they're one and the same." Blake pointed at the paper he'd given Joe. "Now if you don't go on and get that story set up, Mrs. Wigginham won't see her name in the *Herald* tomorrow and I won't ever get invited to any more of her newsworthy events."

Joe started to turn away, but then stopped to ask, "You been invited to this wingding tonight?"

"Not officially, but I'm sure Coleman Jimson wouldn't mind if I decided to show up. He hasn't given up on the idea of pulling me and the *Herald* into his camp yet."

"I ain't seeing that happen, but if you do go, you tell Addie hello for me, boss. Maybe if you make eyes at her, she'll forget young Stanley." Joe shot another grin at Blake before he moved back toward the galley table.

Blake watched him a moment and then let his eyes stray around the shop where the men were getting the press ready for the first run. He loved this part of putting out the paper, when all the words were ready and it was time to start cranking them out.

He even liked it when he was a boy helping his father put out their weekly back in Castleton, Virginia, and they'd done all the cranking by hand. His father would always grab the first sheet off the press and look at it with a hint of wonder. "By golly, it's done it again," he'd say. "Look here, boy. That press has transformed our ordinary old words into news."

Then he would lay the sheet reverently aside to run his hand gently along the frame of the press before they started in cranking out the copies again.

"A newspaperman can never break trust with his readers, boy," he'd tell Blake as they worked. "He always has to print what he believes is the truth, no matter what the consequences." And his father always had, up until the day an angry reader, taking offense to that truth, shot him out on the street.

Blake still missed him all these years later. Hardly a week went by that he didn't wish he could ask his father's advice about the stories he wrote. And there were times when he almost felt his father peeking over his shoulder as some long-forgotten bit of his homespun wisdom would surface in Blake's mind while he was trying to get down the words of a story.

He wondered what kind of advice his father would have about Adriane. Blake smiled a little as he could almost hear his father's words echoing in his mind. "A newspaperman has to gather as much information as he can before he can make the right decision about how to go with a story. If a man's thoughts are fuzzy, his words are going to be like a pied tray of type."

That's just how Blake's mind felt right now. Like a tray of type dumped out on the floor and scattered every which way. And Adriane Darcy was the sole cause.

He'd go to that party tonight. Adriane couldn't have been as beautiful as he'd thought, and seeing her again would help him put everything in proper perspective. He wouldn't let his thoughts just stay jumbled like that pied tray of type because of a woman.

That night when Blake arrived at the Jimsons' house, the street was crowded with carriages and the party was already in full swing. Music and laughter spilled out to him even before a servant ushered him into the long, ornate parlor. Gilt-framed mirrors on every wall reflected the gay colors of the ladies' dresses as they swirled among the dark suits of the gentlemen.

Meta Jimson stood just inside the parlor greeting late arrivals with a stiff smile that didn't soften when Blake spoke of the happy occasion they were celebrating. He was relieved when she turned away from him to the next arriving guest and he could move past her on into the room where, at last, his eyes fell on Adriane.

He'd thought her beautiful that afternoon at Mrs. Wigginham's, but now in a dress the same vibrant blue as her eyes with a neckline that revealed an enticing amount of creamy white skin, she took his breath away. Her dark brown hair was swept up in soft waves and caught high on her head, and his fingers tingled at the thought of pulling out the jeweled combs that held it there to let it cascade down around her shoulders. Blake had a sudden understanding of why men tried to pen poems. Not that he had the gift of poetry, but looking at her, he wished he did.

He was sure she saw him the minute he entered the Jimsons' parlor, but she pretended to be unaware of him as she turned to smile at another guest. Wade Darcy made no such pretense. For a moment Blake thought the man was going to barge across the room and demand he leave, but after a whispered conference with Coleman Jimson, Darcy simply scowled and turned his back on him.

Coleman Jimson, on the other hand, came hurrying over to make Blake welcome. "Mr. Garrett, it's so good of you to come to our little gathering."

"I couldn't miss an event of such note." Blake did his best to match the man's enthusiasm as they shook hands. "Even if I wasn't invited."

"You need no invitation, sir."

"I'm not sure Mr. Darcy agrees," Blake said.

"Don't mind Wade. He's never handled competition well, and you've been giving him a run for his money lately with Chesnut's rag." Coleman Jimson laughed as he clapped Blake on the shoulder. "Of course if you print anything unfavorable about his daughter tomorrow, he may call you out, and I must warn you he's a superb marksman with a pistol."

Blake's eyes drifted over to Adriane. "He needn't worry about that. It would be hard to write anything the least unfavorable about such a vision of loveliness. Your son is an extremely fortunate man."

"Not everybody agrees with that, but it just so happens that I do. If anybody can make a man of Stanley, our Adriane can."

Jimson noted how his words took Blake by surprise. He laughed and pounded Blake on the back again as he went on. "And if you quote me on that, Mr. Garrett, I'll swear on my mother's Bible you made it up. Every word. Now come along and I'll take you over so you can congratulate the couple in person. That is why you came, isn't it?" Jimson's eyes were suddenly sharp on Blake.

"That and the chance for some free refreshments." Blake pushed a bland smile out on his face.

"There's plenty of that for the taking." Jimson led the way across the crowded floor to where Stanley and Adriane were greeting people.

"We have a surprise guest, children," the elder Jimson thundered in his booming voice, catching the attention of everyone in the room. "Blake Garrett from the *Herald*. I'm sure you know my son, Stanley, Mr. Garrett, and this is our Stanley's lovely intended, Miss Adriane Darcy."

Adriane smiled a little, but she refused to meet Blake's eyes directly as she greeted him politely. "How nice to see you again so soon, Mr. Garrett." She looked over at Coleman Jimson to explain they'd just met for the first time that very afternoon at Mrs. Wigginham's gathering for the Library Aide Society.

When she glanced back at Blake, he was ready for her, and he grabbed her eyes before she could turn away. Caught by surprise, she met his look fully, hiding nothing, and something like an earthquake tore through Blake's heart and mind, rearranging everything about his life.

By the time she lowered her eyes an instant later, Blake's thoughts were no longer scrambled but crystal clear. He knew exactly what he was going to do. He just didn't know how he was going to do it.

8

With the coming of the warmer days of April and May, everyone in Louisville who was anyone threw open their windows and doors to let in the fragrance of spring and to hold some sort of social to welcome the season. The snows and cold of winter were forgotten as blooming trees, bushes, and flowers transformed the residential streets, but in spite of the fragrant lilacs and the fresh white beauty of the abundant dogwoods, there was no spring in Adriane's heart.

She went to the unending parties with Stanley. She smiled until her face hurt and admired countless gardens, but inside she felt cold and untouched by it all as the relentless passing of the days moved her ever closer to her wedding day.

Sometimes in the shop helping Beck put together the day's issue, she could almost forget that anything had changed. There was still the news to gather as always and the need to beat the *Herald* to the headlines as the two papers fought for readers.

While no more Irish girls were murdered, a tragic explosion sank the steamship *Independence Day*, and the *Tribune* won the day when Duff rounded up an eyewitness. A few days later a storm blew the roofs off several houses on the outskirts of town, but both papers got out similar reports the same day.

Helena Poteet, a renowned singer from New York, came to Louisville, and the *Tribune* ran stories about her, the concert, and the exorbitant price of the much sought after tickets. However, the *Herald* printed a personal interview with the diva that people talked about for days.

So in her next Sally Sees column, Adriane hinted of a possible relationship between the handsome *Herald* editor and the beautiful singer. Adriane rarely mentioned herself and Stanley in the column as if, by pushing the whole affair out of her mind, she could forget that each day brought September nearer. But then Lucilla would insist on taking her on a shopping expedition or she'd have to stand like a statue while Nora fitted her for a dress. Worst of all and what made her impending marriage hardest to forget, Stanley would put his arm around her and caress her shoulder on their carriage rides to this or that party.

There had also been kisses in spite of Adriane's every attempt to avoid them, but as Stanley was wont to remind her, they were betrothed to be married. That certainly gave him a few rights of intimacy. At such times he'd look at her in that new way she so detested, and Adriane would pull her wrap tighter around her in an attempt to escape his eyes.

That wasn't all she wanted to escape. The thought of marrying Stanley, of actually having to submit to a marital relationship with him, was haunting her sleep at night. The heart-pounding dreams of Henrietta shoving her in a dark closet had given way to nightmares of her wedding night. She could not bear the thought of lying down beside Stanley, allowing him the intimate touches that would be his right once they were married.

When one of those dreams jerked her from sleep, she would stare up at the dark air and whisper the Lord's Prayer out loud. That's what Beck had taught her to do years before whenever she was scared about something.

She had never been sure if Beck knew about the dark closets

of Henrietta's punishments. She hadn't told him. Talking about it seemed to add to the shame. Her father wouldn't talk about it either. Even to Adriane. He would simply let her out of the closet, roughly wipe away her tears, and tell her to stop doing whatever it was she kept doing to upset Henrietta. At last, he must have realized there was no way she could ever please Henrietta, and he began letting her tag along with him to the *Tribune* offices.

Her life changed there when Beck took her under his wing, introducing her to the newspaper business with gruff kindness. By that time, he was a confirmed bachelor and already seemed old to Adriane. He told her he'd been married once a long time before, but his wife had died in one of the cholera epidemics that swept through Louisville. He didn't have any children. The *Tribune* was his life, perhaps even more so than her father's. Not the gathering of the news, but the printing of it. He took pride in filling the galley trays and then seeing the words pressed out on the newsprint.

Adriane and Beck had taken to one another right away. A lonesome old man and a forlorn child who both needed love in their lives. But Beck had given her even more than that. After the papers went out and while he waited for her father to bring in the next day's news, Beck liked to sit next to the window and read his Bible. She would sit on the floor beside him in the sunshine filtering through the grimy window and write stories on scraps of newsprint paper. Then when she finished her stories, they'd switch. Beck would read what she wrote while she would read some story he pointed out in the Bible.

She went to church with her father and Henrietta. She sat on the hard pew and tried to swallow her yawns while the preacher went on and on, but nobody had ever shown her how the Bible told stories sort of the same as newspapers. Not until Beck.

"You just keep it in mind, Addie, that the good Lord is with us everywhere. In the morning when we get up. And at night when we lay our heads down on a pillow to sleep. Daylight or dark, he's there. So if you ever feel scared, you just whisper a prayer and reach right out and feel the good Lord holding your hand."

"What if I don't pray the right way?" Adriane had said. Henrietta was always telling her the Lord wouldn't listen to her because she was so bad. She didn't want to tell Beck that. She didn't want Beck to know how bad she was.

"Ain't no right and wrong ways, child. The Lord hears our very groans and knows our every tear. He'll hear you. But there is a prayer he told us to pray." He leafed through his Bible, making the pages whisper softly, until he found the verses of the Lord's Prayer. "You learn this and then ever' time you don't know what prayer words to say but you're needing some help, you can say this."

She read the verses he pointed out to him. When she finished, he echoed the amen she read before he told her to read it all over again. This time he said the words along with her. Then he pointed to the last verse.

"You take a good look at those last words the good Lord give us there," he told her. "It's plain as the ink on my fingers that he must have known we'd be facing some hard times. That's why he has us asking to be delivered from evil. He takes care of us. You can count on that."

She must have looked doubtful, because Beck had put his big hand softly on her head and said, "Trust me on this one, Addie. He's always took care of me, and if he'll help an old geezer like me, I'm knowing for sure he'll be helping a sweet, innocent little girl like you. Just remember to say the prayer if something scares you."

The prayer had helped on the days when she had to stay home with Henrietta. But now whispering it in the night as she looked toward her future as Mrs. Stanley Jimson, the words just rang in her ears and didn't soothe her heart. *Deliver us from evil*. Stanley wasn't evil. It was simply that she didn't love him. That she would never love him. That she couldn't even bear to think of his lips touching her cheek, much less embracing him as a wife was required to do.

Worse was the feeling that she wasn't going to be delivered from having to marry Stanley. There was no escape. She'd faced that fact the day their engagement had been announced. She kept telling herself Stan would make a wonderful husband and that she was truly fond of him. She thought that given a few more months she might even be able to convince herself it was true.

But every morning she went down to the pressroom and threw herself into getting together another issue of the *Tribune* the way a condemned person might attempt to absorb each new sunrise as the day of his execution drew nearer. At night she dutifully knelt by her bed to say her prayers, but the words seemed to mock her. That innocent faith she'd known sitting beside Beck while he read his Bible had been eroded by doubts. She had no hope of a reprieve. No right to ask one.

Honor thy father and thy mother. How many times had Henrietta screamed those words at her as she locked Adriane in the closet under the stairs?

"The Lord can't bear the sight of bad little girls," Henrietta told her over and over as she shut the door and closed out the light. "Bad little girls who won't obey their parents. Bad little girls like you."

She could shrug off Henrietta's words these years later. They hadn't been true. She hadn't been a disobedient child. She couldn't be a disobedient child now. *Honor thy father*. Her father wanted her to marry Stanley Jimson. More even than that, her father's future with the *Tribune* depended on her marrying Stanley Jimson. A good daughter obeyed her father.

And she would. That didn't mean she had to think about what the end of summer would bring. In the shop as they worked on the paper, she and Beck never talked of the

92

wedding. She didn't even write in her journal about all the plans being made. Instead she wrote of the changing weather, the new steamboat Duff had smuggled her aboard, and the old black dog that now slept in a spot of sunshine out in the back and listened for her footsteps.

When her father caught her petting the dog one morning, he shouted and clapped his hands at the dog to chase it off. He minced no words telling her that showing affection for the stray mongrel was not something a lady would ever do. His frown grew darker when she claimed to not care about being a lady.

"I won't abide such talk from you. You are a lady and you will behave like a lady. Lucilla would take the vapors if an animal like that got within three feet of her."

"I'm not Lucilla, Father. I will never be like Lucilla," Adriane said quietly. She didn't bother to add that she didn't want to be like Lucilla. She'd already upset him enough saying she didn't care about being a lady.

His eyes narrowed on her. "Perhaps not, but that doesn't mean you have to behave like some street vagrant with no breeding." His voice softened a bit as he touched her arm. "You are going to be a Jimson. This is a wonderful opportunity for you."

When she simply stared at him without saying anything, his face hardened again. "I will not let you squander this opportunity, Adriane. I will expect you to act like a proper lady. And you can be sure if I see that mongrel around again, I'll have Beck shoot it. Do you understand?" He didn't expect an answer and she didn't give one as he went back in the house, slamming the door behind him.

Adriane waited until she heard him go out the front door, slamming that door too. Then she looked down the alley to see if she could spot the old dog. Beck wouldn't shoot the dog. She had no worries there. And her father rarely came out in the back alley. He'd forget about the dog. As long as she kept playing her part as Stanley Jimson's intended.

After she caught sight of the dog peeking out at her from the side of a wooden box behind the house next door, she went back in the kitchen to get another biscuit out of the warming oven. The old dog was there waiting when she stepped back outside.

Honor thy father. The words whispered through her head as she let the dog take the biscuit out of her hand. But what possible harm could it do for her to scratch the old dog behind the ears and talk to him while he looked at her as if he understood her every word?

"I need somebody to understand," she whispered to the old dog. "You know that, don't you, old boy? You can't change anything for me, but at least you can listen."

The dog stared up at her. He cocked his head as if trying to hear her better.

"You're right. Beck would listen too, but it would make him too sad. And maybe too mad at Father. That wouldn't be good. Not for either of them. I just have to do what I have to do. What Father wants. Well, except for not petting you." She ruffled the dog's ears and gave his head another pat. He didn't smell good and he probably did have fleas, but she didn't care.

The dog wagged his tail back and forth once.

"You're a smart dog. You just stay out of sight when he's around and everything will be all right. You can do that, can't you?"

He looked up and bared his teeth at her in a dog grin. She had to laugh. "I knew he was wrong about you. You come back tonight and I'll give you another biscuit."

She went inside and washed her hands before she headed to the pressroom to help Beck. Her father was wrong about the dog. It didn't hurt a thing for her to feed him a few biscuits. He was wrong about Stanley too, but she had about as much chance of convincing him of that as convincing him to let the old dog come in and sleep in the kitchen at night.

9

*T*he first week in June, Adriane received the note she'd been dreading from her friend Grace Compton inviting her to lunch. Grace had been away in Philadelphia working for the abolitionists for the last three months, and though they had exchanged letters, Adriane had carefully avoided mentioning anything about her engagement and upcoming wedding to Stanley. Grace was not going to approve.

Adriane had been nearly sixteen when her father decided he might have neglected her proper education and so sent her to Grace Compton's newly opened girls' academy. The school only lasted a few months, because while the parents wanted their daughters taught music and the proper social graces, Grace loved teaching history and the appreciation of literature and art far beyond what was considered proper for a young lady to know. Worse, she sometimes mentioned the need for social or political reforms.

One by one, the girls were withdrawn from the academy until only Adriane was left. Their student-teacher relationship quickly developed into a fast friendship. Grace was almost twice as old as Adriane, but age didn't matter. Grace was a big sister, a mother figure, a teacher and friend all rolled into one.

So when Adriane's father decided there was no longer

money for the lessons, Grace insisted that Adriane keep coming. That she still had much to learn. She claimed the joy of teaching was more than pay enough and she could always manage to eke out a living by making a few hats. Each of Grace's hats was a unique design and quite in demand by the ladies in the social set who considered owning a Grace Compton hat something of a status symbol. Grace might have lived comfortably, except she hated making hats and only did so when her cupboards were nearly bare.

Now as Adriane hurried toward Grace's house, she shut out the sound of the carriages and wagons passing on the street and practiced a smile as she tried to figure out how she was going to explain her upcoming marriage to her friend.

Adriane sometimes felt as if her face might break if she had to push one more smile onto it. She would promise herself she wouldn't smile for a week, but then there would be another round of socials. So she kept smiling and pretending to be happy and excited by this wondrous miracle of the Jimsons allowing her to become part of their family.

Of course Stan's mother only thinly disguised her displeasure with Stan's choice. Sometimes when they were at a tea or social together, Adriane would note Meta Jimson's eyes resting longingly on this or that more appropriate candidate for the position of her daughter-in-law. Adriane's eyes would follow hers and have to agree with the woman each and every time.

Coleman Jimson, on the other hand, boomed his approval of the match to anyone who would listen and had taken to hugging Adriane with much affection since she was already so very nearly part of the family. The embraces did not seem in the least fatherly, but then Adriane and her father had not shared any sort of embrace since she was a small child. Perhaps she didn't know what a fatherly embrace was like. Her father never showed any sign of disapproval when the man engulfed her in his arms. Of course, he seemed to approve of anything and everything the Jimsons did.

Her father and Coleman were becoming very close as they not only celebrated the betrothal of their children but were working together on a campaign to assure Coleman Jimson's election to the state senate in August. Their constant meetings produced an unending stream of rhetoric.

Adriane's eyes fell on an old campaign notice from the city elections in April still tacked to a signpost on the street. With the fervent support of the *Tribune*, the Know Nothing party had swept the elections from mayor to alderman. For weeks before the vote, the *Tribune* had carried little else but political speeches, letters, and editorials. Adriane usually liked elections, but this year it had seemed all the candidates' speeches sounded alike. Their readers must have agreed as the *Tribune*'s circulation dropped.

Blake Garrett, on the other hand, had kept the *Herald* cautiously neutral in the April elections almost as if he feared taking sides, something that surprised Adriane and heightened her interest in the man's motives.

Not that she allowed her curiosity to make her do anything foolish. If they turned up at the same social, she did her best to avoid him completely. It wasn't hard. Stanley hovered around her, and Blake was continually surrounded by a gaggle of hopeful young belles. Even so, somehow he always knew if she allowed her eyes to stray toward him and was ready with that piercing look that seemed to sear the air between them and demand some sort of response from her. A response she could not give.

Adriane shook her head a little to dismiss all thoughts of Blake Garrett. She looked across the street toward where Grace's small house was nestled two blocks away. As memories of the many times she'd hurried along these streets to spend a few pleasant hours with Grace flooded her mind, she no longer worried about what Grace might say about the engagement. She couldn't wait to see her again and hear firsthand about her work in the North. Perhaps they would have no need to talk about Stanley at all.

In her eagerness, she forgot to pay attention to the traffic on the road and stepped into the street directly into the path of two matched bays smartly pulling a light carriage. The driver shouted and jerked hard on his reins to keep from running her down. Spooked, the horses fought against the driver and reared up in their traces. At the sight of hooves flashing above her head, Adriane froze, not sure which way to run. Strong hands grabbed hold of her and just in the nick of time yanked her back up on the sidewalk to safety. The horses found their legs and took off in a wild gallop as their driver kept yelling and pulling on the reins.

With her heart pounding, Adriane's knees went weak, and she leaned heavily against her rescuer as the carriage bounced past them. Two pale, wide-eyed faces peered out at her.

"My dear lady." The man's voice sounded very familiar in her ear. "Do be more careful. I would hate to beat your father to the headline that his own daughter had been run down by a team of high-spirited horses."

Adriane gasped as she looked up at Blake Garrett smiling down at her. Even though her knees felt even weaker, she attempted to push away from him. But he kept his arms tight around her waist.

"Give yourself a moment to recover from your scare, Adriane," Blake said. "It would be quite ungentlemanly of me to allow you to crumple on the sidewalk."

His body felt rock solid against her, and her heart started pounding even harder although the carriage was disappearing from sight. She felt the urge to just lean closer to this man and let him hold her as long as he wanted.

The thought brought her up short, and she immediately stepped away from him. Her eyes darted to his face and away. She took a deep breath and managed a polite smile. "Thank you, Mr. Garrett. I can't imagine what I must have been thinking."

"I'm sure you know exactly what you were thinking, Miss Darcy. Your problem was that you were not watching."

"I suppose you're right." Adriane kept the slight smile on her face as she stared somewhere a bit to the side of his face and went on. "At any rate, I am grateful that you were. Watching, I mean."

"I guess this is one time you can be glad you weren't able to avoid me."

"Avoid you?" Her eyes flew to his face in surprise. "I can't imagine what you mean, Mr. Garrett."

"Can't you?" Blake's eyes burned into hers. "You're afraid to talk to me."

"That's ridiculous." She knew she should turn away from him, but she seemed rooted to the spot.

"That it may be, Miss Darcy, but we have been attending the same social functions for weeks, and any time I attempt to speak to you, you always manage an escape." His look didn't waver. "Even so, I hardly expected you to be so fearful of meeting me that you'd step in front of a team of horses."

In spite of feeling a bit breathless, Adriane managed to keep her voice steady as she peered up at him. "Have I need to fear you, sir?" She tried to sound coquettish as though they were merely sparring meaningless words at a social.

Every trace of a smile disappeared from his face as his eyes probed hers until she was sure he was seeing into her very soul. She wanted to close her eyes, shut him away. She wanted to flee across the road toward Grace's house where she would be safe. But she couldn't allow him to win so easily.

After a long moment, he finally spoke. Not in the haughty voice she expected, but softly, almost kindly. "There are things you should fear, Adriane, but I am not one of them. Remember that. I always stand ready to rescue you."

"I should hope I will not need to be rescued again, Mr. Garrett." She attempted a smile. His kindness was even harder to bear up under than his disparagement.

He didn't smile back. "I think you need rescuing even now."

She arched her eyebrows at him. "From you, sir?"

"Perhaps so, dear lady." At last he smiled fully, and again as it had that first time she'd seen him smile at Mrs. Wigginham's, the light exploded from his eyes. "There are ladies who think I'm more than a little dangerous."

Adriane began breathing easier as if she'd just tiptoed safely away from the edge of a chasm. "I wouldn't wonder." She kept her tone light as she turned from him to look up and down the street for carriages or wagons. "Perhaps if I'm careful, I might be able to make it across the street now."

He held out his arm to her. "Please allow me to escort you. I'm going that way anyway."

"Which way?" she said even as she slipped her hand under his elbow. It would be childish to refuse to walk with him.

He grinned down at her. "Whichever way you're going."

"If I didn't know better, I'd think you were trying to turn my head, Mr. Garrett. Or perhaps you think I'm on the track of a news story that you've somehow missed buying from some poor unfortunate soul."

He laughed easily as they made their way across the street. "It never hurts to keep an eye on the competition."

On the opposite walk, Adriane stopped and looked at him. There hardly seemed any reason to avoid meeting his eyes now. "Alas, Mr. Garrett, I'm not on the track of a story, but simply on my way to visit a friend."

"In this part of town?" Blake looked around at the small houses. "Hardly the place for a social."

"Neither is the newspaper shop where I live."

"But all that will soon change." His eyes came back to hers.

"So it seems." She looked away from him toward Grace's house. "At any rate, my friend's house is right around the corner, and I fear I'm late, so I must hurry on."

"I'll walk you to her door." When she hesitated, he went on. "It really is the way I'm going."

"Very well." She gave in gracefully and began to walk beside him. After a moment of silence, she said, "I have been meaning to compliment you on your interview with Helena Poteet. It was the talk of the town for days."

"She's an old friend," he said. "And if we're handing out compliments, you're due one for your story about the *Betsy Layne*. I hear there was a line down at the dock the next day to get tickets for its first trip down the river."

Adriane looked over at him. "What makes you think I wrote that and not my father?"

"You did, didn't you?"

"Well, yes," Adriane admitted. "I do love the steamships and I managed to get aboard the *Betsy Layne* for a look around without anyone knowing." She laughed. "If only I could stow away on her for her maiden voyage. I think she will beat the record to New Orleans without any problem."

"You keep up with the records?" Blake asked.

"Don't you? People love reading about record-breaking runs." Adriane glanced at him again. "That and murders, of course."

"I don't write about the murders to sell papers." His eyes were suddenly piercing again.

Adriane looked down at the sidewalk as if she needed to watch her step. "I didn't say you did."

"Your father has said it, and more than once." Blake's voice was hard.

"So he has," Adriane agreed, still watching the sidewalk in front of her instead of looking at the man beside her. "And he probably will again. Father actually prefers the old-style papers where the news was mostly political. He sees the need to carry other sorts of stories now, but that doesn't mean he's happy with the way newspapers are changing."

"In the newspaper business, an editor prints the news. That's what his readers want to read whether they know it or not. If you don't show them what's happening, there's not much use in putting out a paper at all." Blake's voice changed then, until he sounded almost sad as he went on.

"You can be sure I have no desire to print stories about how these poor girls lost their lives at the hand of some monster, but it happened. What happens is the news."

"Tell me, Mr. Garrett, and believe me, I'm not trying to steal your story, but do you think the river slasher will strike again? It's been over two months." Adriane looked up at him.

"I don't know any more than you've read in the *Herald*." A frown creased his forehead. "I don't think anyone does. Certainly not the police."

"It must be awful for those girls down there to wonder if every stranger they meet might be the one." Adriane stared back down at the plank walkway.

"What makes you think it's a stranger?"

Adriane's eyes flew up to his. "I don't know. Except it would be worse to think it was someone you knew."

"Much worse. But a stranger would be caught or move on to another town. And this man has already killed three times."

"And you think he'll do it again, don't you?"

"I do," Blake said.

Adriane couldn't keep a shudder from running through her. Her father kept saying that no proper young lady had anything to worry about, but it could be some young girl somewhere did. "I sincerely hope they catch him soon," she said.

"I didn't mean to distress you with all this talk of the murders, Miss Darcy." He was looking at her with concern.

"No, no, I brought it up. And it's sometimes refreshing to talk to someone who's not always fearful of disturbing one's tender sensibilities." Adriane stopped in front of Grace's small house. "And now I must thank you for seeing me safely here. It was really most kind of you."

"My pleasure, Miss Darcy." Blake smiled.

Before he could turn to leave, Grace's door flew open and the little woman came running down the walk to embrace Adriane. Grace Compton was only five feet tall with her shoes on and so slim that the angles of her bones showed through her skin, but she did everything with enthusiasm, as though the energy of a woman twice her size was coiled tightly inside her and she had to let it out every way possible.

"Dear Adriane, I thought you'd never get here." Grace held Adriane at arm's length for a moment, looked her up and down, and then pulled her close for another even tighter hug.

Adriane laughed and hugged back as happy tears ran down her face. For the moment, she forgot to worry about what she'd tell Grace about Stanley. Now she was just too glad to see her friend again after so many weeks.

Two hugs later, Grace at last noticed Blake Garrett still standing beside them, watching their display with amusement as he waited to be properly introduced. She looked him up and down before she said, "One thing for certain, this is not Stanley Jimson."

10

*G*race, please! There's no need to shock Mr. Garrett with your disdain of the social niceties." Adriane sent a pointed look at Grace, even though she knew that would do nothing to stop her friend. Grace enjoyed throwing all the established rules of proper behavior out the window and absolutely relished any social upheaval that might cause.

Indeed Grace didn't even glance over at Adriane as she kept eyeing Blake. "Don't worry, dear. I don't believe Mr. Garrett is the type to be so easily shocked."

Blake laughed easily. "That's certainly true, madam, and since Miss Darcy appears to be somewhat flustered by your admirable frankness, please allow me to introduce myself. Blake Garrett, editor of the *Herald*."

Grace's eyes sharpened on him. "Yes, I remember reading about John Chesnut taking you on at his paper before I left for Boston." She held out her hand with an amused smile. "Grace Compton, teacher, abolitionist, dedicated campaigner for the rights of the downtrodden, especially women, and last and certainly least, occasional hatmaker."

Blake barely hesitated before he clasped Grace's slender hand in a manly handshake. "A pleasure, Miss Compton."

Grace laughed delightedly as if he'd just passed a test of some sort, and Adriane, watching them, began to believe that if she walked away up the street, neither of them would notice. Blake gave every appearance of being enchanted by Grace, and Grace in return seemed totally captivated by his frank smile.

Adriane was a bit disappointed but hardly surprised. After all, Grace was a woman, even if she did have some unconventional ideas about a woman's proper role in society. And just the thought of the light exploding out of Blake's eyes when he smiled at her was enough to make Adriane's own heart do a funny spin.

She brought her thoughts quickly under control. She needed to remember that this man, no matter how charming and handsome, was attempting to destroy the *Tribune*. Smiles and talk of rescues did not alter that fact.

Grace was inviting him to stay and lunch with them. "Nothing fancy, you understand. Just tea and bread and cheese. I do fear I haven't made any hats for some time now."

Blake looked at Adriane, who was ready with a polite smile that slid easily onto her face after all the practice the last few weeks. "And what do you say, Miss Darcy?" he asked. "I wouldn't want to impose on your visit."

"It's hardly for me to say," Adriane said crisply. "It is Grace's house and her tea and bread. However, I must warn you she only wants to feel you out about publishing some news of her work in the North. She's been away from Louisville for several months so can hardly know how carefully you tiptoe around any and all controversial issues for fear of stepping on the wrong toes."

His smile was gone in an instant as anger tightened the lines on his face. "Do you really believe that, Miss Darcy?"

Grace stood to their side, now the one completely forgotten.

"It doesn't matter what I believe, Mr. Garrett. All that matters is what I read in your paper, and I do read your paper. I fear you care more about entertaining your readers than enlightening them."

The lines of anger grew deeper. "A good editor waits to be sure he has the facts before he enters into the fray."

"Such a careful editor might well miss the fray altogether." Adriane stared at him boldly.

"So he might," Blake said softly. Some of the anger drained from his eyes to be replaced by rock-hard determination. "But you can be assured, Miss Darcy, that when I do take a stand, it will be because of what I believe to be right and not because I have been told what to believe or do by someone else."

All the fight drained out of Adriane, and she was sorry she'd initiated the whole confrontation. He was right. She didn't know what she believed anymore. Perhaps she never had. She lowered her eyes to the ground. "I do apologize, Mr. Garrett. I don't know whatever came over me to criticize you in such a way. I must beg your forgiveness."

Beside them, Grace took the matter into her capable hands. "Of course he forgives you, Adriane. Don't you, Mr. Garrett?" She didn't wait for him to answer as she rushed on. "And I fear I must withdraw my invitation to lunch, because Adriane is right in trying to discourage you from staying. It would not, I suppose, be proper, and a lady in her current position does have to maintain appearances, unlike myself who worries not a whit about what the other ladies might say if I entertain a gentleman in my parlor. That is, if I had a parlor to entertain a gentleman in. But you do understand, don't you, Mr. Garrett?"

"I'm trying to," Blake said.

Adriane slowly raised her eyes to look at him again. Even though he still frowned, he no longer looked angry, simply puzzled. "Perhaps Grace would be good enough to invite you to lunch on another day," she said.

"Anytime, Mr. Garrett," Grace concurred quickly. "We could talk about the possibility of you publishing a small news report or perhaps a letter to the editor in regard to my causes. Even Adriane's father is foolhardy enough to do that on occasion."

Blake looked at Adriane. "If indeed it is Mr. Darcy who picks the letters for the *Tribune*. I wouldn't be a bit surprised to discover Miss Darcy was the foolhardy one."

"Not at all," Adriane said, even though he'd hit on the truth. She was the one who slipped Grace's letters into the paper whenever the opportunity arose, but she saw no reason to reveal that fact to Blake Garrett. "Father favors a bit of controversy on his editorial pages."

"Controversy can be an editor's best friend." Blake's smile returned. "Now if you good ladies will excuse me, I've kept you from your tea much too long already. I'm sure we'll all meet again, and perhaps next time it will be proper for us to lunch together."

"One can only hope," Grace said as she allowed Blake to take her hand in his again.

Adriane did not offer her hand, but he stepped close in front of her and took it anyway. Before she could pull it away, he brushed the top of her fingers with his lips. A streak of fire flashed from her hand straight to her heart.

"Please be careful on your way home, Miss Darcy. I must confess that I rather look forward to these duels of words we seem to have whenever we meet," he said before he turned and briskly set off back down the walk the way they had come, giving lie to his words that he had been going the same way as Adriane.

Grace watched until he was out of sight. "Well," she said as she put her arm around Adriane's waist to turn her toward the door. "I do believe we have a great deal to talk about, you and I, but first we'll eat before we both faint from hunger."

"Good." Adriane turned her full attention to her friend. "I am famished. Not only for your tea but also word of the gains you've made in the North."

She followed Grace through the front room where bright-colored ribbons and flowers spilled off Grace's worktable. Unadorned hats were piled in one chair, while the only other chair was stacked high with books the small bookcase against the wall was too full to hold. The kitchen held another table with two mismatched chairs that looked as if they might have been salvaged from a rubbish pile. The table was strewn with papers and pamphlets. Grace pushed them to one side to make room for their teacups.

"Regretfully there haven't been all that many gains." Grace sounded discouraged as she poured their tea and set bread and cheese on the table. "While a handful more papers in the North are taking up the cause of the Negro, very few feel there is any merit in the fight for the rights of women."

"So it didn't go well." As Adriane sipped her tea, she noted the new lines on her friend's face and the tired droop of her shoulders. "I'm sorry to hear that."

"Oh, it's not all bad." Grace straightened a little and squared her shoulders. "I heard Lucretia Mott speak. Not so many years ago a woman speaking out in public would have been totally ostracized, perhaps even arrested. Then there's Elizabeth Cady Stanton in New York. I think I wrote you about her. Anyway, she's taken up the cause and does a beautiful job of eloquently outlining our aims and purposes in words. She even dares to put forward the desire to gain women the vote, although some of the workers fear such a radical objective might very well make all of us a laughingstock."

"Unfortunately it's obvious from what most newspapers print that there are plenty who already think that about those who fight for women's rights." Adriane ran her finger around the rim of her cup. It was only chipped in a couple of places.

"I know. Those at the helm of the papers, at the helm of most everything, are men who seem to be of the belief that all their readers must also be men." Grace sighed and stared down at her cup. "I sometimes despair of men ever admitting we women have minds capable of more than child rearing and needlework."

Adriane reached across the table to pat her hand. "Write something about your work the last few months, and the *Tribune* will publish it."

"I have something already written." Grace looked up at her. "It concerns the battle being waged in New York to allow women in that state to maintain ownership of their property and to have the rights to their own earnings after marriage. There's a strong petition before the legislature, and I think in spite of all the talk against the proposal, it will pass. Maybe not this year but soon."

"See, there is progress being made," Adriane said.

"You always were able to cheer me up, Adriane." Grace visibly brightened as she nibbled on her bread and cheese. "And maybe I'll send something to the *Herald* as well. I promised my abolitionist friends a reading in Louisville."

Adriane's smile stiffened as Grace's eyes sharpened on her. "I'd really prefer not to talk about Blake Garrett or the *Herald*, Grace. He's causing a lot of turmoil at the *Tribune*."

"I don't think it's only at the *Tribune* that he's causing turmoil." Grace peered at Adriane over the rim of her cup.

Adriane concentrated on cutting a small piece of cheese before she said, "I told you I didn't want to talk about Mr. Garrett. He may smile and act charming, but he cannot be trusted."

"Are you sure about that, Adriane?"

"Of course I am. He's trying to steal all our readers." A bit of fire jumped into Adriane's eyes as she stared at Grace.

Grace merely smiled. "Surely the *Tribune* doesn't fear a little competition. I've always thought your father rather relished it."

Adriane looked down to position her cheese exactly so on her bread while carefully considering her next words. "Yes, well, sometimes things change."

Grace set her cup down and reached across the table to put her hand over Adriane's. "Come, come, Adriane. You have no need to be so careful with your words to me. Out with it. What's going on with the *Tribune*?"

Adriane looked up with a sigh. "It's just that Father's changed so much since he became engaged to Lucilla. Or maybe it's this Know Nothing political party he's taken up with. He hardly writes of anything else these days."

"And Mr. Garrett, as I understand it, has been skipping the political speeches and entreaties and instead has been writing about events and happenings the ordinary man wants to read and not just what the poor soul thinks he ought to read." She pulled back her hand and picked up her cup again.

"I fear that is so." Adriane broke off a tiny bit of the cheese, but didn't put it in her mouth. "Our sales have dropped the last two months in a row. I'm sure Mr. Garrett is gaining each reader we lose. His coverage of those dreadful murders has people entranced as if they were reading one of Mr. Dickens's continuing sagas."

"I see." Grace set down her empty teacup and studied Adriane for a moment. "And how do you feel about him, not as an editor, but as a person?"

"I really couldn't say. I've only talked to him twice," Adriane answered casually as she looked down at her plate. She stuck the bite of cheese in her mouth in hopes that her chewing would keep back the color threatening to rise in her cheeks.

"And dueled with him both times if I understood him correctly." Grace sounded amused. "You always did have a sharp tongue. Your father used to say it was due to me that you learned to use it so well."

"There could be truth to that." A smile played around Adriane's lips as she raised her eyes back to Grace's face.

"You would have learned without me, just not so quickly or so well." Grace laughed a little as she fetched the teapot from the small stove to refill their cups.

The kitchen was tiny with hardly room for the one cabinet, the stove, and the wobbly table and chairs. Yet it was in this very room that Adriane had first glimpsed the vastness of the world as she learned the most amazing things from an even more amazing teacher. Freedom had sat beside her at this small table and made her believe she could do anything she wanted. Now she yearned to recapture that exhilarating feeling, but she feared it was gone forever.

They drank their tea in silence for a moment before Grace finally said, "You are going to have to tell me about it, Adriane. And I fear the fact that you do not want to bodes ill."

"Not at all." Adriane pulled forth one of her practiced smiles. "Stanley and I are to be married on September 15th, I think it is. It's to be quite the event. Lucilla has her woman, Nora, already at work on my dress. She guarantees I'll look beautiful." Adriane puffed her hair and struck a pose.

"You're beautiful right now in your everyday working dress."

"You only think that because you love me." Adriane looked down at her plain brown dress.

"If you don't believe me, ask Mr. Garrett."

Adriane kept her eyes away from Grace's. "I doubt he'd agree," she said before quickly hurrying on to talk of Stan. "Anyway, as you know, Stan has been escorting me to socials and various events for some time now. It was just a natural progression of events for us to decide to marry."

"A convenience." Grace studied her cup, fingering the handle a moment before asking, "Is that what you're saying?"

"You could say that, I suppose." Adriane glanced at Grace and quickly away. "I have to consider my future now that Father is marrying. He and Lucilla plan to marry in October, you know, but Lucilla seems more excited about my wedding than her own. She insists I need an armoire full of new dresses, and not only does she have poor Nora working double time, but she somehow convinced Father to part with the money for all the fabric."

Grace ignored Adriane's prattle about dresses. "What kind of future do you expect to have with Stanley Jimson?"

While Grace's voice stayed calm, almost gentle, Adriane began to feel as if she were a girl again trying to pass one of Grace's tests of her knowledge of history or art. She wanted to ignore this question, pretend she had not heard it, but Grace would demand an answer. Finally Adriane forced herself to say, "A very secure one, I'm sure." The word "secure" tore through her, and for a moment she thought she might cry.

"Security is a very nice thing to have." Grace's eyes traveled around the small kitchen. "That's what I always feel when I come home to this dear little house. Secure and safe. It was all my Aaron left me when he died, you know."

"I know." Adriane had heard every story Grace could tell about her beloved husband, Aaron Compton, a dozen times, but she hoped now that Grace would want to tell her some of them again. She didn't know how much longer she could keep smiling while they spoke of her upcoming marriage to Stanley.

But Grace's tests had never been easy, and Adriane realized this one would not be either as Grace went on. "Still, I couldn't stay here forever making my silly hats, not doing anything meaningful, and you won't be able to either."

"It's certainly true I don't want to make hats." Adriane forced out a laugh in an attempt to lighten the moment.

Grace didn't smile as she pinned Adriane with her bright eyes. "Do you love him, Adriane?"

Adriane looked away from Grace down at her cup, as if she expected to find an answer for her friend in the tea leaves floating on the bottom. After a moment, she moistened her lips and said, "Father says romance has little to do with real marriages. That it is just the stuff of silly women's novels."

"Does he indeed?" Grace didn't bother to hide the disdain in her words. "He's certainly one to comment on what makes a happy marriage with his fine record."

"Grace, please don't start on Father. You know he only married Henrietta so that I would have a mother to care for me."

"And we know how wonderfully that turned out, don't we?" Grace didn't wait for an answer. Instead she commanded, "Look at me and stop pretending, Adriane."

Adriane obeyed the teacher's voice. Her practiced smile slid off her face. "I may not be happy now about it all, Grace, but I will learn to be happy."

"Oh, Adriane, think." Grace poked her own temple with a finger before she stood up and began circling the tiny kitchen as she lectured Adriane. "You cannot marry this man. I don't know why you think you should. I'm sure security has little to do with it, and in any case you'd have precious little mental security in that family. Money is not important, has never been important. You may not want to make hats. I don't want to make hats, but making hats is how I survive."

Adriane smiled. "You know I can't sew and that the few times I've tried my fingers were all thumbs. Even if I did attempt to make hats, no one would buy them. And I can't teach music. You never even tried to teach me to play because you said my aptitudes lay elsewhere."

"And they did. They do." Grace paused in front of Adriane to look down at her. "You cannot marry Stanley Jimson." She spoke the words one at a time and very distinctly.

Adriane stared up at her old teacher and friend and steeled herself to her arguments. Grace wasn't telling her anything Adriane had not already told herself time after time late at night when sleep eluded her, but morning had always brought the truth. "I must," Adriane said.

"You must not." Grace stressed her words by banging her hands down in the air. "It would be better for you to become an honest prostitute than to prostitute yourself for social position."

Adriane had long ago stopped being shocked by the things

Grace said. Now she only smiled a little as she said, "You know I cannot become a prostitute."

"Of course you can't." Grace waved her hand dismissing the idea. "I only said that to make you think."

"I have thought, Grace. And I am going to marry Stanley Jimson in September. I have no choice."

"No choice?" The words seemed to almost choke Grace. She took a deep breath before she went on in a softer voice. "There's always a choice, Adriane. One only has to search for it."

"Not this time, Grace."

Grace sat back down and looked at Adriane for a long moment before she spoke again. "Your father has made this choice for you, hasn't he?"

"He approves of the match." Adriane picked her words carefully. "He and Stanley's father have become very close."

"Coleman Jimson is a scoundrel," Grace said flatly.

"You think all rich people are scoundrels," Adriane said with another smile. "Especially slaveholding rich people."

"As they are. Scoundrels, miscreants, immoral men with no consideration for anything but their own comfort and wealth."

"Few in this town would agree with you. The Jimsons are very respected, as you know, and Mr. Jimson is running for the state senate in August."

"God help us all." Grace rolled her eyes as she threw her hands up in the air. Then she reached across the table to grasp Adriane's hands. "I'm just going to be here a few weeks to make as many hats as I can and then once they're sold, I'll be going back north." Her eyes burned into Adriane's. "Come with me. There's always a need for people who can write well in the cause. You won't have much, but you won't starve."

Tears pushed into Adriane's eyes as she squeezed Grace's hands. "Please try to understand, Grace. Father did not desert me when I was born and my mother died. He protected me

114

from Henrietta as much as he could. He's taken care of me all these years. I must do what he wishes now."

"He should not wish this upon you." Grace's grip on Adrianne's hand tightened.

"He thinks I can be happy with Stan."

"And what do you think?"

"Stan has promised to allow me to continue to write. As long as I can do that, I can endure anything."

"Marriage should not be something to endure but a reason for joy."

"Don't you think I know that, Grace?" She pulled her hands free from Grace and sat back. "Don't you think I'd choose joy and love if I could?"

"I'm not yet convinced that you cannot."

When Adriane started to say something, Grace waved aside her words and went on. "But I am unfortunately convinced that you believe you cannot. I will pray for you every day, my dear girl. You must pray too. That there will be another way. Promise me that."

"I am praying. But the only answer I know is to marry Stan."

"That is not your answer. Keep praying and watching for a better way." Grace took hold of Adriane's hands again and gripped them as though she'd never turn loose. "And don't forget that you always have a place with me if you should need it."

11

*B*lake Garrett stared at the newspaper articles about the murders spread out across the top of his desk. It had been over two months since Kathleen's murder, but Blake had the uneasy feeling the river slasher would strike again and soon. Chief Trabue's claim that the murderer had surely been scared off by the show of strength on the part of the police force was nothing but empty rhetoric.

As Blake's eyes fell on the chief's direct quote in a story on the *Tribune*'s front page, he tried not to let thoughts of Adriane disturb his concentration, but he had just as well attempt to stop breathing. She tiptoed around the edge of his mind all day, every day, ready to explode out into his thoughts at the slightest invitation, and the sight of the *Tribune* masthead was more than invitation enough.

It had been a week since he'd pulled her out from under the rearing horses and met her friend Grace Compton. He'd asked around and found out that while all the society ladies wanted one of Grace's hats, Grace herself was pitied, scorned, or laughed at in turn, according to who was speaking about her.

The older women recalled how Grace's family had lost their fortune when Grace was young, but that Grace had had her chances and squandered them by marrying the wrong man. A few of the younger women remembered her fondly as a music teacher. Others collapsed into peals of laughter as they mocked how Miss Grace would spin in a little circle around them at the piano and briskly clap out the time of the melodies.

Blake had planned to ask Adriane about the little woman the next opportunity he had, but Adriane had made sure they had no opportunity to talk the two times he'd seen her since. The last time at a gathering at Mrs. Wigginham's, he'd planned to lie in wait for her and do whatever necessary to force another conversation, even if it turned into one of their duels. But Adriane, with young Jimson at her side, had quickly circled through the guests before making her exit. They had not skipped Blake. Adriane smiled and greeted him pleasantly enough while sliding her eyes quickly across his face.

Jimson hadn't bothered to smile at all as he tightened his hold on Adriane's arm as though he feared she might slip away. Blake wanted to tell him he had reason to fear, for each time Blake saw Adriane with Stanley Jimson, his resolve to do anything necessary to keep their wedding from ever taking place became stronger. Anything.

Still, Blake saw no reason to do something foolhardy this early in the game. There was yet time for circumstances to change. There might even be time to get Adriane to fall in love with him. At the foolish thought, Blake smiled a little and reminded himself he couldn't even get her to talk to him unless he pulled her out from in front of runaway horses. No matter how he might follow and watch her, such opportunities to rescue her were not apt to often present themselves.

With a sigh, he forced his attention back to the news articles in front of him as he made a list of the murder victims' names, ages, and dates of their deaths.

Megan Doyle, 18, January 5
Brenda Quinlan, 19, February 15
Kathleen O'Dell, 22, March 21

All Irish, unmarried, and at home in the Irish taverns. All killed by the same man. No one who had seen the bodies could doubt that.

Blake's eyes caught on Kathleen's name. She'd always been ready to repeat any bit of gossip or rumor about the murders.

"You'll remember poor Kathleen when you catch the monster, won't you, Blake, me lad? It'd be a wonder sure seeing me own name on the front page of a newspaper, especially one as grand as the *Herald*," she had told him more than once. "Almost as much a wonder as having a handsome lad like you to walk me home." Then she would flash her eyes at him in invitation.

Blake felt guilty when he couldn't remember the color of those eyes. He picked up the article in the *Herald* detailing Kathleen's death. Poor Kathleen. Her name had made more than his paper, but it was a wonder she hadn't gotten to see. The black words on the papers began running together, and Blake leaned his head in his hands. He had to be missing something.

"Hey, boss," Joe called to him. "A lady here to see you."

For one crazy moment Blake's heart bounded up inside him as he turned, half expecting to see Adriane presenting herself to him for rescue, but instead Grace Compton pushed past Joe to smile at him.

"A woman at any rate, my good sir, and I do hope I've not come at a bad time." Her eyes touched on his cluttered desk.

Blake scrambled to his feet to properly receive her. "No, of course not, madam. Please do have a chair, such as it is." He moved a pile of papers and dusted off the seat of the chair with his forearm before he presented it for Grace's use.

"Don't put yourself to any bother, Mr. Garrett. I assure you I have sat on worse." She smiled as she sat down, settled her skirts, and allowed her lace shawl to drop off her shoulders. The little woman looked even smaller than Blake remembered as she perched primly in the straight wooden chair and looked over her shoulder at the press in the room behind them. In her lap she carefully held a small package.

"Newspaper offices are such grand places," she said before Blake could ask the nature of her visit. "I've thought so ever since I first visited the *Tribune* offices years ago. I'd dealt with words all my life as a reader, you know, and then a teacher, but I'd never imagined the excitement of churning them out on newsprint."

"A lot of it is merely hard work."

"A lot of nearly everything is merely hard work." Grace's eyes came back to rest on Blake's face. "But to give life the proper meaning, we must make sure it's work that has a purpose."

"I intend for the *Herald* to be a service to the community."

"I have no doubt of that, Mr. Garrett." Again a smile lit up her small, angular face.

"How may I be of service to you this morning, Mrs. Compton?"

"Well, sir, I've never been one to wait too long on anyone, so when you didn't show up on my doorstep for your promised bread and cheese, I brought it to you." She held out the package. "Actually not bread and cheese, but a few tea cakes. While they cannot compare to Mr. Silverman's confections down the street, I do promise they won't break a tooth."

With a laugh, Blake took the package, tore it open, and pulled out one of the cookies. "Won't you join me?" He held the package out toward her.

"Oh no, I ate quite more than my share while baking them."

He chewed slowly, knowing the cookies were not free. He'd read the woman's pieces in the *Tribune*. Well written, to the point, but totally out of step with the accepted thinking in the city. Most of the city's finer citizens felt owning slaves a divine right and did not welcome an abolitionist view even in a short letter buried on the back page. As for the rights of women, no one anywhere was giving that cause much credence.

That aside, Blake liked the little woman in front of him and the way she was studying him as intently as he was studying her without showing the least bit of unease. Even more important, he had a feeling she might prove a powerful ally in his fight to keep Adriane out of Stanley Jimson's clutches. As he swallowed the last of the tea cake, he decided he'd publish whatever she gave him. A few angry readers would be a small price to pay for such an ally.

"That was delicious, Mrs. Compton." He smiled and leaned across his desk toward her as he asked, "How can I repay your kindness?"

She laughed as she pulled a folded paper out of her reticule. "I thought it would take at least two tea cakes." She quickly popped up from her chair to hand the article across his desk and then remained standing as he skimmed through it. "It's not too inflammatory. Just a bit of a treatise in regard to the evils of slavery with the focus on how that institution has bogged down the South." She came around the desk to peer over his shoulder and point out a couple of lines. "Here we have the convincing argument that all men were guaranteed freedom by our great Constitution."

"Did you write it, Mrs. Compton?"

"No, no. The author is Mr. Harrison Fremont of the Philadelphia organization for the freedom of the slaves. He's a very talented lawyer and a trusted friend of the downtrodden." She reached into her reticule yet again. "I have a letter here stating his desire to have this published in your worthy paper."

Blake looked at the second letter. "Very well. It will appear in the *Herald* tomorrow if space permits. The next day if space runs short."

Grace Compton's face lit up. "Thank you, sir. I could tell you were a forward-thinking gentleman when I first laid eyes on you. Do I dare hope you might have some abolitionist leanings?"

"You might hope so, but it's not a fight I wish to take on in this city at this time. I prefer to pick fights I might have a chance of winning." Blake laid the two letters on his desk.

Grace's eyes followed. Then she quickly stepped closer to peer down at the articles spread across his desk. "These are the stories of those dreadful murders Adriane told me about." Without asking permission, she picked up his list of the victims and the dates of their deaths. "The same killer?" she asked.

"There's little doubt of that."

"Any connections between the girls?"

"Nothing notable other than being poor and Irish."

"And young." Grace peered up at him. "Pretty?"

"So their friends say. I only knew Kathleen. She was pleasant enough." Blake hesitated before he went on. "How can I say this without offending you?"

"My sensibilities are not that easily offended, Mr. Garrett. What you're trying to say is that poor Kathleen was not adverse to sharing her favors for a price." Grace raised her eyebrows at him. "True of them all?"

"Perhaps, although Megan's friends are reluctant to say so."

"I read in the *Tribune* that Chief Trabue says we no longer have reason to worry." Grace's eyes swept over his desk. "Obviously you do not agree."

"No. I fear the murderer is out there, biding his time and waiting for the proper opportunity to strike again."

"And what is that opportunity, Mr. Garrett?"

"If I knew that, I wouldn't be rereading these articles for the hundredth time."

"Of course not. And at any rate, it's hard to guess what is

in the future." Grace stared down at the paper in her hand for a long moment. "What you must determine is what opportunity presented itself on these other dates. You need to not only study the papers on the days the bodies were discovered but the news on the days preceding as well. What was going on in the city on those days? Was it storming? Was the moon full? What?"

"It's not the moon. I checked that," Blake said.

"It's doubtful it would be that easy." Grace placed the paper back on his desk. "Besides, there may not be a pattern, or even if there is, one only the wretched person who did the crimes could possibly determine. Our best hope and prayer is that Chief Trabue is right, and the murderer has been scared away."

"We can hope so," Blake said.

"If it can be figured out, you'll be able to do it." Grace lightly touched his shoulder before she began gathering her shawl closer about her. Then she smiled and pointed to the article she'd brought in to him. "Your kindness in helping our just and honorable cause will not go unnoticed in the North."

"Or in the South, I daresay." Blake stood up. "I'll see you to the door, madam."

"Would you be so kind?" she said with another smile. "I don't want to disturb your work, but as a matter of fact, I do have another favor of a more personal nature I would ask of you, and I wonder if you might not walk out into the sunshine with me for a moment. I've always favored a bit of a constitutional to clear the cobwebs out of one's mind, and perhaps it will help you to think more clearly about these dreadful murders."

Outside on the street, Grace kept her eyes straight ahead with a small frown wrinkling her brow as she spoke. "I never had children, Mr. Garrett. My husband and I did not worry over that unduly in the first years of our marriage as we put all our efforts into gaining him some recognition for his paintings. My Aaron was a very talented artist. The two of us were much in love and thought the Lord would bless us with children in his own good time. But then war fever swept the city as the reports came in from Texas of the Mexicans invading. Aaron was not a soldier, but he had a brother in Texas and he felt compelled to volunteer to fight." She peered up at him. "Did you serve in the Mexican War, sir, or were you too young for that conflict?"

"I was old enough," Blake said. "And young enough to think it would be the opportunity of a lifetime for a reporter."

"And did you find that to be true?" She kept her eyes on his face.

"The stories I sent back gained me some notice, and since I was lucky enough to live through the war, I suppose it was."

"Aaron was not so lucky." Grace turned her eyes back down toward the sidewalk. "I, of course, was reluctant to see him march off in his royal blue colors with the Louisville Legion, but at the same time, I don't think I could have felt any prouder. He was stepping up for his country. For his family." The woman's small sigh was a whisper of sadness. "I have since come to realize that the heart-swelling response to the playing of a patriotic tune can be most dangerous and one politicians are not hesitant to use in order to gain their ends."

"Was Mr. Compton killed in one of the battles?"

"No. Nothing so glorious. Disease. His health had never been very strong." She shook her head a little as if to clear it of worrisome memories. "At any rate, I knew then I could never be disloyal to the memory of what we had shared by remarrying. So there would be no children. I opened a girls' school, which with my enlightened views did not find a welcome place in this city, but it did bring me Adriane. She was fifteen at the time and so totally fresh and open, unmarred by the accepted social restrictions usually taught little girls from an early age."

"Hadn't she been to school before then?"

"Just the school of her father's library of books and the newspaper office. She learned to read before the age of five. She was never sure how, but could remember Wade reading the newspaper to her. Even as a little child, she must have had an extraordinary gift for words. A certain unusual maturity if you will." Grace walked a few steps in silence before she went on. "Whatever it was, her stepmother could never accept Adriane as she was. I think she was a bit frightened of such a child, and she punished what she feared."

"Her father allowed that?" Blake said.

"He did what he could, often taking Adriane to the shop with him where Beck watched out for her. Dear Beck." Grace smiled. "He became an adoring uncle of sorts to Adriane, and I, eventually when our paths crossed, an equally adoring aunt."

"And her teacher as well."

"I suppose so, although it was always debatable which of us taught the other the most new things. When she first came to me, her mind was filled with the most amazing facts. She knew the schedules and records of dozens of steamboats. She knew the names and political leanings of most of the senators and representatives in Washington and the names of the mayors in all the bigger cities. But only the most basic math."

"She's a very interesting young woman," Blake said as they neared the end of the first block from his offices.

"Do you think so?" Grace glanced sideways up at him, but gave him no time to answer her inquiry as she went on. "Do you know the Jimsons?"

Blake's voice hardened a bit. "I know them."

"It's odd how having a fortune, no matter how that fortune might have been obtained, can make a man seem respectable to his fellow citizens."

"What do you mean?"

"My father was associated in business with Coleman Jimson once. I was young at the time, too young to understand exactly what happened, but I do know the man stole my father's business." Grace paused a moment. "And destroyed his will to live. Father shot himself in what they kindly called a hunting accident not very long afterward and Mother had to take in boarders to survive. I learned to make hats."

"Your father is not the only person Jimson has destroyed on his way to the top, but you can rest assured that his road to the state senate will not be clear," Blake said. "I have been gathering information and will soon be ready to reveal to the voters exactly the sort of man he is."

"You'd best be very ready, Mr. Garrett." Grace gave Blake an appraising look. "Coleman Jimson is not an adversary to take on lightly."

"I'm keenly aware of that." Blake's jaw tightened.

"Yes, I can see you are." Grace turned her eyes away from him and stared straight ahead as she continued. "I've never told any of this to Adriane. There hardly seemed any reason to. It all happened so long ago. And as much as I dislike Coleman Jimson, at least one can understand the basic greed ruling him. Stanley is not so easily understood, but the young man worries me."

"In what way?"

"I'm not sure. He has money, position. He could have married any girl in the city, and yet he chooses Adriane who has no connections, no family wealth."

"Perhaps he loves her. She is a beautiful woman." A vision of Adriane floated into his mind.

"I suppose that is possible, but from what I hear about town, I can't see young Stanley going against the social conventions for love. He would want a proper wife. And though her beauty is hardly in doubt, there are times when Adriane—as you have discovered—does not bother to practice sweetness and light. I have difficulty believing Stanley is not a man who would prefer sweetness and light. I sense some sort of deal going on here."

"Surely Adriane's father would not bargain her hand in marriage."

"Not unless he thought it was for her own good, and you can see why he might think such a match with Stanley Jimson would be to Adriane's advantage. The worst part of it is that Adriane thinks she can handle Stanley. She thinks he is weak."

"And you do not?"

"Again I'm not sure. I don't really know Stanley, only what I've heard from my hat customers. You know how some ladies do enjoy repeating tidbits of stories and rumors they've heard in the parlors, especially when it's about one of the better known families in the city."

"What stories?" Blake asked. Maybe he could add to his arsenal of weapons against Coleman Jimson.

"Nothing I could substantiate since one can't really give such stories much credence. But of one thing I am absolutely sure." Her voice got a bit stronger and took on the tone of the teacher she had once been as she went on. "Stanley is not a good match for Adriane."

"I can agree with you there," Blake said. "Although of course, I'm barely acquainted with Adriane."

"Acquainted enough, I daresay." Grace sent another sideways glance up at him. "However, at last, I come to my favor, Mr. Garrett. I'll only be in town a few weeks. Since Adriane knows I disapprove of this union, it's doubtful she will write me anything about it. So I was wondering if I might count on you to keep me informed if the date is moved up or anything untoward befalls."

"Of course, madam."

"And I know it's more than I have a right to ask." The little woman touched his arm and stopped walking. She stared up at him intently. "But I beg you to watch out for her. She needs a friend right now, and I rather feel I'm deserting her in her hour of greatest need, but I must return to Boston. I have commitments."

126

Ann H. Gabhart

"I fear the lady doesn't want me as a friend. She avoids me at all costs." Blake saw no reason to sashay around the truth.

"Then you have to find a way to make her talk to you. Your newspapers are warring. Make that war more personal so she'll have to respond."

"Are you suggesting I intentionally make her angry with me?" Blake raised his eyebrows as he looked down at the woman.

Her eyes twinkled a little as she answered him. "Last time the two of you had a duel of words, it ended with you kissing her hand. Who knows how the next duel might end?"

"You're taking a lot for granted, madam," Blake said.

"So I am, Mr. Garrett, and I will pray that yours and Adriane's paths will often cross." She looked up at him with guileless sincerity. "Do you believe in prayer?"

"I don't spend much time on my knees," Blake admitted.

"There are many postures of prayer. But never fear, I will pray doubly hard for your endeavors in the weeks ahead." Her mouth twisted in an amused little smile as she reached out to squeeze his hand. "I will send you my address when I return to Boston."

As the slight woman walked swiftly away, head high, others on the street gave way to her determined progress. Blake shook his head and turned back toward the *Herald*'s offices. With women like Grace Compton leading the charge, who knew what women would be asking for next?

She'd certainly asked enough of him, although making Adriane angry should be easy enough. But he didn't want her to stay angry. Perhaps some kind of trick might not be out of line.

All at once he remembered an old New Orleans paper he had come across when he was gathering the river slasher articles. He'd read it because it detailed a murder as well. Nothing like the Louisville murders, but it had made sensational headlines in New Orleans. He would press the wrinkles

127

out of the paper and send it by messenger to Adriane as if it had just arrived on one of the steamboats from New Orleans. Then just to be sure she realized the story was suspect, he'd credit a record-breaking run to one of the slowest, leakiest steamboats in the harbor, the *Douchester*. That should get a response.

Perhaps she would even storm into the *Herald* offices to demand he apologize for his subterfuge. Which he would readily do. Then if the moment was right, he could offer more than an apology. He could offer her a way to escape Stanley Jimson. He could almost feel her head against his shoulder, her soft hair brushing his lips. He'd be more than willing to go down on his knees if he thought prayer could make that happen.

He let out a short laugh at the idea of praying Adriane into his arms. His father had been a praying man and what had it got him? A bullet in the street for printing the truth. Blake pulled open the door and went back inside his building. The clank and rumble of the press greeted him like an old friend as he made his way back to his desk to find the old New Orleans paper. What was it someone had told him once? That sometimes a man had to give his prayers legs.

12

Adriane had been dreading the Jimsons' summer ball for days. The annual event on the second Saturday in June was as expected in Louisville as the summer heat. The party known for its elaborate spread of food, fine music, and ostentatious decorations drew guests from far and wide with so many beautifully bedecked belles in attendance that it was rumored more than half of all Louisville marriages could trace their roots back to the ball.

Last summer, Adriane had made a long enough appearance to get an acceptable list of names for an enthusiastic report of the event in the *Tribune*. This year, as almost one of the family, she was expected to lend her support by being present hours earlier than necessary.

So now she sat with Stan, three of his sisters, and his mother in the parlor amid the smilax-bedecked mirrors and doorways as they awaited their guests. Adriane tried to console herself with the thought that there should be plenty of political talk at the party later. She'd be sure to overhear something she could use in a Colonel Storey letter.

Adriane slowly waved her fan back and forth in front of her face and managed to swallow yet another yawn as one of the sisters repeated an inane comment one of her children had made the previous day, or so the nanny had reported. Even Meta Jimson seemed bored by her daughter's recital. Over the top of her own fan, Mrs. Jimson's eyes kept flipping from Stanley to Adriane.

No one expected Adriane to talk, which was a relief. For about the tenth time Adriane smoothed the folds of her silvery blue dress, yet another one Nora had finished in record time. Adriane had picked the fabric chiefly because it was so different, and now here among the more ordinary yellow, pink, and cream dresses of Stan's sisters, she wondered if once again she'd chosen poorly. Perhaps it would serve her better to strive for the ordinary.

She certainly hadn't liked it when she'd come down the stairs to check on how the paper was coming before she left and Beck had barred her from the pressroom as he'd looked at her in wonder.

"You make a vision in that dress, Addie. One that don't belong in here."

She'd looked down at the flowing yards of fabric that seemed to pick up and reflect the sunlight streaming in the window next to the front door and knew he was right even if she didn't want him to be. Then Duff, pounding in from outside with some bit of news, had stopped in his tracks at the sight of her.

"Is that you, Miss Adriane?" He whipped off his hat and stared at her with wide eyes. "You look like a princess out of a storybook."

The way they had stared at her as if she were not only someone they didn't know but someone they were afraid to meet had been much more distressing to Adriane than the look of disapproval in Meta Jimson's eyes. The woman's lips curled down now as she said, "That's a most unusual color for a dress, Adriane."

"Yes, it is," Adriane agreed mildly.

"But it is lovely, isn't it, Mother?" Stan spoke up quickly, his eyes lingering a long moment on Adriane.

"Very lovely if one doesn't mind being so conspicuous." Mrs. Jimson sniffed with disapproval and turned her eyes from Adriane to Stanley. "Fetch me another cushion, Stanley dearest. All this sitting is straining my back."

Stan had already fetched her a glass of tea, a fresh handkerchief, and a low stool to prop up her feet under her dark purple silk dress. Each time Stanley jumped to satisfy one of his mother's whims, she smiled a little at Adriane as if she were winning some kind of point. Adriane wanted to tell the old dragon she didn't care if Stan did handstands in the middle of the floor for his mother. In fact it might even be amusing. Heaven only knew something amusing needed to happen before they all fell out of their chairs with boredom. Another of the sisters began talking about the trouble she was having with her cook. The woman just could not learn to make a proper meringue dessert and couldn't Papa possibly give her a new cook.

Adriane turned her mind away from the conversation before she could think too much about what she would do when "Papa" started giving her and Stanley cooks. Adriane hadn't thought at all about what would happen after the wedding since that seemed hurdle enough to face, but now it dawned on her slowly and not very pleasantly that she would be expected to have slaves as servants.

She suppressed a sigh. Here was yet something else about which she and Stan would have to come to an understanding. Her eyes drifted over to Stan. He hadn't been very understanding about anything of late. They had argued three times during the last week. Twice about how Adriane needed to take more care styling her hair before they went to socials, and once about Blake Garrett pulling Adriane from the path of the carriage horses.

The morning following her visit to Grace, Stanley had stormed into the newspaper offices, almost shouting about how she'd been seen in Blake Garrett's arms out on the streets.

Adriane had pulled him back into the hall before her father could wonder at the commotion and come out of his office. In the process she smeared ink on Stan's sleeve. For a moment she was uncertain which upset him the most—the thought of her in Blake Garrett's arms or the ink stain on his sleeve.

As she rubbed ineffectively at the ink with her handkerchief, she did her best to calm his anger. "I was careless, Stan, and stepped into the street without paying proper attention. Mr. Garrett was good enough to pull me out of the way of a carriage."

"I suppose he just happened to be on the walkway beside you," Stan said with a sneer of disbelief.

"I have no idea where he was. I didn't see him until he pulled me back up on the walk before I could be run down." Adriane concentrated on breathing in and out slowly. It would do little good for her to let her temper rise to match his.

"Even if that's so, it hardly explains why he had to hold you while two carriages passed by." Stan's voice was still too loud.

"I felt faint," Adriane said.

"Faint? You've never felt faint in your life, Adriane Darcy." Stan glared at her.

"I've never before been nearly run down by a team of spirited horses. The sight of hooves slashing the air above one's head is a bit unsettling." Adriane kept her voice calm. "And while I might have preferred to be rescued by someone other than Mr. Garrett, I can hardly claim to be sorry I was rescued, can I?"

"I suppose not," he conceded. "But you shouldn't have even been in that part of town unescorted. You need to remember your position."

"My position, yes," she echoed his words as despair swept through her the way it did every time she thought of what that position was. She pushed out one of her practiced smiles in an attempt to appease him. If she could mollify him, perhaps he would be on his way to whatever he did during the

132

daytime hours when he wasn't escorting her to socials. She realized she didn't know what that was, and moreover, she didn't care. She simply wanted him gone so she could return to her work in the pressroom and forget for a few hours the untenable position she was in.

But he wasn't through. "And I do have to insist you not be seen speaking to that man Garrett ever again."

She managed to suppress her resentment at his demanding tone as she chose her words carefully. "That might prove difficult, since he does seem to be at every event we attend lately. I don't know how he could have been in Louisville for months without our paths crossing and now I see him everywhere I go."

"I daresay it's by design." Stan's face grew darker.

"I can't imagine what you mean, Stan." Adriane started to lay her hand on his arm again, but he flinched away before she could touch him. She looked at her ink-stained hand, then dropped it to her side. "Mr. Garrett is quite aware of our engagement."

"Perhaps he has other reasons," Stanley said with an odd, distracted look. So distracted that he left without kissing Adriane's cheek or giving her any sort of farewell.

Adriane hadn't worried about it then as she returned to the pressroom and the story he'd interrupted, but now remembering it, she looked over at Stanley. Before he asked for her hand in marriage, she would have said she knew him as well as any person in the world. Since then, he was continually surprising her.

Even today he was surprising her. He was handsomely dressed as always in a dark coat with his collar stiff and pristinely white, but his cheeks were flushed and his eyes were strangely animated as if he knew some sort of secret that no one could know but him. The most surprising thing about him was the way he looked when he satisfied his mother's many whims. Even as he fetched and carried without complaint, his every movement carried a hint of defiance, and he practically radiated with that defiance whenever he looked at Adriane sitting there in their midst in her exotic gown.

A commotion in the hallway cut short the idle chatter among the sisters. A woman's voice, strong and confident, carried into the parlor. "Dear Alec, what are you doing still here? Papa promised me he was going to give you your papers."

"Now, Miss Margaret, don't go fretting over me. Massah Coleman says he can't get along without me." The black butler's voice was soft and friendly as he greeted Stan's sister who had come down from the North to the summer ball.

"We'll see about that. A promise is a promise." Her voice was strident.

Inside the parlor, Meta Jimson stiffened and stopped fanning for a moment as she and Stan exchanged an uneasy look. Two of the sisters appeared totally unnerved, and even Pauline, the oldest, looked up from her needlework with a concerned frown etching lines between her eyes.

Stan recovered first. He stood and managed a smile as he said, "That's our dear Margaret. Isn't it wonderful she could make it down to our little party this year?"

The sisters all pushed their smiles back into their proper places as they bobbed their heads in agreement. Even Mrs. Jimson pushed out a smile as she looked toward Adriane. "I'm sure she made the special effort because she's so anxious to meet dear Adriane."

Before Adriane had time to decide whether that remark was supposed to frighten her, the sister from Ohio swept into the room, looking a bit formidable in her plain, dark brown traveling costume among their ball gowns. She was nearly as tall as Stanley, and though she was not exactly fat, the trunk of her body was uniformly thick and appeared totally free of the constraints of a corset of any type.

She wasn't pretty. Her dark hair was yanked back in a tight bun with no hint of curl at her temples to soften the severity of the style. Her nose was too large and her chin too jutting, but her face was interesting. The woman's eyes practically slammed into Adriane as soon as she entered the room, and Adriane rose from her chair to meet this new, very different sister.

"My heavens, Stanley, she's beautiful. How in the world did you get her to say she'd marry you?" the woman said.

The color drained from Stan's cheeks and then rushed back redder than ever. Adriane almost felt sorry for him as he sputtered for something to say.

His mother came to his rescue. "Don't be rude, Margaret. Come kiss your mother and then Stanley will properly introduce you to his intended."

Margaret obediently pecked her mother on the cheek before turning to offer her own cheek to Stan. "Do forgive me, brother, but I was assuming you had warned your fiancée about my unladylike habit of saying what I think." Her eyes gleamed with the pleasure his discomfort was giving her, but the sparkle faded as she turned to Adriane again.

Their eyes locked as they sized one another up. After a moment, the sister's appraising look changed and seemed to become almost sad as she reached out to grasp Adriane's hands in hers. "So you're Adriane Darcy."

Stan watched his sister warily as he said, "Soon to be Adriane Jimson."

"I've heard so much about you." Margaret kept talking as if Stan had not spoken. "And I'm Margaret Jimson Black. I rather doubt you've heard anything about me." Her eyes slid sideways toward Stan, then back to Adriane.

Adriane searched for something to say that might relieve the strange tension in the room. "Of course I have, and I've looked so forward to meeting you. Stan told me you have four sons. Are they with you?"

"Heaven forbid, no," Margaret said. "They travel poorly, and since I must go back tomorrow, it didn't seem worth the aggravation to drag them along, especially since Papa's summer gala is hardly a fitting place for youngsters. Their heads would be quite turned by all the pretty belles, and I intend to keep them in the schoolroom and nursery a few more years yet."

"What a shame you can't stay longer, Margaret," Stan said with no regret at all in his voice.

Her eyes went back to him. "Yes, a real shame." Then she glanced around at her mother and sisters. "You look like lovely roses sitting around waiting to be picked."

"Honestly, Margaret. The things you say," her mother said. "When you know we've all already been picked."

"Yes, I suppose you have." Again there was the wicked grin. "And deflowered. Except of course for Adriane who looks more like an elusive moonbeam in that dress than any kind of rose."

"Elusive now, perhaps." Stan slid his arm around Adriane's waist to draw her as close to him as the fullness of her skirts would allow. "But not for long."

Adriane thought icy thoughts but could not keep a blush from climbing into her cheeks. Stan noticed and laughed as he tightened his arm around her.

Adriane forced herself to continue to breathe calmly and keep smiling while she deliberately and carefully turned her thoughts back toward what would be happening at the *Tribune* offices. The galleys would be ready unless her father was holding one for some late story entry. Beck and Duff would be checking the presses, which would soon be clanking out the words. They'd run through the first copies, and her father would check them to be sure they were right since she wasn't there to do it.

The *Tribune* would get out without her there. That wasn't the problem. The problem was she wanted to be there instead of here. The problem was she wanted to be anywhere but here today or any day, but she made herself keep smiling at Margaret as if she were the happiest girl in the world.

The woman squeezed Adriane's hands tighter. "The two of us must talk, Adriane."

"That will have to be later," Stan said quickly. "You barely have time to dress before the first guests arrive."

Margaret laughed. "Yes, I'd best go see if I can disguise my thorns and attempt to turn myself into a rose as well. Even if I too have already been plucked."

When she bustled out of the room, she seemed to take all the life with her. Unable to bear the thought of sitting back down to another session of fanning and hiding yawns, Adriane sweetly asked if she might explore the gardens. After a quick glance at Stanley, Pauline offered to accompany her.

The Jimson garden was noted for its blooming plants and bushes from the earliest bit of warmth in the spring to the first snow in the winter. Now the roses and flowers along the bricked path had erupted in blooms to fill the air with bright colors and sweet fragrances. A green hummingbird darted between the red and pink clusters of hollyhocks while a black and yellow butterfly nearly as large as the tiny bird floated lazily back and forth in front of Adriane and Pauline as they walked.

"It's always so lovely out here. So quiet and peaceful," Adriane said. The sun began to sink low in the west behind a bank of dark clouds, withdrawing its rays slowly, almost reluctantly from the garden.

"It is. Mother had the garden designed for both beauty and privacy." Pauline frowned as she glanced up at the sky. "I do hope it doesn't rain and spoil some of the romance our summer gala is so noted for." Her smile returned as she nodded toward an iron bench surrounded by an arbor of greenery. "That's one of the so-called proposal benches because of how many young men are said to have gone down on their knees in front of their sweethearts here. Is this where Stanley proposed to you?"

"No." Adriane wondered what Pauline would think if she

knew how Adriane had forced Stan to propose to her in the carriage. Pauline was the sister who never said much, except for an occasional quiet word to keep the peace between her two younger sisters, and while Adriane hadn't exactly figured out which of the children might belong to her, all of them listened immediately when she spoke.

Adriane knew she was expected to listen too, and so she wasn't surprised when Pauline began talking about Margaret.

"You mustn't pay too much mind to Margaret or anything she says." Pauline paused on the path to pluck a bloom from a hollyhock stalk. She ran her fingers over the silky smooth pink petals as she added, "Especially about Stanley."

"Oh?" Adriane said.

"All families have their little difficulties getting along at times, don't you think?" Pauline looked at her a moment before she dropped the hollyhock bloom and began walking again.

Adriane kept in step with her without answering. She had no idea what Pauline expected her to say, and she had no desire to start off on the wrong foot with this sister who appeared to be the one most willing to help Adriane fit into the Jimson family.

Pauline didn't seem to notice her silence as, after a few steps, she went on. "Margaret's the youngest besides Stanley. I suppose since she'd been the baby for five years, it was hard for her to relinquish that favored spot. And dear Stanley was so fragile as a child that Mother had to give him all her time and attention. We older sisters didn't resent that, but I fear Margaret did. Not only that, but before Stanley was born, Margaret had rather taken it upon herself to try to fulfill Papa's desire for a son by becoming rather boyish in her activities. She was always climbing trees and catching toad frogs or crickets. Why, one time she even tried to keep a squirrel as a pet."

"Do they make good pets?" Adriane thought of feeding a

squirrel a nut from her hand the way she fed the old dog the extra biscuits she baked for him.

"Oh goodness, no," Pauline said. "Papa had one of the houseboys carry the creature out to the country and bring Margaret back a kitten. A much more suitable pet."

Adriane smiled at Pauline, and as they turned back toward the house, one of the servants came out to light the gas lights along the pathways. The black boy stopped beside Pauline with his gaze on the ground. "Miss Pauline, the Missus says to tell you and the other missy that the guests is beginning to gets here."

"Thank you, Samuel." The boy went on about his work, and Pauline and Adriane walked a bit more quickly on toward the house where light and the beginning strains of music were spilling out the double doors. As they started up the steps to go inside, Pauline laid her hand on Adriane's arm and stopped her a moment.

"So you do understand?" Pauline asked. "I mean, we do love Margaret dearly, but I fear living in the North has caused her to pick up some of the Yankees' lack of civility. You won't allow her careless talk to bother you, will you?"

"Of course not," Adriane said, although she was beginning to doubt she understood anything and especially this family.

Pauline rewarded her answer with a warm smile. "Our Stanley is a very fortunate man."

As they moved on up the steps toward the wide double doors, the sound of distant thunder followed them. Pauline glanced up at the spreading clouds again.

"Father will be furious if it rains. He rather expects the weather to cooperate with his plans, and strangely enough, it usually does. I can't remember a storm ever spoiling our summer gala. Stanley says Father tells the Lord what kind of weather he wants, and the good Lord's afraid not to comply." Pauline laughed a little then as, the clouds forgotten, she led the way into the house.

13

The party was every bit as tedious as Adriane had expected. She tried to fade into the background and eavesdrop on the political discussions as she'd done so easily in the days before she became Stanley Jimson's intended, but now eyes and sometimes whispers were always following her, especially tonight.

Perhaps Meta Jimson had been right. Perhaps she was too conspicuous in the silvery blue dress. Men she'd never seen before kept appearing at her side to tell her how lovely she was. Then they stared at her with dazzled expressions and were completely unable to carry on any sort of sensible conversation.

At first she'd been worried about Stan's reaction to all these admirers, but as the evening progressed and he kept positively beaming at her, she realized he was enjoying the men's bedazzlement much more than she was. Adriane began to feel as if she were no more than another amazing decoration the Jimsons had found for their summer gala, second only to the mountain of exotic fruits in the middle of the banquet table.

Her smile grew stiff and tired as she tried to think of acceptable responses to the inane talk of the men on her dance card. So when her scheduled partner was slow to claim her for the upcoming dance, she slipped through the French doors out into the garden where she embraced the slight chill in the air. Although the rain had held off, clouds hid the stars and lightning continued to flash in the distance.

Adriane rubbed her cheeks to wipe away every trace of smile from her face as she sat down on a deeply shadowed bench not far from the steps without worrying about whether her skirts were nicely arranged or not. Perhaps she could stay hidden there the rest of the evening. While it might be more interesting to be hiding behind a chair in the library where Coleman Jimson and his cronies were talking, this pocket of darkness was the next best thing.

She peeked around the thick evergreen tree behind her toward the house. The musicians were playing again, and couples were sweeping by the windows in a new redowa. Adriane watched for Stan, who was being careful to dance with a different lady each song, but she couldn't spot him. She decided to dare a few more minutes of solitude.

When two people began talking on the other side of the trees behind her, she pulled in her breath and sat as quietly as possible. She smiled a little, wondering if she was about to overhear one of the famous Jimson garden proposals, but as the voices continued, her smile drained away. There was nothing loving about these familiar voices.

"I'm warning you, Margaret," Stanley was saying. "Don't try to fill Adriane's head with your foolish lies."

"Lies?" Margaret said with a short, unpleasant laugh. "I don't lie, dear brother. That's one family trait I was not blessed with, I'm afraid."

"You missed out on a lot of family traits."

"Yes, praise the Lord," Margaret said. "But surely it can't matter what I tell Adriane if she loves you."

"You don't have to sound as if you don't think that could be possible. She is marrying me."

"So you say." Margaret managed to inject a heavy sound of doubt into her words.

"She practically begged me to propose."

Stanley sounded smug, and Adriane couldn't say he was lying. She thought back to the awkward carriage proposal and wished she'd never heard any sort of proposal from him.

"Do you love her?" Margaret was asking on the other side of the trees.

"Of course," Stan answered easily. "Adriane is beautiful and quite charming."

"Charming?" Margaret interrupted. "Mother seems to think she's brash and independent and not at all suitable."

"She is a bit different from other girls I've known."

"Are you sure you'll be able to handle her, Stanley?"

Stan's voice was cold when he answered. "I've yet to meet a woman I couldn't handle."

"Really?" Again Margaret barked her short laugh. "How about me?"

"Have you forgotten your cat?" Stanley's voice sounded almost casual, but even without seeing his face, Adriane knew the words were intended to wound his sister.

"I'd think that would be something you'd pray I had forgotten." All hint of laughter was gone from her voice now.

"Oh no, my dear sister, far from it. I want you to remember forever how I strung up your stupid cat. Muffin, wasn't it?"

Adriane wanted to run back into the house to escape the hatred in their voices, but instead she sat motionless, hardly daring to breathe for fear they'd discover her eavesdropping on them.

"You can't hurt me anymore, Stanley," Margaret said after a moment. "Or control what I say."

"Perhaps not, but it might be well for you to keep in mind that Father wants me to marry Adriane."

"Why? She's not rich, is she?"

"Hardly," Stan said with a short laugh. "Her father is a great man with words but a fool with money."

Adriane started up on the bench as if to defend her father, but then what could she say? Stan spoke the truth.

"Then why is Father so in favor of the match?" Margaret was asking.

"You saw her. He'd like to have her for himself. Since he can't, he plans to have her vicariously through me."

"How can you even insinuate such a thing? Father would never be such a cad."

"No? You remember as well as I seeing Mother nudge our dear Papa awake with a gun to his head." Stanley sounded like the memory amused him.

"That was years ago, and besides, that had nothing at all to do with women. Mother was angry because Father had cut off your curls and high time. You were nearly six."

"That was not the first time," Stan said slyly. "Or the last."

"How could you know such a thing?" Margaret sounded disbelieving.

"Mother tells me things." Stan laughed softly. "Sometimes I wonder how our dear Papa has managed to live through so many dangerous nights."

Behind them the doors of the house opened, and music and noise spilled out as a young man led a giggling belle down the steps to the garden. Stanley and Margaret quickly moved away down the path. Adriane barely waited for the whispering couple to pass her before she jumped to her feet and fled up the steps and back into the house. A lively polka was in progress, and she could only hope all eyes were on the dancers. She pushed the smile back onto her face as she searched through the guests for her father or Lucilla. She would feign illness and ask to be taken home.

"But my dear," one of Lucilla's friends finally told her. "You know how Lucilla can't bear such an awful crush of people, so when your father retired to the library with some of the men, she decided to go home alone."

"I see." Adriane forced a smile as she moved past the woman.

Across the room Margaret came in from the garden alone and peered about until her eyes caught on Adriane. With a determined look on her face, she started across the floor toward Adriane. She'd not gone two steps when a man grabbed her arm and pulled her toward the dance floor. At first Margaret appeared reluctant, but the man was insistent. Margaret gave in with a smile and joined the dancers. Adriane sent up a silent prayer of thanks for the reprieve. She couldn't talk to Margaret. Not until she had time to think.

But the reprieve wouldn't last. The music would end and Stanley would come in from the garden to claim Adriane for their dance. She'd have to smile at him and pretend that she could continue this farce. The very thought of his voice in her ears or his hands touching her as they danced made her throat tighten and her breath come hard. She couldn't do it. Not tonight. She had to get away from this house, from these people. In the morning light she might be able to bear it, but now the darkness was closing around her. She had to escape.

When Adriane spotted Pauline watching the dancers not far from the front entrance hallway, she hurried over to her. "Pauline, I do hope your mother will forgive me, but my father's fiancée is not feeling well and we must leave. You will convey my farewells to your mother and Stanley, won't you?"

"Oh my dear, I'm so sorry. But I'm sure Stanley will want to accompany you." Pauline looked around with a little frown. "Where is he?"

"I'm not sure. Perhaps he is with your father and their friends in the library." Adriane managed a small smile. "You know men. They must have their pipes and cigars."

"And their politics," Pauline agreed.

"It would not be wise to interrupt them. Lucilla and I will be fine. Now please do forgive me, but I shouldn't keep Lucilla waiting. I will explain everything to Stanley tomorrow." As the music ended, Adriane touched her cheek quickly to Pauline's and moved away before the woman could voice more delaying protests. From the corner of her eye, Adriane could see Margaret pushing her way across the room toward them.

Adriane fled from the house without taking time to even collect her wrap. She told herself she should want to talk to Margaret. And perhaps she would. Tomorrow.

Carriages were crammed all along the street in front of the house as the drivers and horses waited patiently for the party to be over. One carriage was moving away, but Adriane couldn't see it well enough to tell if it was Lucilla's. Behind her the door opened again, and Adriane stepped into the shadows. Margaret's thick body was outlined in the light spilling from the house as she stared after the departing carriage for a moment before going back inside.

Adriane waited in the shadows until the music starting up again drifted out the open windows. Then she began walking down the line of carriages as if the very next one was the one she sought. She kept her head high as if it were perfectly normal for a young lady to be wandering alone among the rows of carriages without an escort.

When she got to the end of the carriages, she just kept walking. The gas lamps had been lit long ago, and the streets were not dark. She could walk the few blocks home. Perhaps if good fortune smiled on her, everyone who might recognize her was still at the party, and there would be no one to see or report her outrageous behavior to her father or the Jimsons.

She had gone only a short way down the street when a small carriage pulled to a stop directly beside her and Blake Garrett jumped down in front of her.

"Adriane." He grabbed her arm and pulled her around to face him. "It is you. For a moment I thought you might be Cinderella searching for her coach."

"Mr. Garrett," she murmured as if they'd just chanced to meet on the street in the middle of the afternoon. "I did not see you at the party."

"Trouble with the press delayed me," he said. "It appears

you are not at the party either. What in the world are you doing out here alone?"

"I felt ill." Adriane touched her forehead and tried to look faint. She didn't have to try very hard. "I came out to catch my father's fiancée's carriage to ride home with her, but she was already gone. So I decided to walk."

"Young Jimson allowed this?" Blake sounded incredulous.

Adriane dropped her eyes to the street. "I didn't want to trouble him. This gala is so important to him and his family." She was entirely too aware of his hand on her arm.

"Surely not as important as you," Blake said. "Don't you know it could be dangerous out here on the street? You haven't forgotten there is a killer loose in the city, have you?"

"It's only a few blocks to my house. I'm sure I'll be quite safe." Adriane tried to step back away from Blake.

Blake held her arm tighter and stared down at her. "My dear lady, if you think I'm going to allow you to wander off in the darkness alone, you have another think coming. It appears you are in need of rescue once again."

Adriane looked around her. Outside the scattered pools of light from the streetlamps, it was very dark. She shivered not entirely from the cool evening air, and Blake stripped off his cloak to drape it about her.

"I fear you are right, Mr. Garrett." Adriane lost all resistance to his help as she pulled the cloak carrying his warmth and manly odor close around her. It was ridiculous to take such comfort in the feel of the cloth. "And once more I'm grateful. Please, if it would not be too much of an inconvenience, I beg you to escort me home."

"You don't want to go back to the party and wait for Stanley?" Blake's eyes burned into hers.

"If that would suit you better." She forced herself to say the words, although it was the last thing in the world she wanted to do. "I suppose it is unfair of me to ask you to forgo the party to see me home."

"Who gives a whit about the party?" Blake said as he put his hand under her elbow. "Come."

He helped her into the carriage, then spoke with the driver before he climbed in beside her. The carriage seat was so small Adriane couldn't keep her skirts from spilling over on his legs.

When she tried to pull the flowing material back, he touched her hand and said, "Don't concern yourself." Then he lightly stroked the silky fabric. "It's almost as if I am being wrapped in moonlight. Hardly something I could mind, now is it, Adriane?" His eyes came up to her face. "It is all right if I call you Adriane, isn't it? I feel as if I know you so well."

Adriane looked down at her hands. "You really don't know me at all, Mr. Garrett. I'm not always so muddled that I need rescuing."

"I have no doubt that's true, but any gentleman would be honored to rescue such a beautiful princess."

Adriane sighed. "Do you know how many times I've been told I was beautiful tonight?"

"No more than were true, I'm sure," Blake said with a smile in his voice. "But obviously more than you could bear. Forgive me. As a man of letters, I should be more original, but I was never much of a poet."

"Cinderella was almost poetic." Adriane tried to smile but didn't quite succeed. She felt a bit like Cinderella, except that instead of discovering her true love at the ball, she had opened the wrong closet door to let a pile of family skeletons fall out on top of her.

"Merely inspired by the way you were hurrying panic-stricken down the street." He was quiet a moment before he went on. "Do you want to tell me what happened?"

His voice was so soft and kind that for an insane moment she wanted to lean her head on his shoulder and tell him everything. How she didn't think she could bear marrying Stanley Jimson. How she was afraid to be part of a family

147

that could hide so much hatred for one another. How if she didn't go through with the wedding, her father would be ruined.

She stared at Blake Garrett's face in the dim light filtering through the carriage's windows and reminded herself that this man would be happy to see the *Tribune* and her father fall. It was foolish of her to want to tell him her troubles. It was best to stick with her first lie.

"I told you already. I felt ill."

"You don't impress me as someone given to the vapors."

She dropped her eyes back to her hands in her lap. "As I said, you don't really know me that well."

He put his fingers under her chin and gently lifted her face back up until she was looking at him again. "But I want to know you better if you'll only let me," he said after a moment.

His touch on her chin set off a fire inside her, and instead of pulling away from his hand the way she knew she should, she only waited and even hoped for what might happen next. Slowly he dropped his head toward hers and gently covered her lips with his.

His lips were soft, warm, and insistent, and her lips responded shamelessly as they had never responded to Stan's cool kisses. His hand stroked down her neck and found her shoulder under his cloak. He began to pull her closer to him, and her arms seemed to rise of their own volition to wrap around his neck. She buried her fingers in his dark wavy hair, and suddenly his lips on hers demanded more.

Her own lips answered, and if the carriage hadn't suddenly stopped, jolting her out of whatever spell his touch had put her under, she wasn't sure what might have happened. She pulled away from him and tried to jerk the door open.

He grabbed her and pinned her gently against the seat. "Don't run from me, Adriane." His eyes burned into her.

"I can't do this." Her heart was beating madly and her breath was coming in gasps. Worse than any of that, she thought she might burst into tears because she so missed the warmth of his arms around her.

"Kissing me is the only right thing you've done for weeks," he said. "What you can't do is marry him, Adriane."

"You don't understand."

"I understand more than you think."

His breath was soft on her face and she knew that if he tried to kiss her again, she wouldn't be able to stop him. Or herself. "Please let me go, Blake," she whispered.

"Don't marry him."

"I must. My father wants me to."

"Do what you want to do."

"I want to get out of the carriage," she said.

"Do you?" he asked softly before he turned her loose and opened the door. As if nothing at all had happened between them, he handed her down to the street.

Adriane tried to follow his lead. "You've been so kind to see me home, Mr. Garrett. You need not walk me to the door."

"Your father won't shoot me if I do, will he?"

"Of course not. Especially since he's still at the Jimsons'. But it's entirely unnecessary. You've already done your duty as a proper gentleman." She started to take off his cloak to hand it to him.

He put his hands on her shoulders to keep the cloak around her. "No, keep it. I'll come around for it. We may have a story to talk about at any rate come morning."

"A story?" Newspaper stories were the last thing on her mind, but it might be safer talking about stories than to think about what had just happened between them in the carriage. "There hasn't been another murder, has there?"

"I pray not in Louisville," he said. "But stories come from all over. Just remember that some of them should be thoroughly checked out before they're printed."

"Of course." She looked at him and tried without success to read his expression. "You're a puzzle this evening, Mr.

Garrett. One I'm much too exhausted to solve. I think it might be best if we go back to dueling, don't you?"

"Not at all, my dear lady. And you called me Blake earlier. I liked the way that sounded." They had reached the door and he took her hands in his to keep her from fleeing inside. "I liked a lot of things about this evening."

"I'm sure you did, but now the evening is over." Adriane kept her voice cool and polite as if the kiss in the carriage had never happened. "Good night."

He laughed and tightened his grip on her hands. She wasn't at all sure he would not have tried to kiss her again if Beck hadn't appeared in the door behind them.

"Addie, are you all right?" Beck said.

Adriane pulled her hands free and whirled toward Beck. "I'm fine, Beck. Mr. Garrett was kind enough to see me home when I missed my ride with Lucilla."

Beck's eyes sharpened on the man beside her, but he only said, "Well, as long as you're all right."

He started to go back inside, but Adriane said, "Wait, Beck, I'm coming in." She turned quickly back to Blake. "Thank you again, Mr. Garrett. I do hope I didn't put you to any great inconvenience."

He smiled at her. "It was my pleasure, Adriane. Be assured that any time Cinderella needs a ride, my coach will be available." Then he turned and left her there.

Inside, Beck stared at her curiously. "Sorta odd him bringing you home, ain't it, Addie?"

"Everything's been sort of odd tonight, Beck."

"You want to talk about it?"

"I can't, Beck. Not tonight anyway."

Beck looked at her a long moment before he nodded a little. "We got the paper out. We was a little late because a big story come in from New Orleans at the last minute and the boss held everything up while he changed the headlines. Didn't hardly none of us have time to read it."

"Will the headline sell papers?"

"It should. A big murder in New Orleans. You want to see?"

"I'll look at it in the morning." She gave the old man's leathery cheek a quick peck. "I just need some sleep now. Good night, Beck."

But up in her room she didn't go to bed. Instead after she stripped off her dress, crinolines, and corset, and pulled on her nightdress, she sat down at the little writing table. She opened her journal and quickly flipped past all the filled pages without letting her eyes touch on a single word.

She stared at the blank page a long time before she finally put the tip of her pen in the ink and began writing.

I think at last I know what Grace means when she speaks of love. But how can I love Blake Garrett? My father's enemy. My enemy. Then again, how could I have allowed him to kiss me as if I had no shame if I do not love him? What am I going to do? What can I say to my father? What will Stanley do?

As she wrote Stan's name, the memory of his and Margaret's words caused a chill to chase through her. Adriane got up and wrapped Blake's cloak around her. She felt better at once.

She did not pick up her pen again but went to the window to stare out at the rooftop across the alley while pulling the cloak closer around her. It carried the scent of the outdoors, of ink, of the man himself. She thought again of Blake pulling her close, of his lips on hers, and with the thought, a delicious warmth spread through her. This was how love was supposed to be. She knew that instinctively.

For a minute she thought of how Grace had told her to pray for another way. Could this be her answer? Blake Garrett. But then her father pushed into her thoughts. *Honor thy father.* How could she so betray her father by embracing his enemy?

She lowered her eyes from the window and whispered,

"Dear Lord, what in the world have I done? Please forgive my wantonness."

She went back to her desk and picked up her small Bible there. She opened it to search for the Ten Commandments to read the verse about honoring her father, but the Bible fell open to Isaiah. Her eyes seemed to be drawn to one of the verses. *For I the Lord thy God will hold thy right hand, saying unto thee, Fear not; I will help thee.*

That's what Beck had told her so often. That the Lord would hold her hand through whatever happened to her. But did that include love? A wrong love?

She shut her eyes and tried to think of what to pray. Her mind refused to yield any words, but she felt no condemnation for that. She opened her eyes and laid her hand on the Bible page for a moment before she turned out the lamp. It was as if the Lord was telling her the problems could wait for the sun to rise. That now for this brief moment in the soft darkness, with the lightning flashing outside and the sound of thunder drawing closer, she need feel no shame for drawing Blake's cloak tight around her and dreaming of what might be.

With the morning, perhaps the Lord would show her a way.

14

$\mathcal{T}$he sun was streaming in Adriane's window when she awoke the next day. She dressed quickly in her work clothes but then took her time brushing and folding Blake's cloak as she thought about when he might come pick it up. The situation was impossible. Her head knew that. Her heart did not.

Downstairs the newsboys were long gone with the morning's papers, and her father and Beck were drinking coffee before starting in on the new day's news.

Her father's eyes lit up when she came in the room. "Adriane, you didn't have to come down so early this morning."

"It's not early," Adriane said as she poured a cup of the strong coffee. "It's late."

"Not so very," her father said. "I was just telling Beck about how fine the Jimson gala was."

"Anytime you get to talk politics you're happy, Father, and the place looked like a convention for the Know Nothing party." She took a sip of the coffee as she studied him. "I assume from the look on your face everyone expects the party to do well in the August elections."

"The party has the abler candidates. So as long as there is a fair election, no one expects any problems." Her father

153

waved his hand in dismissal as if politics were the farthest thing from his mind. "But it's you, my dear, who has put the smile on my face. You were quite the belle of the ball last evening."

"So it seemed." Adriane dropped her eyes to her cup.

"I don't know who's happier about the coming wedding, Stanley or Coleman."

"Or you," Adriane said softly.

"Or me," he agreed. "How could I keep from being happy about it? You couldn't have made a better match."

Adriane searched for the right words to tell him she no longer thought she could marry Stanley Jimson, but before she found them, he went on. "I know you don't like to mention your own name in the paper, but it will look odd if you don't write something about you and Stanley in your Sally Sees column."

Sally had seen or at least heard too much last evening, Adriane thought before she abruptly changed the subject. "I hear we have a winning headline this morning."

"Indeed." Her father's smile got broader. "We've beat Garrett on this one for sure, haven't we, Beck?"

"That's right, boss," Beck agreed, but Adriane caught a hint of worry in his voice.

She looked at Beck sharply. "What's wrong?"

"Nothing's wrong, Adriane," her father said. "It's just that the story didn't come in through the usual channels. You must have made a friend on one of the steamships."

"I made a friend? What do you mean?"

Beck spoke up. "The story came in to you, Addie. By special delivery from the captain of the *Douchester*."

"The *Douchester*?" Adriane's voice was faint, and the coffee tasted like lead in her mouth.

"They made a record run up from New Orleans," her father was saying. "And the captain promised this was an exclusive."

"Let me see it," Adriane managed to say as she reached

for a copy of the paper. She swiftly read over the headline "Shocking Double Murder in New Orleans" and scanned the rest of the story while her heart grew heavy. When she spotted another column on the front page detailing the record-breaking run of the *Douchester*, Adriane felt sick.

"Duff must not have been here," she said almost as if talking to herself.

"His mother took a turn for the worse, and he had to go fetch a doctor for her." The furrows between Beck's eyes deepened. "Have we been duped?"

Adriane licked her lips and looked at her father, whose smile had fled.

"Duped? What do you mean?" he demanded.

She stared down at the paper again and pulled in a deep breath. It did little good to delay telling him the truth. "Father, this story is a fake."

"That can't be. I have the copy of the New Orleans paper right here."

Adriane took the clipping he held out toward her. "There's no date, Father. True or not, the story is not new."

"How do you know?"

"Because the *Douchester* can barely steam out of harbor without sinking from all her leaks." Adriane looked at Beck. "You knew that, didn't you, Beck?"

"I ain't no good with all those boat names, Addie. You know that. I'm just good at setting type."

The color drained from her father's face and then flooded back as he snatched the paper out of Adriane's hands. He stared at it a moment before ripping it apart and slinging the pieces to the floor. "Garrett did this," he screamed. "I'll kill him."

Adriane's heart sank even more because she knew it was true. Blake had sent the story. "He didn't intend for us to publish it." She said it as much to convince herself as her father. "He knew I'd know about the *Douchester*."

Her father paid no attention to her as he knocked over his stool and stormed toward his office. "He's gone too far this time," he said.

Beck looked sadly at Adriane. "Your pa's right, you know. The *Tribune* will be the laughingstock of the city."

"I know." Adriane stared at the pieces of the paper scattered on the floor while her father began slamming desk drawers open and shut in his office. Adriane glanced over her shoulder at him. "What's he doing?"

"It'd be my guess he's getting his gun. I figure the boss means to shoot the man and the sooner the better."

The color drained out of Adriane's face. "What are we going to do, Beck?"

"Right now I don't much care whether he shoots him or not," Beck said, his eyes sharp on her. "But from the way you look about to keel over, I reckon there's even more to this story than has already been told."

Adriane stared toward her father's office. "I just don't want him to get hurt." She turned back to Beck and added quickly, "Father, I mean."

"I ain't so sure that's who you're so worked up about." Beck stood up slowly. "I'll do my best to calm down the boss, but it could be you might ought to run warn Garrett just in case I don't make no headway."

Before she could decide what to do, Duff came in with a strange look on his face. "Visitor to see you, Miss Adriane."

Blake Garrett was right behind the boy, and at the sight of him, Adriane's heart began doing a strange dance inside her chest. For just a second she forgot the fake story and her father's rage. All she could think of was Blake's arms around her the night before.

His clothes were rumpled as if he'd snatched on the first thing he touched, and when he swept off his hat, his hair was even more mussed than usual. He came straight across the room toward her as if no one else was there. "I'm sorry,

Adriane. I didn't mean for this to happen. I thought you'd know."

"Get him out of here, Addie." Beck's voice was low, not much more than a growl. "Or there's gonna be bloodshed."

Beck's words were like a splash of cold water in Adriane's face. "You've got to leave before Father sees you." She tried to push Blake toward the door.

"But I want to apologize to him too," Blake said, not moving an inch.

"That wouldn't be a good idea right now." Adriane took a quick look over her shoulder toward her father's office.

Beck stepped up beside Adriane and shoved his face into Blake's. "Listen, Garrett, if you want to see the sun go down tonight and come up again in the morning, you'd better shove off."

"I can't leave until I apologize," Blake said.

"Dead men can't apologize," Beck told him.

"Step out of the way, Beck, and we'll see." Wade Darcy's voice was icy. He had found his gun.

"Father," Adriane cried, stepping between Blake and her father. "Don't be crazy. You can't shoot an unarmed man."

"I'm satisfied the man is armed," her father said. "Are you not, Mr. Garrett?"

Adriane's eyes flew from her father to Blake and back to her father. "You've been campaigning for years in the *Tribune* for an end to duels. You can't do this now."

"Step aside, Adriane. This does not concern you," her father said.

"Do as your father says." Blake's voice was firm and sure behind her.

"No." Adriane looked over her shoulder at him.

Blake's eyes touched hers softly as he pushed her gently toward Beck before he turned back to speak to her father. "I won't pull my weapon on you, sir."

"Then you'll stand there and die like the cowardly dog you are," Wade said.

Blake showed no sign of fear. "I don't think you're the sort of man who would shoot a man over a misunderstanding."

"No misunderstanding. Just the honor of my name."

Her father raised the gun and leveled it straight at Blake's chest. Adriane gasped as the two men locked eyes.

"I'll print a story tomorrow taking full blame for the mistake. The honor of the *Tribune* will be restored." Blake paused a moment before he added, "At least as much as it can be with Coleman Jimson pulling the strings."

Adriane's father shifted the gun a few inches to the left and squeezed the trigger. The bullet flew past Blake to bury itself in the window facing behind him.

Adriane jerked away from Beck and stepped between the two men again. The blood thumped through her, and she wasn't sure whether the ringing in her ears was from the noise of the shot or the rage consuming her as she glared at her father until he lowered the gun. Then she turned on Blake.

"I think you've caused enough problems for one day, Mr. Garrett." Her voice was tightly controlled. "I must ask you to leave."

"Not until we talk, Adriane," Blake insisted.

"I have nothing to say to you." She met his eyes coldly, thankful her anger was burning away any trace of tears.

"You have to believe me. I never intended to embarrass you or your father," he said. "It was only a silly prank. I thought we could laugh about it. I promise you I'll print a story tomorrow accepting full blame."

"Don't bother," Adriane said forcefully. "The *Tribune* is quite capable of handling any problems caused by inaccuracies in its stories without any help from the *Herald*."

"You have to believe how sorry I am." He reached toward her, but she stepped deftly away from him.

"We have no need of your pity." Adriane's eyes flicked to Duff, who stood just inside the door with his mouth hanging open. "Duff, there's a cloak on the table in the hall. Fetch it for Mr. Garrett and see him to the door."

"I can find my own way out, but it isn't over, Adriane." Some fire jumped into Blake's eyes to match hers. "By no means, will it ever be over between us."

He stared at her a moment longer before he turned and pushed past Duff to go out. He didn't pick up his cloak.

After the front door slammed behind him, Adriane looked at her father. "Put that gun away, Father. You're not going to shoot anyone, and especially not Blake Garrett. This war will have to be won with words, not bullets."

Her father sank down on one of the stools and stared at the gun in his hand. "But what are we going to do, Adriane? Everyone in town will be laughing at the *Tribune*."

"Yes." The anger drained out of Adriane in a rush and left her legs weak, but she couldn't give in to her feelings now. She had to think.

"Perhaps instead of Garrett, I should just shoot myself."

"Stop your foolish talk, Father," Adriane said. "It's not the first time we've printed an inaccuracy."

"It's the first time we've looked like complete, absolute fools," her father said. "We'll be ruined."

"It'll take more than this to bring down the *Tribune*." Adriane grabbed up another copy of the paper and stared at it a moment before she said, "What we have to do is turn this prank to our favor, and make sure that if everyone is laughing, then so are we. And laughing first."

"What do you mean, Addie?" Beck asked.

"We'll print a retraction. Take full blame for the whole fiasco. Throw ourselves on the mercy of our readers. And laugh as loudly as possible at ourselves for being so easily duped."

Her father looked up at her, his eyes narrowing as he considered what she said. "It could work."

"But we have to make sure we beat the *Herald*. While we can certainly give Mr. Garrett credit for his part in the whole affair, we need to avoid blaming anyone but ourselves."

"We could put out a special issue this afternoon with the real news," Adriane's father said thoughtfully.

"What news?" Beck asked.

"There's the gala last night," Adriane said.

"There's more news than that," Duff spoke up. "The police pulled poor Dorrie Gilroy out of the river this morning. The river slasher again."

Wade stood up, in charge once more. "Beck, go find out everything you can about the murder, and Duff, locate the newsboys and tell them to come around here about noon, but don't say why. We want this to stay a secret till the extra issue hits the streets. Adriane, get your Sally Sees column about the Jimsons' party ready." He looked at Adriane and smiled as if he himself had thought up the whole fake story to get some attention. "I knew we'd figure a way out of this."

"Don't we always?" Adriane tried to return his smile, but her lips couldn't seem to make the right moves.

Her father didn't notice, but Beck stopped beside her on his way out the door. "When this is over, we'll figure a way to fix the rest of it, Addie. You'll see."

She blinked her eyes to fight back the threat of tears and shook her head before she turned to her work desk. She pushed all thoughts of Blake Garrett out of her mind as she picked up her pen. First she had to worry about the reputation of the *Tribune*. Later would be time enough to worry about her own reputation.

Her father must have thought the same, because he waited until after the surprised newsboys had taken the extra issue out the door at noon before he followed Adriane to the kitchen.

"The extra issue may do the trick," he said as he watched her slice cheese and bread. "Keep us from looking like total idiots."

"I think it will work," Adriane agreed. She looked up from the block of cheese. "As long as you remember to control your temper and laugh every time anybody mentions the story."

"That's a lot to ask." He glowered at her for a moment, then sighed. "But of course you're right, and people will be ragging me about it for weeks. Perhaps I should have just shot him and been done with it."

Adriane tried to keep her face impassive as she handed him a plate. "That would have solved very little."

He was studying her closely. "What is there between you and Blake Garrett?" he asked suddenly.

"Nothing." She didn't try to avoid her father's eyes. "I hardly know him."

"Then why did you have his cloak?" Her father's eyes sharpened on her.

"I forgot to fetch my own before I rushed out to try to catch Lucilla's carriage to leave last night. When she was already gone, I decided to walk home."

"You what?" Her father's voice went up an octave.

Adriane kept her voice calm. "Unfortunately the storm was coming up, and when Mr. Garrett saw me on the street, he insisted on seeing me home in his carriage. Since as I said, I'd left my own wrap at the party, he was kind enough to loan me his."

Her father was staring at her as if he'd never seen her before. "My stars, Adriane. How could you? What will the Jimsons think?"

"Quite frankly, Father, I don't care." Adriane carefully sliced another piece off the block of cheese.

"You can't mean that. You're going to marry Stanley."

Adriane stared at the cheese a long moment before she laid it on her plate. "What if I decide I can't marry him, Father?"

"We've already been through all this. Marrying Stanley Jimson is the best thing that could ever happen to you. I won't let you throw away such an opportunity."

Adriane chose her words with the same care she might if she were expecting to see them in print. "Stanley is not the man I thought he was when I first agreed to marry him."

"This is Garrett's doing too." Her father stood up and began pacing back and forth across the kitchen floor. "Stanley told me the man has been following you around, trying to alienate your affections from him."

"Stanley has managed to do a sufficient job of that all by himself."

Her father waved off her words impatiently as he stopped pacing to stare at her. "Before you allow Garrett to ruin your life, you should know he has tried this before."

"Tried what?"

"To gain control of a paper by wooing the daughter of the owner. I sent out a few inquiries. It appears he was once engaged to a Vandemere girl whose father owns one of the New York papers until the father, sensibly enough, put a stop to the whole affair. My sources—very reliable ones you can be sure—tell me Garrett is ready and willing to do anything to get what he wants, and he wants to have the premiere paper in Louisville."

"The way his readership is growing, he hardly needs to court me to achieve that end," Adriane said drily as she sliced another piece of bread.

"Or send us fake stories," her father said.

"He really didn't intend for us to publish that." She brushed the bread crumbs off the cabinet and dropped them in the bucket of scraps she kept for the old dog.

"So he would have you believe. But you must keep in mind Blake Garrett is a man of many talents, and subterfuge is only one of them."

"What do you mean?" Adriane laid the knife down and looked up directly at her father. She didn't see how things could keep getting worse, but at the same time she dreaded hearing whatever her father was going to say. She wanted to just go out the back door and sit on the stoop with the old dog's head in her lap. Maybe if she could sit there in the quiet, the Lord would take hold of her hand and show her a way out of this mess.

But her father kept talking and with each word, Adriane's heart sank more. "Garrett is intent on seeing the *Tribune* fall, and if spoiling your chances to marry Stanley Jimson will accomplish that goal, then of course he will do that. You heard what the man said about Coleman controlling the *Tribune*." Her father sat back down and looked intently at Adriane.

"Does he? Does Coleman Jimson control what we print?" Adriane hardly dared breathe as she waited for her father's answer.

"Of course not," her father said a bit too quickly. "But I do know Garrett has been trying to find out everything he can about Coleman. He could have learned about the money Coleman has put into the *Tribune*."

Adriane studied her father as she carefully formed her next words. "Has Coleman Jimson bought the *Tribune*?" When her father dropped his eyes to the tabletop and didn't answer right away, she went on. "Has Coleman Jimson bought me?"

"Don't be ridiculous, Adriane," her father said as he got up to begin pacing again. "I only want you to marry Stanley because it's in your own best interest." He stopped beside her and touched her hair lightly before dropping his hand back to his side. "I don't want to see Garrett destroy all that for you because he thinks it will bring down the *Tribune*."

Adriane looked down at her hands a long moment before she raised her eyes back up to her father's face. "I know you say love is not important for a good marriage, Father, but I'm not sure I can marry a man I not only don't love but am beginning not to even like. I'll go north and work with Grace first."

"So that's who has put these ideas into your head. I should have known." A flash of anger colored her father's face again. "You'd starve with Grace Compton."

"I'm beginning to think there might be worse things than starving."

"Not when you're starving." The anger left his face, and he awkwardly stroked her hair again. "Just promise me you'll wait awhile and think about it, Adriane. I can see that you and Stanley must have had some sort of disagreement, but don't throw the man and all your chances over without giving him the opportunity to make it right."

Without waiting for her to answer or eating the first bite of the bread and cheese, he turned and headed back to his office. There was still the regular issue of the *Tribune* to get out.

Her own appetite gone as well, Adriane put away the untouched food. Perhaps her father was right. Blake could be playing loose with her affections. The thought stabbed her, but it was true that Blake wanted the *Tribune* to falter. It had been his aim ever since he took over at the *Herald*.

Adriane looked toward the door to the pressroom but instead went upstairs to her room. She touched the cover of her Bible and felt a prayer rise inside her. *Our Father in heaven, help me.* How many times had she whispered those very words into the darkness while locked inside a closet as a child? And eventually help had always come. Her father would open the door and let the light flood in around her. It was her father she could always trust.

She had to trust him now. Blake had sent the fake story. Blake did want her father's paper to fail. Her paper. Her father was right. She knew nothing about the man. Nothing except that she loved him. But what did she really know about love?

She opened her journal to stare at the words she'd written about love the night before. Tears popped up in her eyes and made the letters of the words run together. She blinked her tears away as she very carefully tore out the page before ripping it into tiny pieces. After gathering every piece up in her fist, she went to the window and opened her hand outside to let the pieces of paper scatter to the wind. She would not let her heart fool her the way the New Orleans story had fooled her father. Then she stepped back to her desk to close the journal firmly as if to keep out any more foolish words about love before she went back downstairs to help get out the next day's issue of the *Tribune*.

15

*B*lake Garrett stared at the noon issue of the *Tri-bune*. It would be expensive with the extra paper and printing time, but it might work. The readers would still laugh about the morning's blunder, but the *Tribune* would survive the laughter.

He almost had not. There had been a few minutes that morning when Blake had wondered if he was going to die the same way as his father. Not because of something he'd written to try to make his town better the way his father had, but all because of a stupid prank he'd pulled to get Adriane to talk to him. A ruse it turned out he hadn't even needed to try.

She'd already talked to him the night before. She'd done more than talk. Blake shut his eyes remembering yet again how softly her lips had yielded to his. How could she kiss him like that and still think of marrying Jimson?

Blake opened his eyes and stared down at Adriane's Sally Sees column. He skimmed through the flowery praise about the beautiful decorations, the exotic fruits, the lively dances. She waxed poetic about the dresses of several notable young belles, but made no mention at all of the couple of note, Stanley Jimson and his intended, the stunning Adriane Darcy.

Adriane had been the belle of the ball. He hadn't had to

read his own correspondent's account of the event to know that. He'd seen her in that spun moonlight dress, racing up the street as if she'd just stepped out of one of his dreams.

She and Jimson must have had a fight. Blake had passed Stanley's carriage just minutes before he'd spotted Adriane on the street.

Blake frowned. It didn't matter what had happened between Adriane and Stanley. What mattered was finding a way to convince her to talk to him again. To give him another chance to explain. To give him another chance to kiss her.

Blake sighed and rubbed his eyes. That was about as likely right now as him catching the river slasher. Again he stared down at the *Tribune*. It was the first headline Darcy had beaten him to for weeks, but the *Tribune*'s facts were sketchy. Blake's readers would be ready to grab his paper first thing in the morning to find out more.

He just wished he knew more to tell. Oh, he knew more facts about Dorrie Gilroy. She was eighteen. Irish like the rest. A pretty little slip of a girl who never had a bad word for anyone, not even her father when he was in his cups and knocked her about a little. The father had been frantic with grief that morning at dawn when the police had brought him down to the river to identify his daughter's body.

"She never hurt nobody," he kept saying over and over. "Not little Dorrie. Why would anybody want to do that to her?"

Nobody had any answers for him. Blake wasn't sure there were any answers to have. Whoever was doing this didn't have a reason. No sane reason a person could speak. The monster was killing because he took pleasure in the act of killing. And a person like that would strike again as soon as the memory of this murder faded and he felt safe enough to do it again. Unless somebody stopped him.

Blake turned and stared at the presses. He'd make sure the police didn't ignore little Dorrie's murder. He'd push and prod them with editorials until they found this killer.

Not only that, but he was ready to take on Coleman Jimson. Even now Joe was setting an editorial questioning some of Jimson's business tactics. Blake made no actual accusations, but still the wording was strong enough that Joe had looked it over and then given him a worried frown.

"You sure you want to print this, boss?" he'd asked. "You go against Jimson and the Know Nothings, you could find yourself out of a paper and fast."

Blake knew Joe was right. Feelings were running high all through the city, but whatever the consequences, Blake was going to use his paper for what he thought was right, be it catching murderers or keeping the wrong men out of political office. So far John Chesnut had given him free rein to print whatever he wanted as long as they were selling papers. He just had to make sure people kept buying those papers.

He put down the *Tribune* and slapped his hat on before he headed back down to the riverfront. His steps slowed as he passed the street that led to the *Tribune* offices, but Adriane wouldn't listen to him today. Not after the morning. He'd write her a note later begging to see her again so he could explain.

He'd never written a letter begging for anything before, not even when he'd supposed himself in love with Eloise. Instead Eloise had been the one to write the letters begging for help. Her last letter was still in his pocket when he received the news of her death. But he was ready to beg now. He would get down on his knees if he had to. Anything to make Adriane understand.

As the days of June passed, Blake sent note after note to Adriane in between writing ever stronger editorials against Coleman Jimson and haunting the taverns to hear what people had to say about the murders. He heard all sorts of theories about who the murderer might be. A riverboat gambler. A traveling merchant. A slave trader. A Southern plantation owner in town for the big Jimson gala the night Dorrie was killed.

But no matter how much talk he heard, that's all it was. Talk. No one had seen Dorrie Gilroy with anybody. No one had seen any of the girls with anybody on the nights they'd been murdered. They'd left the taverns as usual and been swallowed up by the darkness. Sometimes when Blake was reading through his notes or listening to yet another rumor, he felt as though he was lost in a maze. He kept turning corners and discovering new paths, but none of them ever led anywhere.

He wasn't getting anywhere with Adriane either. He wrote her a new note every day until the end of June. It got to be something of a joke to the newsboys he paid to deliver them to Adriane. They fought for the job, because on the other end Adriane paid them to carry the notes back unopened.

Blake stopped sending the notes the first week of July. He hadn't given up. He would never give up no matter what happened. It was just time to come up with a new approach.

He began practically haunting the social scene, attending any and every event he could, but though he saw Stanley Jimson a few times, the man was always alone. That fact didn't go unnoticed by the other guests, and soon there were as many rumors about Stanley and Adriane being whispered around at the parties as there were about the murders floating around the taverns.

Finally the second week of July, Mrs. Wigginham invited Blake to her last Library Society Aide meeting before she left town to spend the hottest summer weeks at one of the resorts. The invitation came in late, only a couple of hours before the event. Blake stared at the neatly printed words and wondered if Mrs. Wigginham was perhaps playing games with him again, as she had at that first library aide meeting when she'd arranged for Blake and Adriane to meet. He could only hope so.

Blake was nearly ready to return to the *Tribune* offices and break down the door if necessary. Just the week before, he'd tracked down Duff Egan, the young Irish kid who worked for Darcy, to try to buy some information about Adriane.

At the sight of the money in Blake's hand, the boy had glared at him and balled his hands into fists. "Ye can't be buying me, Garrett, any more than you're gonna be able to bring down the *Tribune* no matter what you might be pulling out of your bag of tricks. Miss Adriane won't be letting you."

So although he could go batter down the door at the *Tribune* offices—and he hadn't ruled that out—he would be less likely to get in the way of a bullet if he managed a chance meeting with Adriane at Mrs. Wigginham's instead.

As soon as he entered the door, Blake took a quick survey of the ladies in attendance. Adriane wasn't there. He was making his way over to greet Mrs. Wigginham and perhaps find a way to politely ask about Adriane when Stanley Jimson made an entrance with his mother in tow. Fans fluttered and came up to cover faces as whispers swept around the room.

Mrs. Wigginham rose from her chair before Blake reached her. She laid her hand on his arm briefly in passing. "I do appreciate you coming to my little gathering, dear boy," she said. "And I don't mean to be rude. We'll certainly have to talk later, but now I must rush over to ask dear Meta and Stanley where Adriane is. I did so want her to come. I sent her a special invitation just a couple of hours ago."

"As you did me," Blake said.

"As I did you." Mrs. Wigginham smiled up at him. "One can never have too many friends among those who print the news when one is trying to advance a good cause. Don't you agree?"

"Absolutely," Blake said as he wondered what the little lady was up to. One thing he was sure of as he watched her scurry across the room to greet the Jimsons. It had little to do with securing more books for the library.

He was easing back across the room himself to try to overhear what excuses Stanley might be giving for Adriane when he was captured by Priscilla Bowberry.

"How delightful to see you, Mr. Garrett," Priscilla said. "I don't mind telling you I was beginning to despair of there being any person here who could carry on an intelligent conversation."

Blake pushed a smile out on his face as he turned to Priscilla. Tall, slim to the point of bony, and going on thirty, Priscilla was beginning to despair of more than the chance for intelligent conversation. While Blake did sometimes enjoy her blunt and often amusing views of the social set, he took pains not to encourage her to think he might be her last best hope for matrimony.

But Priscilla was nobody's fool. She knew her attributes, and though she might not be a beauty, she did have a lively wit. Even more telling, her family had money. Quite a bit of money. The last time she latched onto him at one of the socials, Blake had the uneasy feeling Priscilla was preparing to make him a proposition, and he dreaded the day he would have to find a polite way to refuse her.

"Priscilla," he said. "You look lovely as always."

She smiled, pleased. "And you, sir, lie like the true gentleman you are."

"Hardly. My father used to say that a man cannot be a good editor and a gentleman at the same time."

Priscilla raised her eyebrows slightly, making her face appear even more angular. "From the way Stanley Jimson is glaring at you, I do believe he would agree with that."

Blake turned to look at Jimson, who quickly averted his eyes. "That's another thing my father used to say. A good editor must of a necessity make a few enemies."

"Indeed," Priscilla agreed. "The way you're going with

your paper's campaign against Coleman Jimson, I hear you won't have any friends left before long. Or at least friends who might buy papers and advertisements. Coleman Jimson is a very influential man in this city."

"Then he hardly needs to worry about a few editorials in my paper, does he?"

She smiled again. "I admire a confident man," she said before she glanced back toward Stanley Jimson. "Young Stanley certainly appears to have lost his confidence lately."

"Oh." Blake kept the tone of his voice neutral. "What makes you say that?"

"This unfortunate affair with Adriane, of course."

"What unfortunate affair? I thought they planned to marry in September."

"Oh, they do, or so everyone continues to say. But you've surely noticed how Adriane has completely vanished from the social scene. They say her father is so worried about the possibility of her throwing over our sweet Stanley that his beard has turned white practically overnight."

"I thought that was because he was worried about the *Herald* stealing all his readers." He kept his voice light.

Priscilla laughed as he had intended before she went on. "You are a concern to him, I'm sure, but not as much of one as Adriane. The poor man is caught in a difficult predicament. There are some who say if he fails to marry Adriane off, Lucilla Elmore may refuse to go through with their own wedding plans this fall." Priscilla's voice lowered a bit. "And even worse, I've heard the poor man is in some financial difficulty. It's rumored he owes Coleman Jimson a good deal of money, and that if Adriane doesn't marry Stanley, he could very well be ruined."

"Are you saying their marriage was arranged by the fathers as a kind of business deal?"

"Good heavens, I didn't say that exactly, did I?" Priscilla twisted her mouth to hide her amusement as she fluttered her fan. "I suppose I shouldn't be telling you any of this. The way the *Herald* and *Tribune* are battling lately, I'm apt to see my words on your front page tomorrow and be roundly condemned by the whole of Louisville society for having such a loose tongue."

"A newspaperman never betrays a confidence," Blake said.

She raised her eyebrows at him. "Another of your father's sayings?"

"No. Mine."

"At least I would pray you'd not mention names." Priscilla looked back at the Jimsons. "But it's all just too delightful not to talk about it. I've even considered paying a call on Adriane to see if I can determine whether she plans to honor her promise to marry Stanley, but I've heard she isn't receiving callers. That wrinkled little man who works for her father comes to the door and says she's indisposed, and we all know what that means."

"Perhaps she really is ill," Blake said, suddenly unable to completely keep his worry at bay.

At his words, Priscilla's eyes sharpened on him. "Do you know Adriane well?"

"Our paths have crossed a few times at various socials," Blake said casually. "The first time at just such a meeting as this here at Mrs. Wigginham's."

"Yes, I remember." Priscilla was studying him closely. "We all quite expected a bit more reaction from one or the other of you that day, but as I recall, the two of you hardly argued at all."

"Only enough to please Mrs. Wigginham, who I'm sure had arranged the meeting as an amusement."

"That sounds like our Mrs. Wigginham. She's always planning something exciting and imagines herself quite the matchmaker." Her eyes widened a bit as if she'd just figured out something that had been puzzling her.

"We must let her have her fun." Blake avoided Priscilla's eyes. The woman was altogether too quick.

Priscilla's lips straightened out in a rather grim line as she studied Blake's face for a moment. Then she fluttered her fan again as she asked, "Do you believe in love at first sight, Mr. Garrett?"

A bit startled by her question, Blake hesitated before he said, "I've never given it much thought."

She didn't seem to care what he answered as she went on. "Mrs. Wigginham does, you know. She says that sometimes when a couple first meets you can practically see a spark fly between them. I used to pray such an occurrence would happen to me."

"I doubt it happens to very many people," Blake said.

"But it does happen to a few, doesn't it, Mr. Garrett?" She stepped a bit nearer to him to look directly in his face.

He quit trying to lie to her. "It does happen to a few."

She smiled a little. "You and I would make an interesting couple. We would always understand one another."

"You're a lovely lady, Miss Bowberry, but unfortunately I have no interest in such a commitment at this time. All my time must be spent building the *Herald*."

"If only that were true, sir," she said with a sad shake of her head.

Blake had no answer to that and so instead offered to fetch the lady a glass of lemonade. It seemed the least he could do.

A few minutes later he made his excuses to Mrs. Wigginham, claiming a heavy workload at the paper. She patted his hand as she said, "At least you made an appearance. That's more than we can say for dear Adriane, isn't it? However, Stanley has sweetly offered to carry a report of my little event to Adriane for me. It seems she hasn't been feeling well." She lifted her eyebrows. "All this hot weather, I suppose. It's quite trying dear Stanley's patience, I do believe."

"The weather or Miss Darcy?" Blake asked.

"Dare we say both, Mr. Garrett." She raised her fan up to hide her widening smile, but there was no hiding the smile in

173

her eyes. "If you happen to see Adriane, please tell her how much I've missed her the last few weeks."

"I doubt I will be seeing Miss Darcy."

"One never knows, does one?" Mrs. Wigginham peered at him with no hint of a smile now. "Sometimes the most unexpected things happen. Especially if we take things into our own hands."

A little later without actually planning it, Blake found himself going up the steps to the *Tribune* offices. Beck met him at the door with a scowl.

Blake could have pushed the old man out of the way easily enough. Both men knew that as they stared at one another, but it wasn't something Blake wanted to do. Instead he said, "I have to know if she's all right. That she's not really ill or anything."

"She ain't sick." Beck narrowed his eyes on Blake as he considered him for a long moment before he added, "She just needs some time, that's all."

"It's been weeks."

"Addie will have to be the one to say how much time she needs."

Blake's eyes burned into the little man. "Tell her one thing for me."

"Addie don't listen to nobody she don't want to listen to."

"She'll listen to you." In fact the longer Blake stood there, the surer he was that Adriane was just on the other side of the door hearing his every word. He raised his voice a little as he went on. "Tell her, and be sure she understands. Tell her that if I have to, I'll kill Stanley Jimson before I let her marry him."

The old man's eyes changed then, and for a brief moment, Blake thought Beck realized they were on the same side. Then the old man was pushing the door closed in Blake's face. "I'll tell her."

16

Adriane was sitting frozen at her work desk when Beck came back into the pressroom. He looked at her and said, "You heard?"

"I heard."

"The man appeared to mean every word."

Adriane kept her eyes away from Beck's face. "Perhaps," she said. "Though he's already proven he can't be trusted. Don't forget the *Douchester*."

"I think you can trust him on this one." Beck stepped over to her desk. "You want to talk about it, Addie?"

"No." Her hand shook as she dipped her pen in the inkpot and a splatter of ink smeared her paper.

Beck watched her blot up the ink before he said, "You can't just keep pushing it away, girl. You're going to have to face it sooner or later."

"I know. Father tells me the same thing every day. How I need to snap out of this 'unladylike' lethargy and come to my senses before it's too late." She stared down at the paper on her desk until the words ran together. The page was already a mess before she'd spilled the ink on it. Three sentences written with two of them crossed out. "Maybe he's right. I can't even write anymore."

Beck reached over to pat Adriane's shoulder. "It'll come back, Addie. The writing. You just have to get this other stuff straightened out."

"I'm not sure I can, Beck."

"There ain't nothing you can't do, Addie, if you set your mind to it." He leaned down to look her straight in the face. "You know I'm praying for you."

"I know." Adriane blinked back tears and put her hand over Beck's on her shoulder. "I'm praying too, but maybe I'm not praying hard enough or for the right thing."

"The right thing? Sometimes we can get all mixed up on what the right thing is."

"But isn't that why we pray? So the Lord can give us answers? The right answers that let us know what we should do." She stared at Beck's face, wanting to find the answers there she couldn't seem to get to her prayers.

"I reckon that's true enough, but the trouble is them answers don't always come down clear as newsprint." He pulled his hand away from her shoulder to wave toward a stack of the day's papers in the corner of the room.

"But why not? Why does everything have to be so hard?" *Honor thy father.* Those words slid through her thoughts a dozen times an hour. How could she pray for the Lord to open a way to her that her father would never understand? Or forgive.

Beck gave her a long look before he pulled a stool over to sit down in front of her. They were alone in the pressroom, as they were so often in the afternoon these days with her father off to his endless political meetings.

"That's a question that used to bedevil me some," he said. "Especially after my May died. So young and all. Didn't seem to me for there to be a bit of reason for that to happen. You have to understand that I loved her as much as a man could love a woman. I always thought it was a kind of a miracle that she made out like she loved me back. But the one she loved the most was the Lord. It was her that taught me about him. She did everything right."

Adriane forgot her own troubles for a moment as she tried to imagine Beck as a young man so terribly in love. The grief was plain in his voice even after so many years. She reached out and took his hand. "And then she died."

A single tear slid out of Beck's left eye and made a trail down through the wrinkles on his cheek. "And then she died."

"I'm sorry, Beck," she said softly.

"It was a long time ago," he said. "And I ain't telling you about it to make you sad for me. I'm telling you so that maybe you can understand how the good Lord keeps on reaching down his hand to help you even when you think he's forgot about you. Worse than forgot you. That he just plain don't care. That's what I thought when he didn't make May get well. I got mad. I didn't want to have no more to do with God if he couldn't come up with no better answers than taking my May away from me. Because you see, I prayed while she was sick. Down-on-my-knees prayers that I thought ought to be answered. My way."

"But they weren't."

"No, my May died. Same as hundreds of others died from the cholera in Louisville that year. But I wasn't worried about nobody else's prayers not being answered. Only mine." Beck was quiet for a moment before he went on. "It pains me to admit it, but I shut my Bible tight and turned away from the Lord. I know May was looking down from heaven, grieving over my hard heart as much as I was grieving over her being gone."

Adriane's eyes went to the Bible Beck kept on his worktable. "I've never known a time when you didn't read the Bible."

"That's just it, Addie. A feller might turn away from the Lord, but the Lord, he don't turn away from you. The good Lord, he just waited me out. Kept on walking along beside me. Understanding. Knowing my hurt. And after a while, I felt his hand on my shoulder again. He helped me see cholera happens. People die."

"He could have healed her. The Bible is full of miraculous healings," Adriane said.

"It is. But that wasn't the answer he had for May and me."

Adriane looked at Beck. She was glad he'd told her about May, but she couldn't see what his story had to do with her own troubles. Her own lack of answers to her prayers. "So what answer does he have for me?"

"I don't know, Addie. But I know he ain't turned his back on you. He's gonna help you find a way. This ain't like the cholera. You just keep on praying, and with the good Lord's hand on your shoulder, you'll figure it out. The right thing."

"One thing I already figured out a long time ago."

"What's that?"

"That I don't know what I'd do without you, Beck." She smiled as she tightened her fingers around Beck's hand.

"You'd do fine," Beck said gruffly. "'Cepting, of course, you'd have to learn to set type a heap faster if the paper got out on time. Fact is, we'd best get to work now if we aim to have the galleys ready to run when your pa gets back from his meeting."

Later, after Adriane had given up on writing her piece and given Beck a filler to use instead, she went out to sit on the back step in the late afternoon sunshine. The old dog came slinking out of the shadows to peer up at her hopefully.

"Sorry, I don't have a biscuit, Mr. O'Mallory, but I can scratch your ears," she said as the dog looked at her with dark brown eyes before he poked her hand with his graying muzzle. She smiled a little and rubbed his ears. "You look like you've been around. I'm thinking you've heard a lot of troubles in your time. You want to listen to mine?"

It was silly of her to want to pour out her heart to a dog, but she needed someone to listen. "I don't know what to do, Mr. O'Mallory. It's all such a mess."

When the dog cocked his head as though to hear better, she rubbed his ears again, before he settled down contentedly at her feet. Adriane leaned back on her arms to raise her face to the sun. As her skin warmed, she remembered how as a little girl, she had tried to soak up the bright light of the sun to carry with her the next time Henrietta locked her in the closet. But she had never been able to store enough light inside her, and the time always came when she had to face the monsters in the darkness again.

Beck told her it was time she faced her problems now. He thought she could. With prayer. Dear Beck. He had kept people away from her and given her these weeks of near solitude. The only person he couldn't keep away was Stanley who came by nearly every day to alternately beseech and threaten her.

She hadn't told Stanley yet she would not marry him. She had rather hoped he would be the one to say he wouldn't marry her when she stopped playing the part of his happy fiancée at all the social functions. But he did seem determined to marry her. Much more determined than she'd ever dreamed he could be about anything. And all the while September drew closer and closer.

Soon she would have to do something. She often thought of joining Grace Compton in Boston. She had written Grace more than one letter asking if she could, but each time Adriane tore the letters up instead of posting them. Her father was right. Grace was barely able to support herself, and Adriane would be a heavy burden on her friend's slim resources.

Besides, she didn't want to go to Boston. She wanted to stay here and put out the *Tribune*. She wanted things to be the way they'd always been. Even as she thought it, Blake Garrett's face pushed into her mind, and she knew that wasn't exactly true.

Adriane had refused Blake's letters through the end of June and then just when she began to weaken and think about opening one of them, he stopped sending them. He surprised

179

her by coming to the door today. Just hearing his voice had made her blood race, and it was all she could do to keep from running to the window to catch a glimpse of him as he left.

I'll kill Stanley Jimson before I let her marry him.

Of course, he hadn't meant it. Not literally. But what had made him come to her door to tell her such a thing? Could it be he truly cared for her enough to contemplate such a desperate move? Cared for her more than his own reputation? More than his newspaper? She dared not believe that.

What her father had said about Blake courting the daughter of a newspaper owner was true. She'd read the letter her father had gotten from Willis Hastings, an editor in New York, telling of Blake's engagement to the daughter of the owner of the *New York Post*. The father had fired Blake and the daughter had married someone else. Hastings concluded his letter by writing that if Wade was asking about Blake Garrett because the man was looking for a job, to send him back to New York since he didn't have any daughters to worry about. Just a newspaper to get out. The letter left a lot of questions unanswered.

If you want answers, you can ask Blake, a voice whispered in her head. But how could she be sure he'd tell her the truth if she did? Even worse, how could she be sure she wouldn't believe whatever he said simply because she wanted so much to believe him? No, it was better to wait here in this small, quiet space of her own making a bit longer. To send up her prayers and wait for the Lord to show her the right thing to do.

She had a little time yet. With the election less than a month away, her absence by Stan's side would surely go almost unnoticed in the heat of the political races. The election and the political rallies were the news, the only news. Even in the *Herald* the murders had slipped to the back pages, although Blake managed a front-page mention at least once a week to be sure no one completely forgot a murderer remained on the loose.

Meanwhile her father was furiously writing editorials in favor of Coleman Jimson and the other Know Nothing candidates. Blake Garrett was as furiously writing editorials against them, especially against Coleman Jimson. If indeed he'd ever lacked editorial courage, he'd found it now. Adriane's father said it was more like editorial idiocy, and not just to her but in print for all of Louisville to read.

In answer, Blake blasted the *Tribune*'s editor for being nothing but a mouthpiece for the Know Nothing party. He accused her father of writing only what the party approved with no ability to think on his own. So the words flew like bullets between the editors, and the sales of both papers increased. Their readers, on the other hand, began choosing sides and shooting their own volleys of words in letters to the editors.

Now as she stared up at the blue summer sky, Adriane thought she should try to write a Colonel Storey letter calling for cool heads. But even if she was able to reach inside herself past the odd blankness of her mind and find the right words, she doubted if such a letter would do much good. It was as if the whole town was not only ready to explode, but wanted to.

Adriane sighed and kept staring at the sky until her face began to burn and sweat trickled down between her breasts. She touched her cheek and smiled a little as she imagined Lucilla's shock and horror if she were to catch Adriane exposing her face to the sun. Adriane would no doubt sprout freckles, but what did it matter? No one was going to see her but Beck and her father and the hands. And Stanley.

When the rumble of the press started up, she gave the old dog a last pat and stood up to go back inside. There was news to print.

As the days passed, the editorials of both the *Tribune* and the *Herald* became more and more heated until Beck sometimes shook his head as he set type. "I sure do hope the boss's words don't set the paper on fire." His words were only partly in jest.

Coleman Jimson's speeches that the *Tribune* published verbatim helped fan the flames. Jimson was working the crowds feverishly for votes, making promises that a *Herald* editorial claimed Jimson wouldn't be able to keep even if he were—God forbid—elected president of the United States.

In spite of the *Herald*'s insistent opposition, Stan told Adriane he didn't see any way his father could lose unless he dropped dead campaigning, and even then he'd probably still get the majority of the votes.

Stanley had reluctantly stayed in Louisville to help his father with the campaign instead of making the rounds of the resorts with his mother.

"It's all terribly tedious," Stan confided one afternoon when he came by to deliver a copy of his father's speech for the next day's *Tribune*. "I've heard all the speeches a hundred times, but Father wants me there to start the cheers if the crowd seems cold."

As Adriane quickly scanned the speech, she said, "I thought the crowds were enthusiastic."

"Oh, they are." Stan brushed at a few specks of dust on his hat. "But Father isn't one to leave anything to chance. He even makes sure he has a few men scattered through the crowd to handle any hecklers."

"Handle them?" Adriane looked up at Stanley. "How?"

"Money. Whiskey. A swift kick or maybe a gun in their ribs. I'm sure I don't know or care." Stan looked bored. "The less we hear from those people, the better."

"What people?"

"The Irish mostly. They're trying to stir up trouble, and Father says, if it's trouble they want, then it's trouble they'll get. And believe me, Father knows how to give people trouble." Stanley's lips turned up in a tight little smile as his eyes narrowed. "If you happen to see your friend at the *Herald*, you might do him a favor by telling him that."

"If you're referring to Mr. Garrett, I don't expect to be seeing him." Adriane kept her voice cool.

"I should think not, since as it is, you'll barely allow me a few minutes of your time. When are you going to be through with this charade, Adriane? Ever since our summer gala, you've been acting as if you practically fear being alone with me. Even Mother is beginning to worry there might be some problem."

Hope, you mean, Adriane thought, but she didn't say the words aloud. "What could be wrong?" She widened her eyes with a pretense of innocence.

"You tell me, my dearest. There are times I can hardly sleep for worrying I might have done something that night to offend you."

"I told you, Lucilla was feeling ill, and I thought it best if I accompanied her home."

Adriane was sure Stan knew that was a lie, but she'd stuck with her story all these weeks. She wasn't about to change it now. In fact she had told it so often and so convincingly that even Lucilla was beginning to believe Adriane had actually ridden home in her carriage.

"Perhaps you should see a doctor," Stan said, concern drawn in careful lines on his face. "My sister Margaret fears you may be suffering from some sort of nervous vapors. Has she written you suggesting as much?"

"She did write me." Adriane almost smiled at the flicker of worry in Stan's eyes. "But just a note saying how glad she was to finally meet me and that she hoped we'd have more time to talk the next time she is in town. She only inquired politely about my health as one is wont to do. I'll fetch the letter if you would like to read it yourself."

"No, no, that's hardly necessary," Stan said. "But everyone is so worried about you. Mrs. Wigginham especially asked after you last week at the Library Aide Society meeting. She was extremely disappointed when I gave her your regrets."

"You brought me quite enough facts for a nice mention in the *Tribune*. I'm sure that pleased her."

"Yes, my dearest, but I have no desire to be a news correspondent." Stan reached out and laid his hand on her arm.

Adriane forced herself to not shrink away from his touch.

"And you should be spending your time planning our wedding and not worrying about little fillers for your father's paper. September is drawing very near."

"Yes, I know, Stan, and I've been thinking. Christmas would be such a beautiful time to have a wedding, don't you think?" Adriane knew she should just tell him straight out she couldn't marry him, but perhaps with a few more months her father would be able to gather the money he owed to Coleman Jimson. If not by Christmas, then perhaps she could hold out for a spring wedding.

Stanley laughed. "I do believe you are getting cold feet on me, my dearest Adriane." He put his fingers under her chin and raised her face up until she was forced to meet his eyes. "But we are marrying in September. I won't allow you to go back on your promise."

He continued to smile, but there was something almost fierce in his eyes. And looking at him, the truth slammed into her. She had promised. Not only Stanley, but her father. The Lord was not going to provide her an escape, and the darkness she so dreaded closed in around her heart.

"Why do you want to marry me, Stanley?" she asked.

"Love, of course, my dearest," he said.

"Besides that," she said.

"Why does there have to be a besides that?"

"I don't know, but there is, isn't there?"

"You don't realize how beautiful you are, Adriane, or how your kind of beauty affects a man." He let his eyes slide down the length of her dress, then reached out to finger the buttons on her bodice with much too much familiarity.

"Really, Stan." Adriane jerked back from him as blood rushed to her face.

"Yes really, Adriane, my dearest." His smile grew broader and even less appealing as he lowered his voice. "If I didn't know your old Beck was listening from the other side of the door, I'd take you now. It would be my right."

"You have no rights to do any such thing until you're my husband."

"A matter of a few weeks. No one would condemn me for being a bit impatient." Stan's gaze went from her face to her body again. "You're going to be so soft. So good."

"Stanley, you're embarrassing me." Adriane backed up against the wall to get away from him.

He stepped closer to her. "Surely not, my dear. You've grown up in a newspaper shop with very little training in the art of being a lady. You can't make me believe you're that innocent." He came at her with both hands.

Adriane slipped past him before he could touch her again. "I think you'd best leave, Stanley," she said coldly.

The look on his face changed as though he realized he might have gone too far. "Please don't be angry with me, my dearest," he begged. "You know I'd never intentionally upset you about anything, but sometimes just the sight of you makes me forget myself. You will forgive me, won't you?"

"Only if you promise never to behave so abominably again."

"Oh, I do promise," he said. "I don't know what came over me. It must come from being in such close contact with all these common men on the streets at Father's rallies. It's enough to make a man fear for his own safety and thus want to gather as much of life to him as he can. And you, Adriane my dearest, are life to me." He took her hand and kissed it, not even appearing to notice the ink stains on her fingers.

"Do you feel the streets are actually that dangerous?" For a minute she forgot his near attack as she noted the unmistakable worry in his eyes.

185

"They are." Then his look of worry was gone as he smiled and kissed her hand again. "But you needn't be worried about me, my dearest. If there's trouble, I know how to take care of myself."

A few days later, the trouble that Stanley expected finally broke out at a political rally. When hecklers interrupted the speech of Humphrey Marshall, the Know Nothing candidate for United States Senator, his supporters began throwing rocks and gunfire broke out.

The rally was not far from the newspaper offices, and after Adriane heard the gunfire, she paced the hall until Beck finally came in safely and reported her father safe as well.

"It weren't much. Just some folks letting off a little steam on both sides," Beck said. "'Course some of the fellers did go check on that rumor going around about the guns in the churches. They somehow got the keys to that Catholic church on Thirteenth Street and searched it."

"Were there any guns?"

"Nah. Most all of what's being said is nothing but hot air. The Irish ain't got nowhere to get that many guns or the wherewithal to get them. The most of them ain't hardly got money to buy food."

"Did you see Duff?"

"Don't you be worrying about Duff. If I know him, he's at home standing guard over his sisters and mother. That last girl that got murdered, that Dorrie Gilroy, you remember? Seems she was somebody they all knew real well, and while everybody else might have forgotten the river slasher with all this electioneering going on, our Duff ain't."

"He and Blake Garrett should get together."

Beck looked at her with a sad smile. "They ain't the oniest ones."

Adriane changed the subject quickly. "Do you think there's going to be more trouble, Beck? With the election, I mean."

"I'd be surprised if there wasn't. The boys just lacked a

little making a mob out there tonight, and if they'd come up on any guns, who knows what might have happened." Beck shook his head again. "The way I see it, about the only good thing that's going to come out of this election is that we're sure to sell a pile of papers."

17

The last hot days of July whipped by in a blur of speeches and newspaper print. A parade was planned for the first Saturday in August as a final show of strength for the Know Nothing candidates before the election on Monday. When her father demanded and Stanley pleaded that she carry a transparency in the parade, she surprised both them and herself by agreeing.

Stanley was pathetically jubilant when she told him she'd march in the parade with his sisters Pauline and Hazel, who had come back to Louisville expressly to take part.

"I'm so happy, my dearest Adriane, and Father will be too," he said, squeezing Adriane's hand. "Can I assume then, that you will be your wonderful old self again and ready to take your rightful place by my side at all the social functions? Mother and Pauline are planning a grand dinner party to celebrate Father's victory, you know."

"That sounds interesting," Adriane said noncommittally, deciding to take one step at a time.

First she'd quit hiding and go back out into the world where she could see firsthand what was happening. Then maybe the strange stupor that had seized her mind and stolen the words from her pen would be broken. It had been days since she'd been able to write much more than a stilted report of the weather in her journal. Her prayers seemed every bit as stilted. She didn't know what to pray or even what to hope for, but that was no reason to shut herself in a dark closet of despair. She needed to gather the light while she could. And wait for the answers that Beck kept assuring her would come.

The day of the parade she dressed carefully and fixed her hair with even more care while trying not to think about the probability of seeing Blake Garrett somewhere along the parade route. It did little good to think of Blake. After the last few weeks of editorial attacks and counterattacks between the *Tribune* and the *Herald*, the prospect of even a casual friendship with Blake had gone from unlikely to surely impossible.

She shoved thoughts of Blake Garrett from her mind and went downstairs to meet Stanley. A storm had lashed through the city just an hour earlier, and the newsboys were bringing in reports of downed trees and roofs off barns on the outskirts of the city. For a while it looked as if the parade might be canceled, but then the setting sun began turning the retreating storm clouds a deep rosy hue as if supplying elaborate decorations for the event.

Not only had the streets been washed and swept clean of refuse by the rain, the storm had freshened the air with an invigorating hint of coolness after the heat of the day. The Know Nothings could not have ordered a more perfect evening for a parade, and the streets were clogged with carriages and people on foot converging on the courthouse where the parade was to begin.

After Coleman Jimson and a couple of the other candidates made impromptu speeches from the courthouse steps, the girls unrolled their transparencies as the band struck up a lively tune. A charge of excitement seemed to be leaping from person to person and bringing shouts and laughter to everyone's lips, even Adriane's, as the parade began.

People along the route cheered as they passed, although Adriane wondered how anybody could be left to cheer as the

Words Spoken True

parade stretched out behind her farther than she could see. Adriane was marching near the front of the winding column between Pauline and Stan who had stuck close to her side all evening. As family of one of the candidates, they had an honored spot in the parade directly behind the actual candidates themselves. The band followed them, and in between the cheers, the pounding drumbeat seemed to echo Adriane's own heart that kept jumping up into her throat every time she spotted a man with dark curly hair in the crowd along the street. Her banner sagged a bit each time the man turned out not to be Blake Garrett.

When they passed by the *Tribune*'s offices, Adriane shouted a greeting and waved at Beck, who watched from the doorway. Not too much farther down the street, she spotted Duff and couldn't keep from worrying that he shouldn't be there. He did look so Irish. Even as she watched, a couple of men laughed and shoved the boy roughly out of their way. Adriane's steps lagged, but then Duff saw her and tipped his cap before he grinned and melted back into the crowd. Stanley put his hand on her elbow and urged her forward.

They were almost back to the beginning of the parade's circuitous route through the city when at last she spotted Blake. The charge of excitement that had been playing over the marchers seemed to concentrate and sear the air between them as their eyes met. For a moment she thought Blake would push out into the street and grab her. For a longer moment she wished he would. Then his eyes shifted a bit to the left and took in Stanley close beside her, and his face turned hard.

"He should be shot for staring at you so brazenly," Stan muttered into her ear as he moved closer to Adriane.

With a heavy heart, Adriane forced herself to look back to the front of the parade. The strength drained out of her legs and arms in such a rush she thought she might have to sit down in the middle of the street and let the parade pass around her.

190

But somehow she managed to keep moving her feet, although she allowed the transparency she carried to droop as she answered Stanley. "If you mean Mr. Garrett, I'm sure he wasn't staring at me but at Father." She nodded slightly toward her father, who was walking directly in front of them. "No doubt he's considering his next attack."

"Perhaps, but it'll do him little good," Stan said with a short laugh. "He took on the wrong family when he took on the Jimsons, and I wouldn't be a bit surprised if we were soon to see the last of our Mr. Garrett."

"Really?" Adriane glanced over at Stan. "Mr. Garrett doesn't impress me as the type to leave town because of a little opposition."

"A little opposition?" A furrow formed between Stan's eyes. "The man's turned everyone who matters in Louisville against him. If he knows what's good for him, he'll leave town now. Tonight. Before the election. It would be much safer for him."

"Safer?" Adriane stared at Stanley as her throat tightened. She could barely get out her next words. "What do you mean safer?"

"Why, my dear, you sound almost distressed." Stanley smiled at her. "I can't believe you'd waste your compassion on the likes of Mr. Garrett after the things he's printed the last few weeks in that travesty he calls a newspaper."

Adriane kept her voice level and free of the trembles that were awakening inside her. "I'm hardly worried about Mr. Garrett. I'm sure he is quite capable of taking care of himself, but I would hope nothing is being planned that would reflect badly on the *Tribune*." She slid her eyes across Stan's face and added somewhat belatedly, "Or you or your father."

"I'm touched by your concern, my dear." Stan's smile changed, twisted a little until something about his perfectly shaped features became almost alarming. "I had begun to fear you didn't care for me at all. It's such a relief to see how mistaken I was."

Adriane looked down at the street and chose her words carefully. "I wouldn't want to see you do anything foolish that might end in you getting hurt."

"Jimsons don't get hurt. People who try to hurt the Jimsons are the ones who live to regret it. Remember that, my dearest."

On the other side of Adriane, Pauline turned from her sister Hazel in time to hear Stan's last remark.

"For heaven's sake, Stanley," she said. "You sound positively grim and on a night when there's no reason for anything but celebration. Father has won the election every way but at the ballot box and that is just a matter of a couple of days. Monday night Father will be our new state senator, and with this exhausting campaign over, we can turn our thoughts toward preparing for the wedding." Pauline squeezed Adriane's arm. "It's going to be the perfect finale to a wonderful summer."

"Perfect," Stan agreed. A confident smile chased the strange threat from his face.

Adriane was relieved when they reached the end of the parade route and she could plead exhaustion and escape from the midst of the Jimsons. Later in the quietness of her room, she sat in front of her open journal. For the first time in days words were ready to flow from the end of her pen, even if they were words she was almost afraid to write.

Honor thy father. The words slipped through her mind as she glanced over at her Bible on the corner of her desk. Those words were there. She couldn't deny that. But other bits of verses came to mind. *For love is of God. Blessed are the pure in heart. Walk in truth. And the truth shall make you free.* Nothing about her life would ever be true again if she promised to love, honor, and obey Stanley Jimson. The Lord was showing her the answer. The only answer.

At last she allowed her hand to begin moving the pen to form the words.

I cannot marry Stanley Jimson. Even if Father loses the Tri-
bune, I cannot marry Stanley Jimson. Even if Father completely
disowns me, I cannot marry Stanley Jimson.

She stared at the words and felt as if she'd just pushed open
a door that had been locking her into this small corner and
now light was flooding in to surround her. Her heart felt free to
beat again. Her mind could take wing and leave the darkness
behind. She laid her hand on her Bible and whispered a grateful
prayer as another Bible verse came to her mind. *And the light*
shineth in darkness. Beck had shown her that in the first chapter
of John years ago and she had embraced the light.

She pulled another sheet of paper to her and once more
wrote a letter to Grace in Boston, but this time she didn't tear
the letter up as soon as it was written. This time she folded
it and stuffed it in an envelope. She'd stay with Grace until
she found some sort of position. She was not totally without
talents. She would find something. Perhaps there would even
eventually be some way to continue writing. It would not be
like helping her father and Beck get out the paper. Nothing
ever would be, but the *Tribune* would survive without her.
She would survive without the *Tribune.* She could not survive
as Mrs. Stanley Jimson.

She dug through the papers on her desk to pull out a piece
of her finest stationery. She studied the smooth whiteness of
the page a moment before she carefully dipped her pen into
the inkpot.

Dear Stanley,

I am deeply sorry to be writing this letter, but after a great
deal of thought and much soul searching, I realize I will not
be able to marry you on September 15th or on any other date.
I beg your forgiveness for the unforgivable, and deeply regret
any pain my decision may cause you. You are a fine gentleman

and I rest assured there are any number of young ladies much more worthy of your affection than I.

> *With deepest regret,*
> *Adriane*

She stared at the written words. She was sure Stan had guessed weeks ago that she did not want to marry him. Worse, she feared he had guessed her feelings for Blake Garrett, though she hardly dared to admit them even to herself. That's why he had tried to frighten her with his threats against Blake. And he had. They weren't idle threats.

Adriane pulled yet another sheet of paper to her—this time the plainest she could find—and in large block letters printed,

PLEASE BE WARNED! THERE ARE THOSE WHO THREATEN TO DO YOU HARM DUE TO THE STRONG OPINIONS EXPRESSED IN YOUR PAPER. A CONCERNED CITIZEN.

She folded the sheet of paper and tucked it in her pocket. Tomorrow she would get Duff to deliver the warning and post the letters.

The next morning Blake Garrett read the printed words and knew Adriane had sent the message. He would have known even if one of the hands hadn't seen Duff Egan slipping away from the building early that morning. Blake stared at the note and imagined her hand forming the letters of the words. Was she really concerned about him, or was this just a clumsy attempt to frighten him into taking the fire out of his editorials? It was really too late for that. The election was the same as over. Even though no one had yet cast a vote, there was little doubt of the outcome. Coleman Jimson had won. Blake had lost.

John Chesnut had just left the *Herald* offices. The old man had been so upset he'd had to keep pausing to recover his breath so he could continue his tirade. It was one thing to attack the *Tribune* and Wade Darcy. It was quite another thing to alienate every businessman in Louisville. People would refuse to buy a paper that published such unpopular opinions. Not only that, but how did Blake expect to keep the *Herald* going without selling any advertisements? It couldn't be done.

Mr. Chesnut had wiped a sheen of sweat off his forehead and insisted Blake moderate his attacks on Coleman Jimson and the Know Nothing party. Of course he'd been going through the same tirade every morning for weeks, and Blake had been able to talk him around to his point of view. But today, Blake hadn't had the words to convince him. Had not even tried.

He'd seen his defeat the night before as he watched the parade file by. And then when he'd spotted Adriane finally out of seclusion and so tight in with the Jimsons, all the fight had drained out of Blake.

It was over. Chesnut was ready to renege on his promise to let Blake buy into the *Herald*, and even if he did hold true to their bargain, Coleman Jimson was determined to prove there wasn't room in this city for any views opposing his.

Blake had known what he was risking when he took Jimson on, and though he might have lost the battle, he had no doubts his position was the only right one. Coleman Jimson lacked the character and proper morals necessary for public service. It appeared the constituents in this district were determined to learn that truth the hard way.

All that was bad enough, but it wasn't what had Blake thinking about going back to New York. He could keep the *Herald* going. New stories, new headlines would pull back his readers even if they did disagree with his politics. And he wasn't worried about the advertisements. The way Louisville was growing, he could find plenty of new businessmen anxious to take out advertisements to replace any business-men who might be coerced into boycotting the *Herald*.

What he couldn't fight, what he couldn't stay in Louisville and watch, was Adriane becoming Mrs. Stanley Jimson. Blake leaned his head in his hands and tried to keep from seeing her so close beside Stanley the day before. It was one thing to say he'd kill Stanley Jimson before he allowed him to marry Adriane. It was quite another thing to actually do it.

If she wanted to sacrifice herself to Stanley Jimson to please her father, to keep the *Tribune* going, for the security of the Jimson money, for whatever reason, there was no way he could stop her any more than he could stop Jimson winning the election. He raised his head and looked at Adriane's printing on the note once more. It might be over, and if so, he was ready to admit defeat. But first he'd be sure. First he'd confront her one more time. He'd make her look him in the eyes and tell him face-to-face that she was going to marry Stanley Jimson.

When that happened, he'd give John Chesnut a couple of weeks to find someone to take his place at the *Herald*, but he'd make sure to be far away from Louisville long before September 15. Else he might really find himself holding a loaded gun pointed at Stanley Jimson's chest.

"Hey, boss, are you all right?" Joe asked, coming up behind Blake. "You ain't letting Chesnut get you down, are you? All that old man's worried about is numbers. He'll come around."

"I don't know, Joe." Blake looked up at him. "I think maybe I fell on my face with this Jimson thing."

"That ain't so, boss. You're right as rain about that scoundrel, and you know it."

"Trouble is, nobody else wants to believe it." Blake blew out a long breath.

"So you lost this round," Joe said. "Ain't no editor any-where ever won every round."

"No editor's ever lasted long losing every round either."

"You ain't fought but one that I can tell. And even if Wade

Darcy and the *Tribune* did win this one, in the long run, it'll be better to be right."

"Wade Darcy thinks he's right."

"I ain't so sure about that." Joe shook his head. "I talked to old Beck the other day."

"You talked to Beck?" Blake's eyes sharpened on Joe.

"Yeah. If I didn't know better, I'd say he hunted me up on purpose," Joe said. "Anyhow even he's a little worried about the way Jimson's pulling the strings over at the *Tribune*."

"Beck said that?" Blake asked.

"Not in so many words, you know. He wouldn't never be that disloyal to Wade Darcy, I don't reckon, but he got to talking up this really weird idea. Something about how the *Tribune* and the *Herald* combined would make a paper that nobody or nothing could ever bring down."

"He said what?" Blake stared at Joe.

"I know. I couldn't believe it either. I asked him if he'd had his head under a barrel these last few weeks while the two papers had been going after each other. He just laughed." Joe shook his head again. "I never knowed Beck to drink, but I figured he must have had a cup or two too many that night even if I couldn't smell it on him."

Blake looked thoughtful for a moment. "The *Herald* and the *Tribune* merged. Old Beck may have something."

"Yeah, it's called getting funny in the head. Chesnut and Darcy ain't spoke in ten years, maybe more. You ain't never gonna get them two to shake hands on nothing unless'n it's just before they plan to have a shooting match."

"You could be right there, Joe, but then surprising things sometimes happen." Blake laughed, surprising himself already. Maybe it wasn't completely over. Maybe there was still hope and time to fight another round. Beck hadn't hunted Joe up for no reason. That was sure.

18

onday, Election Day, dawned clear and hot. Adriane was downstairs when the newsboys came in wide-eyed and full of wild talk already about what might happen that day. They could hardly wait to grab their papers and get back on the streets to be part of it all.

Adriane caught Duff and pulled him aside before he could make his escape. When he cast an anxious eye at the door, she promised, "I won't keep you long."

"I wasn't worrying none. Me papers will be easy enough to sell today what with the men out on the streets waiting to vote." The boy pushed his cap back to a jaunty angle on his dark hair.

Adriane couldn't keep from smiling as she remembered overhearing Duff bragging to the other hands about how the new cap was a sure girl-getter. The other hands made unmerciful fun of him, but they liked him. Even her father seemed to almost forget from time to time that the boy was Irish.

Adriane's smile faded. The men out on the streets didn't forget. Twice in the last week Duff had been set upon by bullies who scattered his papers and tried to steal his money. So now she said, "Promise me you'll be careful out there today."

"Don't you be fretting about me, Miss Adriane. I'll stay clear of them bullies for sure and certain."

"But today there may be more of them out there than usual."

"There'll be trouble. You can go ahead and write that down. That's all anybody could talk about out on the streets around home last night. Plenty of folks is looking for a fight on both sides."

"Just make sure you're not in the middle of it."

"You can count on that," he said with a grin. "I'll be running in so many reports for you and Beck all day that I won't be having time to get in no trouble."

Adriane gave him a quick hug. "If I had a little brother, I'd want him to be just like you."

Duff's grin got broader. "And there's plenty of times I might be wishing me own sisters was more like you. They don't always see me best qualities especially now that I'm making them tell our mother everywhere they go and who they might be stepping out with."

"Your sisters are all older than you, aren't they?"

"That they are." Duff's grin disappeared. "But me da told me to look after them before he died, and I ain't aiming to let them be taking any chances with this river slasher still on the loose."

"It's been a long time since poor Dorrie was killed. Maybe she was the last."

"Maybe. Maybe not. I won't feel safe for me sisters till I see the murderer swinging from a rope."

"The police will catch him," Adriane said.

"I ain't putting too much faith in the likes of them, but I am thinking that Mr. Garrett at the *Herald* might yet smoke him out." Duff looked at her and quickly added, "I don't mean to be upsetting you by saying that, Miss Adriane, but he isn't letting the whole thing be forgot like some others."

"I know." Adriane looked down at the floor and hesitated a moment before she asked, "Did you get the message delivered?"

"I did just like you said, Miss Adriane, and didn't let no-body see me when I slipped it under the door," Duff said, guessing which message she meant.

"Thank you, Duff." Adriane kept her face down to hide the blush burning her cheeks.

"And I got your other letters sent and delivered."

"Delivered?" Adriane asked faintly.

"Aye, I took that one to Mr. Jimson by his house this morn-ing. I thought it'd be quicker than posting it," Duff said. "Now if you don't need nothing more, I'd best be on the streets before people start to missing their papers."

As she watched Duff go out the door, she thought of how Stan might be reading her letter at that very moment and a disturbing uneasiness crept over her. She hadn't wanted him to get the letter until after the election was over. Then again, perhaps it was better this way. Stan might be too busy today with everything else going on to make a scene, and with the passing of enough hours, he might come to accept her deci-sion as best for both of them.

She could hope that, but she didn't really believe being rid of Stanley Jimson would be that easy. Besides, she owed him a face-to-face explanation, even if she didn't exactly look forward to it any more than she looked forward to telling her father what she'd done. Adriane drew in a deep breath and squared her shoulders in anticipation of her father's anger as she went in search of him.

He wasn't in his office, and the breakfast she'd left out for him was untouched. Beck told her, "He left before daylight this morning. Some kind of strategy meeting for the party. He says some of the men are worried the Irish and German immigrants are going to try to stuff the ballot boxes against the Know Nothings." Beck looked up from the type he was cleaning. "Something wrong, Addie?"

"Sort of," Adriane said with a frown. "I needed to tell him something."

"Bad news?"

"He'll think so." Adriane sighed. "I sent Stanley Jimson a letter telling him I can't marry him."

Beck didn't smile, but a few of the lines around his eyes eased out. "Good," he said before he turned back to his type.

"Father won't think so." Adriane stared down at the type and put a couple of letters back in order before she said, "And I'm not sure what Stan will think."

"You worried about him coming around here?" Beck looked up at her again. "I can always send him packing."

"No, I'll have to talk to him. I owe him that much."

"You don't owe him a thing, Addie. You changed your mind, and that's the end of it."

"I rather doubt he'll agree. I'm not exactly sure why, but he did seem bound and determined to marry me." Adriane paused before she went on thoughtfully. "He may not want to take no for an answer."

"I can fix that." Beck wiped his hands on his grimy printer's apron and went back to his room just off the pressroom. He came back carrying an ancient-looking pistol and laid it on the table next to the trays of type.

Adriane stared at the gun. "I don't want to shoot him."

"It don't hurt to be ready for whatever might happen," Beck said.

"I didn't even know you had a gun, Beck."

"I ain't never found much cause to bring it out. A man like me tends to look for the peaceful way." Beck went back to cleaning type as though the gun there beside him was nothing out of the ordinary. "But I carry it on occasion."

"What occasions?"

"One like today." Beck looked up at her. "You can be sure there won't be a man on the street today without a gun or a knife in his pocket."

A tremble raced through Adriane at Beck's words. It was a day primed for violence. "You're scaring me, Beck," she said.

201

"It's a day to be scared, Addie. To maybe send up some extra prayers for our town, but you don't have to worry about young Jimson. If he's fool enough to come by and try to give you any kind of trouble, we'll just use this to persuade him to go back out the door." Beck tapped the gun with an ink-stained finger. "There ain't nothing in the Good Book that says a man can't protect hisself. Or herself."

As the sun came up and began pushing its heat through the dirty windows into the pressroom, Adriane did her best to ignore the gun on Beck's table. But she couldn't. Its very presence in the pressroom signaled unease, the same unease that seemed to be settling over the city as reports began coming in. Early on, Duff brought in the news that armed Know Nothing party men were standing guard at the polls all over the city.

"They ain't letting none of the Germans or the Irish vote," Duff told Adriane and Beck. He was still panting a little from his run through the streets back to the offices.

"They can't keep qualified voters from voting," Adriane said.

"A gun in your face is a pretty powerful discourager," Beck said with a glance at his own gun.

"Some of the men ain't being scared into giving up so easy," Duff said. "They're lining up in front of the polls to wait. One of me sister's friends told me he'd wait all day to cast his vote if he had to. That he was entitled. He said he didn't care how hot the sun got, and it is hot." Duff wiped the sweat off his face.

"Where are the police?" Adriane asked.

"I didn't see none," Duff said. "You can't hardly be blaming them. There's an ugly feel out there on the streets."

"Any fights yet?" Beck asked him.

"Some pushing and a lot of yelling, but it could be things might get worse before long." Duff looked out the window. "That sun could burn the patience out of a saint."

"Did you see my father?" Adriane asked.

"No. He's probably down at the Know Nothing head-quarters on Jefferson Street. I'm hearing that they're running everything from there." Duff headed for the door, his eyes alive with excitement. "I'll be back."

As they watched Duff lope off down the street, Adriane said, "I wish I could see what's happening for myself."

Beck frowned at her. "You ain't stepping foot out of this house, Addie. You understand?" There was no give in his voice.

Adriane sighed. "I understand, but I don't have to like it. I wish I were a man."

Beck laughed. "It ain't the first time you've wished that. You recollect the time you chopped off your hair and wanted to be called Jim. What were you? Ten? Eleven?"

"Eleven," Adriane said.

Beck chuckled as he turned back to his work. "You were a sight."

Adriane didn't laugh. Even now all these years later, the memory of that time was cold and hard inside her. Her father had raged at her, then at Henrietta, who took to her bed after telling Adriane's father no one could control Adriane. She'd moaned over and over that his wayward daughter would be the death of her.

A month later, the poor woman had stirred two weeks' worth of sleeping powders and some arsenic into a glass of milk and gone to sleep for the last time. Adriane was consumed by guilt. So much so that she was sometimes drawn to the hated closet under the stairs where she stared at the door while Henrietta's words echoed in her head. *The good Lord doesn't listen to bad little girls' prayers.*

Adriane wasn't sure which had frightened her most in the days after Henrietta died—that Henrietta was right and the Lord didn't hear Adriane's prayers, or that Henrietta was wrong and he did. Hadn't she prayed often enough to be rescued from Henrietta and her dark closets? Perhaps she *had* been the death of Henrietta. It wasn't until years later that Adriane could completely believe the woman's death had more to do with the baby she'd lost six months earlier than with anything Adriane had ever done or prayed.

The loss of that last baby had been the reason for Adriane's rebellion against being female as well. Henrietta had carried that child months longer than any of her other poor lost babies. Hope had brought new life to her face, and she'd even attempted to be nice to Adriane. Then the tiny boy baby had been born dead after a difficult confinement.

Afterward, any time Adriane was alone with her, Henrietta would fix a piercing stare on the girl and tell her that someday she'd suffer the same fate. That babies brought their mothers nothing but grief. Hadn't Adriane's own mother died giving her life? And wouldn't it have been better if one of Henrietta's sweet babies had drawn breath rather than Adriane? But God had preordained all women be punished for the sin of Eve. No woman could escape that punishment. It was written so in the first book of the Bible.

Henrietta would open her Bible to Genesis and point at the page. "In sorrow thou shalt bring forth children," she'd say without looking at the words. Then her eyes would burn into Adriane as she said, "We're all Eves. All of us."

After a while Adriane decided not to be an Eve but an Adam. It was a matter of a few snips of the scissors to chop off her waist-length hair. A boy down the street gave her an old pair of trousers, and Adriane happily discarded her petticoats.

That night when her father came home, she'd actually run to meet him, sure he'd be glad to have a son instead of a daughter. He wanted a son to carry on the *Tribune* someday. She'd heard him say as much often enough.

But he was not glad. Instead he had banished her from his sight. He not only stopped taking her to the newspaper offices, he ordered her to stay in her room whenever he was in the house until her hair was a respectable length again. As the days dragged by and her hair showed no sign of growing, her room began to shrink around her and changed from a once welcome haven to a room of confinement almost as bad as the punishment closet.

Then, Henrietta, lost in her own darkness, drank her poison, and hours later, Adriane tried to wake her and could not. In the days that followed, the length of Adriane's hair became less and less important until it was as if she'd never cut her hair at all. Of course some of the newsboys had called her Jim long after her hair grew back out, but only when her father wasn't around to hear.

Now as Adriane looked up each time the door opened, half hoping and half dreading to see her father, she feared his rage over her decision not to marry Stanley might match that rage of long ago. He wouldn't understand. He'd already dismissed her doubts as so much romantic nonsense. He was in thicker with Coleman Jimson every day as the man's election and the purposes of the Know Nothing party consumed him and the *Tribune*. He would not forgive Adriane's rebellion easily or soon.

Adriane tried without much luck to push it all out of her mind as she fixed the workers sandwiches and wrote down the reports pouring in from the streets. A little after one o'clock, Duff reported the German and Irish men were finally beginning to give up and leave the polls.

"The sun's too hot," he said before gulping down a glass of water. "And the crowds of Know Nothings blocking the polls keeps growing. When somebody they aim to let cast a vote shows up, they just lift him up over their heads and pass him inside."

Duff grabbed a sandwich and was gone again almost as soon as the words were out of his mouth. When the door banged open again minutes later, she and Beck both looked up expecting to see Duff back with some bit of news he'd forgotten to tell them, but it wasn't Duff. It was Stanley.

He'd lost his hat, and a few strands of pale blond hair looped down over his forehead. His face was flushed and damp with perspiration. Even the knot of his cravat was a bit off center.

"What is this?" His voice was high and strained as he rushed across the room toward Adriane, wildly waving the letter in front of him.

Adriane stood to meet him. Out of the corner of her eye, she saw Beck easing over to the composing table where the gun lay.

"I believe the letter is self-explanatory," she said.

"This is a breach of promise, Adriane." Stan shook the letter in her face.

"Calm down, Stanley," Adriane said.

"Calm down?" Stan's voice went up to a squeak. "Calm down? What are people going to say when they hear I've been spurned by Wade Darcy's daughter? Wade Darcy who doesn't have a nickel to his name. Wade Darcy who would have lost the *Tribune* months ago if he hadn't been riding on my father's coattails."

Adriane squared her shoulders and stared straight at Stan. "I daresay they will say you've made a lucky escape if Wade Darcy's daughter is so very unsuitable."

Stanley leaned toward Adriane until his face was inches from hers. So close that she felt the moisture of his words when he spoke. "Unsuitable or not, I intend to have you for my wife. This letter means nothing."

Adriane didn't give ground to him as she pushed out her voice strong and sure. "That letter means just what it says. I will not marry you, Stanley. If it will save your injured pride, I am perfectly willing to have you say you broke the engagement. Wade Darcy's daughter surely has little pride in any case."

He grabbed her and shook her as he shouted, "You have no right to end our agreement. I won't allow it."

"Take your hands off the girl." Beck's voice was cold as he poked the gun against Stanley's ribs. "I'd rather not pull the trigger, sir, but I will if I have to."

Stanley's eyes flicked over to Beck's face and then down to the gun. Very deliberately he turned loose of Adriane and backed up. "You, my dear man, will live to regret this."

"I doubt it," Beck said. "Now I advise you to get out of here."

Stanley looked back at Adriane again, and there was something chilling in his eyes. "You have been promised to me, Adriane. A few words on a sheet of paper cannot change that. You're mine."

Adriane found her voice. "They have already changed it, Stanley. Now please do as Beck says and leave. I have nothing more to say to you."

"And your father? Will he have nothing more to say to me or my father either?" Stanley spoke calmly enough now, but somehow he sounded even more threatening than he had when he was shouting.

"I will not marry you," Adriane said firmly. "That is my decision to make, and I have made it."

Stan surprised Adriane by laughing suddenly. "Women. You're such foolish creatures and so easily controlled."

"Was your sister so easily controlled? Or your mother?"

He looked puzzled for a moment before comprehension dawned in his eyes. "So you did overhear my conversation with Margaret in the garden. Pauline said you looked a bit discomfited when you rushed away that night." He looked at her, his wide smile anything but pleasant as he smoothed his hair back into place and straightened his collar and cravat. "That's good. You need to know the lengths I will go to get what I want. And I want you, Adriane." His eyes swept down her body.

Beck waved the gun at Stanley menacingly. "If you don't get out of here, mister, you ain't never going to get anything you want again unless'n you want to be dead."

Stanley's arm slashed out and slammed the gun out of Beck's hand. He mashed his forearm tight against Beck's neck and shoved him up against the wall. "Threaten me, old man, and you'll be the one who ends up dead."

Adriane grabbed the gun off the floor and leveled it straight at Stanley. "Let him go, Stanley."

Stanley turned Beck loose and brushed himself off. When he had his jacket straightened once again, he looked from Adriane to the gun. "I doubt you even know how to use that, but it doesn't matter. You seem to be in need of some time to come to your senses."

"My mind is made up. Nothing can change that."

"Nothing?" He raised his eyebrows at her. "My dearest Adriane, I'm sure there is something. Perhaps your father . . ." He let his final words trail off.

"No, Stanley, not even my father."

He looked toward the window. "The streets are very dangerous today." He turned his eyes back toward her and smiled as if they were talking about nothing more important than whether it might rain. "Anything could happen out there. Somebody might even get shot."

"You wouldn't hurt my father," Adriane said.

"Of course, I wouldn't." Stanley looked wounded. "How could you even think such a thing, my dearest? But there are others on the street not as kind as I am, unfortunately."

He stepped nearer her, paying no attention at all to the gun she kept pointed toward him, and laid his hand on her cheek. When she jerked away from his touch, he laughed and said, "Marriage to me will not be so horrendous. You'll see."

19

*S*tanley left calmly, even pausing at the door to smile back at Adriane as if he'd just brought her home after a social. "September 15th will be the happiest day of your life, my dearest Adriane," he said. "You'll be a beautiful bride. My beautiful bride."

For several minutes after he went out, she kept the gun pointed toward the door. When she was sure he was not coming back, she slowly lowered her arm until the gun was pointing toward the floor. Then it was as if some vital bit of energy was draining through her and out the barrel of the gun and into the floorboards until she hardly had the strength to remain standing.

"I should'a shot him when I had the chance," Beck growled as he glared at the door.

"You couldn't shoot him just because he was yelling at me." Adriane thought she preferred the yelling to the quiet threats. What had she done? More importantly, what was Stanley going to do?

"The Lord would've forgive me." Beck was still scowling at the door, but then he dropped his head down to stare at the floor. "I'm sorry, Addie. The man surprised me. Moving so fast like that. I always figured he was more talk than action."

"You're not the first person Stanley has fooled," Adriane said softly. She had to pause a moment to gather the strength to go on. "He may be able to do it, you know. Why he wants to, heaven only knows, but he may find a way to force me to marry him."

"How could he do that?" Beck looked up at her and forgot all about his question. "Whoa there, Addie, don't you be fainting on me, and give me that gun before you shoot your foot off." He took the gun out of her hand and pushed a chair up under her. "Now, don't you worry about that blackguard. I'll be ready for him next time. You can be sure of that."

Adriane hardly heard his words. "Father will be every bit as angry as Stan," she said.

"Your pa will understand."

"Will he, Beck?" Adriane looked at the old man, who didn't quite meet her eyes. "Even if it means losing the *Tribune*?"

Beck looked at the press, the table with its rows of type, and the stacks of blank newsprint waiting for their words. When he finally looked back at Adriane, his eyes were sad. "The boss the same as lost the *Tribune* some months back, Addie. Coleman Jimson owns it now in every way but name. You marrying Stanley Jimson couldn't do nothing to change that."

Adriane wanted to deny the truth of Beck's words, but she knew he was right. "Even if that's true, Stanley will still try to have his revenge on us. You heard him."

"I heard him. But it was just talk."

"No, he meant it." Adriane had no doubt of that. She pulled in a deep breath as some of the strength began to come back into her arms and legs. "Father has to be warned." Adriane stood up so quickly the chair fell back with a loud clatter.

"Hold it, Addie. You ain't setting foot out on them streets." Beck caught her arm as she moved toward the door.

"But Beck, Stanley the same as threatened Father's life."

"Young Jimson ain't got it in him to shoot nobody."

210

"Who knows what Stanley might do," Adriane said.

"I reckon that's true enough, but you still ain't going out on them streets today. Not with the way feelings is running so high among the fellers." He looked at her a moment before turning to take his hat off the rack. "If it has to be done, and I reckon it does, I'll go find the boss and let him know what's going on."

After Beck left, Adriane paced back and forth across the printing room, pausing every time she passed the window to peer out at the men hurrying past, shouting back and forth at one another and waving guns or clubs in the air. The looks on their faces frightened Adriane. Still, in spite of her fear, Adriane wished she could be out there to see what was going on for herself. It might be bad, but it would be news. Not just news. Headline news. Four-inch headline news. Plus she needed to see her father with her own eyes to be sure he was all right.

Adriane jumped at the sound of banging on the back door. Beck had made her lock all the doors after he left, something they never did when the boys were running in their reports. For a long moment, Adriane stared at the gun Beck had left on the table, but she didn't pick it up. It had to be one of the boys, she told herself as she rushed toward the back door.

Like a shadow, Duff slipped inside the minute she cracked open the door. "Miss Adriane, I was getting worried you wasn't coming." His eyes were wide, and he was panting in ragged bursts as if he'd run a long way.

"Are you all right, Duff?" Adriane reached out to touch a bright smear of blood on his cheek.

"Ain't nothing but a scratch." Duff roughly rubbed away the blood on his cheek. "But things are turning bad out there, for a truth."

"What's happening?"

"The Know Nothings have took over the streets and are jumping on anybody that don't look right to 'em and that's everybody but them."

"There are always fights on election day."

"This ain't the normal bit of fisticuffs. I'm not so sure a body could even call them fights. Leastways not fair ones. It's a dozen of them to one of us."

"Us?"

"You know, the Irish and Germans," Duff said. "Last I seen them, the mob was headed for Armbrewster's brewery, but they won't be forgetting us Irish. So I just came back to be letting you know I couldn't be running in no more stories. I've got to get on home and see that no harm comes to me mother and sisters."

"Of course, Duff, but are you sure it's really that bad?"

"I don't want to be worrying you, but they're like animals out there. I ain't never seen the likes of it before." His eyes got even wider.

"Did you see Mr. Darcy?"

"Aye. He's with the mayor. The last I seen them they was trying to talk the men into going home, but the whole thing's past words now. Too many of the men are wanting to throw their torches. Fires are burning all along Shelby Street already."

"Can't the police stop them?"

"Ain't no use depending on the watch." Duff made a sound of disgust. "Them I seen were shedding their coats and jumping right in with the rest of the crowd."

"Surely not all of them." Adriane didn't want to believe his words.

"Maybe not, but them that aren't can't fight the whole crowd. Nobody could fight this bunch. They ain't even letting the firemen through to put out the fires."

"This can't be happening, Duff. Not here. Louisville is a civilized town."

He stared at her with his wide, dark eyes a moment before he finally said, "Not tonight, Miss Adriane. Not tonight." Then as if to back up his words, in the distance they heard a resounding boom. "They must've torched the brewery."

Adriane listened and knew he was right. Whatever was going on out on the streets couldn't be stopped. She looked at Duff, and though she wanted to keep him there with her where she could be sure he was safe, she pushed him toward the door instead. "Be very careful, Duff."

"You don't need to be worrying none about me, Miss Adriane. I can keep from being seen."

As if to prove it, he slipped out the back door and practically melted into the shadows against the buildings. He was gone from her sight in seconds, but she kept standing there staring out the open door until the old dog came up and stuck his nose against her leg. She reached down to touch the dog's head. "You'd best hide, Mr. O'Mallory. It's a night for everyone to hide."

Gunfire sounded in the distance, and as the last traces of daylight gave way to night, an unnatural glow lit up the sky to the east. Even before she shut the door and headed back toward the front of the building, she knew what she was going to do. Who knew when Beck would return? She had to see with her own eyes that her father was safe.

She grabbed her father's dark gray hooded rain cloak off the rack and wrapped herself in it. It was hot, but at least no one would recognize her. She had watched Duff. She would do the same. Stay in the shadows that were growing deeper in spite of the streetlamps beginning to come on. And if there were no shadows, the cloak would be shadow enough.

As she opened the front door and looked out on the street that was deserted now, she remembered her promise to Beck to not leave the building for any reason. She stood there, hesitating, while a burst of gunfire tattooed the air in the distance and then flames were leaping for the sky only a few streets away.

She stared at the sparks flying up above the buildings. The *Herald* offices were in that direction and Adriane thought Blake Garrett could be his own eyewitness to that story. He could simply step out on his doorstep and take it all down. Of course he wouldn't be there. He would be down where the news had been happening all afternoon. If the Know Nothing mob saw him, they'd have no mercy after the way he had blasted them in his editorials the last few weeks.

At the thought, Adriane's heart froze inside her, and without really thinking about what she was doing or why, she went back in the pressroom to pick up the gun and slip it down into the deep pocket inside the cloak. When she went back out on the street, fire alarms were clanging as the firemen rushed toward the blaze. She remembered what Duff had said about the men on the street not letting the firemen through, and she felt a chill as she looked back at the flames rising above the buildings. The whole block could burn.

Dear Lord in heaven, protect us from ourselves.

She looked to the east where the sky glowed ever brighter and wondered if perhaps the entire city might burn. Then she pulled the hood of the cloak well over her face and began walking toward the sounds of sporadic gunfire. Smoke drifted through the streets, seeming to carry with it the roiling, grumbling noise of the mob somewhere up ahead.

At the first sight of a gang of men pushing along the street waving their guns and clubs and shouting, Adriane shrank back into a recessed doorway to hide. The roar of their voices and the looks on their faces as they rushed past left no doubt they were looking for trouble. Adriane hardly dared to breathe for fear one of them might notice her there.

At last when they were well past, she eased out of the doorway and, staying far back, trailed after the men. There looked to be maybe a dozen of them before a couple of men came out of a building to join up with them. Then three more ran up from a side street. Without pausing, the group absorbed the new additions and kept going in a determined rush forward toward the even greater roar ahead.

Suddenly Adriane was terrified of this feeling that had

captured the city and was leaping like a live thing from man to man. The group of men in front of her made her think of a flooded river picking up more water as it rushed along until it jumped its banks and started knocking down everything in its path.

A small carriage pulled by one horse burst out of a side street directly in front of the men. With a yell that sent chills down Adriane's back, they moved in front of the carriage. The horse skittered sideways and stopped. The driver slashed with his carriage whip first at the horse and then the men closing in around him.

Without Adriane really seeing how it happened, the carriage overturned, spilling out the driver and taking the horse down. In a panic the horse kicked and struggled against the tangled harness. The men stood back, and the driver wasted no time disappearing down one of the side streets. A few of the men started after him, but turned back at the edge of the deeper shadows in the alley. Behind them the other men were slashing open the carriage seats as if they thought gold might be hidden in the stuffing.

When they didn't find anything, one of the men touched the stuffing with his torch. Flames shot up at once, and Adriane guessed that the oil from the lamp on the side of the carriage had spilled out. The horse, still on the ground trapped in his harness, whinnied with terror. Some of the men laughed. But then one of the men threw his jacket over the horse's head and another swiftly cut through the harness lines. The horse found its feet and raced wildly away while the men moved on down the street.

Adriane lagged farther behind them now, scurrying from shadow to shadow. Beck was right. The street was no place for her tonight. No place for anyone who wasn't out to find trouble.

And yet she didn't turn back toward the offices. She kept following the men almost as if she felt the same pull they did toward the shouting, screaming mass of men ahead. Smoke was thick in the streets now, more smoke than just that from the burning carriage cushions. Suddenly the carriage behind her was engulfed in a whoosh of flames, lighting up the air around her, but none of the men looked back.

Instead they began shouting and running toward something in the street ahead. Their words floated back to Adriane.

"Irish pup."

"Trying to get away."

"Grab him."

Adriane barely caught sight of the young boy as they yanked him out of the shadows. She did see the boy's hat before the men surrounded him. A cap like Duff's.

She wasn't sure how she got to the middle of the group to stand in front of the boy. Perhaps the prod of a gun barrel made the men instinctively give way. Whatever happened, one minute she was watching the backs of the men as they prepared to punish the boy for being Irish, and the next she was staring into their faces, the gun in her hand pointed at the nearest man's chest.

"Stand back," she ordered.

"Look there! It's a woman," one of the men shouted, and Adriane realized the hood of her cloak had fallen back in her push through the men.

"Rush her," a big man in the front said.

Adriane turned the gun toward him. "Do you want to be the body the others step over to get to me and the boy?" She felt no fear, only cold anger.

"Aw, she probably can't shoot," another man said.

"Don't count on it." Somebody spoke up from the back of the group. A familiar voice. "That's Wade Darcy's girl. If he taught her to set type, he might've taught her to shoot."

Adriane's eyes searched through the men, but she saw no face she recognized. She couldn't worry about that. She had to be sure she held the gun steady with her finger caressing the trigger while she stared at the men closest to her. She shifted the gun slowly and deliberately, pointing it at first one of them, then another.

"Which of you wants your name in the paper tomorrow morning?" she asked. "Man shot while attacking a woman."

There was a roar from the next street over. "They're burning Quinn's Row," the man in the back of the group shouted. "We're going to miss it all."

The big man in the front suddenly turned away from Adriane. "I didn't come down here to shoot no woman."

"Or be shot by one," the man in the back said. He split away from the group and began running. The other men barely glanced back at Adriane and the boy as they followed.

The boy wasn't as old as Duff. His eyes were enormous in his face as he looked at her and said, "Thank ye, missy. Our mothers must have been praying for the both of us tonight." Then without waiting for her to say anything, he slipped away from her and was gone.

Adriane was still standing there on the street not sure what to do next when she heard footsteps running back toward her. She didn't even have time to raise the gun again before the man grabbed her and spun them both into the shadows.

"What in heaven's name are you trying to do? Get yourself killed?" Blake Garrett gripped Adriane's shoulders and glared down at her.

"Blake," Adriane said weakly. She had to fight the urge to lean against him as she realized it had been his voice at the back of the group. She should have known. "Once more it appears I have reason to be grateful to you, sir." She tried to pull away from him so that he wouldn't feel the way she was trembling, but he kept his grip tight on her.

"Don't trot out your society manners for me, Adriane. I want to know, and I want to know now, what you think you're doing out here on the streets in the middle of this rabble."

A little fire pushed through her at the tone of his voice.

"I don't know that it's any of your concern, Mr. Garrett," she said, her voice tight and controlled. "But if you must know, I thought the boy might be Duff, and I could hardly stay hidden in the shadows and let those animals have him without a fight."

"So you thought you'd just let them have both of you."

"I daresay, given time, they would have listened to reason." She tried to make her words sound more confident about that than she felt. He was right. She couldn't have held off the men.

"There is no reason this night. Only madness," Blake said. "You shouldn't be out here at all."

"I know," she admitted. "But I must find Father. I have to warn him."

"Warn him about what? I can assure you he knows about the riots. Men from his party of choice are the ringleaders, the ones who got this mob going."

"Father didn't want any of this to happen." Adriane's throat felt so tight she had to force out her words. "He would never advocate this kind of mayhem."

"Maybe not, but surely you've been reading his editorials." Blake looked away from her toward the noise of the crowd. "It's evident the men on the streets have been as well, and now the Irish and Germans are paying."

A spattering of gunshots sounded a few streets away. "The *Tribune*'s not to blame for this."

His eyes came back to her. "Can you be so sure?"

She met his look fully and after a minute whispered, "No." She felt dangerously close to tears, and she wanted nothing more than to be back at the offices putting together a normal front page full of nothing but the dullest stories.

All of a sudden, his look gentled and he folded her into his arms. "I'm sorry, Adriane," he whispered into her hair. "I have no right to accuse you or the *Tribune*. We're all to blame."

It felt so good there in his arms, so safe. The noise of the shouting crowd faded away. Even the gunshots sounded distant and unimportant. Nothing mattered but his arms holding her, his voice soft in her ear.

He went on. "But I've been half out of my mind ever since I saw you marching beside Stanley Jimson in the parade, and then tonight when I saw you surrounded by those men, I didn't know what to do."

Stanley's name brought back in a rush why she was on the streets. Why she had to find her father. Beck may have thought Stanley's threats were just words. Adriane knew better.

She jerked away from Blake to ask, "Have you seen him?"

"Who? Stanley?" All the gentleness disappeared from Blake's face.

"No. Father. I must find him."

Blake's face was still hard as he answered, "I saw him earlier with Mayor Barbee's group when they stopped the mob from burning the church at St. Martin's."

She grabbed hold of the front of Blake's jacket, and when she spoke, she was shamelessly begging. "Could you help me find him? Please, Blake. I'll do anything."

20

"Anything? You shouldn't make idle promises, dear lady, especially not on a night like this." Blake stared down at Adriane for a long moment, expecting her to turn her eyes away. When she didn't, he said, "You don't love Stanley Jimson."

"No," she said. "It would be better if I did."

"That could never be better," Blake said.

Adriane dropped her eyes from his. "You don't know everything."

"Then tell me."

"There's not time now." She looked back up at his face again as she pleaded, "And I know I have no right to ask your help, but I have to find Father. Please, I beg of you, Blake, help me."

He stared down at her. Even as he agreed to go with her, he knew it wasn't what he should do. He should take her straight back to the *Tribune* offices and lock her inside. She wasn't safe out here. Nobody was safe on the streets this night.

He'd seen riots before. He'd been witness to how hatred could ignite and spread like a flash fire through a group of ordinary men, burning away their consciences and turning them into a massive instrument of destruction, but those other times he'd only been a reporter scribbling notes about what was being destroyed. This time he was one of the forces behind the riot. His words. His editorials. It wasn't beyond the realm of possibility that the mob might turn on him if he was recognized.

He was ready to take that chance as he stayed out on the streets. What was happening might not be news he wanted to happen, but it was news. So with his hat pulled low over his face, he had been doing his best to blend in with the fringes of the crowd while watching the havoc.

Then he'd seen Adriane, her head thrown back defiantly as she stood between those men and that poor Irish kid, and his heart had almost thudded to a stop. She'd never looked more beautiful to him than she did standing there trying to stare down the men. She couldn't have done it, not even with the gun. The men had been like a pack of hungry wolves with the scent of a cornered doe in their noses.

He looked over at her now as they moved silently toward the terrible roar of the mob and the chilling screams of its victims. With the hood of her cloak pulled back up over her head, he was only able to catch a glimpse of her pale face, but he could see how she was straining to see ahead to whatever was happening farther down the street.

Once again, he told himself he was crazy to be taking her toward the mob. Her father wouldn't be there. He thought they both knew that, but they were drawn to the noise. Even if she had a sudden change of mind and begged him to take her home, he wasn't sure he could turn his back on the story unfolding on the other side of this line of buildings. And though he wasn't touching Adriane now, he sensed she was feeling the same pulse quickening mixture of dread and excitement, the same reporter's hunger for the story, no matter how bad that story might turn out to be.

When at last they were close enough to see, it was even worse than anything Blake could have imagined. At least half the buildings on Quinn's Row were already burning, and men were torching the rest of them with no concern for the faces peering frantically out the windows. A few women and children were allowed to slip out of the burning buildings, but when a man tried to escape the flames, a gunshot rang out. The man fell and a roar from the crowd sounded approval as if somebody had just hit the bull's-eye at a shooting contest.

Beside him, Adriane trembled as she said, "Can't anybody stop them?" She was nearly shouting, but he barely heard her words over the noise of the crowd as more shots rang out.

He looked down into her face and told her the truth. "No."

Suddenly he was sick of the news. Sick of his fellow man pushing against him on both sides. Sick of himself for watching. He took hold of Adriane's arm under the cloak and pulled her back away from the crowd. "Come on." He leaned down to speak close to her ear. "Your father's not here. No one with any honor is part of this."

She went with him without protest. They were two blocks away from the screaming crowd before she spoke. "I still need to find Father."

"Your father's probably back at the *Tribune*, frantic with worry about you. Worse, he'll no doubt try to shoot me again when we get there."

"I'll explain how you rescued me yet again."

"He won't listen." Blake looked at her in the light of one of the streetlamps.

"No, he won't listen." A frown tightened Adriane's face.

Blake wished he could believe her worry was for him, but that he sensed had nothing to do with him. "Tell me what's wrong. Maybe I can help," he said.

"How? By writing an editorial in tomorrow's *Herald* about our troubles?" The words hinted at their former verbal duels, but her voice carried no fire, only sadness.

He had no heart for dueling words with her either, so he answered softly, "There'll be more than enough headline news tomorrow without your father and me attacking one another."

"We're leaving the headlines behind." Adriane glanced back over her shoulder.

"We saw enough."

"Yes," Adriane agreed. She shuddered as yet another gunshot sounded behind them. "Duff was right. The men are like animals. Animals with guns and torches."

He tried to reassure her. "They won't come back this way."

"Some of them may have already come this way. There was a fire a few streets over when I left the *Tribune*."

A needle of worry jabbed Blake. Joe was watching over the *Herald* offices, but maybe he should have gone back and guarded the press himself. "Where?"

Adriane hesitated before she answered, "It may have been close to the *Herald*, but I heard the fire alarms. I'm sure they got it under control."

"Nothing's under control tonight."

They didn't say anything more then as they rushed back through the almost deserted streets. Sometimes he glimpsed a white face peeking out around a pulled back curtain or heard the click of a door shutting as they passed, but most of the buildings loomed dark and empty around them.

They were almost back to the *Tribune* when they practically ran headlong into Beck. The old man barely glanced at Blake before grabbing Adriane. "Addie, you promised you'd stay put."

"I know, Beck, but I couldn't stand not knowing what was happening. I wanted to be sure Father was all right." Adriane's words came out in a rush. "You did find him and warn him, didn't you, Beck?"

Beck hesitated a second as though he didn't want to answer before he said, "I found him, Addie, but I was too late to warn him."

"What happened?" It was easy to hear the panic in her voice.

"I don't rightly know if anybody could say exactly. I had just spotted the boss up on this platform trying to reason with the men, but I couldn't get close to him for the crowd of people around him. Some of the men went to shouting, and then somebody started shooting. The boss took a hit to the shoulder that knocked him clean off that platform he was on. Things still might not have been so bad 'cepting the crowd was like a mad herd of bulls. They ran right up on top of him. It took five of us to beat them back so's we could get him out of there. He took a bad knock to the head besides the gunshot in the shoulder."

"He's all right, isn't he?" she demanded.

Beck's voice was sad. "I don't know, Addie. He ain't dead, but he ain't never come to. I ain't sure he's going to. All I can tell you is the doc's on his way."

"No." The word exploded out of Adriane as she jerked away from Beck to run toward the *Tribune* offices.

"Wait, Adriane!" Blake started after her, but Beck put a hand on his arm to stop him.

"I'm obliged to you for bringing Addie back safe and all, but you'd best let her be right now." Beck's eyes sharpened on Blake as if he was only now realizing exactly who he was. "Besides, from what I hear you've got troubles enough of your own."

"What do you mean?"

"You ain't heard?"

"Heard what, man? God only knows the whole town has troubles."

Even in the dim light, Blake could see the pity on the old man's face as he looked at him. "The *Herald*'s burning down, Mr. Garrett. And that ain't all. They say when your boss heard about the fire, he dropped down dead on the spot."

"Chesnut dead?"

"That's what I heard, Mr. Garrett. A funny thing. Chesnut and the boss going down so close together like that after all their years of fighting one another in their papers."

"But you said Darcy's not dead."

"Not yet." Beck shook his head slowly. "Not yet."

Blake looked toward the *Tribune* building. Adriane had already disappeared inside.

"Don't worry, sir," Beck said. "I'll be taking care of her. You'd best go take care of your own."

Blake wanted to tell the old man that Adriane was his own, more important to him than anything that might be burning up a few streets over, but he had no assurance Adriane would welcome him beside her right now.

"Tell Adriane I'll be back," Blake told Beck. "And don't let Stanley Jimson talk her into anything she might regret."

The lines on the old man's face tightened. "That no-good shows his face around the *Tribune* offices again tonight, he'll be the one doing the regretting."

Before Blake could ask what the old man meant, the doctor's buggy clattered past them, and Beck ran after it.

It took Blake fifteen minutes to cut through the streets and get to what had been the *Herald*'s offices. The building was a gray mass of smoldering debris with an occasional flame flickering to life as if the fire wasn't quite ready to surrender completely to the firemen milling about on the street. Blake spotted Joe, his head in his hands, sitting on a pile of sodden newspapers somebody had pulled out into the street.

"You all right, Joe?" Blake asked him.

"Boss." Joe looked up and some of the hopelessness went out of his face as if he expected Blake to be able to fix things. "I guess one of the boys finally found you then."

"No, but I heard." Blake looked at the gutted building. The sight of it seemed to take all the life out of him, and he sank down beside Joe. "What happened?"

"I guess I let you down, boss," Joe said.

"Don't worry about that, Joe. Just tell me what happened."

"Well, it was like this. I heard something in the back of the building. So I got the gun you give me 'cause of how you'd told me to be ready for trouble. Anyhow, I went back there to look around and somebody banged me on the head. The next thing I know I hear somebody shouting my name, and the smoke's choking me and it's hotter than the stoking room on a steamboat. I reckon if one of the boys hadn't found me to pull me outta there, I might not be here talking to you now."

"Did you save anything?" Blake stared across the street at the smoldering remains of the building.

"Not much. It was just too hot."

His files gone. All his stories and ideas up in smoke. The press gone. Everything gone. Jimson was going to have a victory all around. "And how about John? Is he really dead?"

"So they tell me, boss. I didn't think he looked hisself when he come by this morning. I reckon hearing about the fire and all was just too much for his heart." Joe stared down at the street.

Blake was silent a moment before he said, "Wade Darcy got shot trying to reason with the crowd."

"You don't say. He dead?" Joe jerked his head up to look at Blake.

"Not yet, but his man Beck doesn't think he'll make it."

"Poor Miss Adriane. She'll take that hard. Seeing as how she doted on her pa." Joe turned his eyes back toward the ruins of their building. "I reckon there's trouble enough to go all around tonight."

Again there was silence between the men as they considered those troubles. Finally Blake asked, "The boys been running in any stories?"

"A few before the fire. Was things really that bad, boss?"

"Worse."

"We've got enough headlines for two papers, don't we, boss?"

"And nothing to print them with, Joe. Nothing to print them on." Blake stared across the street at the ashes of his dreams of having his own paper.

"Maybe one of the other papers would let us use their presses till we can get set up again," Joe suggested. "We might not be the first issue on the street, but we'd get on the street sooner or later."

"Most of the other papers will be cheering when they hear about us getting burned out." Blake's voice was bitter.

"Oh, I don't know, boss. This ain't the big town. Around here folks sometimes give other folks a helping hand even when they don't agree with them."

"Wasn't much of that happening on the streets tonight."

"That's different, boss, and you know it. Decent folks is going to be so ashamed come mornin', that they'll go out of their way to help somebody. Old Beck might even let us run off a couple of issues, especially if Mr. Darcy ain't able to have a say in it." Joe looked sideways at Blake. "I hear you and Miss Adriane is sometimes half friendly."

"Jimson controls the *Tribune*."

"True enough. But it could be he'll be so busy celebrating his win tonight that he won't be paying no whole lot of attention to anything else. A man who can move quick might just surprise a lot of people. Maybe Jimson most of all."

Blake was still staring at what was left of his building, but he wasn't seeing the burned pile of rubble now. The wildest idea was taking shape in his head. "You know, Joe," he said after a long silence. "You may just have something."

"You want me to try to round up the boys, boss?"

"They'll be coming in soon enough." Blake stood up. "I'll be back." He started away, but then turned to put his hand on Joe's shoulder. "I'm glad you got out, Joe. Real glad."

"You ain't the onliest one, boss."

Blake tried to figure out exactly what he would say all the way back through the streets to the *Tribune*. He'd never been one to beg, but if it came to that, he would.

Beck came to the door, and when he let him in without a word, Blake knew there wouldn't be good news about Wade Darcy's condition. "How is he?" Blake asked anyway.

"He ain't woke up, but he ain't stopped breathing," Beck said shortly. "The doctor weren't too sure which might happen. Said it was hard to tell in these kind of things. That he'd seen folks linger like this for days, weeks even."

"I'm sorry," Blake said.

"Yeah, me too. Me and Wade go way back. Way back." Beck turned his eyes to the floor. After a minute the old man looked up at him again. "Did Joe get anything out for you?"

"Himself. Barely."

"Folks is playing rough tonight."

"But the game's not over." For a second Blake thought about telling Beck his plan to try to get the old man on his side before he talked to Adriane, but it was Adriane he had to convince. She was the one who would have to say yes.

Beck gave him a considering look. "No, I can see it ain't. I reckon you're wanting to see Addie."

"Yes."

"She might not come down."

Blake met his look fully. "Then I'll go up there."

Beck gave him another long look before he said, "I'll tell her you're here."

"Tell her I'm not leaving until I see her."

21

Adriane sat beside the bed, watching her father's chest rise and fall. The doctor had dug the bullet out of his shoulder. He'd poked and prodded around on her father's head and pulled up his eyelids to peer at his eyes. He'd listened to his heart and checked for broken ribs.

Through it all her father had shown no sign of life other than the rising and falling of his chest. But surely as long as he was breathing, there was hope. She had to believe there was hope, even though Dr. Hammon wouldn't quite meet her eyes as he packed up his instruments and told her to send for him if there was any change. She had to believe there was hope in spite of the way Beck was walking around with his shoulders hunched over as though somebody had punched him in the stomach.

Her father would come to. He'd look up at her and want to know why she was sitting there beside him when there was a paper to get out. He'd tell her to bring him a pen and paper so he could write down what he saw happen. He'd say the people had to know the truth.

The truth. What was the truth? Had Stanley done this because she refused to marry him? Or had her father simply been in the wrong place at the wrong time? Bullets were flying everywhere out on the street. She wouldn't be the only woman keeping a prayerful vigil over a loved one this night.

She didn't turn her head when Beck came into the room and said, "There's somebody here to see you, Addie."

"I don't want to see anyone, Beck. Send them away."

"I don't think I can."

Adriane finally turned her eyes away from her father to look at Beck. "Is it Lucilla?"

"No. Mrs. Elmore sent word that she'd be here in the morning. I reckon as how she's afraid to come out tonight."

"I suppose that's sensible." She was just as glad Lucilla wasn't coming. Adriane wanted to be the one beside her father when he opened his eyes.

She looked back at her father's face, so still and pale it didn't even look like him. He was always smiling or frowning over a story, always trying to drive home his point. There was never this stillness. Never.

Beck came over to stand beside her at the bed. He stared down at her father a moment before he said, "It's Blake Garrett, Addie. And he ain't going away till he sees you."

Adriane's heart quickened at the thought of Blake Garrett downstairs in the hallway demanding to see her, but then she shook her head. "I can't leave Father's side."

Grief deepened the wrinkles on Beck's face. She knew what he was thinking. That she couldn't hold her father there if it wasn't meant to be, but he didn't say it out loud. Instead he said, "I'll sit right here beside the boss and holler for you if he shows the first sign of coming out of it, Addie." Beck touched Adriane's shoulder. "Go talk to him. The man's had problems enough of his own tonight, and I ain't wanting to turn him away."

"All right, I'll see him." She couldn't argue with Beck. She didn't want to argue with him. She wanted to see Blake even if it did make her feel like the worst kind of traitor to stand up and turn from her father's sickbed, perhaps his deathbed, to go downstairs to meet his enemy.

Blake was standing just inside the front door, his face smudged with black and his dark hair tumbling wherever it wanted. Adriane caught a brief glimpse of herself in the hall mirror and noted her own disheveled hair and bloodstained dress. But it didn't matter. Blake's eyes were fastened on her face. He didn't care about her hair or clothes.

"I'm sorry about your father, Adriane," he said.

"He'll get better." Adriane pushed confidence into her words.

"What if he doesn't?"

Adriane wanted to turn away from him and the truth his eyes were forcing on her. She'd been able to ignore Beck's worries, but Blake's eyes refused to allow her to pretend.

"I don't know," she said. "Right now I have to believe he will."

"The fire you saw." His voice was low, almost expressionless. "It was the *Herald*."

"Oh, Blake, I am sorry." She reached a hand out toward him, but then let it drop back to her side without touching him. "What will you do?"

"That's up to you."

"To me?" His eyes were growing even more intense on her.

"I need a press. You need an editor. The *Tribune-Herald* has a nice ring."

"The *Tribune-Herald*," she repeated after him as though she couldn't believe what he was suggesting. "You know my father would never agree to that."

"Your father doesn't have to. Nobody has to but you. Marry me, Adriane."

"What?" Adriane wasn't sure she'd heard him correctly.

"You heard me. Marry me."

"Just because you need a press?"

"No, because we need each other." Blake stepped closer to her, and she didn't back away. "You don't want the *Tribune* to die any more than I want the *Herald* to die. Together we can make a great newspaper."

"Are you proposing we marry as some sort of business deal?" she asked faintly. "Just to merge the papers?"

"No." His eyes burned into hers. "No," he repeated. "It would be a marriage in every sense of the word. A man and woman becoming as one."

He put his hand on hers, and she thought her skin might catch fire from the heat passing between them. His breath caressed her face. His scent filled her head. She could almost feel his desire leaping out at her and forcing her body to respond until every inch of her skin desired his touch.

She whispered, "When?"

"Now. Tonight. This minute."

She tried to rein in her runaway emotions. She reminded herself that just a few hours ago she'd told one man she couldn't marry him. She could hardly marry another man the very same day. Especially a man she barely knew. And not with her father battling death upstairs in his room. The last thought was like a dash of cold water in her face, and she pulled her eyes away from Blake's to stare at the floor as she said, "I couldn't."

He put his hand under her chin and raised her face back up until once more he captured her eyes. "You must. There's no other choice. There's been no other choice since that very first day in Mrs. Wigginham's parlor. Perhaps even before that. We both know that."

"I know nothing of the sort," Adriane managed to say, even though the heat was racing through her again stronger than ever. The dash of cold water evaporated without a trace in the power of the flames.

"Don't lie to yourself, Adriane. Not tonight. You want to marry me. I can see it in your eyes."

"I need time," Adriane said weakly.

"Time is what we don't have. We have to grab hold of what we want tonight. Marry me."

"But Father . . ." she began and hesitated.

"He'll understand. We'll make him understand, and when he gets used to the idea, he may even be glad."

Tears pricked at her eyes in gratitude. He'd allowed her to keep hope for her father's recovery. Even so, how could she marry him? Now. Tonight.

As if he sensed her questions, he said, "I'll send Joe for a preacher. We'll take care of whatever else needs to be done tomorrow."

The word *yes* was rising up from the core of her being. She wanted to marry Blake Garrett, but while the thought of being with him freed a certain wild passion inside her, it also let loose dark memories from her childhood. She knew so little about what happened between a man and woman.

Grace had tried to explain it once, but Grace's straightforward common sense had completely deserted her as her face had turned red and she became tongue-tied. She'd managed to explain very little of the mechanics, although she had assured Adriane that with the right man the act of love would be as natural as breathing. But would it be? And even if it was, it would still bring babies. What was it Henrietta had said about her mother? Nine months from the marriage bed to the deathbed.

"I'm afraid." The words slipped out past her guard. She hadn't planned to say them no matter how true they were.

Blake's eyes gentled. He pulled her close and wrapped his arms around her, and she surrendered to his embrace gladly. "You'll never have anything to fear, my darling. Not with me."

His lips softly touched her hair, then her cheeks and eyelids. Adriane thought her insides were melting, but she couldn't let go of her fear. She made herself remember her father upstairs and pulled away from Blake.

He let her go, the first doubt beginning to show in his face, and somehow that doubt gave Adriane courage to say the words she wanted to say. "I will marry you."

Joy leaped into his eyes to replace the doubt, and once more he tried to pull her close. But she wouldn't allow it.

"Wait, Blake," she said. "I will marry you tonight as you ask, but I still need time. My father needs me with him right now. I must stay by his bed."

"And not come to mine. Is that what you're trying to say, Adriane?" Blake's voice lost its gentleness. "I told you I wasn't proposing a simple business arrangement. I won't settle for that."

"And I understand and accept that. But I need time." As she met his eyes fully, it was as if everything inside her tried to keep her from saying her next words, but she pushed them out. "I will also understand if you want to withdraw your proposal."

He studied her a moment. "How much time?"

"I don't know."

Again his eyes probed her before he finally said, "I would never force you to do anything you didn't want to do, Adriane. Will you accept that as a promise of whatever time you need?"

"Yes," she said.

"Then it will be as you ask. I'll send Joe to find a preacher who will do the ceremony. Once that's over, we'll get out the paper."

"The headlines must be written," Adriane said, a bit dryly.

"That's what you want, isn't it?" Blake's eyes bored into her.

"Yes," she admitted. "Yes, it is. And what my father would want."

His eyes were still searching her face. "Do you want to write a Colonel Storey letter while you sit with your father?"

Adriane gasped, too surprised to deny she wrote the letters. "How did you know?"

"I know you, Adriane," he said simply. Then for the first time since she'd pushed him away, he reached out and touched her cheek. "May I kiss you, Adriane? It only seems proper to kiss the woman who has just agreed to become my wife."

Without a word, she held her face up to him, and he gently touched his lips to hers. The very softness of the touch set off the fire inside her again, and when he wrapped his arms around her, her own arms crept around his neck as his lips became more insistent.

Then he was pulling away, looking down into her face before he gently brushed her forehead with his lips. "Don't need too much time, Adriane," he whispered before he abruptly turned her loose and went out the door.

For a moment, she stared at the closed door, trying to wrap the memory of his embrace around her to keep away the fear, but the fear won out when the unnatural stillness of the house pressed down on her. She went back up the stairs to where her father lay pale and unconscious upon his bed, and she felt shame for the minutes she'd nearly forgotten him.

Beck looked up at her. "What did he want?"

"Our presses," she answered. "He wants to merge the *Tribune* and the *Herald*."

Beck didn't look surprised. "What did you tell him?"

"I said yes. You'll need to reset the masthead page."

"I can do that." Beck studied her face closely a moment before he went on. "You ain't telling me everything, Addie."

"No."

"Are you going to?"

Adriane looked at her father as if she were afraid he might hear her. "He's sending Joe for a preacher."

A slow smile broke over Beck's face, but no answering smile came to her own lips as she asked, "Did I do the right thing, Beck?"

"Not only the right thing, Addie. The only thing. That right thing we've been praying for."

"I don't know." Adriane sighed as she looked down at the floor. "What will we do about Coleman Jimson and the money Father owes him?"

"We'll worry about that after we put out this first issue.

That's the way it's always been in the newspaper business. One issue at a time."

"It's not just the newspapers we're merging," Adriane said softly.

"He's a good man, Addie."

"You don't even know him. I barely know him myself." A bit of panic edged into her voice.

"You know him good enough, Addie. You love him. I can see that all over your face. That's all that really matters."

After Beck left to go downstairs to get the presses ready, Adriane thought that was the one thing neither she nor Blake had mentioned. Love.

Adriane looked at her father and noted the even rising of his chest. Then she turned her eyes to the darkened window on the far side of the bed. While she couldn't see into the future any more than she could see what the darkness held outside the window, she could make herself face the truth in her heart.

She loved Blake Garrett. More than she loved life. More than she loved the *Tribune*. Adriane's eyes returned to her father's white face. More than she loved her father. There had never been any answer but yes inside her to Blake's demand that she marry him. It was the depth of that feeling that frightened her most.

She slipped to her knees beside her father's bed and prayed for light to take away the darkness of her fear. Love was good. Not something to fear.

Her father used to tell her the same thing about the dark. "There's no reason to be afraid of the dark," he would tell her. "The dark can't hurt you, and you know I'll come. I always come."

"But sometimes it takes you so long," she'd told him.

"Then think of the light."

So she had, and when Beck had started reading the Bible to her, he'd pointed out Scripture about light as though he knew exactly what she needed. Beck always knew. She'd memorized those verses so she could whisper the Bible words like a mantra when Henrietta shut her inside the closet. She thought if she could repeat enough verses, the Lord would know she wasn't bad all the time. That he wouldn't turn his face from her and would bless her with light. He would send her father to rescue her sooner.

But now it was her father who needed to be rescued from the dark. The familiar verses rose up in her memory. *God saw the light, that it was good: and God divided the light from the darkness . . . And the light shineth in darkness . . . I am the light of the world: he that followeth me shall not walk in darkness, but shall have the light of life.*

The light of life. That was her prayer.

22

They stood up together in the pressroom with Beck on her side and Joe on his. Adriane had washed her face and changed into a clean dress since she couldn't bear the thought of marrying in a dress stained with her father's blood.

Blake had combed his hair back from his face, and he looked strangely solemn without the stray curls falling down on his forehead. He wore the same jacket still smudged with black and smelling of smoke.

Reverend Cassaway, the preacher Joe had dragged from his bed to perform the ceremony, kept peering at them anxiously as if he expected one of them to back out while he recited the marriage ceremony.

Adriane said "I do" when the man asked her if she would love, honor, cherish, and obey. She felt a deep stillness inside her as she stared at the worn Bible in the preacher's hands and listened for Blake to make the same promise.

When the silence lengthened, Adriane noted a tremble in the preacher's hands as he waited for Blake to say the words. Her heart began to pound in her ears. Why didn't Blake answer?

Blake gently touched her cheek to tip her face toward him.

As his eyes captured hers, she knew he'd been waiting for her to look at him before he said the words. She had no doubt as he spoke his "I do" that he was making a promise for life no matter what the reason was for this wedding.

Reverend Cassaway must have felt the same thing, because he looked relieved as he smiled and pronounced them man and wife and told Blake he could kiss the bride.

Both Beck and Joe were smiling along with the preacher as they waited for the kiss. Blake put his hands on her shoulders and stared down into her eyes. Even now they shared no smile. With a sudden flash of understanding, Adriane knew Blake was as afraid of what might be expected of him as she was of what might be expected of her.

At last he kissed her softly before he whispered in her ear, "Thank you for doing me the honor of becoming my wife, Mrs. Garrett."

The name jolted her, and she pulled back to look at his face. Suddenly a smile was exploding from his eyes and wrapping warmth around her. She reminded herself of the serious-ness of the moment. She thought about how upset her father would be that she'd married his enemy. She told herself she and Blake had not shared any spoken words of love. Yet in spite of all this, a smile was bubbling up from deep inside her and pushing out on her face in answer to his. And she felt surrounded by light.

For one magical moment she didn't think she needed any time at all. She was ready to give herself to Blake without conditions.

Blake's own smile became a laugh as he grabbed her up in a sweeping hug that lifted her off her feet. By the time he set her back down on the floor, she felt dizzy from more than the spinning hug. The feel of his body was burned into hers. Then Beck and Joe took turns kissing her flaming cheeks before slapping Blake on the back.

The moment did not last. Even before someone knocking

on the door interrupted the explosion of joy, Adriane had remembered how unseemly her conduct surely must be with her father so near death upstairs. She let the worry and sadness flood back through her, almost welcoming them, because she knew and understood those feelings. This joy that filled her when Blake touched her was too new, too strange. She again needed time.

The knocking turned into a frantic banging and brought them all back to the realities of the night. Outside on the streets there was a riot.

Beck picked up his gun from the table. "I'll see who it is," he said.

Blake followed him out into the hallway while Adriane stayed frozen in her spot waiting.

Beside her Reverend Cassaway cleared his throat nervously and looked at Joe. "I think I've performed the necessary service for these two as requested. Perhaps it would be best if I just hurried on home now. Mrs. Cassaway will be worried."

"Sure, preacher." Joe slipped the man some money before he pointed the way to the back door.

Reverend Cassaway tucked the bills in his vest pocket and wasted little time making his escape, pausing only a bare few seconds to say, "I do hope that's not trouble of any sort and that you'll be very happy, Mrs. Garrett."

After the man scurried off down the hall, Joe looked over at Adriane with an embarrassed grin and shrugged a little. "Sorry, Miss Adriane, but he was the best I could do this time of night."

Adriane was only half listening to Joe as she heard Beck open the door. What if it was Stanley? Or worse, his father. Coleman Jimson could have somehow heard of their troubles and be coming to demand payment of the money her father owed him. Adriane's eyes went to Blake's broad back between her and the door. She, at least, could no longer be that payment.

She was relieved and surprised to hear Duff's voice out in the hallway. "Where's Miss Adriane?" he said.

Adriane's relief vanished at the sight of the boy's face as he brushed past Beck and then Blake to find her. She met him at the door of the pressroom and wrapped her arms around him. "Oh, Duff," she said. "What's happened?"

He tried to answer, but all he could get out was another "Miss Adriane" before the sobs choked out any more words. She'd never seen him like this. He was always so tough, old beyond his years, as he worked to take care of his mother and sisters. But now, this moment, he was a heartbroken child in her arms even though he was nearly as tall as she was. She held him and waited, her own heart growing heavier inside her.

As quickly as the sobs came, they stopped. Still, she kept her arms around the boy and waited for him to share his sorrow. At last he raised his head off her shoulder. "It's me sister, Miss Adriane. Lila."

The tears were gone as if they'd never been, but Adriane almost wished them back. She could hold him while he cried. She knew no way to ease the terrible hopelessness on his face, and even before he spoke the words, Adriane knew there was no chance his sister would wake again.

"Tell me what happened, Duff," she said gently. "Was she caught out on the streets in the riot?"

"No, I could've protected her from the likes of them." His face went cold. "It was the slasher. He must have grabbed her as she left work. I should've never let her take that job at the tavern, but she promised she'd be watchful." Despair washed over him as he repeated in almost a wail, "She promised."

For a minute he looked ready to break down again, but then his voice hardened. "I left me mother and sisters with neighbors to come be telling you, Miss Adriane. At least with me own sister, the *Herald* won't be beating us with the headlines."

"We won't print the headlines at all if you don't want us to, son," Blake said quietly behind the boy.

Duff whirled to glare at him. "How could you know about it already?"

"I didn't," Blake said, but Duff wasn't listening.

He threw himself at Blake, flailing him with his fists and screaming, "Maybe it's true the rumor I been hearing. Maybe you are the slasher yourself. Killing the poor girls, killing me own sister for to sell more of your newspapers."

"Duff!" Adriane tried to grab the boy's arms.

"It's all right, Adriane," Blake said without looking at her. He allowed Duff to hit him a few more times before he caught his arms and held him. "You don't believe that, Duff, but it could be you're going to find the truth of why I'm here just as hard to believe."

Duff quit fighting and looked up at Blake. They studied each other a moment before Blake said, "You saw her, didn't you?"

"I had to make sure it was her, don't you see? I thought maybe they could be wrong. So much was happening out on the street. I thought maybe Lila was just fearing to come home."

"But it was her."

"It was her." The look on Duff's face as he spoke the words sent a chill through Adriane. His voice changed as he begged Blake to help him make sense of it all. "Why'd he have to be doing that to her, sir? Why couldn't he have just killed her easy without slashing her all up like that?"

"The man's a monster." Blake's face turned rock hard. "But we're going to catch him and make him pay."

Duff's shoulders drooped as he stared down at the floor. "Ain't no way to catch him. Nobody cares about an Irish girl. Just look what happened out on the streets tonight. Nobody tried to stop that."

"Some people did," Blake said.

"But they couldn't," Duff said.

"No, but this killer is not a mob. He's just one man."

When Duff kept his head down, Blake ordered him, "Look at me, Duff."

Duff slowly raised his eyes back to Blake's face.

"We're going to catch this killer," Blake said. "He's going to pay for what he did to Lila. And Dorrie and Megan and Brenda and Kathleen."

"How are we going to do it, Mr. Garrett?" Duff asked.

"I don't know, Duff, but we'll find a way. You, me, Miss Adriane. Maybe we can make the headlines work for us. You see the *Tribune* and *Herald* are the same paper now."

Duff looked from Blake to Adriane. "The same?"

"We merged the papers," Adriane said. "It's too long a story to tell right now when you need to get back to be with your mother, Duff."

"I can explain it quick like, boy." Beck came over to put his arm around Duff. "They done gone and got hitched up together a few minutes ago. Now come on. I'll go with you back to your ma's house. Mr. Garrett and his crew can get out the first issue of the *Tribune-Herald* without us. Course not as easy, but they'll get it done." He shepherded the boy out of the pressroom with his arm still around his shoulders.

"Beck will take care of him," Blake told Adriane. "You'd better go see about your father."

She had started toward the stairs when he stopped her again. "And take some paper and ink and write something. I'll send one of the boys up for it when we're ready."

She looked at him. She hadn't been able to write anything worth printing for days, even weeks. How could she expect to write anything now when she felt so totally drained by everything that had happened in the last few hours? "My father wrote the stories for the *Tribune*," she told Blake.

"Then write the stories your father would have written. Better yet, write a story about your father and how he was standing up to the mob trying to stop the madness. Write about how he never intended for the men to take his words so far." His eyes softened on her. "It's a story that has to be written, Adriane. And one that should be written by you."

Upstairs one of Blake's men—Adriane thought his name was Calvin—met her at the door with a relieved look.

"He ain't come around, miss," he said. Then the man on the bed behind him forgotten, he peered past Adriane toward the stairs. "Sounded like more than a wedding going on down there. I started to come find out, but I figured I'd better not since the boss told me to stay here till you got back."

"Mr. Garrett has everything under control."

The man smiled a little. "The boss always does, miss. It's a real talent of his getting things to go the way he wants."

For some reason his words bothered Adriane. "I don't suppose he wanted your offices to burn down."

"Well, not that for sure. I reckon Jimson played rougher than even the boss expected, but he ain't give it up. There'll be an issue of the *Herald* on the streets in the morning just the same as every other day since he come to Louisville."

"Not exactly," Adriane reminded the man. "The *Tribune-Herald*."

"For sure, miss," Calvin agreed quickly with an embarrassed bob of his head. "And a fine paper it'll be."

She let him make his escape down the stairs without saying any more. Adriane didn't know why the man's words rankled her. Then she sighed. Perhaps because he was right. The truth was the masthead might say *Tribune-Herald*, but it was the *Herald* editor, the *Herald* men putting out the first issue, the issue that would set the tone of this new paper.

Adriane went to her father's bed and watched his chest rise and fall a few moments before she took his cold hand in hers. "I love you, Father," she whispered softly. The noise from the pressroom drifted up the stairs, but she shut it out as she went on. "I can't remember a time when I didn't want to please you, but I couldn't marry Stanley. I couldn't."

She paused and studied her father's face. There was no change. "Marrying Stanley Jimson would be like going into a dark closet, one nobody could ever rescue me from the way you used to rescue me from Henrietta's closets. I don't know what being married to Blake will be like, but I know it won't be like that."

She fell silent, rubbing her father's hand as if she could rub life back into it. Finally she said, "I think you might like Blake if you didn't already hate him so much." She smiled a little at the contradictory words. "He has a way of getting things done. Even now, with his press nothing but a pile of rubble and ashes, he's printing a newspaper on our press, on our newsprint, Father." She half expected her father to rear up out of the bed in rage at that, but he was as motionless as ever.

Tears pushed up in her eyes. "I'm sorry, Father. I knew Stan would be angry, but I didn't think he'd go this far. I wouldn't have written him the letter if I'd known. I would have done what you wanted." She held his hand to her cheek a moment. Then she took the rag from the pan beside the bed, wrung it out, and carefully bathed his face.

Adriane heard footsteps pounding up the stairs, and then Joe was in the doorway. "Sorry to disturb you, Miss Adriane, but the boss says to tell you to hurry up with that piece. He's holding up page two for it." Joe's eyes caught a moment on the blank paper she'd laid on the end of her father's bed before he kept talking as if he saw the page half full of words. "And he says maybe something about the two of you marrying and joining up the papers might not be out of line. But he says that's up to you."

"All right, Joe. Tell Mr. Garrett I'll work on it."

"The boss said to tell you we ain't gonna put the paper on the street without something about Mr. Darcy in it. Something you write."

After Joe went back downstairs, she stared at the blank sheet for a long moment before she made herself dip her pen in the inkpot. Then as if a dam had broken inside her, she could barely keep enough ink on the nib of her pen to keep up with the words flowing out of her.

She didn't try to make her father into a hero. She simply wrote of him as a man who knew his part in the tragedy that had played out on the streets during the terrible night and who had done everything he could to stop the insanity, even to standing in front of a mob bent on violence. Violence that had not spared him. She wrote about the strength of his beliefs and the power of his words and in the last paragraph begged their readers to pray for his recovery. Then she signed it Adriane Darcy Garrett.

She stared at the name on the paper for another long moment before she got a fresh sheet of paper and quickly wrote a short editorial announcing the merging of the two papers.

This joining together of two so disparate newspapers will usher in new opportunities for growth as our great city prospers in the years ahead. The Tribune-Herald *will ever be open-minded on any and all issues as we attempt to illuminate the truth.*

She quickly reread what she'd written, and though she thought it could be better, she didn't have time for rewrites. Once more she signed her new name. This time it did not look quite so strange, and she decided the name itself would have to serve as the announcement of her marriage. Due to her father's grave condition, it would hardly be proper to print a formal announcement of the event. The very fact that she had married at such a time would be considered highly improper and scandalize the townspeople quite enough without flaunting an announcement in black and white in front of their eyes.

For a minute she considered scratching out her name at the bottom of both stories, but then she went to the doorway to call to Joe downstairs. When he rushed upstairs, he looked a little surprised to see all the words. She smiled to herself. It wasn't going to be the first time she surprised Joe. Or Blake.

The *Tribune* may have been merged, but its spirit wasn't dead. Then sadness overwhelmed her, first for her father, then for Duff and his family, and finally for the whole city.

She returned to her chair by her father's bed and began once again watching for the rise and fall of his chest. She was sitting just the same two hours later when Blake came into the room as the first light of morning was pushing through the window.

"It's done," he said. "The boys are picking up their bundles."

"How does it look?" she asked without taking her eyes off her father.

"Not bad considering how we threw it together. If Beck hadn't come back, we'd have never gotten it ready on time. You want to see an issue?"

"Not now." She still didn't look up at him.

"You should rest." He came over behind her and laid his hands lightly on her shoulders. "I'll sit with him."

"No. He's my father."

He didn't argue with her. "Then if you don't need me here, I'll go with the boys to see if there's anything to salvage at our building. Maybe some of my files didn't burn completely. There might be something. And I want to go talk to Duff and his mother."

"Duff?" She finally turned her head to look up at him.

His face was fierce as he answered. "I made him a promise. I intend to keep it."

"How?" she asked. "No one ever seems to see or know anything about whoever it is who kills these girls. It's as if he rises out of the river like some evil wraith that can appear and disappear at will." She wanted to weep when she thought of what Duff's sister had suffered.

Blake tightened his hands on Adriane's shoulders as his frown grew even fiercer. "The man doing this is no apparition. He's real enough and we can catch him." But then he sighed as if he knew words alone couldn't make that

247

happen. "If we can only figure out a way to bring him out in the open."

Her hand came up almost of its own volition to touch one of his on her shoulder. "Thank you, Blake."

"For what?" He looked surprised.

"I don't know." She searched for something to say that would make sense. "For rescuing me, I suppose."

A smile chased some of the dark worry off his face. "You do seem prone to needing rescuing, for a fact." He leaned over to lightly kiss the top of her head before he left. "Beck will be downstairs if you need anything."

23

After Blake left, the room was too quiet with only the shallow sound of her father's breathing. Adriane stood up and busily straightened her father's covers and fluffed his pillow. Then she tried to pour some of the medicine the doctor had left down her father's throat, but it slid out the corners of his mouth and trickled across his cheek to his ear. After she carefully wiped off his face, she laid a fresh, cool cloth on his forehead. When she could think of nothing else to do, she put her ear down on his chest to listen to his faint heartbeat and try to pull hope from the sound.

"He ain't no better." Beck stood in the doorway, a cup of coffee in one hand and a plate of bread, apples, and cheese in the other. A paper was tucked under one arm.

It wasn't really a question, but Adriane straightened up and shook her head slightly anyway.

Beck's mouth tightened a little as he handed her the food. "Blake told me to make sure you ate something."

Adriane looked at the plate and then at Beck. "Blake?" she said. "What happened to Garrett, the enemy?"

"He weren't never my enemy. Just the *Tribune*'s. And I reckon the two of you brought all that to an end last night."

Adriane broke off a piece of bread and stared at it. "His

249

man, Calvin, said he had a way of getting things to go his way."

"What're you getting at, Addie?" Beck studied her as he waited for her answer.

"I don't know." Adriane turned her eyes toward the window as though she might see some truth come floating in with the morning sunshine. Finally she said, "I'm just not sure I did the right thing."

"Weren't nothing else to do."

"You mean because of getting the paper out?"

"I don't think the *Tribune* had all that much to do with it, Addie. Or the *Herald* either." Beck's wrinkles softened a bit, but he didn't actually smile.

Adriane stared down at the piece of bread she had reduced to crumbs, and Beck went on. "But if you did just get hitched to keep the paper rolling off the presses, you picked a good man. You should have seen him putting them stories in the galleys straight out of his head. The man knows what makes a good paper same as the boss. I brought one up for you to look at."

Adriane's eyes went from the folded paper still under Beck's arm to her father on the bed. "Do you think we should send for Dr. Hammon again?"

"I'll fetch him if you want me to."

"But you don't think it will do any good."

The old man shook his head sadly as he looked at her. "No, child. I think the boss has done gone off and left us. His body just ain't figured out it's supposed to stop breathing yet."

Adriane didn't try to deny his words. Instead after a moment she asked, "Will you stay with me, Beck?"

"Me and the boss, we go back a long way, Addie. Before you were even born. I ain't going nowhere."

So they waited together. The doctor came, shook his head, and left. A little later, Lucilla made an appearance. She followed Beck up the stairs, but then hung back in the doorway as she offered to send a servant over to help them.

"I've never been good in sickrooms," she said. "The smells, you know." She held a dainty white handkerchief to a face almost as white. "You do understand, don't you?"

"Of course, Lucilla." Adriane quickly ushered her away from the room before the woman fainted.

Once out of sight of the sickbed, Lucilla quickly regained her composure. By the time they reached the bottom of the stairs, the color was back in her cheeks as she turned to Adriane and demanded, "What exactly have you done, Adriane?"

Adriane wasn't sure what she meant until Lucilla pulled a copy of the morning paper out of her reticule and opened it to point at Adriane's new name. Adriane Darcy Garrett.

She kept her eyes on the printed words. She seemed to need to see them to believe it was true as she answered, "I married Blake Garrett last night."

"How could you?" Lucilla looked a bit faint again as she began throwing out questions without giving Adriane time to answer. "What about Stanley? What about your father? And what about your future, my dear? Did you never think of your future?"

"I've thought of little else for weeks. I had no future with Stanley."

"And what kind of future do you expect to have with this man? Especially after this affront to the Jimsons. The *Tribune* cannot survive that. You surely know your father owes a rather substantial amount of money to Coleman, don't you?"

"Yes," Adriane said.

"I won't be able to help you." Lucilla looked truly distressed. "Most of what the late Mr. Elmore left me is tied up in trusts his lawyers handle. Your father understood that and was working out other avenues of repayment."

Adriane felt a deep sadness as she answered, "I know. Poor Father. It seemed so simple to him. I would marry Stanley, and all his problems would be solved."

Lucilla looked at Adriane as though if she only tried hard

enough, she might be able to understand. After a long uncomfortable moment, she said, "My dear, have you been indiscreet? Is that the reason you married Mr. Garrett so hastily?"

For the first time in hours, Adriane felt the seeds of a smile on her lips, but she didn't allow it to grow. "No, Lucilla. I'm still quite pure."

Lucilla's eyes narrowed on her a bit. "And quite foolish." Lucilla jabbed her finger at another spot on the newspaper she still held. "This story is proof of that if nothing else. Even if you did take leave of your senses and venture out on the streets last night, you should have never admitted to that foolhardiness in paper."

"I don't know what you're talking about," Adriane said.

Lucilla read the headline aloud. "Lady risks life to save Irish boy."

Adriane quickly scanned through the story before she looked up at Lucilla and said, "I see no names in the story."

"But it is about you, isn't it, Adriane? You did go out on those streets last night when all decent ladies were locked in their houses on their knees praying."

"I knew Father was in danger. I wanted to warn him."

"Adriane to the rescue," Lucilla said with a wry little smile. "But you didn't save your father, did you?"

When Adriane didn't say anything, Lucilla went on, her voice gentler now. "My dear girl, who is going to save you from your own folly?"

Again Adriane made no answer, and Lucilla put her small slender hand on Adriane's arm. "I will help any way I can, my dear. I am fond of you, but you do understand I can't go against the Jimsons. You should have married Stanley."

Adriane stepped back away from her touch, and Lucilla's hand hovered a moment in the air before she began adjusting her dark blue lace shawl over her lighter blue, crisply pressed, morning dress. After a moment, she said, "Do send a messenger at once if Wade shows the slightest change."

"Of course," Adriane said without smiling. Then as Lucilla turned toward the door, Adriane blurted out, "Do you love my father?"

Lucilla turned back toward Adriane, her small smile appearing to be affixed to her lips much the same way the sapphire brooch was fastened on her collar. "Is that what this is about? Love? My poor dear, you surely weren't foolish enough to throw all your chances away simply because you fancy yourself in love with Mr. Garrett."

As Adriane silently watched Lucilla go out the door, she wondered why she'd even bothered to ask the question. Lucilla would not be leaving if she loved Adriane's father.

Adriane was halfway up the steps when she heard the front door open again, quietly, softly. Thinking it might be Duff, she turned on the stairs and went back down.

But it was not Duff. Instead when she stepped back out into the hall, she almost bumped into Stanley, who was standing in front of the hall mirror checking his hair as she'd seen him do dozens of times when he came to pick her up for a social event. She gasped and stepped back quickly.

"Adriane, my dearest," he said, showing not the least bit of surprise at her sudden appearance beside him. "The very person I wished to see."

Adriane took a deep breath to regain her composure, and when she spoke, it was coldly. "What are you doing here?"

"I wanted you to know how very sorry my father and I both are about your father. It's so unfortunate that he had to be the victim of such random and unreasoned violence."

Adriane stared at him, trying to see through his polished exterior to the truth underneath. He met her eyes as though welcoming her study and even smiled a bit. Suddenly Adriane did see, and her heart began to pound. Stanley's smile grew wider, and she knew he was not only aware of her fear but relishing it.

"You're despicable," she said.

"At last, my dearest, you are beginning to understand me."
He stepped closer to her.

Adriane wanted to run up the stairs away from him, but
she forced her feet to stay planted on the floor as she pointed
toward the door. "I must ask you to leave. You are not welcome in this house."

"But Adriane, my dearest, it is probably more my house
than yours." His smile didn't waver as he moved away from
her to peer into the pressroom and wave his hand toward the
presses. "We the same as own all of this, you know. Unlike
my own father, your father unfortunately has never had much
of a head for business, and now he has failed to deliver the
promised payment." Stanley looked directly at her again, his
eyes traveling slowly up and down her body.

She crossed her arms in front of her in a vain attempt to
hide from his eyes. "Whatever debt is owed your father will
be repaid. You can tell him that."

"I don't think it will be that easy." Stanley casually picked
up one of the papers and scanned the print on the first page.
"I see another poor Irish girl was murdered last night. What a
shame, but I must say I am surprised to see the report on the
front page with so much other news to report. But then your
new editor seems to enjoy stories of young women coming
to a bad end." Stanley looked up at her, and his eyes were
chilling. "Has he told you about Eloise Vandemere?"

"What he has or has not told me is no concern of yours."

"Oh, my dearest Adriane, you couldn't be more wrong. I still
care deeply for you in spite of the heartless way you have spurned
me, and while I certainly don't mean to upset you unduly at
such a time, I would be remiss in my duty to you as a loving
friend if I did not warn you to be careful of our Mr. Garrett. I
believe Miss Vandemere's father owned a newspaper as well."

"Get out, Stanley," Adriane said as forcefully as she could
without raising her voice. "You and I no longer have anything
to say to one another."

"Oh, I have to disagree, my dearest. I believe you are quite wrong on that count. We have a great deal yet to say to each other, and a great deal yet to do, you and I."

He grabbed her, moving so quickly that he had her pinned up against the wall just inside the pressroom before she could much more than gasp. She kicked at his legs and tried to twist loose of his hold, but he only smiled and pushed her harder against the wall. His fingers dug into her upper arms as he pressed his body against hers. "So soft," he whispered as he touched her cheek with his lips.

She couldn't fight him. He was too strong. She stood perfectly still then as she demanded, "Let go of me, Stanley."

"Oh, I'll turn you loose." His laugh sent chills of fear up her back. "When I'm through with you. And not one second before."

"Turn loose of me now," Adriane hissed through clenched teeth.

"Or what?" He looked amused. "Do you think Blake Garrett can protect you? Is that why you married him?"

Adriane stared at him coldly without answering.

"But where is he?" Without loosening his hold on her, Stanley made a pretense of looking around. "I don't see him." He looked back at her. "If I were you, my dear, I wouldn't count too much on Mr. Garrett. Women have counted on him before and ended up dead."

Suddenly Beck was calling to her from the top of the stairs, "Addie! Addie."

At the same time the front door swung open with a bang. Stanley loosened his grip on her arms the slightest bit, and with a sudden, sharp twist, she scrambled away from him. She grabbed the first thing her hands touched, Beck's stool, and held it out between them as Stan reached for her again.

Then Blake was in the doorway. When he saw them, he dropped the boxes he was carrying. Papers with blackened edges spilled out. "What are you doing here, Jimson?" He kicked the papers out of his way as he came into the room.

Stanley straightened his jacket coolly and looked around at Blake. "I might ask you the same question. After all, Adriane was my betrothed yesterday."

Blake's eyes went from Stanley to Adriane still holding up the stool, and a dark angry red appeared in his cheeks. "That was yesterday, Jimson. Today she is my wife."

"So it appears." Stanley casually picked up one of the day's newspapers and studied the masthead. "And it also appears you managed to find a way to publish your version of the news in spite of the unfortunate fire that destroyed your presses last evening."

When Blake took another menacing step toward Stanley as though he might try to squash him like a pesky bug, Adriane dropped the stool and swiftly moved in front of Blake. "Stanley was just leaving," she said.

"Was I?" Stanley asked with a smile, then answered his own question. "Perhaps I was. But you and I, Adriane my dearest, will see one another again." He reached out and touched her cheek as his eyes swept up and down her body again.

Blake moved Adriane aside as if she were no more than a feather to grab Stanley by his coat lapels and propel him out into the hall. "Don't you ever touch my wife again, Jimson," Blake said as he shoved Stanley toward the door.

Stanley stumbled a bit before he caught his balance and looked at Blake coldly. "And you too, my good man, should be extremely careful whom you touch." He straightened his jacket once more, carefully brushing off his arms.

"You don't scare me, Jimson. You're just a little boy playing in his daddy's shadow."

Anger blazed in Stanley's eyes, then as quickly disappeared as he laughed. "You may discover I have my own shadow. One you'd best be careful to not let fall over you or yours." Again Stanley lazily took in Adriane, who had followed them out into the hallway.

Blake's hands curled into fists as he took a step toward

Stanley. "You ever so much as lay a finger on Adriane again, I'll kill you."

"Why, Mr. Garrett, that sounds decidedly like a threat," Stanley said with yet another laugh.

"No threat," Blake said flatly. "A promise."

"Oh, I am frightened," Stanley said. Still smiling, he turned his gaze toward Adriane once more. "Do take care, my dearest. Things are not always as they seem."

With that, he plucked his hat off the hall table and went out the door as though nothing the least untoward had taken place. Adriane looked at Blake, but only met his eyes briefly before she stared down at the floor.

"Did he hurt you?" Blake's voice was gruff.

"No," Adriane lied.

"You shouldn't have let him in." His voice was hard and angry.

Adriane jerked up her head to stare at Blake. "Let him in?" Blood rushed to her face as she felt ready to blow into a thousand pieces. "You think I let him in?"

"He was in here." Blake glared back at her.

Beck appeared at the bottom of the stairs and frowned at the two of them. "I don't know what's going on here, but Addie, you'd best come along. The boss is sinking fast."

24

lake wasn't sure Adriane wanted him beside her, but he followed her up the stairs anyway. He was going to be there when she needed him. And she was going to need him. She might never admit it. She might even fight against it, but she was going to need him. She already had. Just moments ago.

When he'd come in and seen her with Stanley Jimson, Blake had been surprised. Not because Stanley was there. Blake had expected trouble from the Jimsons when they heard about the merging of the *Tribune* and *Herald*. What he hadn't expected was the look on Adriane's face. It was almost as if she'd been afraid, even though Blake couldn't imagine anyone being afraid of Stanley Jimson, who had to be the most useless man ever born. Then when she'd stepped in front of Blake to protect Stanley from him, he'd felt as if a hand had hold of his heart squeezing it.

Even so, he shouldn't have yelled at her. Not when what he really wanted to do was take her into his arms to protect her and shield her from hurt.

Of course, he couldn't. Even now sorrow was barreling down on her with absolutely no way for him to stop it. He could only stand back and watch as Adriane cried and clung to her father's hands while the dying man gasped for breath. The memory of watching his own father struggling to hold on to life stabbed through him sharp and fresh. As if in a dream, he saw Beck put his hand on Adriane's shoulder and say, "Let him go, Addie."

She kept her eyes on her father's face. "I can't."

"You have to," Beck said gently. "It's his time."

Beck's words echoed in Blake's mind. His stepmother had said the same thing when his own father lay on his deathbed, but it hadn't been his father's time. Somebody had stolen his life from him. It had taken Blake years to accept the fact he could do nothing to change that. His father had gotten shot. His father had died.

It was the same with Wade Darcy. It wasn't his time. He had simply fallen victim to the riot that had raged through the city the night before. No amount of tears or regret could change that now. Blake pulled himself away from his memories to kneel beside Adriane. He put his arm firmly around her in case she tried to pull away, but she didn't.

Instead she looked over at him with a hopeless expression on her face. "I shouldn't have left him to go downstairs with Lucilla."

"You're here with him now, Adriane." Blake tightened his arm around her. "Talk to him."

"It's too late," Adriane said.

"No, you still have time. Tell him he was a good father. Tell him how much you love him." Blake looked at the man on the bed. "Make his leaving good."

Haltingly at first, she did as he said.

Darcy's breath stopped coming in gasps, and then it stopped coming at all as the man seemed to slip away from them like a raft pulling loose from a tree to slide away down the river.

Adriane jerked away from Blake, threw herself across her father's chest, and cried, "Oh Father, I'm so sorry. It's all my fault. I should have done what you wanted me to do."

Blake began to feel as if he'd come in during the middle of a play and didn't know what was going on as he watched Beck grab Adriane's shoulders and pull her up until she was looking directly at his face. "Ain't none of this your fault, Addie. You didn't shoot the boss."

"I could've kept it from happening, Beck." Adriane's face was bleak as she stared at the old man. "You know that."

"Hush now, Addie." Beck gently stroked her hair back from her face. "There ain't no going back and doing things over. You can't bring him back. He's in the good Lord's hands now."

Long after Beck pulled the sheet up over Wade Darcy's face, Blake wondered about their words, but this was not the time for questions about why Darcy died, even if he'd known what questions to ask.

An undertaker came and managed to politely refuse to deliver a coffin until Blake gave the man nearly every bit of money he had left. He'd have to find a way to pay the hands and buy more newsprint later.

The undertaker had taken Wade Darcy's measurements and was leaving when an old black woman named Mary showed up, saying Mrs. Elmore had sent her to help care for the sick. When the woman saw the undertaker, she shook her head sadly and told Adriane, "Now don't you be worryin', child. I knows how to take care of them that have gone on too. I'll help you lay him out proper."

After the black woman went to the kitchen to heat water, a heavy silence fell over the three of them gathered around Wade Darcy's body. Adriane sat like a statue in the chair next to the bed, her face nearly as white as the sheet covering her father's body. She looked so lost and alone Blake wanted to scoop her up out of the chair and carry her away from this pain.

But when he suggested she might want to lie down and rest a few moments, she didn't even look at him as she said, "I have to take care of Father first."

Blake started to tell her that this woman, Mary, could get the body ready without Adriane's help, but he knew she did not want to be spared this last painful task. So he only said, "Somebody will have to write his obituary."

"There's one on file downstairs." Adriane's voice was flat and controlled. "Father wrote a fresh copy every January on his birthday. He said an editor had to be prepared for any eventuality and that it was a foolish man who counted on someone else to tell the truth about his life." Adriane looked down at her hands tightly clasped in her lap before she went on. "I don't know whether Father told the truth or not, but Beck can read it and make whatever corrections might need to be made."

"Addie, you should do that," Beck said softly.

"No, I won't be able to help with the paper today."

"We surely won't be putting out no paper today," Beck said.

"The readers expect a paper every day," Adriane said. "No matter what happens."

Blake spoke up. "We'll do one page, bordered in black. We'll split the page, print Wade Darcy's obituary on one side, John Chesnut's on the other as the headline stories. I owe that much to Chesnut, at the very least. We can fill in the rest of the space with reports on last night's damage."

"Put in something about Duff's sister." Adriane raised her eyes to stare at a spot on the wall somewhere above her father's body. "You promised him we'd find a way to catch the murderer."

"Ain't nobody going to be too interested in that right now with all this other madness going on," Beck said.

"The murderer might be." Adriane's eyes came away from the spot on the wall to look not at Beck, but at Blake.

"What do you mean?" Blake asked.

A bit of color was inching back into her cheeks. "You could print a report that somebody saw Lila with a man last night before she was murdered."

"How do you know somebody saw them, Addie?" Beck asked.

"I don't," Adriane said.

"But somebody might have. There were a lot of people on the streets." Blake's eyes locked on hers as he considered her words.

Beck was forgotten, something that didn't seem to upset him as he said, "I reckon I'll leave the two of you to figure out what lies we aim to print and go get the presses ready."

"It could be dangerous for Duff," Blake said after Beck went downstairs.

"You mean because the murderer might know Lila was Duff's sister?" Adriane said.

"And that he works for the *Tribune*."

"What do you think the murderer would do if he thought somebody might be able to identify him?"

"He might go into hiding for a while. He might leave town and go to some other city and prey on the girls there." Blake's eyes burned into Adriane's. "Or he might try to kill whoever he thought might have seen him."

All the color drained from Adriane's face again. Finally she asked, "Do you think we could protect Duff?"

"Nobody is needing to protect me." Duff spoke up from the doorway. "I can be taking care of me self."

The boy's face was as pale with grief as Adriane's. Yet he grew even paler as he looked at the sheet covered form on the bed and twisted his hat in his hands. "Beck told me about the boss. I come up here to tell you how sorry I am, Miss Adriane."

"Did Beck tell you what else we were talking about?" Blake asked.

"He said you were trying to figure a way to be bringing the slasher out in the open by printing some story about there being a witness who saw me sister with the murderer." Duff stared first at Adriane then Blake. "There weren't none, were there?"

"Not that we know of," Blake said. "But if we were to print a story that there was and the murderer knew who Lila was, he might think it was you."

"He'd know it was. All the folks down my way are always saying they can't even spit without me noticing and writing it up in the paper."

"It's too risky." Adriane spoke up with her eyes on Duff.

Before Blake could agree, Duff said, "It's me what will be taking the risk, Miss Adriane, and I'm wanting to do it. I ain't sure it might not even be true. I might be knowing the killer if I saw him."

Blake looked at him sharply. "You think you might have really seen him then?"

"I didn't say that, sir. I said I think I'd be knowing him if I saw him now with me sister's blood staining his hands. It won't matter how much he scrubs his hands, I'll see it."

So Blake wrote the story even though he feared Duff was too young to understand the dangers. The boy only knew his need for revenge.

Blake understood. He'd felt the same way after his father died. Like Duff, he'd been consumed with the need to find the man who had shot his father. He couldn't sleep at night for thinking about how he would confront and kill the man. During the days, he walked the streets, sure somehow that if he saw the man face-to-face, he'd know he was the one who had shot his father. Before long, he found reasons to suspect every man he met. If his stepmother hadn't packed him off to New York to work for one of his father's friends, Blake wasn't sure what might have happened.

He wasn't sure what might happen now either, but he had a bad feeling about it all as he laid the type in the galleys. Duff had left again. It was going to be impossible to keep an eye on the boy the way he slipped in and out.

He said as much to Beck when they took the first galley proof off the press, and they were standing side by side scanning the stories.

"The boy knows how to take care of himself," Beck said as if to convince himself as well as Blake.

"But this is asking for trouble." Blake poked at the small headline down toward the bottom of the last column.

"'First lead in river slasher murders,'" Beck read aloud. "'A witness has come forward claiming to have seen two of the unfortunate girls with the same man shortly before they were murdered. When asked why he had not come forward previously, the witness claims to have tried to describe the man to the police but could get none of the officers to listen. This reporter has been unable to obtain Chief Trabue's comments on this new development due to the tragic events of the last day.'"

Beck stopped reading and said, "You'll hear from Trabue about that." Beck looked at Blake. "And probably the mayor as well."

"I wouldn't doubt it," Blake said. "Not that it matters all that much. You and I both know they're going to do their best to run me out of town no matter what we print."

Beck's eyes narrowed on Blake. "I heard they run you out of New York City too. Any truth to that?"

"Nobody ran me out. I just left."

"You made some enemies," Beck said.

"I did." Blake didn't try to explain. If Beck didn't trust him for who he was, he wasn't going to be convinced by a lot of words about a poor girl who had thrown herself off a cliff rather than stay in an unhappy marriage.

Beck didn't ask any more questions as he turned his eyes back to the paper. "The boss would have liked the black edging. Though I ain't so sure what he'd have thought about the masthead. The *Tribune-Herald*." Beck shook his head. "It's sort of like seeing a two-headed cow at the circus. You keep wondering if maybe it ain't just your eyes playing tricks on you."

"He was a good newspaperman before he got so far under

Coleman Jimson's thumb." Blake ran his fingers across the masthead. "He might have seen the two papers could be greater merged than either of them could be by themselves."

"Except you just got through saying Jimson will be finding a way to shut us down before that can happen." Beck looked up at Blake.

"Unless we can stop him," Blake said.

"We won't be able to stop him," Adriane said from the door of the pressroom. "Father owed him too much money."

Blake turned to look at her. "How much?" he asked.

"A lot, I think. Father was never very good with finances. Beck can tell you that."

"That's a fact. The boss was always too ready to buy some newfangled piece of equipment." Beck sighed and mashed his lips together.

"It doesn't matter," Adriane said. "Even if we had the money, that's not what Coleman Jimson wants. It was never the money. It was the paper."

"He's won the election already," Beck said.

"There will be other elections," Adriane said. "I fancy he'd like being called governor."

"Over my dead body," Blake said with fervor.

Adriane's face went pale at his words. "I'm sure he could find a way to arrange that. For all he cared, you might have been in your building last night when it burned."

"True enough. He was probably hoping I was, but I wasn't. And though the election may be over, the fight's not."

"No," Adriane agreed. "Father's death should give us a little sympathy time. He won't pitch us out of his building for a couple of weeks and another newspaper office burning down might look suspicious, even to his supporters."

"He won't forget," Blake said.

"Neither will we," Adriane answered. "And we won't run."

"I don't run from fights." Blake faced her squarely as if expecting a fight right then. "I never have."

265

"Jimson won't have to burn the building down," Beck said as he looked first at Blake, then Adriane. "The way you two strike sparks off one another, you're liable as not to set it on fire yourself."

Adriane dropped her eyes to the floor for a moment before she looked up at the old man. Blake was amazed to see what was almost a smile on her face. "Oh, print the papers, Beck, and hurry up. I just came down here to tell you to let us know when Mr. Mortimer gets here with the coffin. We're going to have Father in here for people to pay their respects."

Beck looked around the pressroom before he said, "The boss would like that, Addie, but I don't know that Mrs. Elmore will think it's proper."

"Proper or not, that's what's happening. If Lucilla is too scandalized, she can stay away." There was no hint of doubt in Adriane's voice. Then her shoulders drooped as she went on. "Added to all the other scandalous things I've done in the last two days, it should keep the gossips happily buzzing for weeks."

25

*I*t was true. Adriane could almost hear the scandalized whispers sweeping through the parlors and drawing rooms. Have you heard what that Adriane Darcy has done now?

She didn't care what anybody said, she thought as she quickly left the pressroom before Beck could think about pushing the paper he was holding at her. Even from across the room, she could see the thick black borders around the page. That by itself was enough to make her heart feel too heavy. She knew her father was dead. Hadn't she just helped dress him in his best for his funeral?

Still, she was afraid that if she saw her father's words telling about his own death, she wouldn't be able to keep back the tears pushing at her eyes. She couldn't cry now. There was too much to be done. No, she'd have to wait until sometime when she could be alone. Then she'd read it.

She didn't think about when that might be, now that she was a married woman. It was hard for her to think about being married at all. None of it seemed real. Not the ceremony. Not Blake and Beck working together on the same paper. Not the funny light-headed feeling she'd had when Blake swept her

267

up in his arms and kissed her after the preacher pronounced them man and wife. None of it.

It was almost as if she were walking around in a dream. Soon she'd wake up and everything would be the way it was before. Her father would be in his office firing off another volley of words against the *Herald*. Blake would be in his office doing the same against the *Tribune*. Stanley would still be expecting her to marry him.

And that's where the dream dissolved and became a nightmare. A nightmare that was only too real. Even now, hours later, Adriane could still feel Stanley's fingers bruising her arms. She could see the look in his eyes when he'd said how sorry he was about her father and hear his words as he'd warned her about Blake. The words were burned into her mind. Who was this Eloise Vandemere? What had happened to her?

Adriane wearily shook her head, but she couldn't shake the questions away. She loved Blake Garrett. There was no use trying to hide from that fact, but it was just as true that she knew very little about Blake before he came to Louisville. What if he didn't turn out to be the kind of man she thought he was, just as Stanley Jimson had turned out to be completely different than she'd thought? A few months ago she would have never believed Stanley would physically attack her.

She told herself Blake was not Stanley. And while she might not know a lot of things about Blake and his past, she did know him. There were times when their eyes met that she felt almost as if she were inside his mind and he inside hers. At moments like that, nothing was hidden.

"You look plumb wilted, missy," Mary told her when she went back into her father's bedroom where his body waited for the undertaker to arrive with the coffin. "You go freshen up, and I'll sit with Mr. Darcy."

"I can't. I'll need to clean the pressroom downstairs when they're through running the papers."

"Don't you be worryin' yo' head about that. Me and the menfolk will take care of what needs doin'. You go on along and get cleaned up cause you wants to be ready when folks start comin' by to pay their respects to yo' pappy."

Adriane did what the old black woman said. It felt odd going back into her room and looking at the familiar furniture and books and knowing that since she'd last slept there everything had changed. At her small desk, she opened her journal and dipped her pen in the inkpot. She stared at the empty page so long the ink dried on the nib of the pen. Finally she laid the pen aside and closed the book. Just as she couldn't yet read the words, she couldn't yet write them.

Instead she laid her hand on her Bible. She didn't open it, but words seemed to rise up out of it to comfort her. *Yea, though I walk through the valley of the shadow of death, I will fear no evil: for thou art with me.*

What had Beck told her? That her father was in the Lord's hands now. He was right. Her father was gone. But she couldn't keep from thinking he might still be alive if she had done something differently. If Duff had posted the letter instead of delivering it. If there had been time to warn her father. If only her father had truly known Stanley, then he wouldn't have promised her to him and perhaps none of this would have happened. If only.

Another Bible verse rose up in her mind. One Beck or Grace had once taught her. She didn't remember which. *Trust in the Lord with all thine heart; and lean not unto thine own understanding.*

Adriane raised her eyes toward the ceiling. "I don't understand, Lord."

Then trust. The words came unbidden to her mind. She could trust the Lord. She could trust Beck. But could she trust Blake?

Wearily she stood up and pulled her good black dress out of the wardrobe and laid it across the bed. She stripped off down to her chemise and drawers. She had just poured cold water from the pitcher into the bowl and begun to sponge off when there was a knock on her door.

Before she could reach for her wrapper, Blake pushed through the door, his arms full of the same boxes he'd been carrying when he'd come in earlier to find Stanley in the pressroom. For a minute, Adriane thought he might drop them again as his eyes swept over her.

"You're so beautiful," he said, his voice strangely husky.

Her cheeks burned as she grabbed her wrapper.

"Don't," he said. "You're my wife. I can look at you."

"It's not the time," Adriane said softly as she pulled on the wrapper.

"Perhaps not." He took a deep breath and seemed to remember the boxes he was still holding. "We were clearing out the pressroom, and I thought maybe I could store these up here somewhere till I get a chance to go through them. I'm afraid they smell of smoke."

"You can put them by the desk," she said.

After he set the boxes on the floor, he stood up and looked around. "The room's small," he said, his eyes on the bed.

"It's large enough for me," she said.

His eyes came back to her. "But now there are two of us."

"Yes." Color bloomed in her cheeks once more. He did seem to fill up all the empty space in the room until the walls needed to give way.

"We'll work out something," he said.

"I can sleep on the settee in the sitting room," she offered.

"I hardly think so." He didn't quite smile, but looked as if he wanted to.

"You promised me time."

"No, Adriane," he said. "I promised you would never have any reason to be afraid of me. You don't now."

One step and he was beside her. She gripped the wrapper closer to her, but he gently pulled her hands away. "I'm not going to hurt you," he said. "I just want to see your arm. It looked as if you had a bruise there."

She couldn't fight with him. She didn't want to fight him. She let him peel the thin wrapper off her shoulders and down her arms, and wanted nothing more than to lean against his chest and rest there for a while. To trust him completely. She was so tired, and the tips of his fingers touching her were so gentle.

Yet she couldn't keep from flinching when he ran his fingers over the place on her arm where Stanley had grabbed her.

"How'd you do that?" Blake asked.

When Adriane saw the marks of Stanley's fingers on her arm, she tried to pull her wrapper up to hide them, but Blake wouldn't let her. He pushed down the other sleeve of her wrapper, with not quite as much care this time, to reveal a bruise on that arm as well.

"Who did this to you?" he asked.

She looked down at the floor as she desperately tried to think of some way to explain the marks. She couldn't tell him the truth, because if she did he might want to go after Stanley, and that thought terrified her.

Blake put his hand under her chin and gently but insistently raised her face until she had to look at him. Even then she tried to shield the truth by not directly meeting his eyes.

He saw it anyway. "Jimson?" he said as if he couldn't quite believe it was possible. "Stanley Jimson did that to you?"

"It doesn't matter." Adriane hastily pulled her wrapper back up to hide the marks. "He's gone now. You sent him away. They're only bruises. They'll fade."

The color drained from Blake's face, and his features turned to granite. "I'll kill him."

She grabbed his arm as he started to turn away. "Please, Blake. There's already been too much killing."

His eyes were hard, and his voice rough as he said, "What's going on here, Adriane? Are you telling me you care what happens to Jimson?"

"No." Her own anger flared up to match his. She was no longer even aware of the fact that her wrapper hung open and her chemise was half unlaced. "But I won't be the reason for another man dying. I won't."

"So I'm just supposed to pretend I haven't seen those." His eyes flicked down to her arms and back to her face. "I'm supposed to forget that he hurt you."

"He won't come back." She tried to sound surer about that than she felt.

"How do you know?"

"He has too much pride."

"Then why did he come today?"

At last she dropped her eyes away from his, but again he lifted her face and made her look at him. "Why did he come?" he asked again.

"He was angry. He didn't think I'd really refuse to marry him to begin with and then . . ."

"And then you not only turned him down, you married me?"

"Yes."

Blake's eyes probed hers. "What did he tell you about me?"

"Nothing much." Adriane didn't want to think about the doubts Stanley had tried to put into her mind. But the name was there. Eloise Vandemere.

"You can't keep secrets from me, Adriane. Not now."

His eyes demanded the truth. She could give him no less. "He told me that I shouldn't count on you too much. That other women who trusted you had ended up dead."

"Did you believe him?"

"I don't know what to believe, Blake. I hardly know you."

His eyes on her were intense. "Yet you married me."

"Yes," she said.

"Why?"

"You asked me to."

Suddenly without warning, he smiled. "So I did."

Relief flooded through Adriane at the sight of his smile. She put her hand on his arm. "Promise me you won't go after Stanley."

His smile disappeared. "I don't understand, Adriane."

"My father is dead because I refused to marry Stanley."

"You think Stanley Jimson had something to do with your father getting shot?"

"I know he did," Adriane said.

"Then why are you trying to protect him?"

"I'm not protecting him," Adriane said. "I'm trying to protect us."

"Us?" Blake looked confused for a moment, then a look of wonder came into his eyes. "You're afraid for me?"

"You don't know Stanley. He's not as he seems."

Blake's smile came back. "I can take care of myself, Adriane. Especially against the likes of Stanley Jimson. We're not talking about his father here."

"No, we're not." She looked at him squarely with determination setting her jaw. "But you have to promise me anyway."

Again his smile disappeared as he studied her thoughtfully. "I don't make promises I can't keep," he said finally. "But I will promise you to wait until we have time to talk about what's going on, because there's more here than I know about."

"And more than I know about as well."

"What do you mean?"

"Eloise Vandemere." The name spilled from her lips before she could think better of saying it.

"What did Jimson tell you about her?" His voice sounded stiff suddenly.

"Nothing. He just said I should ask you about her."

"So now you have."

Adriane looked at him a moment while the barbs of doubt Stanley had planted in her mind dug deeper. "What happened to her?"

"I don't talk about Eloise."

"I see," Adriane said after a moment. She pulled her wrapper tight around her and tied it before she went on in a tightly controlled voice. "If you'll excuse me, I need to dress now."

She thought he might refuse to leave, that instead he might reach out and take her into his arms. For a moment she wanted him to. She wanted to just disappear into his strong arms and forget all the pain.

Yet she couldn't forget. Not her father. Not Stanley Jimson. Not even Eloise Vandemere, a woman Adriane didn't even know, because suddenly her shadow had moved into the room with them. So instead of stepping nearer to him the way she wanted to, she deliberately turned away and picked up her clothes brush to begin stroking the skirt of her black dress.

When Blake left the room without a word, she wanted to call him back, but she bit her lip and was quiet. What could she say anyway? That she loved him and she didn't care what he might have done in the past? That she trusted him without any kind of explanations? That would be the same as asking for more hurt, and didn't she have enough pain pushing down on her already? She had to be satisfied that he was not storming out of the building in search of Stanley.

Then a fearsome thought poked into her mind, and she sank down on the bed. Stanley might come after Blake. As panic began climbing back up inside her, she reminded herself that whatever Stanley had caused to happen the night before during the riots, he had not meant for her father to die. It had been meant as a warning, a way of forcing Adriane to do as he wanted.

Adriane shut her eyes and carefully pulled back into her mind the exact expression on Stanley's face when he had talked about Blake. Stan had looked calm, almost amused that Adriane would be foolish enough to marry a man like Blake Garrett when she could have married him. He wanted

Adriane to pay for that mistake. That was why he'd tried to poison her mind against Blake and find a way to destroy them both.

She'd told Blake the truth when she said Stanley came to the house that morning because of his wounded pride. She had not told the truth when she'd said he wouldn't come back. The next time she'd have to be ready.

With that thought, Adriane stood up and began methodically washing in the basin of cold water. She pulled the black dress over her head and fastened the buttons. She stood in front of the small mirror on the wall and caught her hair back in a tight bun. As she tucked a few loose strands in place with a couple of combs, she wished all the thoughts shooting around inside her head were as easy to tuck away.

She dropped her hands and stood a moment staring into the mirror. The face staring back at her was pale and drawn, the eyes heavy with the pain of unshed tears. She tightened her mouth and blinked back the tears.

So what if there were unanswered questions. She couldn't worry about that right now. She had to worry about making it through the rest of this day and through tomorrow when they would put her father in the ground. After all that was done would be soon enough to worry about being married to Blake Garrett and who this Eloise Vandemere was.

If she wanted to worry about something else right now, she told herself she should worry about Duff and his mother and sisters. Adriane wasn't the only one to lose a loved one this day. Grief hung over the city like the lingering smoke of the burned buildings.

For a moment she imagined she could even smell the smoke though her window was not open. Then she remembered the boxes of files Blake had placed on the floor beside the desk. She looked at them and wondered what clues they might hold to Blake's past.

She was still staring at the boxes when Mary tapped lightly on the door and said, "Miss Lucilla is downstairs, missy. And the undertaker's here. Is you needing help with dressing?"

"No, I'm ready." Adriane turned away from the boxes to the door.

26

By early evening, people had run out of places to sit or stand in the pressroom, and they were spilling out into the hall and kitchen. Some men even clustered in groups in the street in front of the building. Inside, Lucilla's parlor chairs that had looked so out of place in the bare, unadorned room had long since disappeared under the dark full skirts of the ladies who had come with their husbands to pay their respects to Wade Darcy.

Lucilla had not been happy with the arrangement, but she'd given in gracefully when Adriane refused to listen to her pleas to consider a more sensible location. She'd not only sent the chairs but had supplied the food spread on the kitchen table and two more servants to open the door to visitors.

Lucilla, in a high-necked black dress that tightly molded her tiny waist, sat in a padded wing chair pulled up close to the coffin so that she could spring up to greet each new arrival. She would stand with them and peer down at Adriane's father and dab at her eyes with a black bordered handkerchief.

Lucilla's grieving widow act didn't bother Adriane. In fact, Adriane thought her father would have been pleased by the woman's show of tears. He would have been impressed by all the mourners as well.

Adriane stood to the side of her father's coffin and looked around the crowded room. She should have done as Lucilla wanted. It had been silly, childish even, to insist on having her father's body laid out here in the pressroom just because that was where she'd always felt closest to him.

The truth was, the room was entirely too small even after they'd moved everything out except the press, which Beck had draped with black crepe. Now it loomed there in the middle of the room like some kind of brooding ogre standing guard over her father's body. The people closest to it kept glancing around uneasily as if afraid the thing might begin to inch their way.

The two windows were also draped with black cloth, and though the gas lamps were turned up high, the room was murky with shadows. Lucilla and a few of the other ladies had brought in gladiolus and rose bouquets from their gardens, but the flowers brought no feeling of cheer. Instead their abundance emphasized that this was a room of death.

All around Adriane small groups of men gathered in the midst of the flowers to talk about the riots. They kept their voices hushed in respect for the dead, but occasionally a man would forget and speak too loudly, allowing a scrap of sentence to escape.

"Irish shot first."

"Protect themselves . . ."

". . . Fair election."

"Immigrants have to earn the right to vote."

Adriane almost expected her father to sit up in his coffin and add his voice to the discussions. In any group, he was always the most vocal, the best at defending whatever position he picked for the *Tribune* to espouse. It didn't seem possible his voice had been silenced forever.

Once more Adriane mashed down the sadness that threatened to push her tears out into the open. She couldn't give in to her grief now. Too many of the women were watching her, even as they talked every bit as busily as the men. While they kept their mouths hidden behind their fans and handkerchiefs, their words were easy enough to guess as they cast furtive glances at Blake, who had stayed by Adriane's side, close enough to touch, ever since they'd begun receiving visitors.

Adriane liked him there in spite of the way people's eyes widened when they saw them together. Or perhaps because of it. What was it Lucilla had said? That Adriane liked to shock people. Still that wasn't the only reason Adriane liked Blake beside her, and she wanted him to stay there in spite of the questions he had refused to answer, that he might never answer.

"He shouldn't have come tonight," Blake suddenly whispered more to himself than to her.

"Who? Duff?" Adriane asked as she spotted the boy in the doorway, looking around with wide eyes at the people crowded into the room.

"Everybody in here will know he's Irish," Blake said.

"What if they do? He belongs here." She felt a flash of anger, but kept her voice low as she looked at Blake, daring him to deny it.

"I know that." His eyes stayed on Duff. "I find it a little surprising considering your father's politics, but that's hardly the issue right now."

"What is?" She turned her eyes back to Duff.

"The piece in tomorrow's paper about someone seeing the same man with two of the victims on the nights they were killed." Blake held his hand up as though to motion the boy back. Beck must have noticed, because he was beside Duff at once.

"I haven't read it yet," Adriane said as they watched Beck put his arm around the boy and lead him off toward the kitchen.

"I kept it vague, but it may have been a mistake to put it in at all." Blake looked worried.

"Why? You've been printing stories in the *Herald* about the murders for months. Everybody will just think this is something else you've dug up, maybe even made up, to keep the murders before the public eye."

"As a matter of fact, it is." Blake twisted his mouth to the side to hide a little smile. "Something I made up, I mean. But some readers never doubt the printed word, and the murderer, whoever he is, will surely have some concerns that there might be some truth to the report."

"Isn't that what we wanted? To make the murderer so worried that he might tip his hand?"

Blake looked down at her. "Yes, but I'd rather people didn't give my witness a name, especially Duff's name. But here he is. An Irish street kid, the likeliest witness there could be, even without adding in the fact that one of the victims was his sister. They'll remember seeing him here when they read the story in the paper tomorrow and will put two and two together to figure out he's our witness."

"Surely you don't think anyone in here could be the murderer," Adriane said with shock as she quickly looked around at the people in the room. "Or even might know the murderer."

"He's in some room somewhere."

"But not here," Adriane insisted. "These men are businessmen and gentlemen."

"Gentlemen are not always as they seem," he reminded her. "You think one of them is the reason your father is dead."

"Stanley's no gentleman," Adriane said coldly.

"We can agree on that." Blake's voice was almost a growl. "But just as his fancy clothes and parlor manners with the ladies hide his true nature, so others who dress in dark suits and knot their cravat properly may not be as they seem."

"But the river slasher is a monster," Adriane said.

"A monster who probably looks like any other man."

Adriane's eyes swept around the room again. She knew most of these men. They were ordinary businessmen who would be ready to defend themselves and their honor at the drop of a hat, but murder? That was different.

Then again some of these very men could have been part of the mob roaming the streets during the riot, and a goodly number of those men had fired their guns and taken lives without remorse.

Adriane's eyes went back to her father's body. Who would have thought Stanley Jimson would cause this to happen? Not that she believed Stanley had actually shot her father himself or even meant for her father to die, but that didn't change the fact her father was dead.

But those actions, as bad as they were, couldn't compare to the heinous crimes of the river slasher. None of these men could possibly be the murderer.

Nevertheless Adriane looked toward the door that led out through the hall to the kitchen and wished Duff had not come. She wouldn't be able to bear it if something happened to him because of what they'd printed. Whatever that was. Adriane suddenly wanted to go in search of a copy of the newspaper to read the piece herself and try to gauge the danger those printed words might pose for Duff.

She might have done just that if at that very moment Coleman Jimson hadn't come through the door, his voice booming out greetings in every direction. People stopped talking and looked up. Lucilla cast a near panicked look over her shoulder at Adriane before she patted her lips with her black-edged hankie, touched her hair to be sure no strand had escaped its pins, and hurried to greet the man.

Blake's muscles tightened as he stepped closer to Adriane. Beck appeared at the kitchen door, and Joe pushed away from the wall in the back of the room.

"It's all right, Blake," Adriane whispered. "He won't pitch us out on the street tonight."

"You forget he's already found a way to pitch me out on the street," Blake said.

Adriane slipped her hand through Blake's elbow and leaned closer to him. "You're not on the street now, and tonight we have to call a truce in honor of my father's memory. That's why Coleman Jimson is here."

"That's a laugh. He's still campaigning."

"He has no need to campaign now. He won the election," Adriane reminded him. "Promise me you won't make trouble."

"Me?" Blake looked at her. "You should want to see the Jimsons in trouble as much as I do."

"Yes, but not tonight," Adriane said quietly as she watched Coleman Jimson move up beside Lucilla to view her father's body. "Tonight I must respect my father's friendship with the man."

Every eye in the room was on Coleman Jimson as he looked down at Wade Darcy and sadly shook his head. "He was a fine man." Though his voice was no longer booming, no one in the room had to strain to hear his words. He patted Lucilla's shoulder. "You would have had a wonderful life together. Such a tragedy for you, dear lady."

Real tears appeared in Lucilla's eyes, and all around them, ladies sniffled and rummaged in their reticules for fresh handkerchiefs. Even some of the men lifted a hand up to brush away a tear or two. Adriane watched dry-eyed. She would grieve, even perhaps give in to the flood of tears inside her in time, but not because of anything Coleman Jimson had to say.

At that moment Coleman turned toward her, and Adriane met his look fully. She had been prepared to face his anger since she had put his family in an embarrassing situation by marrying Blake. She was not prepared for the genuine disappointment, even sorrow in his eyes.

"Adriane, my girl," he said as he came over to take her hands in his. "You can't possibly know how sorry I am about all this. Your father was one of my closest advisors and friends, and I will sorely miss his presence by my side and his always sound advice on the issues."

"You're very kind to say so," Adriane murmured. She started to ease her hands away, but he held tighter.

"And this other." He paused a moment as he let his eyes go to Blake and then back to her before he said, "I do hope you will be happy with Mr. Garrett, but you must be aware how greatly it saddens me and all of our family. We had so looked forward to you becoming one of us."

Adriane kept her eyes on Coleman Jimson's face as a flush warmed into her cheeks. "I fear I must beg your forgiveness for any inconvenience breaking my engagement to Stanley may have caused you and Mrs. Jimson, but we discovered we had differences that made marriage impossible."

The man raised his thick black eyebrows a bit as he said, "It appears you did not find marriage to someone else nearly as reprehensible."

Adriane could almost feel Blake tensing for an attack beside her. She pulled one of her hands free of Coleman Jimson's grasp and laid it on Blake's arm in what she hoped was a calming gesture. "Mr. Garrett and I have much in common."

Blake spoke at last. "I'm sure Mr. Jimson has little interest in what we might have in common, Adriane. Our new senator has much more important issues about which to concern himself."

Jimson smiled slightly at Blake. "How right you are for once, Mr. Garrett." His eyes came back to Adriane. "And I certainly had no intention of taking you to task for your decision, Adriane, especially at a time like this. I only wanted to let you know how disappointed we are. Not that I can say I'm surprised. I never had much confidence in Stanley's ability to get a woman like you to marry him."

Adriane wasn't the only one shocked by his plain words if the sudden hush around the room was any indication. She tried to smooth over what he said. "I'm sure Stanley will find a lovely girl much more suitable for him than I could ever be."

"Perhaps so." Coleman sighed and shook his head as

though to deny the words he'd just spoken. A long moment passed as he continued to stare at her with his practiced smile, even as his eyes grew cold. At last he lowered his voice and went on. "But of course, you must realize the broken engagement does cause a few embarrassing problems for us all."

"Yes, I'm aware of that." Adriane also lowered her voice, but she knew the people around them were leaning closer to hear every word. "And it is most kind of you to wait to discuss those troublesome matters until after my father's funeral. His death was such a terrible shock that I haven't been able to think about the future." She did her best to appeal to his sympathy. "You do understand, don't you?"

"Perfectly, my dear." Again the man looked almost sad as he squeezed her hand, but then the sympathy disappeared from his eyes. "As I am sure you can understand that my own situation is a bit awkward, to say the least. I can hardly continue to back a paper that condemns me so roundly."

Blake spoke up again. "You surely have no fear of an open discussion of the issues, Senator Jimson, especially now that the votes have been counted. At least the votes of those who were allowed into the polls."

Coleman Jimson's eyes went from Adriane to Blake. "No fear at all, my good man." He paused as if waiting for Blake to say more. When he didn't, Jimson raised his eyebrows and went on. "It's too bad about your building, Garrett. One of your hired hands must have been careless with a lantern."

"Someone was careless, at any rate," Blake said.

The tension crackled the air between the two men, and Adriane was sure that at any moment, Blake would lose his stiff control and take a swing at the other man. She had the feeling Jimson hoped that would happen.

She stepped forward a bit to put herself between them as she said, "It was very kind of you to come pay your respects to my father, Mr. Jimson, and as for this other, we will be glad to meet with you day after tomorrow at your convenience.

Just send around a message as to the time." Adriane pushed a small smile out on her face.

"As you wish, my dear. I'm sure we can work out an amicable agreement."

"Does he own the press?" Blake asked softly after the man moved away.

"I don't know." Adriane was suddenly so tired she wasn't sure she'd be able to keep from swaying as she stood there. "Probably."

Blake peered down at her. "Forget Jimson. He's not important. What you need is something to eat." He put his arm around her and turned her toward the kitchen.

"I can't eat," Adriane protested. "Not now."

"Of course, you can," Blake said briskly. Then his eyes softened on her. "It won't be as hard as you think. I'll be right beside you."

She knew he was no longer talking about food, but she smiled a little anyway as she said, "To help me eat?"

He didn't smile back. "I'll spoon-feed you if I have to."

Adriane's own small smile slipped away as she stared up at him. "He's going to put us out on the street."

Blake's jaw set in a rigid line. "He's going to try."

27

The black-bordered second issue of the *Tribune-Herald* announcing the deaths of the two news warriors, Wade Darcy and John Chesnut, was carried out to the streets by the newsboys the next morning before daylight. A few hours later, a little before noon, Wade Darcy's body was carried out to the cemetery.

By the time they lowered his coffin into the ground, Adriane just wanted it to be over. She had insisted on keeping the long, lonely vigil by her father's body throughout the night, and now dazed by both her grief and lack of sleep, she felt surrounded by a thick, gray fog. She knew the preacher was talking, but his words were nothing more than a muddled mixture of sounds that made no sense to her ears. When he finally stopped and looked at her, it was a long moment before Adriane realized he was waiting for her to drop the first handful of dirt on her father's coffin in the grave.

As the loose dirt scattered and danced on the wooden surface, Adriane had to force her feet to move away from the grave and allow Lucilla to take her turn.

People followed them back to the house, where Lucilla's servants, under Lucilla's direction, saw that they were fed. Adriane sat in a straight chair in the shadow of the press and wished them all gone. She wasn't sure how many more sorrowful smiles or sweaty pats on her hands she could endure.

Blake brought her a plate of food, but when she pushed it aside, he carried it away without a word. He left her alone until all the people were gone. Then he came back and, still without a word, pulled her to her feet and ushered her toward the stairs.

When she saw the set, determined look on his face, she went with him meekly. She couldn't fight him even if he was about to demand his rights as her husband. She was so exhausted it was all she could do to push her feet up the steps, and before they got to the top, Blake was nearly carrying her.

In her room, she stood silent and waited submissively for whatever might happen next, but all he said was "You need to sleep."

When she just stared at him without moving, he went on matter-of-factly. "Do you need help undressing?"

His words were like a dash of cold water in her face. "No, I can manage," she said.

He looked at her a long moment. "That's your trouble, Adriane. You always think you can manage without help, but the truth of it is that neither one of us can manage without the other anymore. We need each other."

"You don't need me. You need the press." Adriane wasn't sure where the words came from, but she wished them back as soon as they were out.

Color exploded in his cheeks. "Blast the press. It's not even yours. It's Jimson's." Then as quickly as it had come, the storm left his face, and he went on in a flat voice. "You're tired. I'm tired. Let's just let it go right now. We can fight tomorrow."

"Will we fight?" She stared up at him.

"About some things." The beginnings of a smile turned up the corners of his mouth. "Maybe a lot of things, but we'll make it, Adriane. It's going to turn out all right."

"How can you be so sure?"

"I don't know. Just a newsman's hunch, but what kind of newspaperman doesn't have a few hunches that turn out to be right." The smile left his lips then, but stayed in his eyes. A gentle smile that was almost like a caress. "Try to sleep."

She listened to his footsteps going back down the stairs, and wanted to call him back to help her with her buttons. She wanted him to tell her again that somehow they would make it even if he couldn't tell her how. She wanted to see him smile. She wanted him to touch her.

The last thought brought her up short, and she made herself remember how little she actually knew about Blake. She made herself remember Eloise Vandemere, whoever she was. Adriane's eyes went to the boxes Blake had stacked in the corner of her room, but even if she could find answers there, she was too exhausted to search through them. Blake was right. She needed to sleep.

Late in the day the noise of the press starting up woke her, and she was somehow comforted by the familiar sound. She thought she should get up to see if Beck needed help, but sleep stole over her again before she could move.

The next time she awoke, it was dark. She still lay on top of her bedcovers in her chemise and petticoats, but someone had spread a light cover over her. She gingerly reached out her hand to feel the bed around her. She was alone.

She hadn't really expected to find Blake in the bed with her, for she surely would have awakened if he'd lain down beside her during the night. But he had made it very clear that they would share the bed.

As she sat up slowly, her eyes began adjusting to the darkness until she could make out the shapes of the furniture. Without a sound, she slid out of the bed, found her slippers, and pulled a wrapper around her. The clock struck two as she stepped out in the hallway, and she used the bongs to cover the noise of shutting her door. If Blake was sleeping in the sitting room, she didn't want to wake him. Of course he could be in her father's room, but somehow she didn't think so. There would be too many ghosts of memories in there.

In fact, the ghosts seemed to come out of the room as she crept past it to follow her down the hall to the stairs. She didn't try to chase them away. She wanted them with her. That was the reason she was up.

The ghosts drifted silently down the stairs, but though she tried to be as quiet, one of the steps creaked loudly when she stepped on it. She held her breath and listened for some answering sound of movement in the house, but when she heard none, she began to doubt Blake was even there.

Downstairs in the pressroom, she lit a candle and shielded the flame with her hand. As soon as she found what she wanted, she moved silently out of the pressroom into the kitchen, where she set the small candle in the middle of the table. The flame flickered and made strange shadows on the walls, and Adriane had no trouble at all imagining the ghosts among them. But she wasn't afraid. She knew these ghosts.

She was here to face them, but the smell of ham and fried chicken still heavy in the air made her remember the old dog. She found some biscuits in the warming oven on the stove.

The back door hardly squeaked at all when she went out of it, but it must have been enough to alert the old dog. Before she could call him, he appeared out of the shadows on the back stoop beside her.

"I'm sorry, Mr. O'Mallory," she said as she put the biscuits down in front of him. "I'm afraid I forgot about you, but if you'll forgive me, I'll find you a juicy ham bone tomorrow."

As if he understood her words, the dog wagged his tail and pushed his head against her hand for a pat before he dropped his nose to the biscuits. For a moment, Adriane was tempted to open the door wide and let the old dog come in to keep her company, but then she went back inside and shut the door behind her. An old dog sitting at her feet wasn't going to make what she had to do any easier.

She sat down at the table and stared at the folded paper for a long moment. The black edges peeped out of the folds, and her hands felt heavy as she made herself open it up. The finality of the dark black headline type screamed at her. "Wade Darcy, 1801–1855."

The obituary her father had written for himself was brief, terse almost, and not at all like something he would have written for anyone else. He gave his birthplace as near Richmond, Virginia, and listed his late parents' names as Joseph and Emma Darcy. There was no mention of brothers or sisters, although Adriane remembered him once talking about a brother who went west. She herself was listed as his only survivor, with one brief line about a wife, Katherine Darcy, preceding him in death. There was no mention of poor Henrietta at all.

He warmed to his subject a bit as he began an account of his accomplishments, especially when he came to how he'd established the *Tribune* in 1841, first as a weekly, then as a daily in 1848. A hint of pride crept into the words as he wrote about the newspaper rising in popularity until it became Louisville's most widely read daily, one that was a beacon of light to all its readers.

As her eyes fastened on that line, she could almost hear him saying the words aloud. *A beacon of light*. That had been the *Tribune*'s creed for years, but her father had never said the words without a bit of awe mixed with his pride.

"Words have power, Adriane," he'd told her more than once as they looked over a story together. "The right words can split the darkness of ignorance and light the way for our readers."

With his voice echoing in her mind, she read the last paragraph Blake must have written, detailing how Wade Darcy had courageously sacrificed his life in an attempt to stop the riots. Then a few lines stated how sorely he would be missed not just by his loving daughter but by the whole community, but it was the last sentence she read over twice.

Today a great voice has been silenced, but the memory of that great voice will live on in the minds of all his friends and readers and long be an inspiration to those who follow in his path.

Adriane dropped the paper and stared at the shadows shifting uneasily around her. Now was when she was supposed to cry. She had saved her tears for just this moment, but though the tears were a crushing weight inside her, her eyes stayed dry.

The candle flame flickered, and the ghosts danced out of the shadows to mock her tearless eyes. Then there was one who was not a ghost.

She didn't know how long Blake had been standing in the doorway before she became aware of him there. He made no sound until she turned her head to look at him.

"Are you all right?" he asked.

"Yes," she said.

"Do you want me to go away?"

She started to tell him yes, that she wanted to be alone, but it seemed to be a time for the truth. "No," she said softly.

As if he'd been holding his breath waiting for her answer, a whisper of air escaped him. He came across the narrow space separating them and pulled up a chair beside her. For a minute he didn't say anything, didn't even look at her, but instead studied the candle that was nearly burned down and the newspaper in front of her. "It was a good, honest obituary," he finally said.

"The part you added was kind," Adriane said.

"Not kind. True. I may not have agreed with everything your father said or wrote, but he was a good newspaperman."

She didn't know why those words caused the tears to break loose inside her, but suddenly her eyes were flooded. She covered her face with her hands as she said, "I'm sorry."

Gently he touched her hands. "Don't hide your tears from

me, Adriane. Let me share them." He slid out of his chair onto his knees beside her and pulled her head down on his shoulder.

With relief, she leaned against him and didn't try to stop the sobs that shook her body. Then after the last tear had emptied from her, he stayed on his knees beside her as he fished out his handkerchief and gently dried her cheeks. She peeked over at him a bit self-consciously as she said, "I'm all right now."

He still didn't climb up off his knees. Instead he looked oddly unsure of himself. After a moment, he said, "I want to properly propose to you, Adriane."

"But we're already married, Blake," she said, remembering how she had forced Stan to propose to her in the carriage. She'd been so foolish then. She tried to pull Blake up. "You don't have to do this."

"Yes, I do." He took hold of her hands as his eyes burned into hers in the dim candlelight. "I don't want there ever to be any doubts in your mind as to why I married you. It has nothing to do with presses or newspapers. It has only to do with how much I love you."

"You love me?" A touch of wonder awoke in her heart.

"I love you more than life itself." There was no way she could doubt his words, because he was opening his eyes to her and letting her glimpse his soul. He spoke his next words slowly and distinctly. "Adriane Darcy, will you be my wife?"

"Yes," she said with no hesitation.

"Without conditions?"

"Without conditions." And with those words she gave up all resistance to the love that wanted to flow out of her toward him.

"No matter what might have happened in the past or what might happen in the future?"

For a moment his words reminded her of all she didn't know about him. What in his past would make him ask for such a promise? But then his eyes were there, promising nothing mattered but his love for her and her love for him. "I am your wife, Blake. The vows said till death do us part."

The candle guttered, and the flame drowned in the melted wax. Darkness fell around them, but neither of them moved as if they did not want to let loose of this moment.

Finally Blake said, "Thank you, Adriane." He stood up at last and reached down for her hand. "There are still a few hours before the newsboys come for the papers." He hesitated for a bare few seconds before he went on. "Come to bed."

She went with him willingly, her fears of what he might expect of her vanishing just as the ghosts who had followed her to the kitchen had dissolved into nothing but harmless shadows as soon as he had come in the room.

She was ready to surrender totally to him, yet when they lay down on her bed together, he demanded nothing. She tried to awkwardly tell him that he could take what he wished.

He gently brushed his lips against her hair, pulled her close to him, and whispered, "When the time is right, there will be no taking. Only giving. But now we'll sleep."

And so she did. When she next woke, the grainy gray light of dawn was slipping through her window. Blake's arms were still warm around her and she lay without moving for a moment as she absorbed the feel of him against her and listened to his soft, even breathing. She had never felt so safe.

She didn't know why. She had no reason to feel safe. She had every reason to believe that life was fragile and easily stolen. Her father was gone. The *Tribune*, which had been the center of her life and her father's for so many years, might soon be gone as well. Yet with Blake's arms around her, she felt safe.

The questions she'd had yesterday didn't matter. Her eyes went to the boxes of files that she could just make out in the dawning light. If there were answers there, she would never look for them. The past didn't matter. Eloise Vandemere, whoever she was, didn't matter. Even if Blake had loved her once, he loved Adriane now, and that was all the answer she needed.

She turned her head slowly to study his face while he slept, but he was not asleep. His eyes were open and waiting for hers. And she knew the time for giving had come.

"I won't hurt you," he whispered.

"I know," she said softly and surrendered herself completely to him in every way.

28

*B*lake's fingers trembled as he fumbled with the ribbons on Adriane's chemise. She was so beautiful, her skin so incredibly soft under his hand. All through the early morning hours, he had held her close, breathing in her fragrance and hardly daring to move for fear she might pull away from him.

Passion had flooded through him more than once, but he had refused to give in to his desire for her. He wanted there to be no bad memory of their first time together. So he would wait until she was ready. He had been prepared to wait however long it took, but then she had surprised him by turning those beautiful eyes on him in the dawning morning light. Eyes that wanted him to touch her even as she feared what that touch might bring. Innocent eyes full of trust.

He wanted to keep that trust alive, but what if his touch didn't bring her the pleasure simply breathing in her scent brought him? That fear of failing her made him clumsy as he tried to undo her chemise. So clumsy in fact that after a moment she reached up and untied the ribbons herself.

He peeled the fabric away and stared at her with the wonder of a boy first aware of the differences between men and women. He could feel her looking at him as if worried he

295

might find her lacking, and he whispered to her how very beautiful she was. She seemed to relax a bit then, and he ran his fingers over the softness of her skin.

When she pulled in her breath sharply, he looked into her eyes. If there was any question left in his mind that she might not really be ready, she answered it by lifting her lips up to his. As soon as their lips touched, the fire consumed them both.

Long after their passion was spent, he held her, not wanting to surrender their closeness. He'd known it would be like this with Adriane, had known from the start their bodies would join as easily as their minds, but he hadn't expected the sheer joy of receiving her love to make his heart feel as if it might burst. He had to wait for it to calm its beating before he could whisper the words of love into her soft hair. Words that, wonder of wonders, she repeated as softly back into his own ears.

The folded issues of the *Tribune-Herald* waiting for the newsboys down in the pressroom were forgotten as the gray of dawn gave way to morning. There was nothing but the feel of Adriane's body next to his with nothing separating them.

At last he pulled away from her to let his eyes soak in the delicious wonder of her body again. He tried to slide his eyes quickly over the ugly bruises still evident on her arms so anger wouldn't spoil this time for either of them, but the bruises were there. Not looking at them didn't make them disappear. Very lightly he ran his fingers across them.

"He'll never hurt you again," he said, softly brushing the purple and green splotches with his lips.

She wrapped her arms around him so that he couldn't see the marks and looked him directly in the eye. "Forget about him. He's part of the past."

"I'm not sure it will be that easy."

"No," she agreed. "But if I can do it, so can you."

"My past and yours are not the same," he said.

She was quiet then, not asking any questions. He couldn't

even see the first question in her eyes, but he knew this was a time for an explanation, if not answers. He had none of those, for he had never been able to find good answers to his own questions about Eloise and whether there had been anything he might have done to save her.

"You want to know about Eloise," he said.

She turned her eyes from him too quickly as she said, "No. Whoever she was, she's not important." She twisted away from him and started to get up. "I should go down and help Beck hand out the papers to the boys."

"The boys have already come and gone." Blake pulled her back down beside him.

She didn't fight against him, but she did jerk the light cover over her up to her chin as if she had become uncomfortably aware of her lack of clothes. He helped her smooth out the corners and covered himself as well, even though he regretted the passing of the easy intimacy between them before he said, "Eloise has nothing to do with us."

Adriane silently stared down at the cover, and although Blake wanted to tip her chin up until he could see into her eyes, instead he talked to the top of her head. "But I was wrong not to answer your question yesterday, even though it is true I don't like to talk about Eloise."

"Then don't. I'd rather you didn't." Her grip on the cover tightened.

He had the feeling she was afraid of whatever he might tell her about Eloise. There was no changing what had just happened between them. He could understand how she didn't want to hear something that would prove she'd made a mistake in giving herself to him so completely. He made himself begin talking, unsure of what she'd think after she knew about Eloise.

"I don't know what Stanley told you about Eloise." His muscles tensed as he said the man's name, and he had to take a deep breath and force himself to relax before he went on.

"It doesn't matter. No one knows the truth about Eloise. Not even me, but I'll tell you what I do know. Then you'll have to decide who to believe."

She finally raised her eyes to his. "That decision has already been made."

"Some decisions have to be made over and over." He pulled his eyes away from hers and stared up at a dark brown watermark on the ceiling. "That's sort of the way it was with Eloise. I met her just after the Mexican War was over."

"Were you in the war?"

"Not as a soldier, but I did carry stories from the battlefields to the papers in the East. We didn't have the wire then and all the papers were in a race to be the first to get news of the big battles for their headlines. I was good at getting the stories through."

"I can imagine," she said a little dryly.

He glanced at her, but then fastened his eyes back on the blob that was beginning to take on the shape of a horse's head. "At any rate, I came back to New York after the war and started covering the police beat and going to the odd social when Harper, the editor, twisted my arm. Nobody printed much of that kind of news then, but Harper's wife liked seeing her name in print. So he would give the parties she went to little write-ups and stick them in when he needed a filler. It wasn't long till all the ladies were clamoring for ink for their own gatherings."

"So you had to go to more socials," Adriane prompted when Blake stopped to catch his breath.

"Harper made it part of my job. And that's how I met Eloise. After all the misery I'd seen in the war, Eloise was like the first spring flower at the end of a long winter."

"Was she really pretty?" Adriane asked, her grasp on the cover tighter than ever.

"Pretty fit her." He looked at Adriane. "Not beautiful like you."

Adriane's cheeks reddened, but her grip on the cover loosened.

For a second he wanted to stop the story and peel the cover away, but he forced himself to look at the dark smudge on the ceiling again and continue. "She took a fancy to me even though I wasn't in her social circle. Who knows why? Anyway we became engaged. Secretly. She said she needed time to decide how best to tell her father about us, and I didn't try to rush her since her father owned the paper where I worked. I wasn't so dumb that I didn't realize the whole thing might backfire on me. But I didn't court her only to get a toehold on the paper the way people said when they found out."

"You wanted a paper," Adriane said.

"Oh yes," Blake agreed without looking at her. "And I had no doubt I'd have one someday, but not like that. I wanted to earn it on my own." He stopped talking again.

After a minute she asked, "What happened?"

"The expected. Vandemere found out about our secret engagement and put a stop to all Eloise's silly games and my chivalrous romantic ideas." Blake shifted uneasily as though something in the bedding had suddenly jabbed him. He had been so young and foolish then.

"Did you love her?"

"I thought I did at the time, but then after her father made her marry a man he considered much more suitable, I discovered that although my pride was sorely wounded, my heart survived intact. I never even noticed a crack."

"You sound heartless," she said, but she sounded relieved.

"You may think that's even truer when you hear the rest of it."

"There's more?" she asked, her relief replaced with a hint of worry.

"A great deal more." He was silent for a moment before he made himself continue. "The man her father chose for her, Lyle Davidson, was years older than Eloise, but he was wealthy and had the proper social standing. Unfortunately for Eloise, he was also insanely jealous. If she so much as smiled at another man at a dinner party, he'd go into a rage. Eloise would have to disappear from the social scene for weeks at a time while the bruises healed. It was like taking the sunlight away from a butterfly."

"Didn't her family know?"

"Her father knew." Bitterness rose up in Blake even after so many years. He might not have loved Eloise, but he hadn't wanted her hurt. "But Vandemere was campaigning to be elected mayor and he was running scared from any hint of scandal that one of the opposing newspapers might dig up. And it could be he did try to help her privately. I can't say. All I know for sure is that she started finding ways to send me notes begging for my help."

Blake paused, remembering his dismay when one of Eloise's friends slipped him that first note. He'd heard the rumors about her marriage, but he hadn't expected her to involve him. He hadn't wanted to be involved.

"I suppose she thought I still loved her. And in her desperation, she imagined I was more courageous than I was."

"What did she expect you to do?" Adriane asked.

She was so intent on his story that she half sat up, letting the forgotten cover slip to her waist. He made himself turn his eyes away from her and keep his mind on Eloise. A sort of sick shame filled him as it did every time he thought about how he had failed Eloise, and now he wanted to get up and leave the room while there was still hope Adriane wouldn't hold him at fault. But in spite of his reluctance to tell the whole story, he kept pushing out the words.

"I'm not sure. She hinted at a duel once, but I wasn't that chivalrous or foolish. I had never actually met Davidson, but I'd heard of his ability as a marksman. I sent notes back to her encouraging her to ask her father for help. I even sent one of her notes to me on to him."

The blob on the ceiling suddenly took on the shape of a man's face under a hat. "A couple of days after that, Harper called me into his office to say that though he hated it, he'd have to let me go. Then I received a polite letter from Vandemere strongly suggesting that if I would leave Eloise alone, he was sure she and her husband could work out any difficulties they might be experiencing. Somehow I became the villain of the piece."

Adriane slipped her hand over his. "It wasn't your fault."

Blake's heart skipped a beat at her touch, but he wouldn't allow himself to look at her. He just kept staring at the dark shape of a man's face as he continued. "It gets worse. In Eloise's next note, she begged me to run away with her. She said she realized her love for me was worth any sacrifice, and she was prepared to go to California or anywhere as long as we were together."

Blake closed his eyes a moment and saw the fancy scroll of Eloise's handwriting. It was so like her. All flourish and no depth. After a moment he went on. "She had never even imagined that I might not love her anymore."

"What did you do?"

"Nothing. She told me she'd meet me at a secluded cliff side not far from their summer home and we could plan our escape. I didn't go." Blake paused a moment before he pushed out the last words. "The next thing I heard, she was dead."

"What happened?" Adriane asked.

"She fell off the cliff where we were supposed to meet. At least that's what they told. When they discovered her packed case and a servant came forward to say he had carried messages to me, the police came round to have a word with me, but I'd just been hired by another paper and had spent the day with my new editor. There wasn't much investigation after that, although rumors of all sorts made the rounds. They held a coroner's inquest, but it was just a formality. Vandemere saw that it was declared an accident."

"And was it an accident?" Adriane asked.

"I don't think Lyle Davidson pushed her, if that's what you mean, but no, I don't think it was an accident. I think Eloise made the only escape she could, since no one would rescue her."

She raised up then and leaned over him until he had to look in her eyes. "And is that why you married me? To rescue me."

He met her eyes. "I told you, Adriane. I married you because I love you. No other reason."

"But you have rescued me." Adriane touched his lips softly with her own. "And for that I'm grateful."

Blake quelled the passion that made him want to grab her and leave all words behind. "You may not think I have pulled off much of a rescue when Coleman Jimson sets us out on the street later today."

She surprised him by smiling a little. "We'll be on the street together." Her smile grew wider. "With Beck and Duff, of course."

"And Joe," Blake said with an answering smile.

A blush warmed her cheeks as she took a quick glance at the sun streaming through the window and then at the door. "Whatever will they think of us still in bed with the sun full up."

His smile became a soft laugh. "I'm thinking they will guess the truth."

"And what truth is that?"

He pulled her down on top of his chest and whispered into her soft hair. "That if there is never another day, this day will be enough."

29

driane surrendered herself to his touch again and rejoiced that her body responded so naturally to his. After their passion was once again spent, she laid her head on Blake's chest. Everything was forgotten except his fingers in her hair and the sound of his heart slowing its mad racing.

The soft knock on her door surprised her, as if she'd forgotten there was anyone else in the world besides them. "Addie," Beck called. "Addie, you awake?"

Adriane stiffened and started to jerk away from Blake, but he smiled and held her closer while he whispered in her ear, "We're married, Adriane. Married people sleep together."

"Surely not all day," she whispered back, her face burning hot.

"If they want," he said with a lazy smile.

But he let her sit up and pull on her wrapper before she answered Beck. "What is it, Beck?"

"I was just some worried about you, seeing as how the morning's half spent. And then there's the paper, and ain't none of us seen hide nor hair of Blake all morning. Joe figures he must have gone down to the riverfront to try to dig up some news about the murders."

Blake looked at Adriane with a smile and raised eyebrows

as he waited for her to answer Beck. Adriane stood up and smoothed her hands over her cheeks as if she could rub away the hot color flooding them. "No, he's here with me," she said.

There was a silence on the other side of the door then, and Adriane imagined Beck's cheeks might be turning red to match her own before he said, "Then I reckon I'm double sorry to be bothering the two of you, but you know I ain't never been no hand at writing out stories, and if we're gonna get another issue of the *Tribune-Herald* on the street before Jimson throws us out, we'd best be at it." Beck's voice changed a bit. "He sent a note around a bit ago."

Blake got out of bed, pulled on his pants, and in two steps was across the room to pull open the door. "What did he say?" he asked Beck.

Beck didn't answer right away as he looked between them without the least sign of embarrassment and grinned so big that his eyes were nearly lost in the explosion of wrinkles. When he did finally say something, it had nothing to do with Coleman Jimson. "I'm feeling like somebody's give me a Christmas gift seeing the two of you like this."

Adriane pulled her wrap tighter, very conscious of her lack of clothes under it. "Oh hush, Beck, and stop looking like you just scooped the headlines for a week. It's not as if we've been doing anything uncommon."

"Now that's a fact, Addie, but all things considered, I figured as how it'd take the two of you a heap longer to get around to it."

"Adriane and I haven't been considering much of anything except ourselves this morning, but I suppose it's time to be getting down to business again." Blake's smile disappeared. "What did Jimson's note say?"

Beck turned serious as well. "He's coming around to meet with Addie at three. I figured if we hurried, we could have tomorrow's paper most done by then."

"And Duff, where is he?" Blake asked as he pulled on his shirt.

"He took his papers out, but he's back now. I told him the press had been running a tad rough and he's taking a look at it. The boy's got a knack for the machinery, but some problems are hard to put your finger on. I figure to keep him busy with it most of the day."

Blake paused in tucking in his shirt and looked up at Beck. "Good. I'd just as soon he wasn't on the streets today."

Adriane felt the flush draining away from her cheeks as suddenly all their problems pushed back into the room to surround her. "We could print a retraction. Say we were misinformed and there is no witness."

Blake turned to her and laid his hand softly on her cheek. "Beck and I won't let anything happen to Duff, Adriane."

"That's right, Addie. Don't you worry none about it. You just stay here and rest up." Again Beck grinned.

Adriane was opening her mouth to say she was quite rested enough when without looking up from pulling on his shoes, Blake said, "She'll have to rest tonight. We need her to get out the paper now."

"I reckon you're right as rain about that." Then with another grin and a wink at Adriane, Beck backed out of the room shutting the door behind him.

Blake turned to look at her. Slowly he reached out and ran his hand softly along her cheek. "I'm not sure I care whether we put out another issue or not," he said as he reached for the tie to her wrapper.

Adriane pushed his hand away. "We've been quite scandalous enough already. I daresay I won't be able to look at Beck without blushing for days as it is."

Blake laughed and grabbed her close before she could step away from him. It only took the touch of his lips on hers to make her abandon all resistance, but even as the fire of passion rose inside her, he pulled back and smiled down at her.

"Till tonight, my darling." He kissed her one more time before he turned her loose and yanked open the door. "Don't be long," he said. "We've a paper to get out."

After he shut the door behind him and his footsteps clattered down the stairs, Adriane sat down on the edge of the bed and put her head in her hands. She wavered between wanting to say a prayer of thanks for Blake to thinking she should ask forgiveness for her wantonness. Surely it was indecent for her to have felt such happiness with Blake so soon after her father's death.

It was all too confusing. Too much had happened too fast. Some part of her found it impossible to believe her father was gone forever. Scraps of arguments kept coming to mind to make him change his mind about Blake. Arguments she'd never get to use, but somehow she needed to believe that with time she could have convinced him.

With a deep breath, Adriane sat up straight, forcing herself to face the truth. Her father had run out of time. There would be no convincing him. The best she could do for him now was to save the *Tribune*, and time was running out for that as well.

Adriane stood up and poured water from the pitcher into the washbowl on her dresser. She needed to be ready when Coleman Jimson came.

She stared at her image in the mirror. She felt stronger than she had in months. No longer was she being carried along in a flood of what other people wanted for her into a life she wouldn't be able to bear. She was Adriane Garrett now, and Blake loved her the way she was.

For a second Henrietta's dour words of warning came back to make her uneasy. "We're all Eves. Every one of us no more than nine months from suffering and death." And now Adriane had been with a man. Even now she could be beginning that nine-month journey. *And the light shineth in the darkness.* That was what she had to think on. The light shining in the darkness. The Lord had helped her bear the darkness of Henrietta's closet until her father could rescue her.

Now her father was gone, but the Lord hadn't left her in darkness. He'd sent Blake to her. Together they could be strong enough to face anything. Together. Side by side. She didn't have to worry about Blake trying to shove her into a small dark closet of conformity.

She smiled a little. In fact he was throwing open doors to parts of herself she'd never even dared to dream about. And even as a new blush climbed into her cheeks, she found herself looking forward to his promise of the night.

"Adriane Darcy," she whispered to her reflection. "What's come over you? Thinking such wanton thoughts." She tightened her mouth to erase the smile and splashed more cool water on her face. But the smile stayed curled deep inside her, waiting without fear or shame for the right moment to uncurl and find its way back to her lips. And she remembered Grace's awkward explanation of what happened between a man and woman in the marriage bed. *It's by God's design. He gave us love. He made us this way for a purpose.*

A prayer came unbidden to her lips. "Thank you, Lord, for letting Blake love me."

Downstairs, Adriane threw herself into the work of getting out the paper. The hours passed swiftly with words and the clatter of type in the galleys. Blake, with Duff safely in tow, had gone down to the riverfront, but they'd come back with little new information.

Blake wrote an editorial calling for accountability for those who had done the shooting, but there was little real fire in his words. As he told Adriane after she read it over, the police could hardly arrest the whole town. Or even all the Know Nothings.

"But mark my words," he added. "The Know Nothings have killed their cause with these riots. Thinking men will leave the party."

"But what about their candidates who won in the election?" Adriane looked up from the paper at him.

"Men like Jimson will be smart enough to note how the wind lies and make new alliances."

At Jimson's name, Adriane felt a cold dread settle in the pit of her stomach as she looked at the clock. It was almost three.

"Don't worry, Adriane." Blake put his hand on her arm. "Jimson may be able to take the building and the press, but he can't take our words. We'll find a way to get those words in front of the readers."

"How?" Adriane asked. She had spent part of the morning going through her father's accounts to try to determine exactly how much was owed to Jimson, but she could find no record of any deal he'd struck with Jimson.

For a brief moment she had thought that if Coleman Jimson had no written proof of money owed him, they would not have to give in to his demands. Then she knew she couldn't do that. She would honor her father's debts.

Besides, even before Jimson came at three and pulled the paper bearing her father's signature out of his pocket, she had known he would have the proof. He was not a man to let such a thing as money owed ride on handshakes and friendship.

"Adriane, my dear, you must know how distasteful all of this is for me," Jimson said, a look of genuine sorrow in his eyes.

Adriane had steeled herself for the confrontation, prepared for anything but sincerity from him, and for a moment she was at a loss for words. She stared down at the paper to regain her composure and went pale when she saw the listed amount. Then she smiled a bit at herself as she realized an amount ten times less would have been just as impossible for them to pay.

Without a word, she handed the paper to Blake, who stood beside her in the front hall. He read the amount impassively and handed it back to her.

Adriane looked from the paper to Coleman Jimson. It was strange how it was almost as if she'd never seen him before this moment. Always before when she had looked at him, Stanley had been in his shadow. Now as she thought about what Stanley had done, she began to wonder which shadow was darkest and just how much Coleman Jimson actually knew about his son.

Adriane laid the paper on the hall table without taking her eyes off Jimson. "You know, of course, that we can't pay you the full amount today."

"I feared as much." Jimson again sounded as though the truth of that gave him no pleasure. "I would have never called in the note as long as your father was living, my dear, but things have tragically changed." He glanced over to Blake before he looked back at Adriane. "We do seem to have somewhat of a dilemma."

Adriane kept her eyes steady on the man in front of her. "Do you know who shot my father?"

He looked at her with a puzzled frown. "My dear, how could I? It was a shot fired at random from a mob of crazed men."

"And how many men in your pay were in that mob?" Adriane stared at him.

"My dear girl, grief has caused you to lose all reason." His surprise was evident. "What possible motive could I have for wanting to harm your father? It was my fondest hope that we would soon be related through your marriage to Stanley. I knew nothing of the broken engagement until after the riots."

"Perhaps not, but Stanley did. He came to the *Tribune* Monday and threatened my father's life if I persisted in my refusal to marry him."

Now it was Jimson's turn to pale, but he pulled himself under control quickly. "Stanley was no doubt distraught when he was here. Normal enough, considering he'd just been rejected by the woman he loves, but anything he said

309

was no more than words. Stanley is much better with words than actions."

"Perhaps you don't know your son as well as you think." Even as Adriane spoke, she realized that Coleman Jimson knew his son very well. Beads of sweat were popping out on his forehead. Even so, she had no proof for her accusations.

"Surely you don't plan to print any of these outrageous allegations." Jimson's alarm was becoming even more visible by the second as he looked at Blake. "You are aware that libel is a serious crime."

"As is arson." Blake's voice sounded harsh after his long silence.

Jimson's eyes narrowed on Blake. "Are you trying to blackmail me?"

"Not at all," Adriane said quickly, sensing Blake's anger in spite of his impassive expression. "We only plan to print the truth in the *Tribune-Herald*, whatever that truth may be."

"My dear girl, truth is often illusive." A new wariness shielded the look in Jimson's eyes. "In fact, truth is something most editors learn to bend this way and that to suit their particular causes. Your own father was very adept at finding the proper truths to publish."

"My father believed in what he printed," Adriane said staunchly and then wondered who she was trying the most to convince. Coleman Jimson or herself.

Jimson smiled a bit as if he sensed her uncertainty. "Of course, but he was wise enough to consider carefully what he believed as you and Mr. Garrett here will also need to do."

"As we will." Blake spoke quietly but forcefully. "You can rest assured of that."

"It is comforting to know that you both have such respect for the truth, but truth will not pay the bills." Jimson looked down at the paper on the hall table.

"Regrettably so," Adriane agreed, trying to take control of the situation again as she changed tacks quickly. "We will turn over possession of the building to you by the end of the month. Until then we will continue to publish the *Tribune-Herald*, but we will concentrate on a healing of the city. An effort I'm sure the state's newly elected officials will support fully."

Jimson looked around. "The building is not in very good shape. I doubt it has the value you imagine."

"And what value would you put on the *Tribune*?" Adriane kept her voice cool. She had expected this.

"The readership numbers have been falling in recent months, I understand. And without Wade, I doubt the paper has much chance of survival in the crowded newspaper market here in Louisville." Jimson looked from Adriane to Blake. "However, the *Tribune-Herald* together is a much more marketable commodity."

"You can't take the *Herald*," Adriane said. "It is not mine."

"Neither is the *Tribune*, as a matter of fact," Jimson said. "When you married, all your property as well as your debts became your husband's."

Adriane's heart sank as she realized what he said was true. She had not only lost the *Tribune* but had caused Blake to lose the *Herald* as well. She lowered her eyes away from Jimson's. She had no more fight.

Blake's hand tightened slightly on her arm as he spoke. "As Adriane has told you, we will vacate your building and if necessary, surrender the equipment. As to the *Herald*, we will have to wait for the reading of Mr. Chesnut's will. In the meantime it's imperative that we continue publishing or else lose our readers. Without readers, the papers, either of them, have little value. I'm sure everyone will take note of your patient forbearance and think highly of you for allowing their newspaper to continue uninterrupted."

Jimson studied Blake a moment before he said, "And there will be no vicious attacks on my character?"

"You have won the election, though perhaps not as fairly

as one might wish." When Jimson started to protest, Blake held up his hand to silence him. "Let me finish. Be that as it may, there would be little need in attacking your character now. As not only an editor but a citizen of this town and state, I would hope that I have been wrong and you will represent our district well. If not, then my duty as an editor would be to point out your shortcomings as our senator."

"And none of that could happen before the end of the month as I won't have taken office by then," Jimson said thoughtfully. "I think this is a deal we can strike. As long as you realize the debt will not be forgiven no matter what you print or don't print."

"A great many things will not be forgiven," Blake said.

Jimson's eyes narrowed as he stared at Blake for a long moment before he said, "I think we understand one another."

"There is one more condition," Blake added before Jimson could turn away.

Jimson looked at him suspiciously. "What's that?"

"You keep your son away from my wife if you want him to keep breathing."

Jimson looked once more at Adriane with sincere sorrow in his eyes. When he spoke it was to Adriane, not Blake. "Stanley is my only son, and his children will carry on the Jimson name. You can't fault a man for wanting those children to be strong, my dear. I had hoped your strengths would counter Stanley's weaknesses."

"So you bought me for him," Adriane said.

"No, my dear," he said sadly. "I only tried to buy you, but he spoiled the deal as I feared he would all along."

"And our deal?" Blake said coldly.

Jimson looked back at Blake. "Stanley will not trouble you or Adriane again. I'll see to it."

Without another word, he turned on his heel and left. Adriane's knees felt weak and she leaned against Blake, thankful for the strong feel of his body.

"It's all right, Adriane," he said softly. "He'll keep his part of the deal. Stanley Jimson won't bother you again."

With Blake's arms strong around her, she could almost believe it in spite of the worry deep inside her that none of them knew what Stanley might do.

30

After Jimson left, Blake called a meeting of the hands in the pressroom. Around them, stacks of the *Tribune-Herald* lay folded and ready for delivery on the morrow. It was early, not much after five in the afternoon, but they had gone ahead and printed the paper before Jimson came in case the man refused to listen to reason and insisted on closing down the press. Why one more issue mattered that much, Blake didn't really know. He just knew it did.

A newspaperman got out his issue no matter what. His father had taught him that, had believed it without question. The news could not be stopped, and so after his father died, Blake had done everything he could to keep their paper going.

It hadn't mattered so much what he printed, but he'd worked night and day to keep a paper out on the streets the same as always. It hadn't changed anything. His father was still dead and the paper he'd published dead with him. All Blake had been able to do was delay facing that truth for a few weeks.

That was all they'd done today with Coleman Jimson. The debt was too large, twice as much as anything Blake might have imagined, and even if by some chance, Chesnut had left Blake some share of the *Herald* in his will, there wasn't much

314

left of the *Herald* of any value. The building and equipment were gone. While the name remained, a newspaper was only as good as its last issue in the eyes of most readers.

It was a losing battle, but one they would fight to the bitter end. With that in mind, he wanted to be fair to the hands. He had no money to pay them today and could give them little guarantee of pay tomorrow or even of a job by the end of the month.

Blake surveyed the motley crew clustered about him in the pressroom. Beck and Duff were all who remained of Darcy's hands, and besides Joe, only three of his own hands had shown up the last couple of days. Calvin, a young kid named Seth, and Herb, a man he'd hired only last week.

Blake frowned at Herb slouched against the wall, his hands deep in his pockets, and wondered why he was still there. The man hadn't received the first sniff of pay and had hardly had time to develop any feelings of loyalty to Blake or the *Herald*.

Herb looked up, caught Blake's eyes on him, and slid his own eyes quickly back to the floor. Something about the man bothered Blake, but he couldn't quite put his finger on what. Even so, it wasn't a time to send men packing without cause. The man did his job. He'd even been the one to pull Joe out of the burning *Herald* building on Monday. For that, if nothing else, he owed the man a job as long as he wanted it.

Blake explained the situation to the men quickly and succinctly. He finished up by saying, "We're going to do our best to keep the *Tribune-Herald* up and running, but if you leave, there won't be any hard feelings."

"I ain't going nowhere, boss," Joe said. "You know that."

Blake allowed himself the faintest ghost of a smile. He had known that. Had counted on it, in fact. And Beck would be with Adriane till he died. He was the same as family, and Duff near to it. If it came to it, that would be enough to get out the paper, but the meeting had been for the other three.

Herb glanced up at Adriane and quickly away as he said, "I always heard tell a woman in the pressroom was bad luck."

Blake glanced at Adriane beside him, but she didn't act as if she'd even heard the man. Ever since they'd struck the deal with Coleman Jimson, she'd hardly said three words to anybody as she helped fold and get the papers ready. Blake looked back at Herb and said, "Mrs. Garrett has been helping her father put out the *Tribune* for years."

"So I've heard." Herb didn't look at Adriane again. "Could be they've had more than their share of bad luck along the way. More than their share lately at any rate."

Across the room, Beck muttered something that Blake couldn't make out. Maybe it wasn't words at all, but merely a growl, as it was plain the old man was only a word or two away from exploding. Surprisingly enough, Adriane made no response at all. She seemed hardly aware of Herb's words.

Blake kept his own voice calm. "If you don't like the working conditions, Herb, you're free to walk out the door right now."

The man slouched lower against the wall. "I didn't say I was wanting to quit. I was just worried some about bad luck."

"The *Tribune-Herald* is going to make its own luck the next few weeks. We're going to put out a paper that will set Louisville on its ear."

"We could do it too, boss," Joe said. "All we got to do is figure out who this slasher fellow is, and what with this witness coming forward, maybe things is finally beginning to break."

Beside him, Blake felt Adriane come to attention as she finally showed some sign of hearing what was being said. He glanced at her and regretted for the hundredth time the story they'd run in the paper the day before.

"Some folks out on the street are saying you just made that up, Mr. Garrett," the kid named Seth said. His face flushed a little as he went on. "I told them you wouldn't print something that wasn't true."

Before Blake could come up with an answer for Seth that wouldn't completely spoil the boy's belief in the truth of the printed word, Herb spoke up. "That ain't the worst rumor going around." Herb's gaze hit on Blake for a second before sliding down to the floor. "I heard a rumor the other day that you were the killer yourself, Mr. Garrett. That nothing like this happened before you came to town."

"That rumor's so old it's growing mold," Calvin said.

"Girls is still getting killed," Herb said.

Duff was across the room and had the much bigger man pinned against the wall before anybody else could move. "Mr. Garrett didn't kill me sister, but he's seeing to it that whoever did has some reason to be worried."

"Easy, boy." Herb's eyes flew full open for a moment, but he didn't try to push the boy away. "I wasn't aiming to upset you about your sister and all. I was just giving wind to some of the rumors I'd heard. There's another going around that it's one of the watch and that's why nobody can ever catch him. Then I even heard it might be some society dandy."

"If you'd seen what he done to her, you wouldn't be talking about it like it's no more than some kind of parlor guessing game." Duff's face twisted as he tried to keep back his tears.

Blake started across the room, but Adriane moved in front of him. With only a bare glance at Herb, she took hold of Duff's hands and pulled him away from the man. Then she put her arm around the boy and ushered him out of the pressroom.

When the door shut behind them, Herb muttered, "I wasn't meaning to trouble the boy. I feel bad for him. His sister too." Without looking at any of the rest of them, he pushed himself away from the wall and shuffled out the front door.

"And good riddance," Beck said.

"I promised no hard feelings," Blake said.

"I make my own promises." Beck sent Blake a hard look before he stood up and went into his room off the pressroom and shut the door firmly.

Joe, Seth, and Calvin filed out without a word. From the way Calvin kept avoiding Blake's eyes, Blake didn't think he'd see much more of him. Blake blew out his breath, glad the meeting was over, and pushed away from the printer's table he'd been leaning against. He'd have to tell Joe to scrounge through the taverns to find some hands.

Maybe he should do it himself. It could be he might find more than new hands. Maybe the piece in the paper had shaken loose a few worries, and new stories would be going around about the murders. Blake hadn't heard the one about the policeman. Of course since the riots, nobody had much good to say about the watch. The rumor about the society gent was old. Blake had heard it even before he'd heard his own name in the rumor mill.

He remembered what his father used to say about rumors. "You don't print rumors, Son. Not if you're an honest editor who cares about the reputation of your paper, but you do listen to them, and sometimes if you look deep enough into what's being bandied about and who's doing the bandying, you can catch a glimmer of the truth. That's what you print."

He needed more than a glimmer of truth to print. He needed a lot of truths. His eyes went to the folded papers ready for delivery the next morning. A dull issue. Readers expected more than that these days, and somehow he'd find a way to give it to them in these last issues of the *Tribune-Herald* if that's what they turned out to be.

But first he had to find out what was bothering Adriane. As he got up to go in search of her, he realized that for the first time in years something was more important than the headlines to him. An unsettling feeling, but one he welcomed.

As he went out to the kitchen, he worried Adriane might be regretting giving herself to him so completely that morning.

The thought made his insides twist. Touching her and loving her had been so good he'd been sure nothing could ever spoil the love between them. Yet now only a few hours later she seemed to be pulling away from him. He couldn't let that happen. He wouldn't let it happen.

He found her and Duff sitting on the back stoop, petting one of the ugliest dogs he'd ever seen. The dog looked up warily at Blake and started to slink away, but Adriane caught him around the neck.

"Don't worry, Mr. O'Mallory. He may look cross, but we won't let him chase you away," she said with a laugh.

A weight lifted off Blake's heart at the sound of her laugh. Whatever was bothering her had nothing to do with their night together, and suddenly the thought of the night ahead made him feel shaky inside. He didn't want to wait for the night. He wanted to pull her up next to him now, touch her hair with his lips, and carry her up the stairs to her bed. Their bed.

Before he could actually grab her, he pulled his runaway emotions to a halt by reminding himself that even if it had nothing to do with him, something was still disturbing Adriane. So he turned his eyes back to the dog. "What are you two doing with a mangy creature like that?"

"He's an ugly thing for certain, ain't he, boss?" Duff glanced up at Blake and then ran his hand across the dog's head gently. "I ain't never had a dog of me own. Never enough food, you know."

"Well, it looks as if you might be able to share this one with Miss Adriane." Blake sat down beside Adriane on what was left of the stoop. "What was it you called him?"

"Mr. O'Mallory," Adriane said. "And I can't say that he'd agree to be anyone's dog. He's an independent character."

"He looks a smart enough dog to know when he's got it made to me," Blake said. "I think he'll be sticking around awhile."

Adriane reached over and took Blake's hand. Duff noticed and grinned a little. "Maybe I'd best be seeing if old Beck has anything for me to do before I go home."

"Tell me before you leave," Blake said as the boy stood up. He didn't aim to let the boy walk home alone.

After the door shut behind Duff, Blake and Adriane sat silently as the last rays of sunshine disappeared behind the buildings and the shadows deepened. The old dog let out a contented breath and settled himself at Adriane's feet. Blake would have felt as happy as the old dog if he hadn't known Adriane wasn't feeling the same peace. Of course it could be simply grief at the loss of her father, but he sensed there was more than that sadness troubling her.

She glanced at him and away as she said, "I suppose I should see if we have anything to eat."

He held her hand tighter. "I'm not hungry." He reached up and turned her face gently toward him until he could look into her eyes. "Is something bothering you, Adriane? Something besides losing your father?"

"I do miss him. I keep expecting him to come in yelling about some new story." She reached up and wiped away a tear.

"But that's not all, is it? It's this with Jimson, isn't it? But he'll stand by his bargain. We have till the end of the month."

"I know." Adriane shifted her eyes away from his to stare over his shoulder toward the side of the building across the way.

He waited a moment for her to say more, but when she didn't, he said, "It's too late to shut me out, Adriane."

Her eyes came slowly back to his. "I'm sorry, Blake. I would have never married you if I'd thought about what it might cost you. I had no idea Father was so deeply in debt."

"Coleman Jimson doesn't worry me. To tell you the truth, with you here beside me, nothing does. He can't really hurt us now no matter what he does. You believe that, don't you?"

"I want to." Adriane lowered her eyes but not before Blake glimpsed more than worry there.

"You're afraid." He couldn't keep the surprise out of his voice.

"Yes." She barely whispered the word as if voicing the fear made it even worse. The dog rose up off the ground and laid his muzzle on her knee.

Blake wrapped his arms around her and pulled her close as he whispered in her ear, "My darling, you don't have to be afraid. We're together now, and together we can handle whatever happens."

She didn't relax against him or make any answer, and suddenly Blake felt a bit of answering fear waking inside him. He pushed away from her and tipped up her face until he was looking into her eyes once again, but the shadows were deep now and hid her thoughts. He pushed out the words. "Is it me you fear? Have I asked too much?"

"No, Blake, you don't understand," she said. "I'm not afraid of you. I'm afraid for you. And for Duff. For all of us."

His voice gentled. "I won't let anything happen to you, my darling."

"Things are not always so easily prevented," she said. "Just last Sunday my father sat in his office writing his editorial for the Monday paper. Duff's sister Lila was happy with her family. You had a press and a building. Now all of that is gone." She looked up at him in the fading light. "What might be gone this time next week?"

"I don't know, Adriane, but I do know one thing. I loved you last Sunday, and I'll love you this Sunday and next Sunday and every Sunday forever. Nothing can ever change that."

"Nothing?"

"Nothing," Blake said. "Just ask your friend, Mr. O'Mallory. He'll tell you." Blake dropped his lips down to tenderly cover hers as the old dog cocked his head and watched.

Behind them the door banged open, and then there was an embarrassed shuffle of feet.

"Sorry, boss," Joe said when Blake pulled away from Adriane to look up at the intruder. "I reckon this ain't a good time to be disturbing you, but a runner just brung around a message I think you might be wanting to see."

31

The strange, nameless fear rushed out of the shadows of Adriane's mind stronger than ever and swallowed up her thinking as Blake took his arms away from her and stood to follow Joe back into the pressroom. A tremble swept through her and she concentrated on breathing in and out slowly to keep her panic under control. She felt like a little girl again with Henrietta dragging her toward the closet to give her over to the dark.

Only this was worse, Adriane thought as she trailed after Blake into the building. This fear had no door. As a child, she'd run her hands around the edges of the closet door, and even though she couldn't open it no matter how hard she pushed, she'd always known, even in her most desperate moments, that eventually her father would come, open the door, and let the light spill in to her.

Now she frantically felt through her mind for some edge of a door, but she could find no hint of light. Instead there was only the consuming dread that she had absolutely no way to fend off whatever was lurking in the dark waiting for her.

And the light shineth in the darkness. The Bible verse echoed in her mind, but maybe Henrietta had been right. Maybe the Lord wouldn't listen to bad girls. Or to a woman

323

who would so disgrace her father's memory that she would marry his sworn enemy while he lay dying. Yet a prayer for light rose within her.

Inside Blake unfolded the note and read it aloud. "If you want to know who the murderer is, be at the docks at nine. A Witness."

"I'm going with you," Duff said.

"No." Blake glanced up at the boy.

Adriane leaned over to look at the large stilted printing on the paper.

"I'm going," Duff repeated.

"I doubt anything will come of this." Blake shook the note a little. "Just some no-good trying to part me from a few coins for a drink or two on the pretense of knowing something. It happens all the time."

Duff clenched his hands into fists, and his face looked old beyond his years as he stared at Blake. "And what if it be the murderer himself? He may think you're on to him, what with this witness story. If it is and I see him, I'll know." It was almost as if Duff had convinced himself he actually had seen the murderer with his sister. That he was the witness.

Blake studied the boy a long moment before he nodded.

Adriane's heart skidded practically to a stop inside her chest, and she had to try twice before she could speak. "I don't want you to go. Either of you."

Blake laid his hand gently on her cheek as he filled her ears with confident assurances. He was strong. He could handle whatever happened. He'd make sure Duff didn't get hurt. Besides, the murderer wouldn't have written them a note. It would surely be a false lead, but one he had to check out.

Even though she heard the sense in what he said, it was all she could do to keep from clinging to him before he left with Duff. As she stood in the doorway and watched them disappear into the darkness on the other side of the streetlight, she tried to block out the thought that she'd never see them come back out of that darkness, but her fear had no reason.

Beck put his hand on her shoulder. "Blake can take care of himself, Addie, and he's no doubt right about it being a false lead. Most leads are, you know."

She took a deep breath and forced herself to turn away from the street and come back inside where Beck and Joe were both watching her uneasily.

She tried to smile, but her lips refused to respond. "I'm sorry. I don't know why, but I have a bad feeling about it all. What if it's some kind of trap?"

Joe picked up his hat. "You want me to follow them, Miss Adriane? I can keep an eye out for trouble and warn the boss if it comes skulking up some way he might not be expecting."

"Would you, Joe?" A bit of light edged into Adriane's dark fear.

After the door closed behind Joe, Beck looked at Adriane. "You want to pray about it, Addie?"

"I am praying, Beck. You will too, won't you? That they'll come back safe. I don't know what I'll do if something happens to Duff because of that story." She met Beck's eyes. "Or to Blake."

"Don't you worry, Addie. Me and you can pray them through." He reached out and took both her hands. Then he looked up and without closing his eyes started talking to the Lord. "God, we know you're up there and that you listen. We're a mite worried down here and we're asking you to watch over them that are trying to do good. To protect them and bring them home to us. Amen."

"Please, Lord," Adriane whispered.

"They'll be back here before you know it." Beck smiled at her as he squeezed her hands and gave them a little shake before he turned her loose. "So why don't you go rustle us up something to eat? They're liable to be hungry when they come in, and as a matter of fact, I'm feeling a mite peckish myself."

Because she knew Beck was trying to make her think of ordinary things instead of worrying, she played along, even managing to smile back at him before she headed for the kitchen. There was no reason to trouble Beck with this nameless fear inside her, but once out of his sight in the kitchen, she dropped down at the table and put her head in her hands. She shouldn't have let Blake and Duff go. Something terrible was going to happen.

"Dear Lord in heaven," she whispered and then couldn't seem to come up with any more words.

Out in the alleyway the old dog growled and started barking. Low, furious barks that brought her to her feet. She peered out the window, but she couldn't spot the dog in the dark. He'd probably cornered a rat.

She didn't sit back down, but instead began rummaging through the cabinets for food. Beck might really be hungry. She pulled out a few apples and a bit of cheese. She had just finished slicing the cheese when she heard Beck's voice in a growl almost as low as the old dog's, followed by a loud crash and a heavy thud.

With the knife she'd been using to slice the cheese still in her hand, Adriane hurried across the hall to push open the door to the pressroom. The darkness slammed into her, and for a second she wasn't sure if it was real or a part of her fear.

She blinked her eyes, but the darkness stayed. The light spilling out of the kitchen behind her seemed faint and far away. "Beck?" she called. Her heart began thudding so hard inside her that she doubted she'd hear Beck even if he answered. And she knew the danger wasn't on the docks waiting for Blake and Duff. It was here waiting for her.

"Beck?" she repeated, her voice not much more than a whisper. The darkness throbbed with silence. A terrible silence that drummed in her ears and breathed on her neck. A silence that wanted to swallow her.

She glanced over her shoulder toward the kitchen. She could run back in there and slam the door on the dark silence. Make her escape out the back door. But what of Beck? He might be hurt and need her help.

She turned her eyes back to the darkness in the pressroom, a darkness made blacker by her glance toward the light. Her grip tightened on the handle of her small slicing knife as she asked the Lord for courage and began edging toward the nearest gas lamp on the wall.

Disoriented by the darkness and the fear throbbing through her, she banged into a stool that fell over with a loud clatter. Her heart in her throat, she froze as if somehow by standing motionless she could become as invisible as whatever else was in the room. The stool rocked back and forth on the floor. When at last it stopped, she heard something else. A furtive footstep.

She peered at the shadows. A bit of light came through the front windows from the streetlamps outside, and now that her eyes were adjusting to the darkness, she saw the shape of a man stepping away from the press.

"Who are you?" Adriane's voice came out stronger than she had expected it to. "What do you want?"

"My dearest Adriane, you know the answer to both questions already." The man moved purposely into the shaft of light coming through the window.

"Stanley," Adriane said. Her throat tightened, and she could push no other word out as her fear took form in front of her eyes.

"You didn't really think I would allow you such an easy escape, now did you?"

Stanley's laugh sent a tremble through Adriane, and she was almost glad she hadn't lit the gas lamp so he wouldn't have the pleasure of seeing her fear. She licked her lips and swallowed twice before she was able to ask, "Where's Beck?"

"Gone on to a better world, we should hope," Stanley said.

Adriane couldn't keep a strangled cry from escaping her throat.

"Oh, my poor dear." Stanley's voice spilled over with fake sympathy. "You were overly fond of the old man, weren't you? But he did have such a way of interfering."

Adriane tried to quell the panic rising inside her. Perhaps he was lying. Perhaps Beck was only hurt. Her eyes swept around the room. That shape slumped against the door had to be Beck. She took a step toward him, then stopped. Instinctively she knew that if she turned her back on Stanley, all would be lost. With another desperate prayer for courage, she fixed her eyes on the man in front of her.

"This is completely all your fault, my dear Adriane." Stanley paused a moment as if allowing her time to consider his words. "You should have married me as you promised you would."

"I would never have married you." She almost spat the words at him.

"Oh, I don't know. I think you would have, given the proper persuasion. It was just extremely bad fortune that your father hit his head when he fell off that platform. If nothing else, I am an excellent marksman. Even my father would agree with that. I've often heard him bragging to acquaintances about my superior shooting ability." Stanley's voice changed, deepened. "'By golly, Stanley may not be good for much, but he can hit the bull's-eye every time.'"

"I thought you didn't like guns." Without moving her head, Adriane shifted her eyes from Stanley to the bulky shape of the composing table between the windows where she'd last seen Beck's gun. She couldn't be sure the gun hadn't been moved, but even if it was there, Stanley stood between her and the table. Her father's gun in his desk was closer. And she still had the knife in her hand.

Almost as if he'd read her mind, Stanley was saying, "As

a matter of fact, they aren't my weapon of choice. I much prefer a knife. The blade is so much more personal and intimate somehow."

"Knife?" Adriane said faintly. Her grip tightened on the knife in her hand until her arm ached to the shoulder.

"A gun is much too quick, and death should be slow, not something to rush, don't you agree, my dearest Adriane?"

"You're mad." Adriane's voice was barely above a whisper.

"There are many who would agree with you on that point, my dearest. Of course, unfortunately most of them are no longer alive to agree with anything." Again Stanley laughed, the sound belonging to the darkness surrounding him.

"You?" Adriane couldn't give voice to the thought rising in her. It could not be. Even with Stanley facing her in the dark, even with his crazed laughter echoing in her ears, she could not believe the man she had danced with, the man she had allowed to kiss her, the man she had once thought she could marry was the river slasher.

"Did you never wonder where I went when I disappeared at those parties, my dearest?"

"No." The word was more a denial of the truth he was pushing through the darkness toward her than an answer to the question he asked.

He went on as though she hadn't spoken. "Perhaps if you had not been so cold toward me, I would not have found it necessary to seek warmer bodies."

Adriane wanted to shut her eyes and put her hands over her ears, but that would not make this monster in front of her disappear. "But you killed them," she whispered at last.

"It somehow seemed to be necessary, my dearest. They might have talked, you know."

"How could you?" Adriane said.

"Actually it was very easy. Family love is so touching, don't you think? The first girls were desperate for the bit of extra money I promised them. Their families needed it, you see.

And then with your young Irish friend's sister, I only had to mention that the boy had been hurt in the riot and she was ready to follow me anywhere." He paused a moment. "When I decide to do something, no one can stop me."

"Someone will," Adriane said.

"Perhaps you think your knight in shining armor will come to your rescue." Stanley breathed out an exaggerated sigh. "But alas, I regret to tell you that is not to be. There are men waiting at the dock for him. He might have found it more advantageous if he had tried a bit harder to accept my father's politics. And considerably safer too. There are those in the party who don't appreciate their candidate, now their new state senator, maligned so forcefully. I personally couldn't care less what your Mr. Garrett writes about my dear father, but one must use whatever resources one has. And what will one more beating, perhaps even killing, matter in the light of what's happened the last few days?"

"The truth will come out." She pushed out her voice stronger.

"Spoken like a true newspaperman. I can practically hear your father's voice echoing your words from the world beyond. But unfortunately, my dearest, you are beyond his help. I fear beyond anyone's help now." His voice was matter-of-fact, almost pleasant.

Adriane whirled and made a mad dash for her father's office. Her hand was on the doorknob when Stanley caught her.

He yanked her away from the door and shoved her against the wall. When he spoke, his face was so close to hers that she could feel the breath of his words. "You can't escape me, my dearest Adriane. You were a fool to ever think you could, and now the time has come to pay for your foolishness."

Adriane stopped struggling against him and tried to quell her panic by taking small controlled breaths. It might help if he thought she was helpless with no fight left. Her hand tightened on the handle of the small paring knife hidden in her skirts as she said, "What do you want from me, Stanley?"

"Everything, my dearest. Only everything." He raised his hand up, and let the long, broad blade of the knife he carried catch a glimmer of light. "It's my due. A promise made, a promise taken."

He softly slid the knife blade flat against the bodice of her dress and began slicing off the buttons. Adriane tried to shrink away from him, but there was no escape. No door to this darkness. Her knees went so weak she thought she might fall.

Stanley lifted up the knife and held the point against the skin under her chin. "I'd much prefer you did not faint, my dearest. Play your part and I will make the ending easy for you. Quick. Merciful. I am not the brute you're perhaps imagining me to be."

He kept the knife under her chin as he ripped open her bodice with his other hand. At the downward tug on her dress, the point of the knife pricked her skin, and she flinched her head up and away.

Stanley's eyes came back to her face. "Oh, what a shame. I seem to have nicked you." He turned the knife to the side and ran the back of his hand down her cheek to the cut on her chin. "Will you ever be able to forgive me, my dearest?"

Adriane desperately clamped down her panic again so she could think. There had to be a way. She couldn't stand there and give herself over to him without a struggle. He had a knife, but then so did she. Nothing to compare with the one he held, but a weapon in any case. She needed to plan her move carefully, for she might have only one chance to free herself from his grasp. She forced her voice out as calmly and firmly as possible. "Turn loose of me this instant, Stanley."

"That was always the trouble between us, wasn't it, Adriane? You thinking you were the stronger of the two of us. But now you will finally understand my true strength." He laughed a little, as though the thought amused him as he lowered his eyes to her torn bodice. "I do hope you haven't allowed your Mr. Garrett any of the pleasures of your body. I did so want to be first with you."

"He is my husband." Adriane inched her hand out from behind her skirt.

"That is a shame." Stanley lifted his eyes back to her face a moment. "But perhaps it will make it easier in the final moments. I do think it's almost a service to the community to rid it of fallen women who tempt the innocent to fall from grace as well, don't you?"

Across the room there was the sudden clatter of another stool hitting the floor, and the hope that Beck might still be alive sent a surge of strength through Adriane. When Stanley jerked his head around toward the noise, she threw up her forearm to shove aside Stanley's knife. The tip sliced into her chin. She hardly noticed the hot pain as she jabbed her own knife into his side. The point was too dull to penetrate very far through his jacket, but the surprise and force of her thrust knocked him backward. Before she could move out of his reach, he slammed his arm down on her wrist and knocked the knife out of her hand. He reached for her, but Adriane twisted away from him and melted into the shadow of the press.

"Well, well," Stanley said with another laugh. "You always were a woman of surprises, weren't you, my dearest? A knife of your own, but it does appear you do lack some skill in its use."

Adriane slid closer to the bulk of the press and clamped her lips together to keep her panting breath from giving her away. Slowly she began to ease around the press toward the composing table. She had to believe Beck's gun was there. It was her only chance. She could see Stanley standing perfectly still in the middle of the room, no doubt listening for her faintest move.

Then he came straight toward the press as if he could see

her there in the shadows. "You can't hide from me for long, my dearest. I will find you."

Even if the gun was there, she'd never reach the table before he caught her. She ran her hands along the press for anything loose she could use for a weapon. There was nothing. She was almost ready to give up hope when her foot bumped into a tray of type on the floor next to the press. In spite of how the rattle of the type gave her away, she blessed whichever one of the hands had neglected to return it to its proper place.

As Stanley rushed toward her, she grabbed up the tray and heaved it at him. The tray crashed harmlessly to the floor in front of him. Adriane thought all was lost as he kept coming, but then his feet were scooting on the spilled type. He went down hard. Adriane raced across the room. Her heart lifted when she saw the gun on the table. She grabbed it and turned toward Stanley, but he was gone. He must have gotten to his feet and stepped back into the shadow of the press.

"You won't shoot me, Adriane." He sounded amused.

Adriane moved the gun toward the sound of his voice without saying a word. She held her breath and listened for his first movement toward her.

"What a picture you are there in the light of the window." His voice changed until he sounded almost admiring as he stepped out of the shadows and held his knife out toward her before letting it clatter to the floor. "You have won. I surrender to you."

"Don't come any closer." Adriane leveled the gun toward the middle of his chest. The gun wobbled slightly in her hands.

Stanley moved two steps nearer to her. "I promise not to harm you in any way. You have my word as a gentleman."

"You're hardly a gentleman." Adriane managed to hold the gun steadier in spite of the way her heart was pounding. She tightened her finger on the trigger. "And if you move one step closer, I will shoot you."

"No, you won't," he said, but he stayed where he was. "It's

a fearsome thing killing someone. Much better if you let the police handle it."

Her silence must have given him confidence, because he began slowly moving toward her again. "Besides, no one will believe I am the slasher unless I'm alive to confess. If you shoot me, you'll be sure to hang."

He had moved into the light of the window now and she could see his face. Amused by her threat. Arrogantly confident of her inability to pull the trigger.

"Then may God forgive me, I'll hang." She steadied her hand as she pointed the gun barrel at the center of Stanley's chest.

But he was right. In spite of, or perhaps because of, how the confident look on his face fled, she hesitated a blink of a second too long. He was on her before she could pull the trigger back.

He pushed her against the wall, the gun trapped between them. She held on grimly as he tried to wrest it away from her.

"Turn loose, Adriane, or you might end up shooting yourself in the chin and marring your beauty." His face was inches from hers, his body trapping her, his hand taking control of the gun.

She didn't turn loose, but it was obvious she was no match for him. She was going to die. Blake's face flashed in her thoughts and regret swept through her that she would never see him again. Even if he did manage to escape Stanley's trap, she would not. At the thought she sagged back against the wall, her hands still gripping the gun but with no hope of pulling it back to point at Stanley again. She was going to die. A prayer rose inside her that she could face that death with courage. And with hope for eternity.

Yea though I walk through the valley of the shadow of death, I will fear no evil. Thou art with me. The verse filled her mind, and she suddenly didn't feel as alone. *Dear Lord, forgive my sins and welcome this child home.*

She surrendered as he mashed the gun against her chest. The end of the gun barrel raked over her cut chin and hot pain sliced through her.

"That's right, my dearest. Accept your fate. The darkness awaits. You'll be glad to enter in." He laughed softly as he relaxed his hold enough to touch her hair with one hand while still gripping the gun with his other hand.

"There will be no darkness. The light shineth in the darkness." Her words were so calm she wondered if somebody else was speaking them.

"Scripture. From you, dear Adriane. I am surprised. Do you think you can convict me of my sins at this last moment?" He laughed. "But alas, I fear your verse is nothing but empty words. The darkness always overwhelms the light. Darkness is all that awaits any of us."

"No, you are wrong. There is light." The end of the verse came into her head then. "And the darkness comprehended it not."

"I know what. Why don't I let you go first to see? But you can trust me on this." He began to wrench the gun out of her hand. "Nothing but darkness awaits you."

His words infuriated her. She refused to let him destroy her hope for light. She would not go easy into the darkness—his darkness. The sure knowledge welled up inside her that it was not now her appointed time to die any more than it had been her father's time. Stanley was trying to steal her life. Steal her light.

"No!" she screamed. She hooked a foot behind his legs, turned loose of the gun, and shoved hard with both hands against his chest.

As he fell backward, he grabbed her torn dress to pull her down with him. With her feet tangled up with his, she couldn't catch her balance and jerk free. The gun went off as they fell. The sound was deafening.

32

*B*lake was nearly a block away from the *Tribune* building when he heard the shot. With a strangled cry almost as if he felt the bullet slamming into his own body, he began running faster, even though he'd been running for what seemed like hours ever since the name Stanley Jimson had been knocked out of one of his attackers down on the dock.

None of the half-dozen men with hats pulled low to shadow their faces had planned to do any talking at all as they surrounded Blake. They'd been so sure he'd be alone, they hadn't bothered to check the shadows where Duff was watching, ready to run for help.

Blake yanked his gun out of his coat, but before he could get it pointed at any of the men, one of them knocked it out of his hand. If Joe hadn't appeared from nowhere to push through the men to stand beside him, Blake might not have been able to stay on his feet until Duff brought help from a nearby tavern. As it was, he and Joe took some hard blows, and Joe's arm looked to be broken.

Bad as that was, it wasn't until he recognized his newest hand, Herb, among the attackers that the terrible uneasiness had begun to rise inside him. Blake grabbed the man by the collar and demanded, "What's going on here, Herb?"

The man stared at the ground. "You should be more careful what you print in your paper, boss. The Know Nothings ain't happy with you."

"Who's paying you, Herb?" Blake demanded.

The man screwed his mouth up tight and tried to jerk free. Blake tightened his grip and twisted Herb's shirt collar until the man was gasping for breath.

"Give him to us, Mr. Garrett," one of Blake's rescuers said. "We'll make him sing whatever tune you want him to."

"I don't want anything but the truth." Blake kept his eyes on Herb as he loosened his hold to let the man breathe. "This was a trap, wasn't it? Who sent you down here?"

When Herb kept his eyes downcast without answering, Blake made a sound of disgust and pushed the man toward the men from the tavern. It didn't take much to shake loose the man's tongue and get him to admit working for the Jimsons.

"It was you that set the fire," Joe shouted and aimed a kick at the man, who huddled on the ground, trying to shield his head from the blows.

Blake pulled Joe back before the kick found its mark. "Easy, Joe. He could've let you burn with the building."

"I wouldn't kill nobody for money," Herb mumbled as he straightened up and finally looked at Blake.

"How about tonight?" Blake asked.

"We were just gonna knock you about a bit. Jimson wanted us to keep you busy for a while."

"Why would Coleman Jimson want you to do that?"

"Never had no dealing with the old man. It was the young dandy what give me my orders."

"Stanley?" Blake couldn't keep the surprise out of his voice even as Adriane's warnings about Stanley echoed in his head.

"That's right. He's a strange one, that one. He finds out I talked . . ." Herb let his voice trail off, visibly trembling now. Then he wrapped his arms tight around his chest as he looked at the men surrounding him and then back at Blake. "I'd done decided I'd do this last job for him and be on my way downriver before I found him slipping a knife between my ribs."

That's when Blake had turned and started running. And sending up desperate prayers that he wouldn't be too late. Dear Lord, he couldn't be too late.

Now with the echo of the shot still searing through his brain, the building was in front of him at last. The front windows were dark, and when he saw the front door ajar, his courage almost failed him, not sure he could bear the sight of whatever awaited him in the dark room beyond.

He leaned against the doorjamb and tried to stop panting so he could listen. It would do Adriane little good for him to rush in and get shot straight away. He didn't even have a gun. He'd lost it at the riverfront.

A carriage rattled by out in the street as the normal noises of the night went on undisturbed by whatever had happened inside. Blake heard nothing at all from inside the pressroom. Nothing. Out back the old dog howled, a sound so full of despair that Blake imagined the dog somehow knew Blake was too late.

He pushed on the pressroom door, but it was blocked by something. Ramming his shoulder against it, he shoved it open a few inches. A groan stopped him. Blake reached through the opening and touched a shoulder. Beck. He ran his hand down along the old man's side until he felt something warm and wet soaking his printer's apron. Blood.

"Adriane!" Blake shouted, all caution forgotten as he pushed Beck back from the door as gently as possible in his panic. "Adriane, answer me."

He was squeezing through the door, stepping over Beck's body when she spoke in a strange, flat voice. "He's dead."

The relief that rushed through Blake took his breath as a

prayer of gratitude filled his heart. She was alive. He could hear her and see her sitting on the floor scrunched up against the composing table. He barely glanced at the body sprawled at her feet as he covered the space between them in three steps. He touched her shoulder, but she flinched away from him.

In the light from the window, he saw the white of her chemise under the torn bodice of her dress, and for a moment his hand turned to stone. What had Jimson done to her? What had Blake let happen? He should have listened to her and not allowed himself to be tricked. He should have been there to protect her. He didn't realize how despair and rage must be warring on his face until she inched farther away from his hand back against the table. She fumbled with the tattered remains of her bodice to pull it together.

"It's all right. I'm here now." He reached toward her, but stayed his hand before he touched her. When he saw the blood on her dress, his throat tightened. She was hurt. "You're bleeding."

She looked down at her front. "Not mine. His blood. He pulled me down with him." Her words were flat and clipped, as if she fought to keep herself under firm control.

Very gently then, he touched her cheek and moved her face around in the light. The terror in her eyes stabbed through him. "It's all right, Adriane," he repeated softly as though soothing a frightened child. "It's over now."

She met his eyes fully, the terror, if anything, growing. "He said they'd hang me if I shot him. That nobody would believe he was the river slasher."

"The slasher?" Even with the man lying dead at his feet and Beck maybe dying on the other side of the room, Blake could nevertheless hardly comprehend what she was saying. "Stanley Jimson?"

She went on as though he hadn't spoken. "He said it was my fault. That I was the reason he killed those girls, because I was so cold toward him. He was going to kill me too." She pulled in a breath, and her voice got stronger as she went on. "I decided I'd rather hang."

"Shh, darling." Blake gathered her into his arms and stroked her hair. "They don't hang people for defending themselves."

She stayed stiff against him as she kept talking. "He grabbed for the gun. He thought I'd given up, but I pushed him back and we fell. The gun went off and there was blood every-where." A shudder went through her. "I didn't know if it was his or mine as he grabbed for my throat. He wouldn't die." She pulled back from Blake to let her eyes touch on the body on the floor. "He wouldn't die."

"He can't hurt you now." Blake tried to pull her close again, but she wouldn't let him as her eyes came back to his. Wounded. Troubled.

"But he's dead," she said. "I—"

Blake didn't let her finish. "You did what you had to. He needed killing." Blake tightened his arms around her, and at last she relaxed against his shoulder and let him hold her.

A few minutes later Duff pushed through the door into the pressroom. He stumbled over Beck's body and fell on his knees beside the old man. "Oh no, not old Beck," he cried.

"He's not dead yet, Duff. Run for a doctor." At Blake's words, Adriane raised her head away from his shoulder to look across the room at Beck.

Instead of running to do as Blake said, Duff lit the gas lamp just inside the door. When light spilled across the room, the boy's eyes widened as he took in Blake holding Adriane and then Stanley's body on the floor.

"He was the one, wasn't he?" Duff said, but didn't wait for an answer. "I see me sister's blood on his hands."

"Get Dr. Hammon, Duff." Some life came back into Adri-ane's voice as she pulled away from Blake. "Beck needs help."

Blake didn't like letting her loose even though he knew she had to see to the old man. She completely forgot her torn bodice as she grabbed a printer's apron from a hook on the wall and folded it to press against Beck's wound. The man groaned, and she talked to him as she tried to staunch the bleeding.

"You can't die, Beck," she told him. "You just can't. You hear me, I know you do, so don't you give up. You can't die!"

Blake heard the terrible loneliness in her voice and knelt beside her. "Let me." He nudged her hands off the makeshift bandage to take over applying the pressure on Beck's wound. "Beck's tough. He'll make it."

She stared down at Beck and her next words were barely above a whisper. "But what if he dies? Like Father. Both because of me."

"You didn't do this. Stanley did."

She didn't say anything then, but it was easy to guess what she was thinking. He pushed his words at her. "You couldn't marry Stanley Jimson. You knew that. Beck knew that. I knew that. In time, if your father had lived, he would have seen that too." He looked over at her bent head, willing her to turn her eyes to him. When at last she did, he went on. "Beck's not dead yet. You told him not to give up. Don't you give up either."

A tear slipped out of her left eye and traced down through the blood on her cheek. She had said the blood wasn't hers, but her chin was dripping blood. It was all he could do to keep pressing the bandage against Beck's wound and not reach over to lift her head so he could see how badly she was injured. But she needed Beck to live more than she needed her own wound seen to.

She looked back down at Beck and picked up one of his hands in both of hers. "I haven't given up, Beck. We'll pray. You, me, Blake." She glanced over at Blake.

"I'm not too good at praying." The words were hardly out of his mouth when he remembered the desperate prayers that had risen up inside him as he was running from the waterfront. Prayers the Lord had answered. "At least out loud."

"You don't have to pray out loud."

"All right. Then I'm praying." And he was. Praying for Beck to keep breathing. Praying for the doctor to get there soon. Praying for Adriane, that she wouldn't have to lose Beck.

She kept Beck's hand in one of hers and put her other hand on Blake's arm as she looked upward. "Dear Lord. Please. Let it not be Beck's time the same as it wasn't my time. Let him live. Please. Amen."

"Amen," Blake repeated after her as she leaned over to kiss Beck's hand.

"He feels so cold," she said.

"He's lost a lot of blood, but his heart isn't giving up. I can feel it under my hands."

Duff came bursting through the door with Dr. Hammon in tow. The doctor looked from Beck to the body across the room. He settled his eyes a moment on Adriane before he told Blake, "You'd best send the boy for the police."

"Not yet." Blake looked up at Duff. "Go get Coleman Jimson." Blake's voice turned hard on the man's name. "Tell him it can't wait till morning. That it has to do with Stanley."

The doctor paled at the name and took another look at Stanley's body. He opened his mouth as if to say more, but after looking at Blake again, he knelt beside Beck without another word. Blake lifted his hands away from the bandage to let the doctor examine the wound.

At the first probe of the doctor's fingers, Beck groaned loudly, opened his eyes, and began fighting to sit up. When Blake and Dr. Hammon held him down, he fought harder. "Let me at him," the old man shouted. "He's got Addie."

"I'm all right, Beck." Adriane leaned over close to Beck's face to calm him. "Now be still, and let Dr. Hammon take care of you."

The old man began breathing easier as his eyes fastened on Adriane's face. "I was feared he was going to kill you."

"That's what he had in mind." Adriane took the old man's hand in hers. "But we stopped him. You and me."

342

Beck's eyes sharpened on her. "It must've been more you than me." Then when she didn't say anything, he went on. "But I reckon there ain't nobody that can beat us in the head-line war tomorrow."

By some miracle, the knife had missed any of Beck's vital organs, and the doctor said with the proper rest and care, the old man had a good chance of making it. Once Beck was bandaged and settled in his bed, Dr. Hammon turned to Adriane. "Now, my dear, it appears that you too are bleed-ing." His eyes touched on the blood staining her torn dress that she had pulled together as best she could.

"It's not my blood." Adriane attempted to keep her voice from trembling as she desperately tried to block from her mind the image of Stanley's face as he died. She failed on both counts.

Blake moved closer to her and put his arm around her waist. She leaned against him, glad he was there beside her. Glad Stanley hadn't been able to steal him away from her by whatever trap he'd set for him down on the waterfront.

The doctor went on kindly, but insistently. "I think some of it may be yours. There appears to be a cut on your chin."

Adriane shut her eyes a moment and remembered Stanley's knife slicing into her face as she jerked away from him. "It's nothing," she said. She reached up to touch her chin and was surprised to feel the warmth of fresh blood on her fingers.

"No arguments. You need stitches." Dr. Hammon's voice was calm and businesslike. "Come out to the kitchen and we'll fix it." When he put his arm under her elbow to usher her out of Beck's room toward the kitchen, Blake's arm tightened around her. The doctor looked at him. "She's safe now, man. There will be plenty you can do for her later, but now I need to tend to that cut."

When Blake turned her loose, the doctor led her out of Beck's room back into the pressroom where the sickening smell of death assaulted her. Adriane felt faint, but she forced herself to keep walking toward the kitchen, her eyes straight ahead.

Beside her, Dr. Hammon glanced toward Stanley's body and then over his shoulder at Blake, who had followed them out. "For the love of mercy, Garrett, do the decent thing and cover the man's body before his father gets here. If I need your help with your wife, I'll call you."

So Adriane was sitting at the kitchen table doing her best not to flinch as Dr. Hammon stitched up the cut when Coleman Jimson came storming in the front hall and into the pressroom.

"What's the meaning of this? Dragging me out this time of night. I don't care what Stanley's done. It could have waited till morning." His voice was loud and angry.

Adriane's heart began to thud back and forth in her chest. Whatever else Stanley had been, he was the Jimsons' only son, and her gun had killed him. His blood would always be on her hands, his dying face forever in her nightmares.

Dr. Hammon looked toward the pressroom for a moment. Then all his attention was back on Adriane. "Try to relax, Adriane. I'm almost finished here."

But although she was no longer feeling the pain of the stitches, she couldn't relax. Not with Coleman Jimson about to look at his son's body.

The doctor must have noted her unease because he began talking in a low, kind voice. "Whatever happened to Stanley, he brought it on himself." He looked up from working on her chin and met her eyes. "I think you can trust your husband to handle this and spare you any additional agony. He seems a decent sort."

From the pressroom she could hear Blake's voice, calm but cold as he told Coleman Jimson his son was dead. Jimson's voice trailed off, and there were no more shouts. Neither were there any sounds of grief. Instead Coleman Jimson only sounded extremely weary as he said, "His mother will take this very hard."

Blake gave the man no word of sympathy. Instead he said, "He was the river slasher."

Dr. Hammon pulled in a sharp breath, but Adriane could hear no response from Coleman Jimson in the next room.

After a moment, Blake spoke again, the shock evident in his voice. "You knew."

Adriane pushed the doctor's hands away from her chin and stood up. The doctor stopped her long enough to tie off his last stitch, then let her go. She paused in the doorway to the pressroom. Trembles ran through her as she remembered standing there earlier, feeling the evil throbbing in the darkness. Stanley's evil. An evil his father had evidently been aware of.

Coleman Jimson was staring at the sheet-covered body of his son. "I didn't really know," he said finally. "I only suspected."

"And you didn't do anything," Blake said.

"What could I do? He was my son."

"And what about Adriane?" Blake seemed to nearly choke on the words. "You were willing to sacrifice her life."

"I never thought he'd hurt Adriane. Never." His eyes flew back to Blake, and even from across the room, Adriane could see the concern in his face. "He didn't, did he? She's all right?"

"I'm alive," Adriane said from the doorway, her voice stronger than she'd thought it would be. "Five other girls are not."

Coleman Jimson stared at her a moment, taking in her torn dress, the blood. Then he looked back at Blake. "You did right to shoot him."

Blake didn't contradict him, and even as Adriane started to speak, Dr. Hammon lightly touched her arm to stay her words.

"It will be better this way," the doctor whispered in her ear.

And so having accepted what he thought was the truth about his son's death, Jimson turned his mind to the future. "You can't print this," he told Blake.

"It's not the kind of thing you can hide," Blake said.

"Maybe not all of it, but some of it. The whole truth would kill his mother."

"And destroy your political career," Blake said harshly.

"Perhaps, but people do not always hold a father responsible for a son's sins," the man said, and Adriane could see him beginning to regain some control. "But think, Garrett, what it could do to Adriane if you publish the truth. The gossip."

"There will be gossip no matter what we print."

"We can control it. We must control it." Jimson narrowed his eyes as he looked at Blake before he went on. "It will give you a certain power over me, and the loan will be forgotten."

"We are not for sale," Adriane spoke up, her words fierce and determined.

Jimson turned his eyes toward Adriane. "I wasn't suggesting that you were, my dear, but I do hope we can be reasonable. For the good of us all. There could be some difficulties for Mr. Garrett here if the circumstances were examined too closely by the police. Plus, I'm sure neither of you would want the matter to go to trial where you might have to take the stand to testify about Stanley's attack on you. Think how distressing that would surely be for you."

Blake's voice was tightly controlled as he said, "What story can we print that people will believe?"

"A duel," Jimson answered quickly. "People will understand that."

"I don't fight duels," Blake said.

Jimson thought a moment before he asked, "Was it Stanley's gun?"

"No." Adriane had difficulty pushing out the words. "He had a knife." She shuddered as she pointed to where it still lay on the floor. "It was Beck's gun."

Jimson stared down at the knife before touching his eyes on the cut on Adriane's chin. His face went white as if fully realizing what his son had thought to do. He shut his eyes and stood very still. After a long silence, he moistened his lips with his tongue and said, "All right. So this is what we'll say. Stanley, crazed with jealousy, breaks in here to confront Adriane. Wade's man pulls out his gun to make him leave. Stanley fights with the old man, and in the struggle Wade's man is wounded and Stanley is killed. We don't have to make mention of the knife."

Blake looked across the room at Adriane. She met his eyes and nodded. There was the germ of truth in the story.

Duff suddenly spoke up from where he'd been watching the men from the door. "But what of me sister? What of the slasher?"

Blake turned and answered him softly, with kindness. "Naming the murderer won't bring back Lila, Duff, but no more girls will die." He paused a moment, his eyes searching the boy's face before he went on. "Will that be enough?"

Duff looked from Blake to Adriane. "If it's best for Miss Adriane this way."

Blake's eyes lifted from Duff to Adriane. "It is."

And so the deal was made, the story planned with silence in regard to the whole truth vowed by all present.

33

*B*efore the police came, Adriane went upstairs where she scrubbed her hands three times in her washbowl. Then she sat on the edge of her bed and stared at those hands in her lap. She thought she should change out of her bloodstained dress in case the police wanted to talk to her. Downstairs she heard the front door opening and then the murmur of unfamiliar voices, but she couldn't make out any of the words. She was glad. She didn't want to know what they were saying.

She remembered how when she was a child locked inside the closet and the monsters had edged too close, she had shut her eyes and whispered the Bible verses about light. *And God said, Let there be light: and there was light.*

She needed light. She needed to block out everything. Stanley slicing off the buttons of her dress, then the sharp point of the knife under her chin. The deafening boom of the gun as they'd fallen. The way even as he was dying he'd reached for her throat to take her with him. His eyes changing into something not quite human as he'd fought for his last breath. And then Blake was there, anger mixed with the fear on his face. She couldn't tell what he was thinking even as he had pulled her close and held her as though worried she might break or perhaps was already broken. Then Beck bleeding. They had to think about him.

She tried to think about Beck now. To pray for him. That was better than thinking about what had happened. She didn't want to think about what had happened. Not even about the deal they'd struck with Coleman Jimson. A deal to tell and publish lies. That didn't seem right. Best for everyone perhaps, but was it right?

The minutes ticked slowly past as she stared at her hands and waited, and though the lamps in her room were lit and light danced all around her, the monsters of the dark lurked in her mind.

It seemed like hours later when she finally heard Blake's step on the stairs. Once again she was the child in the closet hearing her father coming in the house and knowing that soon she'd be rescued from the dark. For a moment she felt that same joyous leap of her heart, but then she mashed it down. This time there might be no rescue. What if the police didn't accept their story? What if they demanded to know the truth? From her. What if they decided she was guilty of causing Stanley's death? She had wanted him to die. That was surely reason for guilt.

She didn't look up when Blake came into the room, but kept her eyes on her hands. Was that more blood under her fingernails?

He came over to stand in front of her. When she kept her head bent, he gently touched her hair. "They're gone."

She made herself ask, "They believed what you told them?"

"It sounded true," he said. "Jimson played his part well. A grieving father distraught over the foolish actions of his son that led to his tragic death. The police were ready to accept whatever he told them to believe. They carried the body away for him."

"And Beck?"

"He's still out from whatever the doctor gave him. Duff's

sitting with him. Joe came in and the doctor set his arm and gave him a ride home in his buggy. Everything is taken care of."

"Everything?" Adriane asked quietly, her eyes still on her hands. That was definitely blood under her fingernails. Maybe Stanley's blood. She clamped her lips together to keep back a scream.

"Almost everything," Blake admitted. He knelt in front of her and with great tenderness lifted her face up, being careful not to touch the stitches in her chin. His eyes probed hers as though looking for answers to unasked questions.

She started to say something, but he put his fingers softly on her lips. "Not now. We'll talk later. First a bath."

He carried in the tub and hauled warm water up the stairs that he must have put on to heat before the police came. He found the towels and soap, and when all was ready, he helped her strip off the ruined dress. She could feel his hands trembling as he eased the sleeves off her arms. While he carried the dress to the door to throw it out of the room, she slipped out of her chemise and pantaloons and stepped into the tub to sink down into the warm water.

She picked up the soap, but he knelt beside the tub and took it from her. Gently he began soaping her shoulders. She kept her eyes straight ahead as she said quietly, "He didn't touch me."

When his hands went still on her shoulders, she turned to look straight at him. "Would it have changed things if he had?" She kept her eyes steady on his. She did not want him to back away from the question. She needed an answer.

He didn't hesitate. "Nothing could ever change the way I feel about you, Adriane. Or the way we belong together in every way."

She was too surprised to speak when his mouth began quivering and his face crumpled as tears filled his eyes. He brushed the back of his hand across his eyes and drew in a shaky breath before he was able to go on. "But I should have been here to protect you from him."

"You can't always rescue everyone." Adriane reached up to touch one of the tears that leaked out on his cheek.

He put his hand over hers and brought it around to his lips. He kissed her palm before he said, "But I want to rescue you. I can't stand to see the wounded look in your eyes. I should have been here to save you from killing him by killing him myself."

"I wasn't holding the gun when it fired, but I did make him fall. That's when the gun went off." Stanley's contorted face was there in front of her again. She shuddered so violently that water splashed out of the tub onto the floor.

"It's over, darling. He can't hurt you now." Blake reached into the tub to put his arms around her.

She stayed stiff, unable to accept his embrace. "But don't you see?" Adriane stared down in the water at her hands just below the surface. The blood was gone from under her fingernails, but would it ever be gone from her memory? "I wanted him dead. I was glad when he died."

"Shh, it's all right. You didn't cause it. The evil within him caused it all. But he's gone now and can't hurt anyone else. That's what you need to keep in your mind. He can't hurt anyone else." He touched his lips to her cheek and then her shoulder. "I'm here with you." He leaned back and looked at her face. "I'll always be with you."

Adriane could see the depth of his promise in his eyes. With him beside her, she'd be able to face whatever was to come. Even the blackest closet of her fears would never be completely dark again, for his love would glow from inside her to push aside the darkness. A gift of light from the Lord who had heard her prayer in the darkness.

"I want to have your baby." She wasn't sure where the words came from or why she picked that moment to say them with death so fresh in her mind. Perhaps that was the reason.

Blake laughed, light exploding from his eyes as all signs of his earlier tears vanished. Suddenly death seemed far away. "I certainly hope so. If we're going to start a newspaper dynasty, we'll need at least six. Three boys and three girls. Think of the money we'll save on hands once Beck has them trained to set type."

"They might not all be as adept with the type as their mother," Adriane said.

"True enough. But as long as they have their mother's fire and courage, that will be enough." Blake dropped his lips down to cover hers lightly before he began soaping her arms and back.

Adriane shut her eyes and soaked in the good feel of his hands touching her before she opened her eyes again and looked straight at him. "I love you, Blake Garrett. I have since the first moment I saw you in Mrs. Wigginham's parlor."

"I know." A smile lingered on his face. "The part I wasn't sure about was whether I could ever get you to admit it."

"And now that you have?" She raised her eyebrows at him.

"I think it calls for at least five-inch headline type."

"I doubt that headline would sell papers." She laughed. A few hours ago, she wasn't sure she'd ever have the chance to laugh again. But with the Lord's help she had escaped the dark closet of evil that was Stanley Jimson. Another laugh welled up inside her as she rejoiced in the light surrounding her now. It was good to breathe. It was good to have Blake kneeling there beside her tub. It was good to have words of love on her lips.

"It will be a limited edition. One issue for you. One for me. And maybe one for Mrs. Wigginham."

"And you?" Her smile faded as she stared at him intently. "I think you may have decided to rescue me that day, but when did you know you loved me?"

"I've always loved you, Adriane. I just didn't know it until I saw you."

She stood up then, letting the last of her fears slide away from her like the droplets of water off her skin. Water couldn't rid her of the stain of Stanley's blood, but Blake's love could.

His eyes widened with surprise, but then his face warmed with love as he wrapped a towel around her and lifted her out of the tub. Water dripped everywhere, but neither of them noticed as he held her close and lowered his lips to hers.

Light, glorious light filled her heart. Nothing could ever steal that from her again. She'd prayed for an answer and now that amazing answer held her in his arms.

"I love you, Adriane Darcy," Blake whispered into her hair.

"You mean Adriane Darcy Garrett, don't you?" She leaned her head back to smile at him.

"I do indeed, Mrs. Garrett. I truly do." Light exploded from his eyes again as he said, "I love you, Adriane Darcy Garrett."

"And I love you, Blake Garrett. For now and forevermore." Never were words spoken more true.

Author's Acknowledgments

A writer spends a great deal of time alone in front of her keyboard as a story spills out of her imagination onto paper or a computer screen. It's a process I've never been able to explain, but one that I'm compelled to attempt over and over as I dip new stories out of that mysterious well of ideas inside my head. But once the story is all written down and polished as well as I can polish it, then I get the fun of sharing it with you, my readers.

That's when I can no longer do it all alone. I'm blessed to have a wonderful agent, Wendy Lawton, who is always just a call or email away to offer encouragement and help while she does her best to see that I don't stumble into any writing business pitfalls. I'm also privileged to work with a wonderful editor, Lonnie Hull DuPont, who had great suggestions about this book that helped me make the story better. I thank Barb Barnes for her editing expertise and also the proofreaders at Baker Publishing who keep me from making bonehead mistakes by careful reading. I appreciate all the Baker team who design great covers and come up with suggestions for titles that will attract the eye of the book shopper. I thank

Michele Misiak, who never fails to direct me to the right person when I have a question and never, ever seems too busy to help. I appreciate the publicity and marketing teams who present my books with enthusiasm to the book buyers and reading public. Without them, my books would not find you, the readers.

And of course, I do want to thank you for reading, for adding your imagination to mine in order to make my characters come to life in your minds and hearts.

I also have to thank my patient husband who has had to suffer through too many deadline crunches lately. I appreciate the wonderful support of my entire family.

Last, but never least, I joyfully thank the Lord who gave me stories to tell and the ability to write them down to share with you. I am blessed beyond measure by you, my readers, and by the Lord who so loved the world. The world—that's me, you, all of us.

Ann H. Gabhart and her husband live on a farm just over the hill from where she grew up in central Kentucky. She's active in her country church, and her husband sings bass in a Southern Gospel quartet. Ann is the author of over twenty novels for adults and young adults. Her first inspirational novel, *The Scent of Lilacs*, was one of Booklist's top ten inspirational novels of 2006. Her novel *The Outsider* was a finalist for the 2009 Christian Book Awards in the fiction category.

Visit Ann's website at www.annhgabhart.com.

Meet ANN H. GABHART at
WWW.ANNHGABHART.COM

Learn about New Books, Read Her Blog,
and Sign Up for Her Newsletter

CONNECT WITH ANN AT
[f] Ann H Gabhart
[t] AnnHGabhart

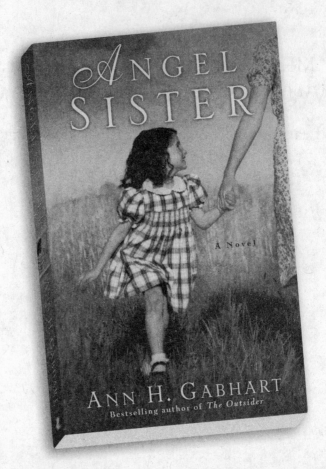

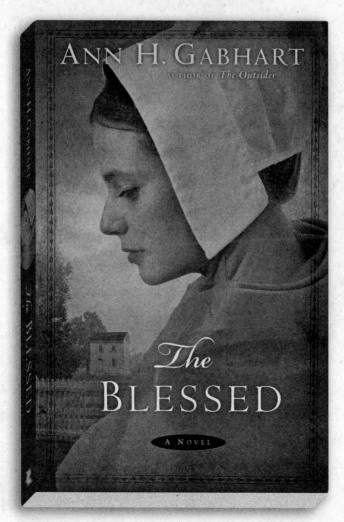

THEY LIVE IN A COMMUNITY WHERE LOVE IS FORBIDDEN, BUT WILL THAT QUENCH THE PASSION IN THEIR HEARTS?

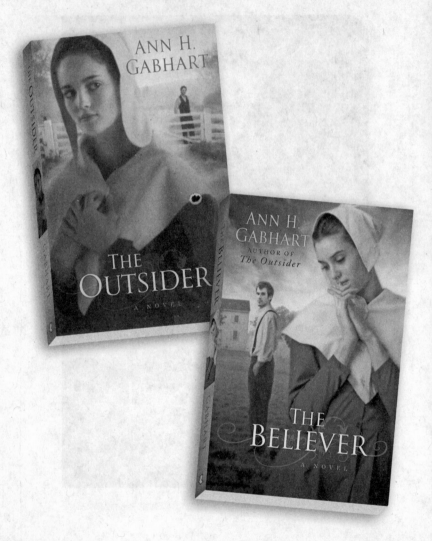

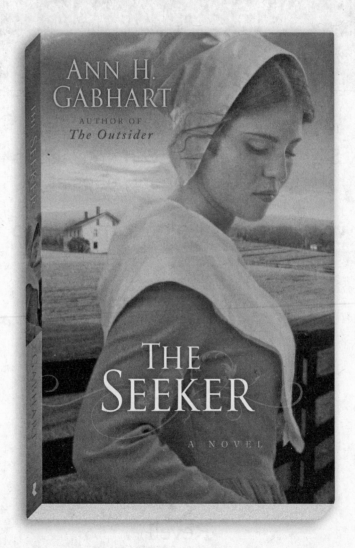